L

'Sydney-base
the bravest
characters s
command.'

MW01706589

West Australian

'*Lunch with the Generals* is a handily crafted novel, the style sparse yet detailed, the sign of a brilliant storyteller.'

Courier Mail

'Hansen has what it takes to become an international bestselling "name" author.'

Who Weekly

LUNCH WITH MUSSOLINI

'Another fine effort from Hansen, with complex characters from wartime Germans and Italian fascists to Australian widows.'

Courier Mail

'This is a book as brilliant technically as it is profound thematically. Yet Derek Hansen has a lightness of touch that contrasts with his sombre yet gripping narrative.'

Canberra Times

'This is *not* a book I could not put down: I deliberately put it down often, in order to make it last longer.'

Glasgow Herald

SOLE SURVIVOR

'Hansen has written an excellent novel — one which can be read on many different planes ... Hansen is a damned fine storyteller whose book is just so easy to read and enjoy.'

Bendigo Advertiser

Other books by Derek Hansen

NOVELS

Lunch with the Generals

Lunch with Mussolini

Sole Survivor

SHORT STORIES

Dead Fishy

Psycho Cat

BLOCKADE

DEREK HANSEN

HarperCollinsPublishers

HarperCollins*Publishers*

First published in Australia in 1998
This edition published in 1999
Reprinted in 1999
by HarperCollins*Publishers* Pty Limited
ACN 009 913 517
A member of HarperCollins*Publishers* (Australia) Pty Limited Group
http://www.harpercollins.com.au

Copyright © Derek Hansen 1998

This book is copyright.
Apart from any fair dealing for the purposes of private study, research, criticism or review, as permitted under the Copyright Act, no part may be reproduced by any process without written permission.
Inquiries should be addressed to the publishers.

HarperCollins*Publishers*
25 Ryde Road, Pymble, Sydney, NSW 2073, Australia
31 View Road, Glenfield, Auckland 10, New Zealand
77–85 Fulham Palace Road, London W6 8JB, United Kingdom
Hazelton Lanes, 55 Avenue Road, Suite 2900, Toronto, Ontario M5R 3L2
and 1995 Markham Road, Scarborough, Ontario M1B 5M8, Canada
10 East 53rd Street, New York NY 10022, USA

National Library Cataloguing-in-Publication data:

Hansen, Derek.
Blockade.
ISBN 0 7322 6466 9.
I. Title.
A823.3

Typeset in Sabon 10/13
Cover photograph: International Photographic Library
Printed in Australia by Griffin Press Pty Ltd on 50gsm Bulky News

6 5 4 3 2
02 01 00 99

Derek Hansen was born in England, raised in New Zealand and now lives in Sydney. After an advertising career spanning thirty years, Derek sold his agency to realise an ambition to write novels.

His debut novel, *Lunch with the Generals*, was an instant bestseller and was published widely in Europe. His last novel, *Sole Survivor*, is to become the subject of a major Hollywood movie.

Having stared down enough concrete canyons to last a lifetime, Derek now works from his home on the northern beaches overlooking Pittwater and Ku-ring-gai Chase National Park, with cockatoos, corellas, galahs, lorikeets, king parrots and penguins for company and hardly another house in sight.

ACKNOWLEDGEMENTS

When I was first contemplating writing this book I was introduced to an extraordinary young woman with pink hair into which were entwined parts of a rather large dead bird. She appeared to be wearing her entire wardrobe yet still looked as though a stiff breeze would bowl her over. She was enveloped in a fug of incense which I later learned performed a similar function to deodorant. Over a series of interviews she introduced me to the world of people collectively though inaccurately referred to as ferals, the people of all ages who are committed to the protection of our remaining forests — almost to the exclusion of everything else. Her name is Isabella and she was the inspiration for my fictional character, Summer. I'm grateful to her for her insights and observations, for her weird drawings and posters, without which I probably would not have proceeded. She is still out there somewhere saving forests.

Thanks are also due to Peter Wright, formerly of the Australian Conservation Foundation and now with the Nature Conservation Council, for his patient explanation of the various roles of conservation groups, loggers and governments, and for showing me how things actually worked. Jill Redwood of Concerned Residents of East Gippsland (CROEG) also contributed hugely to my knowledge bank and sent me dozens of editions of *Potoroo Review* — printed on recycled paper — which proved invaluable. All the above provided a balance to the brochures and fact sheets kindly sent to me by NAFI, the National Association of Forest Industries.

Thanks also to Professor David Tiller at the Royal Prince Alfred Hospital for his assistance on all medical matters, and to my wife Carole and editors Nicola O'Shea and Laura Harris, all of whom gave guidance and advice only a fool would ignore.

AUTHOR'S NOTE

Blockade is a work of fiction. The town of Osbourne does not exist, nor does Little Potoroo Creek, Thirsty Creek, Tathra Heights or the electorate of Tathra Valley.

East Gippsland was chosen as the location for this novel because areas there are still a source of dispute between green groups and timber contractors. That said, the conflicts and events described in this novel are purely imaginary and bear no relation to actual events or conflicts.

The events and characters are all products of my imagination. Any resemblance to real organisations or real persons, living or dead, is unintentional and pure coincidence, the only exceptions being the Australian Conservation Foundation, the Wilderness Society, Friends of the Earth, CROEG and GECO.

PART ONE

DORF FOREST RAVE

CHAPTER ONE

Cheryl Bollok looked into her bathroom mirror and saw a woman who chose the certainty of riches over the possibility of love. She firmly believed that nobody in the world would have chosen differently. Cheryl relinquished all claim to love in exchange for a future immeasurably brighter than her past. Her husband came with a house, washing machine, dryer, an Italian cooktop which ran on both electricity and gas, a wall oven, a four-wheel drive Toyota Landcruiser and a new name that inspired fear, awe and loathing depending upon whose side you were on. But nothing spoke more eloquently of her change in circumstance than her Miele dishwasher. To own a machine that cost thousands of dollars just so she'd never have to wash dishes again seemed to her the ultimate extravagance. Hers was the only dishwasher in Osbourne, other than the one in the pub and that was just for washing glasses. In the dark and lonely hours, loveless and friendless, she only had to look at her dishwasher to be reminded of the worth and wisdom of the deal she'd struck. In her new life there were no more dishes to wash, no mud-encrusted boots to scrape, no mud and tannin-stained work pants and shirts to boil clean, no more torn threadbare clothes, worn sheets or fraying towels to be saved once more by needle and thread, no more lamb necks, no mutton, no grey mincemeat, no tripe to try and turn into a palatable meal, no more gathering and chopping wood for the fire and no more boiling up saucepans of water for the bath.

Cheryl was born at home, in a rude timber cottage built originally as a single-room shack by her grandfather and added on to ever since. As if forewarned about life in her home town of Osbourne, she delayed her entry into it for just over forty pain-filled hours. The local doctor was supposed to help with the delivery but got tired of waiting and retired to the pub instead. Her father hung around for a while longer but eventually became so fed up with his wife's moaning and groaning and the general lack of progress that he went and joined the doctor. He thoughtfully left his wife a glass of water in case things got rough. Cheryl entered the world unaided except by her long-suffering mother, who only just managed to cut and tie the cord before collapsing into exhausted sleep. Cheryl was convinced that the lack of help she had received then would be repeated endlessly for the duration of her life.

Cheryl's father made a tenuous living by felling and hauling logs for the sawmills. It was a hard job to begin with and, ironically, it only became harder the harder he worked. The more logs he felled the further he had to go into the forests to find new ones, and the further he had to haul them out. The yards paid for sawlogs by the foot not by the miles they had travelled. Cheryl's father took his consolation in the pub, hoping all the while for sons who could work with him and make his life a little less hard. When Cheryl was born he couldn't hide his disgust. He never forgave her for being a girl, even though two sons followed.

As she towelled dry, Cheryl examined herself critically and wondered — not for the first time — whether she was even loveable. She was too tall and broad and her bones too heavy for anyone to describe her as beautiful. Men reserved words like 'handsome' for her kind. Yet her features were even and her figure remarkable for a woman of her build, her breasts full but firm and her hips nicely rounded. Her large hands and feet had once been a source of embarrassment, but Cheryl knew they weren't the cause of her real problem. Her real problem was that men didn't find her particularly feminine. Not even the blokes in Osbourne, who had no call to be choosy about anything.

Cheryl moved from her bathroom to her walk-in wardrobe. She dressed slowly, pulling on her thick woollen socks and then her carpenter's jeans with their extravagance of pockets and loops to hang things off. She tucked in a heavy tartan shirt, grabbed her sweater and quilted jacket and wandered into her bedroom. Of course her children loved her, and their photos spread all over her dressing table and tallboy showed as much. She gave her two boys all the love that had been denied her by a father who had no use for a daughter and a mother who was too beaten down to care. She loved her boys unreservedly, indulging and doting on them, and they smiled back at her from an assortment of frames, each one vying for space. They smiled at her as babies, as toddlers, and as strapping lads in school photos. She'd cried for days when the time had come to pack them off to boarding school in Melbourne, but she wanted them to learn about the world beyond Osbourne and, hopefully, one day have the wisdom to make their life there. The highlights of her year were the school holidays when the boys returned, when her loneliness was buried beneath an avalanche of laughter and activity. Yet whenever they were invited to spend the holidays with school friends she always gave her blessing, even though the disappointment at not seeing them was heartbreaking. But she firmly believed the less time they spent in Osbourne or with their father the better.

She picked up her hat and ambled down the hallway, past sweeping landscapes of pristine forest, to the room she called her studio. Her life revolved around this room and it contained the only passion left to her. Unfinished canvases stood propped on easels and against the wall, each with its reference photo pinned in the corner. Throughout school Cheryl had excelled at art, but her father couldn't see the point of it and made her study accounting instead. Even so, she kept up her art and nearly topped the state at the end of Year 12. She could have gone on to university, but universities cost money and weren't on the Doak family agenda. More photos of the boys and a lightbox sat upon a stripped and waxed dining table. A captain's chair and a whitewood plans cabinet were the only other pieces of furniture. Cheryl reached up and took her camera and lens box from their storage place on top of the cabinet. She checked to see that she had all the film she needed as she made her way back down the hallway to the kitchen. There was no urgency for her to do anything. She boiled the kettle, filled a flask with hot water for coffee and cut a sandwich for lunch. The only sound was the gentle murmur of her Miele dishwasher as it washed two breakfast plates, two coffee cups, two knives, two forks, two spoons and a bacon-smeared grill tray. No Miele dishwasher had ever had life so easy. Once packed, Cheryl took a final look around to make sure she hadn't left any lights on, then locked the back door behind her. There was nobody and nothing to say goodbye to. Years earlier, in a bout of loneliness, she'd asked her husband Miklos if she could have a dog. He'd laughed and dismissed her with a comment calculated to hurt as well as deny. 'One dog in the house is enough,' he'd said.

Cheryl climbed into her Landcruiser and set off for the forest. She'd warned Miklos that she wouldn't be home till after dark and told him to get dinner at the pub, which is what he did most nights anyway. She had a long, lonely day ahead of her, but at least it was a loneliness of her choosing. She had no idea that a day which had begun so ordinarily would, ultimately, change her life forever.

* * *

To get to the part of the forest where she wanted to take her photographs, Cheryl had first to drive into town and then through it. She drove past old wooden houses, similar to the one she grew up in and had no intention of ever setting foot in again. Among them, ugly and out of place, were the newer squat square brick and concrete block homes built by families who believed Osbourne had a future. All of them had a scattering of derelict cars and utes cluttering their yards. Families that had outgrown their homes had old caravans on blocks for the extra kids to sleep in. Cheryl tried not to look at the houses as she drove past; the hopelessness and futility that lurked behind the closed front doors reminded her of her own past, and aroused faint feelings of guilt. She'd escaped, they hadn't. She was privileged, they weren't. Dogs barked at her passing.

Cheryl turned down Thirsty Creek Road and headed out of town. Thirsty Creek Road looked like a set for a western movie, except instead of a facade of saloon bars, saddleries and general stores it had a facade of forest. Fifty metres beyond the roadside rows of trees there was nothing but devastation. The land had been ravaged by clearfelling, and the trunks of ancient trees deemed worthless for woodchips or sawmilling lay rotting on the ground. What had once been virgin forest now looked like the aftermath of a nuclear holocaust, courtesy, as it happened, of her husband Miklos Bollok.

Cheryl first came to Miklos's attention through her book-keeping. Her father and brother Arnie were boasting in the pub about how smart they'd been to put Cheryl in charge of finances, how there was always food on the table even when they went weeks without giving Cheryl or her mother any money to buy it.

'That,' said Miklos Bollok, 'is exactly the kind of book-keeper I'm looking for.'

Cheryl grabbed the job without hesitation, as if it were the best thing that had happened to her in her life. She had been in awe of working in an office, of actually dressing up to go to work, of sitting at her own desk with a typewriter, calculator and telephone, and she had been in awe of Miklos Bollok as well. He was by far the biggest and most powerful man she had ever met. But she stood up to him right from the start, just as she'd had to stand up to her father and her brothers — she saw no reason to do otherwise. She smiled when Miklos explained about levies, taxes and his two sets of books. Miklos smiled later, when Cheryl explained her new systems and procedures and how much more money they'd save him. As the business prospered and grew Miklos took her further into his confidence, and came to value her opinions on matters as diverse as business deals and hirings. He asked her straight questions and got straight answers. He appreciated the fact that Cheryl always told him what she thought and not what he wanted to hear. He considered taking her on as a partner but then had a better idea.

When Miklos married Cheryl everybody thought it a good match. A big man should have a big wife, they argued, but there were other considerations. Cheryl was strong, and everybody knew she'd need to be. She was local, came from a logging family and didn't have to be told the score. Neither of them harboured any illusions; it wasn't so much a marriage as a business arrangement. Miklos wanted someone who could give him kids and had the good sense not to interfere with the way he lived his life. He wanted someone who could run his home the way he wanted. He was a man in a man's world and wanted a man's house to come home to. The last thing he wanted was to be married to someone who would frig around with prissy furniture and curtains.

Cheryl looked ahead at a life of luxury and security and didn't hesitate. There was no one better qualified to take her hand. She had no intention of marrying a dirt-poor logger and ending up like her mother. Besides, none of the blokes in Osbourne had fronted up for anything more permanent than a quickie on the back of their ute. Cheryl understood her role and what was required of her. She learnt to take no notice of Miklos's succession of mistresses and to tolerate his drinking.

Even so, she expected some companionship from Miklos. After all they'd communicated well enough in the office and Miklos had enjoyed sharing confidences. But, once married, Miklos cut her out. Maybe somebody told him a wife shouldn't know too much about her husband's business, or maybe he knew that anyway. Their relationship deteriorated to less than that of flatmates. Her few friends deserted her because of her change in station; she was no longer one of them. People passing her in the street greeted her as Mrs Bollok instead of Cheryl. Arthritis took hold of her mother and she refused to set foot outside her front door. Her father grew too old for the hard work and each day left home to take up residence on a bar stool. There were times with the kids away when not even the happy gurgle of her Miele dishwasher could dispel the deadweight of her loneliness.

But at least there was her art.

At the end of Thirsty Creek Road Cheryl turned up the fire trail towards the escarpment and Tathra Heights. As the Landcruiser ground its way up the succession of hills and ridges, each one higher than the preceding, she looked out across an unbroken landscape destined to be clearfelled. Though the forests cried out for a champion and protector, it had never occurred to Cheryl to volunteer. Up until the time she met Miklos, her father and brothers had taken her with them whenever they needed an extra hand. They taught her how to use a chainsaw and cut down trees. The equation was simple: trees were logs and logs were money and money was desperately needed. She learnt quickly, and there was no place for equivocation when saw blades were running and trees falling. But she couldn't help looking ahead at the centuries-old forest, and behind her at the devastation, and feeling a sadness. She took to wandering off to have her lunch among the honey myrtle, acacia and grevillea. She was stunned one day to hear a lyrebird mimic a chainsaw, and ashamed when she realised it was probably hers.

As Cheryl crested a ridge she spotted a tall wiry man on the hillside opposite. He appeared to be waiting for her, as if he'd heard her coming and assumed the offer of a ride. It didn't occur to Cheryl that the man was a feral until she drew close enough to see that he had none of the equipment tree fellers usually carried. She was considering driving on when he smiled. The smile was so spontaneous, so genuine and so unexpected that Cheryl couldn't help but respond with a smile of her own. She slowed to a stop.

'Hop in,' she said and braced herself. She'd given people lifts before, many of whom had talked non-stop as if in payment for the ride. Cheryl didn't want that. At the very least she expected to be assailed by the smell of a sweaty unwashed body. The man climbed in the front seat, sat back and placed his canvas carryall between his feet.

'You're very kind,' he said, smiled once more and closed his eyes.

'No worries,' said Cheryl as she engaged gear. She dared to breathe and was relieved to find the inside of the car smelled no differently. When she stole a glance at her passenger his head was lolling on his chest as if he'd already fallen asleep. Cheryl marvelled that anyone could be so at ease and at peace with the world. As the kilometres ticked past it was easy to forget he was there.

* * *

'Oh my God!' Cheryl let the Landcruiser roll to a halt, struck by the beauty of the valley unfolding below them.

'Your first time up here?'

Cheryl spun around as if seeing her passenger for the first time. It took her a moment to gather her wits and nod.

'They want to turn it all into woodchips.'

'I know,' said Cheryl. 'That's why I brought my camera with me. At least I can preserve it on film.'

'That's very good,' said her hitchhiker. 'But not good enough.' He smiled gently and took both of her hands in his. He began talking, softly and poetically, looking into her eyes and touching her very soul. She sat spellbound as he put her feelings into words, those words massaging parts of her she never knew existed. She'd never heard anyone use words so beautifully. He spoke lovingly about trees and the understorey, made every trunk, stem, leaf and blossom seem as priceless as the Crown Jewels. He spoke about the animals and birds as if they were precious gifts, and Cheryl hardly dared breathe for fear of breaking the spell. He painted mental pictures which expanded the bounds of her imagination and were more moving than any Rembrandt, Van Gogh, Renoir or Monet. Cheryl wanted him to keep talking forever and couldn't quite put her finger on the moment when he actually stopped and let go of her hands. The click of the passenger door opening brought her back to reality.

'Who are you?' she asked.

'Can't you guess?' He smiled at her and his face lit up like Christmas. 'I am God,' he said. 'This is my kingdom.'

He turned and walked away into his valley. Cheryl didn't blink until he had disappeared from sight. Something very special had happened to her, something beyond her understanding. She sat motionless, staring down into the pristine forest as if seeing it for the first time. As the afternoon wore on she realised that the favoured light of sunset would not penetrate beyond the rim, and that she'd have to come back and shoot the magical valley at dawn. It didn't matter. Her journey hadn't been wasted; indeed, nothing could have been further from the truth. Something extraordinary had happened, something she'd been waiting for all her life.

She felt awakened.

CHAPTER TWO

Summer made the mistake of thinking everything she saw, felt and believed was real. A ball lampshade diffused the only functioning bulb in the huge room, a pathetic forty-watt bayonet-socket pearl nicked from KMart, which hung listlessly from a fitting attached to one of the exposed rafters. Strategically placed candles nicked from Woolworths and held upright by rock-hard bagels provided atmosphere and the only other light.

Every cell in Summer's body resonated with the vibes around her, and she felt so high she could have been out in the forests with God. Everywhere she looked she saw people having a good time. Even The Dick with Ears was loose, talking to a guy who'd come down from Sydney to picket the Moscow Circus. Big butch Ciaron had gone to the bucket bong once too often and was lying flat on her face, while one of the Sydney contingent who hadn't twigged to her orientation optimistically gave her a massage. Stretch, the resident muso, had got hold of a chick who wanted to be a singer and they sat staring into each other's eyes, as if expecting a divine revelation.

Summer didn't have a clue what they were on. Austrian Anke and Lyndal were chatting up two guys Summer had never seen before. She figured the way the girls were drooling over them they'd probably see action before the night was out. Thalia, squat mother, Buddhist of convenience and most permanent of the permanents, was doing her tolerant number, as if all the good vibes buzzing around were her doing. Pete was bending her ear about astral travelling. Pete drank five-dollar bottles of Aussie champagne and was often the first guy the timber workers picked on at a blockade. Barry sat alongside him, smiling his perpetual smile, smoking one joint and rolling another. Barry was Thalia's bloke and always smiling because he was always high on the grass he grew on the roof in the old factory's elevator and maintenance room. With the animal rights activists on their way back to Sydney, the WA conservationists heading back to their karri forests, various friends of the squat and half a dozen street kids in need of a feed and a place to sleep, Summer reckoned there were fifty people lying around on cushions or on the old sofa, although the candlelight and the kinetic state of her own mind made an accurate count impossible.

The thump-thump-thump she felt reverberating through the floorboards wasn't from the Vibe Tribe techno; it came from the big room up the steps and out the back where the transients slept. Dougie and his mates were brainlessly bouncing basketballs, maybe even playing a game.

By normal people's standards the squat was a mess. The walls had been painted out with slogans and plastered over with posters — a directory of worthwhile causes dating back the three years the squat had been going. But, by squat standards, the old factory was a palace. Summer had chosen the squat not because of what it had but what it didn't have. It didn't have fascist skinheads getting pissed and abusing everyone who didn't share their racist beliefs. It didn't have hard-core heroin addicts who stole, lied and were only interested in getting loaded. Shooting up was frowned on in the squat, in case anyone overdosed and brought the cops down on them, but those who wanted to usually managed to get ripped anyway.

Tonight was one of those great nights for the squat, when the anarchists, socialists, pro-abortionists, right-to-lifers, pro-drug, anti-drug, vegos and flesh-eaters all put aside their differences in favour of the things they had in common — their independence, belief in conservation and the rights of individuals (and animals), and their deep-rooted distrust of all governments, bureaucracies and multinational companies. Summer couldn't understand why every night in the squat wasn't as good, and why it took the presence of outsiders to unite them. She was thinking about getting out her sketch pad and trying to draw the scene in front of her when The Dick did his party trick. She didn't know what the trigger was, who said what or who did what, and it wouldn't have made any difference anyway. She heard The Dick cry out and jump to his feet.

'Arsehole!' he yelled.

Summer heard the sickening thud and his victim's scream. She closed her eyes. Darren — The Dick — always opened hostilities with a Liverpool kiss and things went downhill from there. All around her people were shouting and trying to grab hold of The Dick before he went totally psycho. Summer tried not to feel guilty because she didn't believe in being responsible for the actions of others. She made no claim on people and ran a mile when people made claims on her. Even so, Darren was sort of her bloke and she'd sort of introduced him to the squat. Some of the guilt found her and settled on her like an Antarctic mist.

'For Christ's sake, talk to him! Calm him down!' Thalia was screaming in Summer's ear, but she made no effort to move or even open her eyes. What could she say that she hadn't said a hundred times before? The truth was, Darren liked a fight, went looking for them and when he couldn't find one, started one. After every fight he'd promise never to do it again and look so contrite and boyish it was impossible not to believe him and give him another chance. But Summer decided that this time there'd be no more chances.

The music seemed louder but that was only because the shouting and screaming had died down, which meant that one way or another The Dick had been sorted out. Dougie and his mates had stopped banging their basketballs. Someone was crying. Summer thought it was the unlucky prick The Dick had picked on, until she recognised the sobbing as Pete's. She opened her eyes and found Lyndal squatting on the floor beside her, wiping champagne out of her hair and eyes.

'They bloody broke one of Pete's bottles over The Dick's head. Stupid bastards picked the full one.' Lyndal licked her fingers. 'Tastes godawful.'

'Where's Darren?' Summer asked.

'They threw him out, the guys I was talking to, Dougie and a couple of others. Jesus, Sum, he's a prick.

What did he have to do that for? Everyone was having a good time.'

Summer ignored the question. Ciaron was back sucking on the bucket bong and there was a queue waiting. Barry was telling anyone who cared to listen that things were 'cool'. Stretch and his little singer were sharing a joint while they waited for their divine revelation. Thalia was tending to Pete who'd got in the way of a stray fist. Things were settling down, but Summer knew it wouldn't be the same any more. The Dick had stuffed it and the magic had gone. There was nothing else for it: he had to go or she did. That was the thing about acid. It cut through all the crap and helped you see things more clearly.

* * *

The cold woke Summer. Her feet were frozen and the slight flesh on her body did little to protect her. It didn't matter that she was wearing her thick cords, a hand-knitted sweater over her thickest shirt over two t-shirts, and Darren's padded plaid jacket on top. Her bones ached with cold. She should have been warm, even though the squat was the coldest hole in Melbourne. She pulled the two blankets further across her, more in hope than in any real expectation of benefit. The cold seeped up through the gaps in the old factory floor and had no trouble penetrating the thin mattress. A sudden angry movement pulled the blankets back away from her. She lost more than she'd gained, but the to-ing and fro-ing had been going on all night. Whose mattress was she sharing anyway? Whose back had she curled against?

Who had curled up against her? Not Darren. The Dick had disappeared into the night. He'd probably get the shits again and worse when he came back and discovered she'd nicked his jacket. Reality beckoned but her mind was still too fogged and confused to grasp it. The only thing she was certain of was that she needed to feel better than she did.

She sat up and tried to feel positive, tried to remember what had made her feel so good and high only a few hours earlier, before Darren had done his trick, but the room remained dark and soul-destroyingly cold. The last time she'd felt this cold was in north-western Tasmania, where she'd been trying to stop the government putting a road through the Tarkine Wilderness. There, she'd had only a tarp and the kindness of strangers to protect and warm her. She'd never been so cold in her life. But she'd had soulmates by her side, ideals, and a cause to fortify her. She'd glowed with self-righteousness and fiery indignation, joined in the chanted demands and proudly taken her place on the blockade in defiance of the weather, hostile locals and grim-faced cops. They'd achieved nothing. The road had gone ahead and a virgin wilderness and precious habitat had been split open for logging and for tourists in cars to gawk at and litter. But the protest itself had been positive. She'd stood shoulder to shoulder with people from every part of Australia, all sharing a common concern and sense of outrage. She'd come away convinced that awareness of the government's crimes would grow and spread. The drops of rain would become a river, and the river a torrent. Maybe next time they'd win, maybe next time the government — any government — would think twice. Even in defeat there was cause for hope. But, as hard as she tried, she could find nothing to feel positive about in the morning gloom of the squat.

Thin light filtered through the cracks in the boarded-up window. Summer had no idea what time it was other than that it was morning. She didn't wear a watch or keep a clock, believing they were just another way the system enslaved and controlled people. The bleak light further depressed her. There were no bold patterns on the floor, no shafts of light that might signal a sunny day. As her eyes adjusted to the gloom she realised there were not one but two bodies lying on the mattress beside her. Three of them sharing a standard double mattress. No wonder she'd had to fight for the blankets. One was Ciaron and she was big enough to occupy the mattress on her own. Summer shivered and got up in search of a toothbrush. It didn't matter how many she stole she always ended up without one. She could go without washing herself or her clothes for a week at a time, but couldn't stand not being able to brush her teeth. Neither could others, it seemed, for they were always borrowing her brush and forgetting to return it. It wasn't theft or lack of consideration. In most cases they simply lent her brush to someone else who lent it to someone else until nobody could remember whose brush it was in the first place. Nobody really believed in possessions anyway.

Summer pulled on her boots and tiptoed as quietly as she could over sleeping bodies and past what had once been the managers' offices, where the squat's permanent residents slept, and slipped into the bathroom. Once she'd closed the door behind her she switched on the light. Someone had got the cocktail wrong and puked. The stench rose as solid as a wall. Summer had to wade through the porridge of vomit so she could squat over the toilet, but that was why she'd pulled on her boots. At least there was toilet paper. Her pee whistled into the bowl, and that was another thing she wondered about. Why did her first pee of the day always whistle? She pulled up her pants and tiptoed to the handbasin, opened the cupboard to see if anyone had been foolish enough to leave toothbrush and paste behind. Someone had. The bristles were yellow and shaggy and buckled under pressure, but a shaggy toothbrush was infinitely better than no toothbrush. Summer closed the cupboard door and stared at her reflection in the mirror. Someone cold and almost anorexic stared back, thin-lipped, squinty-eyed, hollow-cheeked. Someone sick, a shadow of the pretty girl that adorned her school photos. The feeling of unease came back: she looked sick, felt sick. Her red hair colouring was growing out so that it showed pinkish blond where it was undercut. She thought she could still see a greenish tinge on the sides, a reminder of the demonstration outside Victoria's State Parliament when she'd dyed her hair and painted herself green, pretending to be a tree. She untangled her shoulder-length rat-tails which had got caught up in the eagle's talons she'd woven into them. On the whole, the wedgetail eagle she'd found dead by the roadside had looked in better health than she did at that moment.

She tiptoed to the kitchen in the hope of finding a bagel. Most evenings someone from the squat made the trip to the House of Bagels, timing their arrival to coincide with closing time when the staff threw out all their unsold product. The staff were sympathetic to the needy, and didn't throw the bagels away so much as put them outside the back door in plastic bags and cartons for the homeless, destitute and desperate to forage through. Part of the thrill was getting home and discovering what kind of bagels they'd scammed. Plain, boiled, caraway seed, fruit. Nobody could forget the night The Dick had brought home bagels to go with a carton of tinned asparagus Summer and Lyndal had knocked off from Franklins. Everyone was starving and the prospect of asparagus in bagels had assumed the proportions of a state banquet. Then someone had made the gut-wrenching discovery — the bagels were chocolate chip. They'd laughed later, but definitely not at the time. As she rummaged through the rubbish on the kitchen benches Summer would have been happy to find a chocolate chip bagel, but the only ones left were plain, days old, hard as tram wheels and only fit for replacing the candleholders the rats had gnawed. There was milk in the fridge and Nescafé on the bench, but Summer had to get out. It was cold and gloomy and about to get worse. The residents with jobs or early lectures had already gone and she didn't want to be around when the rest woke up hungry, hungover, or needing to score. She couldn't handle any more negativity.

Port Melbourne was on the up with new factories, cafés, shops and restaurants opening daily, but the new prosperity hadn't yet touched the streets around the squat. Pensioners waited to die in ugly little houses, and couples who'd married too young and got themselves shackled with kids moved in when they did. But the newcomers only rented. Speculators and developers bought up every place as soon as it came on the market and then waited for the market to move. The system sucked, it really did. Summer knew she shouldn't have taken Darren's jacket. It would be the first thing he'd look for when he returned to the squat. In a community where owners had, at best, a casual relationship with possessions, everyone understood that Darren's jacket was Darren's. The consequences of borrowing it without his permission — which he wouldn't give anyway — just didn't bear thinking about. It looked like a thick plaid shirt but was padded like a jacket. Darren liked to think it was the sort of jacket rough tough Canadian lumberjacks wore, even though he was anti-logging. He ignored the Quicksilver label that showed it really belonged on the back of a surfie down on the peninsula who he'd had a disagreement with, punched unconscious and robbed. Nevertheless, Darren wore the jacket as if it were the sacred cloth of his calling, believing it identified him with the bush and forests. Summer knew he'd stress but there was nothing she could do about it. She needed the jacket so she'd taken it. It was his problem that he was short so the jacket fitted her as well. Besides, he owed her enough.

She wandered down Arden Street and into Bay Street, her back to the southerly that gusted up from the Antarctic and across Port Philip Bay. Her hands ached with cold even though she'd buried them deep in Darren's pockets. Her ears stung even though she'd turned up Darren's collar. Darren's jacket, she decided, wasn't all that Darren cracked it up to be. People were still grabbing breakfast and knocking back coffees behind the steamed-up windows of cafés. Summer hovered by one run by an Italian family, her practised eye latching onto the customers who were most impatient. She ignored people on their own, looking for people in groups of two and three who were fidgeting or looking at their watches, their slave bracelets. Two young girls, dolled up like secretaries, were hassling a third mid-way down the bar which ran the length of one side of the café. The bar was there for people who were too busy, too important, or didn't have the time to sit. Summer moved in.

'Leave it!' one of the girls said.

'We'll miss the bus,' said the other.

'Orright!' said the third. 'Dunno why they have to make it so hot.'

Before the girls had made it to the door Summer had the abandoned cup of coffee to her lips. It was black and unsweetened. She grabbed the sugar castor and tipped in three spoonfuls. Her hands gripped tightly around the cup, absorbing its warmth. People were looking at her but she was used to that and didn't care. Sensation flowed back into her fingers and her nose began to run. Darren's sleeve rose automatically to wipe it. Her eyes began to water as the scalding liquid was welcomed into her stomach. She dried them with the back of her hand.

'Use this.'

'Ta.' She took the paper napkin Jerry the waiter gave her, dried her eyes and blew her nose.

'You're not going to leave it there for me to pick up, are ya?'

Summer shoved the gluey napkin into Darren's pocket and instantly forgot about it. 'They left you a tip. Here.'

'Ta. Why didn't you pocket it?'

'Money only causes hassles.'

'I thought it was the other way around. The lack of.' Jerry knew he was on dangerous ground and changed the subject. 'You want milk in that?'

'Yeah.'

'I'll see what I can do.'

'Jer. . .'

'Yeah?

'Don't start liking me, will you?'

Jerry was nineteen, a year older than her, but in every other way at least three years younger. He was an Australian-born Italian christened Gianni, who played Aussie Rules in winter, cricket in summer, and still had to speak Italian at his parents' place. He was a bit too straight for her but still as cute as hell with snake hips and a bum women just wanted to grab. Summer knew he liked her. She smiled at him which made him blush and start gathering up empty cups and dirty saucers from along the bar. He took them away to the kitchen. As the swinging door fanned the air behind him Summer caught a glimpse of his mother bustling to intercept and hassle him. She didn't have to listen to know how the conversation would go. Jerry always had to defend her when she stole in for a coffee. His mum, dad and even his brother made it plain they wanted her out and gave him a hard time when he let her stay. In return she didn't abuse his kindness and imposed on each of the other cafés in the area equally. In truth she knew she should have gone somewhere else, but she was cold and desperately needed a friend to pump her up so she could feel positive. Maybe it was tough on Jerry, but he chose to work in his parent's café and that was his problem. At least he knew where his next meal was coming from and didn't have to crawl for the dole.

'Here's your milk.'

'Too late.'

Jerry rolled his eyes. 'Sorry, the service here sucks. I'll get you another.'

'Nah ... your old man will freak.' Summer's lips moved but she didn't.

'There's something I want to ask you about.'

'Okay, then. Cost you a capooch.'

'Sure. One cappuccino with raisin toast.'

Summer never said no to free food, always took what was on offer whenever it was offered because there were plenty of times when she went hungry. Jerry wheeled away and threw buon giornos at new arrivals, as every good Italian waiter is trained to do. She glanced up at his father behind the espresso machine. He looked away in disgust. She crept closer to the wall heater. The warmth had yet to reach her bones, but already she was feeling more positive. Ten minutes earlier she'd been cold and hungry with no prospects of alleviating either. Now she was smiling, standing next to a heater and breakfast was on its way. There was never any reason not to feel positive. Jerry was going to ask her out but that was too bad. As much as she liked him there was no place in her life for him and, if he was smart, no place in his life for her. On the other hand, if he asked her out it could finally push her into doing what she knew she had to do. She began to see the positive side of knocking Jerry back.

'Here you go.'

'Ta.'

The cappuccino had a thick collar of froth and a heavy dusting of chocolate. The butter on the raisin toast looked like it had been laid on with a trowel.

'Heard about this rave over in Collingwood Friday night. You want to come?'

'Love to.'

'Yeah?' Jerry's face lit up.

Summer took her time responding. The cappuccino left a frothy moustache on her top lip for Darren's sleeve to wipe away. Jerry handed her a bundle of paper napkins but she slipped them into Darren's pocket instead, deciding to keep them to use as tissues later. She sniffed to stop her nose from running.

'Where will I pick ya up?'

'You don't. Sorry, Jerry, I'd love to go with you but I've decided to head down to East Gippsland.'

'Give me the coffee back.'

Summer laughed. There, the decision was made and she immediately felt better for it.

'You're not hitchin' are you?'

'No choice.'

'Shit! Don't you read the papers?'

'No.'

'Hang on.' Jerry reached across and picked the morning paper up off a recently vacated table. 'Another hitchhiker's been dumped. This time near Goulburn.'

'I don't want to read it.'

'Cops reckon it's a truckie. A bloody maniac.'

'The cops are lying.'

'About it being a truckie?'

'About it being anyone. It's all lies. Propaganda.'

'Why would they lie about something like that? Look at the pictures!'

'Fake. It's all bullshit, Jer. Think about it. Every time there's a blockade on somewhere along the coast, they make like some hitchhiker's been murdered. Don't you see the pattern? Don't you think that's too much of a coincidence?'

'I dunno what you're talking about.'

'EGCGs, the East Gippsland Conservation Group, are planning a blockade and the cops know that people like me will be coming down from Sydney and Melbourne to join it. They know we hitchhike, so they make like somebody's been murdered to put us off going. It's obvious.'

'Aw, be real!'

'It's the truth! It's all a conspiracy so nobody turns up for the blockade. That way they don't get enough protesters to interest the media. If the media don't take any notice, they can do whatever they like and nobody gets to hear about it until it's too late.'

'Crap! I can't believe some of the shit you come out with.'

'Gino! Attsanuff!'

They both looked around at Jerry's father who'd moved out from behind his espresso machine and was glaring at them. Jerry shrugged and lowered his voice.

'You're so far out of your skull sometimes.'

'It's the truth, Jer, but you're like everyone else. You're so used to being manipulated you can't see it. You don't want to see it.'

'Bullshit!'

'Dorf dorf, da-dum, dorf dorf.'

'Don't do that techno shit.'

'De-oooo de-oooo–'

'Gino!'

'Please, Summer, gimme a break.'

Summer started to laugh. She looked around the café and at the curious faces watching them.

'Just take care, alright. I better go serve some customers before they walk out.'

'Horrrrrrrr . . . piff! piff!' said Summer. She let him walk a few steps away then used her talent for mimicry to imitate the espresso machine. That even got a laugh from Jerry's dad. The whole café came alive. People emerged from sullen morning stupor to smile and look at one another. The good vibes energised her. She beamed. 'Schurrrrrr . . .' she said, 'schurrrrrr . . . piff! piff!' She mimed the action, held cups, pulled levers. Somebody clapped and others joined in. 'Thanks Jerry,' she called. 'You've made my morning. Be nice to wake up alongside you one day.'

His mum and dad stopped smiling.

Summer waited until a couple of young guys left and followed them down to the tram stop. Someone was sure to be busking at the station or the square. Someone was sure to be busking somewhere and wherever they were she'd find them. She felt terrific, positive as all hell. She was on the move again and she always felt good about that. No ties, no attachments, no strings on her freedom, but no money either. She heard a tram rattling towards them.

'Dorf,' she said. 'Ta-dum ta-dum dorf dorf!'

The two young guys spun around.

'Hi,' said Summer. She started laughing. All she wanted was the tram fare to town and she didn't doubt for a second that the guys would provide it. There never, ever, was any reason not to feel positive.

* * *

Summer spotted Matt and Georgie in the mall with a girl called Sky, whose parents had both been hippies and prototype ferals in Gippsland before they caved in to the system. Sky had a sister called River and a brother called Malcolm; it was easy to see which part of the cycle her brother had been born in. Her parents disapproved so much of the way Sky lived that they no longer spoke to her. They knew first-hand about the drugs, the casual sex and the risks, and thought Sky had dropped out just to spite them. Summer snuck in around behind so she could take the buskers by surprise. She shook her head. Nothing was happening and nothing was going to happen. It was a personality thing as much as anything else. All three were good backing but no one had the front to lead. They sounded like losers, and passers-by were justified in not giving. She blew her nose into a napkin, stuffed the messy wad into Darren's pocket and crept up behind them.

'Dorf,' she sang. 'Whee-ooo, whee-ooo, dit-it dit-it, bee, biddle-oo biddle-oo.'

She took off in full flight, doing the licks and riffs that were her trademark. It was all the group needed. They dorf-dorfed and de-dummed, sang counterpoint and came alive for the first time that day. Passers-by stopped with stunned amused looks on their faces, wondering where the ghetto blaster was that they had to be miming to, and grinning foolishly when they realised the group was making electronic machine noises humans weren't supposed to be capable of. Summer played up to the crowd, which was half the trick. She made the act funny, took the mick and worked on the smiles. The smiles became laughs and hands dipped into pockets and purses. It was all so simple when you were positive. Everybody wanted to feel good and all you had to do was show them how. She sang, she danced rigid-limbed like a robot, and the two hats on the pavement began to rattle. The wind still blew mean and vicious but Summer began to grow hot inside Darren's jacket. She did a wind-down like her batteries were dying and burst out laughing.

'Summer!' Georgie threw her arms around her and kissed her. Georgie was like an older sister, a fellow activist and soulmate. She passed Summer on to Matt.

'Jeez, Sum, thank Christ you came along. We were dying here.'

'Yeah, I saw.'

'Need more than three for techno.' Matt kissed her, felt how thin she was but said nothing. Thought if he hugged her too tight she'd snap. He passed her on to Sky.

'Hi Sum.' Sky was new to the life and Summer was already a legend. She hesitated, not knowing how friendly she was supposed to be. Summer's hug left her in no doubt.

'We've taken more money in the last five minutes than we have in the last hour,' Matt said. 'Want to do a bit more then go for a coffee? Yeah?'

'Sure,' said Summer. A tram stopped nearby to drop another load of human fodder to feed the high-rise offices around them. 'Dorf,' said Summer counting them in. 'Dorf, dorf, dorf.'

* * *

'You look like shit.' Georgie said it sympathetically, but Summer did look like shit. They were sitting in an old-style café in Flinders Lane that had steadfastly resisted any concessions to progress or fashion. It still sold canned soups — tomato being its biggest seller — and salad rolls with sweaty ham, slippery lettuce, mushy tomato, thick cucumber wheels and grated shreds of carrot. But there was a market for their product and that market drove courier vans, delivery trucks, worked across in the rail freight yards, or didn't work at all. If nothing had changed over the years neither had the prices and that, plus the fact that the coffee was drinkable, was the reason for the café's continued existence. Darren's coat hung on the back of Summer's chair and without it they could see how scrawny she'd become.

'You're not using, are you?'

'Hey, no way!' She sniffed, reached for a table napkin and blew her nose. Her eyes started running again.

'You should get Gretta to make you up something. Okay?'

Gretta shared Matt and Georgie's flat and fancied herself as a herbalist and walking-talking authority on alternative medicine. She did reiki and had previously spent a couple of years with a French-based outfit that went around harmonising people. She'd studied iridology, colour therapy and naturopathy, but it was as a herbalist and harmoniser that she thought she'd found her true vocation. Gretta made up natural remedies, the only kind of potions that Summer was prepared to take. This was one of life's great ironies. Summer thought nothing of popping amphetamines or dropping acid, yet steadfastly refused to take so much as an aspirin for a headache. Pharmaceuticals were also part of the grand conspiracy, a rip-off perpetrated by foreign-based multinationals, and did more harm than good. She blamed the drug companies not just for thalidomide but for AIDS, Alzheimer's, multiple sclerosis and cancers of every kind. She believed, as all her friends did, that pharmaceuticals poisoned the system and that natural remedies were far superior. She also believed that the truth was being deliberately suppressed by government and big business in the interests of profits.

'How long have you had the cold?'

'Dunno. Ages. Since Tassie.'

'You had a cold before Tassie.' Georgie rolled her eyes and looked helplessly at Matt. 'Have you taken anything for it?'

'Darren brought me some stuff down from Nimbin. Do you know Valda? Yeah? Well, she made it up for me out of some bark and stuff the Aborigines use. Trouble is, Darren took over a week getting down to Melbourne and I think the stuff was off. I drank it anyway but it made me chuck.'

'Anything Valda gave you would make you chuck,' said Georgie. 'She made up a poultice for Matt's troppos once and they got so bad we had to go to a medical centre in Ballina to get them scraped. You never saw tropical ulcers like them. His legs had more craters than the moon. Matt ended up having to take antibiotics and it took months to get them out of his system. Gretta reckons Valda doesn't know the first thing about herbal remedies.'

Summer laughed. 'Valda said the same thing about Gretta.'

'Do you want to come to the flat now or later?' asked Matt. 'We can split the bread now if you like. After the coffee there's around twelve bucks each.'

‘Now, later, I don’t care. I need to go to the DSS.’

‘Yeah, same here.’ Matt stared morosely at his empty cup. ‘May as well get it out of the way.’

They got up and left. Summer needed her dole money, but she also needed to see Gretta. She needed to see someone. The rain picked up just as they left the café, exposing another weakness in Darren’s jacket. It wasn’t waterproof and, worse, it absorbed rain like a sponge. It dragged Summer’s shoulders down and her spirits with them. She stuck her hands into The Dick’s pockets for warmth and encountered the snotty tissues. The day had started badly and was heading back the same way. She tried to be positive. Maybe Gretta could do something for her, maybe she was just run down. But maybe it was something else, something more sinister. She shook her head involuntarily, as if to rid her head of negative thoughts, and stood wet and shivering beneath a shop awning while they waited for the rain to stop. Little Potoroo Creek seemed a long way away. Summer couldn’t help her feeling of unease. She couldn’t wait to get out into the forests so she could feel good again. She couldn’t wait to see God.

* * *

Darren caught up with Summer at the DSS. When he took off his beanie she saw that he had a lump on his head like half a hard-boiled egg. With his buzz cut it stood out like a red light on a cop car, but Summer knew better than to mention it. She just kept doodling away on her sketch pad.

‘Fuck you,’ said Darren by way of greeting.

Summer took off his jacket and handed it over. Matt and Georgie rolled their eyes but refused to get drawn in. The Dick threw his jacket over the back of his seat and started reading a copy of Nexus magazine somebody had left behind. He had a sullen look on his face that warned against any attempts at conversation or apology. Summer wondered what had happened to the boy hero who'd burst into her life in a blaze of glory at a blockade up in the central highlands.

It was only her second blockade and the first one that had turned nasty. Aging hippies from a local commune, whose sense of dress and reality was still rooted in the sixties, were holding the front line, hands clasped, singing 'We shall not be moved'. Coming at them were a couple of mad bastards waving high-revving chainsaws, followed by a mob of grim-faced loggers wielding axe handles. Summer had no faith in the power of song over the power of the mob and was scared shitless. She had no doubt at all about who would be moved. In her heart she knew that the thugs coming at them were just ordinary men, husbands and fathers from nearby towns who were just protecting their livelihood, but they didn't look like husbands or fathers and it was hard to believe they'd be going home to wives, children and dinner at the end of the day. Where were the cops? Where were the hard-hats from the Department of Conservation and Forestry? Summer felt a chill in her blood when she realised they'd all been persuaded to be somewhere else.

The front line was wavering and Summer could see that Ghandi's principles of passive resistance which they'd all got juiced up on were about as useless as her father's pathetic attempts to bribe her into going to university. The sound of the chainsaws ripped through the air, straining nerve ends. Men were shouting, women were crying, and nobody was singing any more. Then, out of the blue, Darren burst onto the scene, bare-chested and as angry as a boil. He marched up to within two metres of the guys with chainsaws, chin out with more aggro than a pit bull. He planted his feet, pulled out his dick and started pissing on the loggers. They scattered and Darren went after them. When he ran out of piss he spat. Great green gobs. The mob couldn't get out of the way fast enough. The tables really turned when one of the guys with a chainsaw tripped over. Darren was onto him in a flash and Summer saw first-hand the effects of a well-executed Liverpool kiss. The logger's forehead split open like a ripe watermelon. Darren picked up the chainsaw and what had begun as a bit of ducking and diving to get out of spitting range turned into a full-scale rout. The loggers legged it. Throughout the exchange Darren's dick poked out of the front of his jeans, growing bigger and harder in direct proportion to the level of violence he generated. Even more amazing — and everyone at the blockade noticed — was how much Darren looked like his dick. The shape of his head, his buzz cut and the hardness of his pale lean body helped, but it was more his attitude. He looked like a wild rampant willy from hell. That was the moment Darren acquired his nickname, and so did his dick. Darren became The Dick with Ears. His dick became Little Darren.

There was no doubting he was rude and vulgar, but in between his bouts of violence he could be extraordinarily sensitive, endearing and self-effacing. The women loved him and Summer was forced to wait her turn. When it arrived she gave him the full-on triple treat: boobs out, belly in and buttocks squeezed tight. But if Summer chose Darren, he also chose to go back to Melbourne with her, which in hindsight wasn't the smartest thing either of them had ever done. He didn't do drugs before he joined the squat, but thereafter did whatever he could scam. Without a cause to fight for, without issues clear cut and in front of him, without an enemy challenging him physically, he didn't know what to do with himself. He became a scrounger and bludged off the squat. Summer stupidly gave him what money came her way when her brain told her all she should give him was the shove. She didn't like relationships, didn't like guys who got into hard drugs, but somehow she couldn't find the energy to do anything about it. That worried her as well.

'Bastards,' said Darren alongside her, but Summer couldn't be bothered enquiring who the bastards were or why. Nexus was full of allegations of conspiracies and cover-ups, and Darren accepted everything the magazine said without question. She said goodbye to Matt and Georgie, who were regulars at the DSS, knew the system and already had their cheques. They were happy to wait for Summer but didn't want to hang around with The Dick.

Summer sniffed, gave up and wiped her nose on her own sleeve. She thought about trying to sneak a fresh napkin out of the pocket of Darren's jacket but didn't want to draw his attention to the ones that weren't so fresh. Her eyes watered and she felt cold, wet and sick. The DSS was also part of her problem. They made her feel worthless and a liar simply for claiming her entitlement. She believed people in Australia — in the whole world — were entitled to live without compromising their beliefs. Everyone was entitled to a living without government harassment or cynical inquisition. So what if she had no permanent place of residence? So what if she hadn't held a job in the past six months? So what if she hadn't been looking for one either? They'd jerk her around and give her more forms to fill out which they could ignore at their leisure until she gave up. Overhead Oprah Winfrey prattled on inanely and, unbelievably, some people actually watched. Summer thought the talk show battering was part of the process of humiliation and dehumanisation. The Dick with Ears seemed not to notice. She scratched away on her sketch pad.

She was only there for the money because she needed money. The drizzle had kept them off the streets, preventing them scamming coins with their singing and fire-eating. She needed money, even though money only brought more problems. Money was a problem and so was Darren, and Summer could feel her frustration with the DSS growing and growing, feel the deadening, steamrolling, unbeatable weight of the system, and knew the system was going to win. Again. She could see it in the doleful faces of the clerks. Yes! She started to smile. The doleful versus the doleless. She decided to share her observation with Darren. He didn't get it.

The real problem was in East Gippsland and she knew that was where she should be, where she wanted to be. Issues crystallised in the forests and her life regained its purpose. What she did there was grand and inspiring and absolutely vital. Did she have a job? Of course she had a job. It just didn't pay. She served a higher cause, one of inestimable value to the country and the whole world. Future generations would thank her, but in the meantime it didn't pay a bean.

'What do you think, audience?' asked Oprah.

'Next,' said a clerk. Somebody got up and shuffled dolelessly forward.

'Bastards,' muttered Darren.

Summer put down her pen and closed her pad. She'd drawn the clerks as grim reapers who cast shadows that spread over the walls and ceiling and settled like a pall over the waiting applicants. Some of the applicants had been waiting so long their limbs had grown around the seat supports like potato vines and sprouted leaves.

'Dorf, dorf do-wee dit dit,' sang Summer.

'Oh Christ!' said Darren.

'Dorf dorf . . .' sang Summer.

'Don't do it,' said Darren hopelessly.

But Summer had counted too many problems and they were all reflected in the mean suspicious faces of the DSS staff. Her drawing had only depressed her further. The system had won. She decided she'd survive without them.

'I'm out of here,' she said and left. Darren grabbed his jacket and followed her.

'Fuck!' he said, but nobody took a blind bit of notice. 'Why?' he demanded. 'Why'd ya walk out? Fuck're we gunna do now?'

'Dorf dorf, tee-wee dit dit.'

'Aw shit!'

It was raining again. They were broke. Darren wrestled his way into his already damp jacket.

'Can't handle them today,' said Summer. 'Why did you walk out?'

'Cause you walked out. I was cool.'

'Then go back. Get your money. I'm not stopping you.'

'Jesus, Sum, you can be a bitch sometimes.'

'Dorf dorf . . .'

'This doesn't make any bloody sense.'

'Then go back. Suck for your money.'

'Stuff you, Sum!' Darren spun away and headed back down the footpath to the DSS. He made the mistake of putting his hands in his jacket pockets. 'Bitch!' he screamed.

'See you,' said Summer amiably and kept walking. She felt good, even pleased with herself. Two problems solved — the DSS and Darren. The problems would recur but she might be in a better state to handle them when they did. All she needed was money and to feel better so she could start hitching to East Gippsland. 'Dorf dorf,' she sang.

Passers-by glanced at her and smiled. She did a little dance and laughed. Why be down when up felt so neat? Somebody would be at the station to give her tram fares to see Gretta. Somebody would scam some food. Somebody would have some grass or acid. She had no regrets and no worries. All she needed to get by was a positive attitude, and that was the greatest gift nature had given her.

Besides she'd made her decision. Little Potoroo Creek needed her and she'd waited too long to answer the call.

CHAPTER THREE

Miklos Laszlo Bollok was looking forward to the blockade at Little Potoroo Creek. He'd have preferred it if the greenies had picked on someone and someplace else, but he was never one to step back from a fight.

Miklos was born a bully. He weighed eleven pounds nine ounces at birth and promptly tried to push his mother out of bed. She took one look at him and swore. She knew immediately what she'd done. Nine months of cruel carrying through a hot Mount Redcliffe summer, nine agonising hours of labour, and all she'd got for her trouble was a replica of her husband. The baby had his large square head, his blunt forehead, his lack of neck, and his short pudgy arms and legs. Doubtless he also had his father's sensitivity and compassion. She wondered how long it would take before the new member of the family started thumping her around, making demands and treating her like hired help. She didn't wonder for long. The baby drew a long shuddering breath and screamed in indignation. He demanded attention. Yelled to be fed. Life was there to be lived, to be grabbed by the scruff of the neck and shaken until it had spewed up all it had to offer. Where the hell was everybody? His mother braced herself as a well-intentioned nurse lifted the baby up and laid him across the top of her belly. Miklos went straight for her nipple, grabbed hold of her breasts and began to suck. His sucking could have stripped the chrome off the bumper bar of a '58 Cadillac. If he'd been born with teeth he couldn't have hurt her more. His mother just accepted that this was the way things would be, and thought briefly about adoption and infanticide. When the nurse asked if she could bring her anything, she asked for a large gin.

Miklos's father, Ferenc, was a giant, a man made for a landscape that was super king-sized. He was a heavy machinery man and worked the mines of Western Australia. He trucked out iron ore in massive Euclids, drove bulldozers the size of a block of flats, and worked drills so huge he could have bored a tunnel through to Budapest to visit his folks. He was right at home with machines and relished his role in ripping up entire mountains and shipping them off in chunks to Japan. His strength was legendary, and he saw no reason why he shouldn't give others regular opportunities to witness and admire it. He never walked into a pub without looking for trouble, and usually found it. But two, three or four opponents at a time were never enough. He'd bludgeon, chop and hurl them into submission. They'd try to fend him off with pool cues, but the shafts just broke against his head and failed to slow him down. The violence helped him enjoy the end-of-day beers his workmates were always eager to buy him. His party trick at the end of the night, if he wasn't letting off steam with the mining town whores, was to sneak up behind cars and lift their rear wheels off the ground. He'd wait until the puzzled drivers fed in the revs then let go. On good nights the cars would suddenly accelerate wildly into the vehicle opposite, a manoeuvre guaranteed to start a fight. Sometimes they'd just break their axle or transmission. Whatever happened, he always got a laugh.

Miklos worshipped his father and wanted to grow up just like him.

Miklos thought he'd found his vocation when Ferenc decided to go into business for himself and leased a truck. His business grew through intimidation: when he asked people for their business they were usually frightened enough to oblige. Whenever he encountered resistance he negotiated. But, on the whole, few were prepared to argue with a man who negotiated with his fists, who laughed as he snapped arms and cracked knees back the wrong way. Before long Ferenc had six trucks running around for him and more money in his hands than he'd ever dreamed of. He even stopped thumping his wife and daughters, until the mining slump hit and mineral prices plummeted.

It was Miklos who came up with the solution. He was doing a school project on Western Australia's natural resources at the time, which required a lot of cutting and pasting and not too much thinking. 'E' words like environment and ecology weren't on the curriculum in those days.

'Bugger 'em, Dad,' he said. 'Tell 'em to get stuffed. We oughta take the trucks south and start cartin' logs. Says here we're shippin' whole karri forests off to Holland. They can't get enough of the stuff.'

The family moved lock, stock and prime movers down to Pemberton, where Miklos's dad beat up a few logging contractors, leaned on a few sawmillers and set up business. The boom days came back, the beatings stopped and Miklos turned fifteen, left school and got his driving licence. The examiner couldn't believe how skilfully the boy handled the heavy rigs. Miklos didn't bother telling him he'd been driving since he was twelve.

On his twentieth birthday he told his father it was time they expanded east. It was good business, he said, a good hedge against bad times. If things got rough in the west they could all head east, and vice versa. All he needed, he said, was one truck to get himself going. Ferenc thought about it and finally agreed. After all, it had been Miklos's idea to switch to hauling logs, and that had been the smartest move the family had made. He began thinking in terms of a continent-wide road haulage dynasty, and realised his eldest son was just the man to get it up and running. The boy was smart and a man after his own heart which, coincidentally, was the only real problem. That thought troubled him because he knew how dark and scheming his own heart was. He resolved his doubts by giving Miklos the oldest truck in the fleet, the first one he'd ever leased. He justified his decision by saying it was the only truck they didn't owe money on.

Miklos didn't argue. He shook hands on the deal and, when his father drove off to work, dropped the motor and transmission out of his old clunker and swapped them for the motor and transmission from Ferenc's new Mack which was up on the hoist for a service. Miklos was almost a thousand kilometres away, past Eucla and heading into South Australia, before Ferenc woke up to what he'd done.

He swore and cursed, picked a fight in the pub and put two blokes into hospital. He didn't feel the least bit proud that his son had grown up to be just like him.

Miklos knocked on doors, punched heads and conscientiously built his business the way his father had taught him. He began by shifting logs in Victoria's central highlands, and made a name for himself ducking levies by running logs to mills at the dead of night — the Victorian equivalent of a Tennessee moonshiner. Some wit in the pub nicknamed him My Left Bollok and the name stuck. The wit was lucky to make it to hospital with his left bollock still attached.

Miklos lobbed into the timber town of Osbourne near Orbost one day, and decided he liked the place. The local timber workers had a neat way of shaking hands with their fists clenched. The negotiations were intense and bloody but Miklos prevailed. As his business grew, so did he, quickly expanding to a size which almost justified him having his own postcode. The locals reckoned if he was up on Tathra Heights when the snow fell they could ski down his belly. Miklos realised that his days of driving trucks were coming to an end. Besides, he was becoming aware of how much more money he could make driving a desk. Miklos was a big man with big ambitions, but never in his wildest dreams had he envisaged a scheme like the one he saw going on around him. The name of the game, he realised, was politics, and the key to the incumbent politicians remaining in power in his far-flung neck of the woods was jobs. For people to remain in jobs there needed to be a healthy timber industry, yet everywhere around him sawmills struggled to survive. The contract loggers and haulers were no better off, being forced deeper and deeper into the forests to find suitable trees to fell. They worked longer and harder just to stand still. The banks and finance companies which advanced money on their rigs and equipment were not sympathetic. Miklos had succeeded by using intimidation to cherry pick the best contracts, but even he was finding the going tough. Yet for every problem there is a solution, and Miklos found it in the pages of the *Melbourne Herald*. He didn't know whether to laugh or applaud. It didn't matter. The sheer nerve of its architects left him speechless.

The news had been presented as another triumph by a caring government. In return for the promise of more jobs, the State government had given away concessions to four hundred and fifty thousand hectares of Crown land to the giant woodchip companies, along with a federal licence to extract and export five hundred thousand tonnes of woodchips every year for the following eighteen years. Miklos had chuckled then laughed out loud. He couldn't help himself. It wasn't just that the government had given away forests they didn't own, it was the promise of jobs. It took a lot of men a lot of time to extract sawlogs from forests in which there were few tracks and even fewer roads, and more men and more time to saw them into top quality timber. But the woodchip contracts were for clearfelling and Miklos had seen clearfelling first-hand. He'd watched the specialised machines and bulldozers with chains mow down football-field-sized slugs of forest in a single day. He knew it didn't take many men to do that, and he knew something else even more amazing: it could take a full day for loggers to haul out a single quality log, and another for a sawmill to cut and dress it. Clearfelling opened the whole forest to loggers and the woodchipping machines could eat a log every eight seconds. Machines did practically everything and didn't need a whole bunch of blokes standing by to watch them. By the time the government woke up to that fact, there'd be even fewer jobs than before and nothing they could do about it. The commitments had been made, there was too much investment involved, too many overseas contracts, and a pressing need to retain the few jobs that were left. There was no political will to do anything. The scam was beautiful. It was outrageous. It deserved to succeed. Miklos just had to laugh.

He sent his men out in their trucks and sat down to do a bit of thinking. He was a firm believer that if people could fall for a scam once, they could fall for it twice. All it needed was a fresh coat of paint. By lunchtime he had his proposal all worked out and rang the State member for the electorate of Tathra Valley, Bernie Dwight. Bernie was also a local man. He'd founded the Right Australia Party when he discovered his extreme right-wing views were so far to the right that neither of the major conservative parties would have him. 'Dwight is Right' had been his election slogan, and he championed the right of all white people to carry high velocity semi-automatic assault weapons against the day when blacks, Asians, pinkos or greenies gave them occasion to use them. Needless to say, he got elected by a landslide.

Miklos had given generously to Bernie Dwight's campaign, so he had Bernie's ear. When Bernie heard what Miklos had to say, he gave him the rest of him as well. Together they took Miklos's proposal to the local bank manager, who was smart enough to refer them to head office in Melbourne. In Melbourne they met with the senior loans officer who was new to the job and anxious to build an empire.

'Listen real close,' said Bernie. 'There's a good buck in this.'

The loans officer thought Miklos and Bernie were a gift from a compassionate God.

* * *

Miklos formed a company with himself as chief executive and Bernie's interest lost in the fine print. He called the company Regional Consolidated Sawmillers, and began snapping up majority interests in ailing sawmills.

'Size is strength,' he argued. 'Together we stand, divided we fall.' The sawmillers couldn't believe their luck. They'd thought they'd have to close down; instead Miklos gave them a cheque and the promise of a steady supply of sawlogs. They loved him. In return, Miklos gained control of their exclusive forest permits, which gave him vast areas of south-east Victoria to plunder.

His generosity extended to logging and carting contractors. 'You guys are gettin' done like dinners,' he told them, and showed them a better way. He bought out the leases on their trucks and logging equipment, and leased everything back to them at better rates. He encouraged them to lease equipment for clearfelling. If Bernie had retired, they would have elected Miklos to replace him. In return, Miklos gained control of their activities, decided who did what and who got what. It didn't take long for recalcitrant sawmillers to fall into line as their supply of logs became erratic or dried up. Miklos's empire grew.

Miklos needed the rights to take pulp logs so he submitted plans for a woodchip mill and applied to the government for a concession. Bernie presented the proposals to a Coalition government who relied on Bernie's continued support to maintain a slim majority. They gave Miklos a definite maybe and copped a battering from the major woodchippers who didn't want competition in any way, shape or form, especially when the competition took the form of an upstart like Miklos Bollok. The government denied Regional Consolidated Sawmillers their application for a new concession, but placated Bernie by giving permission to clearfell the areas to which they had exclusive forest licences. Of course the greenies objected immediately, but the government simply redefined the forests as degraded and insisted that Regional Consolidated Sawmillers were only removing the waste from the sawmill logging. The waste was between ninety-six to ninety-eight per cent of the original forests.

'It'll do,' said Miklos and immediately did a deal to supply one of the Japanese woodchip mills with pulp logs. When the government got around to asking him when building would begin on his woodchip mill he simply pointed to the denied concession and shrugged. 'Economics,' he muttered. 'Viability,' he said sadly. The fact was, the rights to clearfell the licensed areas was all he'd been after all along. 'At least I managed to save the sawmills,' he said, and he had. For the time being at any rate.

For the next few years, Miklos fed sawlogs to the sawmills and pulp logs to the chipmills. He supplemented the ash and other eucalypts he fed to the chipmills with the butts and tops of sawmill logs. When the chipmills asked for more he gave them more, and he didn't care how long the loggers and truckers had to work to provide it. The loggers and truckers didn't mind either, because the longer they worked the more money they made. They'd never had it so good. Inevitably, someone in the local pub renamed Regional Consolidated Sawmillers to reflect the true nature of its activities: Rip, Chip and Ship.

Sawmilling had very little to do with the business any more. The company prospered, but it didn't take long for Miklos to realise his resource was depleting. It was time to offer the government the prospect of more jobs. He repainted his proposal and resubmitted it to government. This time he proposed a pulpmill he had no intention of building to supplement the chipmill which he'd neglected to build, totalled up the number of people the combined project would employ directly and indirectly, talked added-value, export dollars and government coffers swollen by the levies on the trees he logged. The idea was that his pulpmill would supply the local paper manufacturers and help reduce the trade deficit. All he wanted in return was for the government to grant him a hundred thousand hectares of old growth forest, and build a few access roads here and there. Oh, and an export licence to tide him over until the pulpmill was built.

'Listen real close,' said Bernie to the minister in charge. 'There's a good buck in this.'

As luck would have it, Miklos's proposal was exactly the fillip the government needed to revive its flagging fortunes in the run-up to what promised to be another close election. The government granted a concession of eighty thousand hectares. The proposed pulpmill featured prominently in their election campaign.

Miklos immediately hit the bank for a loan to build his chipmill. The loans officer baulked at providing more money, particularly such a substantial amount of money, and referred the matter upstairs. The management understood the situation immediately. They had two choices: they could lend Miklos more money or lose all the money they'd invested to date. They lent the money on Miklos's solemn assurance that he had made no binding commitment to build a pulpmill. Miklos laughed. He couldn't believe people could control so much money and be so naive.

Miklos had learned his business well. The land he'd chosen for his concession was high country, full of mature straight silvertop and mountain ash which produced the beautiful white pulp the Japanese paid a premium for. Of course there were many other species of trees there as well. Ancient communities of mountain plum pine, magnificent five-hundred-year-old messmates, stringybarks, ironbarks, blue gums, grey gums, shining gums, lilly-pilly, sassafras and cabbage fan palms. Many of the trees were unsuitable for either sawmilling or chipmilling, especially the big old fire-blackened trees with their holes and hollows. Miklos regarded them as rubbish to be knocked down and burned, little realising that other people regarded them and the dense understorey beneath them as precious habitats for endangered wildlife and plants. Certainly precious enough to fight for.

The most precious area within his concession bordered on Tathra Heights. It had never been logged because it nestled between two steep ridges and was impenetrable to all but the most ardent and experienced bushwalker. The map on Miklos's wall recorded the precious spot as Little Potoroo Creek.

* * *

'What about this environmental impact study?' Miklos asked Bernie.

'What about it?'

'Well, shit,' said Miklos. 'What about the greenies? Seen the papers? They're trying to get the government to declare half my concession a national park.'

'Normal.'

'What're ya gunna do about it?'

'Done,' said Bernie. 'Spoke to my man in the Department of Conservation and Forestry. He knows the score. Told him there's a good buck in it.'

'So?'

'Jesus H, Miklos, you think this is the only environmental impact study the government has to do right now?'

'Suppose not.'

'Those blokes in DeCaF are busier than a three-legged kelpie with fleas. Regulations say they have fifty days to put in a report on rare, protected and endangered flora and fauna, and most of the time they're lucky if they can spend more than a few days on site.'

'I think I like this.'

'Gets better. There's a team trying to do a report on a couple of hundred hectares up in the central highlands, in mountain goat country. They got choppered out last time they went in because they got caught in a blizzard and nearly died from hypothermia. They've got ten days to finish their report and two of them are still in hospital. My man made sure they got given your job as well.'

'Jeez you're a bastard.'

'Do my best.' Bernie started laughing and Miklos joined in. Their eyes began to stream.

'Fuckin' land of opportunity,' said Miklos.

'Fuckin' oath!' said Bernie.

The two of them retired to the pub for the rest of the day to drink beer, get drunk and press the flesh with their constituents. A young bloke came into the pub while they were there, selling bumper stickers. Miklos liked them so much he bought fifty for the trucks and cars of everyone who worked for Rip, Chip and Ship.

'Fertilise the forest,' they said. 'Doze a greenie.'

* * *

The two men from the Department of Conservation and Forestry flew over the Rip, Chip and Ship concession, drove around in a four-wheel drive as far as existing trails would allow, got out, wandered around a bit and got straight back into their Landcruiser. It was cold, wet and windy and the rain was trying hard to turn into sleet. They sat shivering, wondering why they always got the miserable jobs instead of the fact-finding missions to Rio. Their driver, a department man from way back who'd been primed by Bernie, bided his time then let his guests in on the secret.

'Who do you work for?' he asked.

'DeCaF,' they responded.

'And what does DeCaF stand for?'

'Department of Conservation and Forestry.'

‘Do you put the emphasis on the beginning or end of your sentences?’ he asked quietly and looked pityingly at his guests. ‘Try putting it on the end for a change.’

The two men thought about this and took another look at the forest around them, this time from a new and enlightened perspective. All they saw were a couple of eastern rosellas, a wet butcherbird and an expanse of forest just sitting there doing nothing of benefit to anyone. A definite waste of a natural resource. They raced back to Melbourne and fabricated their report in the light of their new perspective, hedging their findings — as every public servant is trained to do — so that they didn't actually lie. They hadn't seen any sign of spotted-tailed quolls, long-footed potoroos, wallabies, ringtail possums, leadbeater's possums, gliders, powerful or sooty owls, and their report reflected their acute lack of observation. They hadn't seen God, either, but they could be excused for that. At the time, they didn't know he existed.

CHAPTER FOUR

For the first week after her encounter with God, Cheryl felt like a displaced person. She'd awakened but wasn't sure to what. She felt an overwhelming longing one moment and flat the next, and was at a loss to the cause. Some days she just wanted to jump into her Landcruiser and head off up to Tathra Heights, but on other days doubts nagged at her. How would she find him? And if she did, what was her motive in finding him? She created excuses for doing nothing. One day it was a light drizzle, another the need to go shopping. When Miklos brought home some books for her to check to make sure nobody was fleecing him, she welcomed the work for the simple reason that it excused her from having to make a decision.

As more days passed she began to wonder if God really meant as much to her as she had imagined and, if so, what did she mean to him? She began to fear the consequences of a second visit. What if he'd forgotten all about her? What if he ignored her? Worse still, what if he'd discovered who she really was? Something extraordinary had happened up on Tathra Heights, something that had opened her heart and fired her soul. She'd witnessed first-hand the power of love and had been moved to the point of tears, even though that love had been directed not at her but at the forest. Something inside her had reciprocated, but for what? Or whom? It had been a magical, unforgettable moment and Cheryl felt both possessive and protective of it. But what if he'd forgotten about her? What if he ignored her? What if he'd discovered who she really was? Her doubts ate away at her. She grew increasingly reluctant to risk a second encounter with God in case it in any way diminished the first.

She found it easy to justify her timidity. There was something pitifully absurd about a thirty-five-year-old married woman with two kids chasing around a forest looking for a feral dropout whom she knew absolutely nothing about, and for reasons she was not prepared to face. The fact that she was also the wife of Miklos Bollok made it even more ridiculous. So instead she cherished her memory of her meeting with God, clung to it like an old spinster clinging to a faded photo of her lost one true love.

Not a day passed when she didn't think of him. He helped fill her lonely hours. When she stood before her easel, brushes in hand, ready to translate her photos onto canvas, she liked to believe that she was painting the forests for him. It was only when she was preparing to begin a fresh painting that her omission occurred to her: Miklos was going to destroy Little Potoroo Creek and her magical valley with it, and she still hadn't taken the photograph. She was seized by dread and anticipation in equal parts when she realised she had no choice but to visit Tathra Heights once more.

CHAPTER FIVE

Summer began to wonder if coming to the hospital was such a smart move after all. They always tried to suck her into the system and make her take drugs which only made her feel worse. But Gretta's potions had done nothing, except taste like the diarrhoea they'd afflicted her with. She needed help and didn't know where else to turn. The young doctor was surly and clearly disapproved of her. When he took a blood sample he checked her arms for needle marks.

'Your boyfriend come with you?'

'I wouldn't call him that, but yeah, he's waiting for me out there.'

'Might take some blood from him while we're at it. What's his name?'

Summer told him and watched the doctor disappear through the curtains of her cubicle. She rubbed her arms then wrapped them around her. The feeling of dread had come back and there was nothing she could do to dispel it. As she left the hospital a shiver ran through her which had nothing to do with the cold.

* * *

'Hi everybody,' said Summer as if she wasn't scared shitless that she might really be sick. 'Dorf dorf beedle-eep.'

'Hi!' said The Dick. 'I'm from This is Your Life. I'm here to remind you you've got one.' He was still pissed at having to give blood and really pissed at the old bat who'd taken it. She'd spotted the bruises on the inside of his arm where he'd injected his dole money and taken it upon herself to give him a lecture. She'd scoffed when he'd told her it wasn't a habit, just recreation. What would she know? Some of the checkout girls laughed. An old woman turned away in disgust. Most people just looked on bored. Darren started banging on the cardboard box he was carrying, drawing attention to it.

'Ari Krishna, Ari Krishna ...' sang Summer. She danced in and out of the closed checkout counters and round and round the people queueing to buy their way out, deliberately making a nuisance of herself. Darren made the box seem heavy as he followed her. It didn't matter that it made a hollow sound. Who cared enough to notice? The checkout girls smiled, relieved to have a break in the monotony. Summer danced down the aisle looking for any half-filled boxes the shelfstackers had left behind. She found one but it was full of boxes of Kleenex. The next was empty. Empty would do at a pinch. Darren found a box with a dozen cans of John West red salmon in it and swapped it for the one he was carrying.

'Dorf dorf, deedle-eeep, deedle-eeep,' sang Summer as she danced around an elderly couple. 'Have a nice day,' she said. She kissed the old bloke on the cheek, something the couple could talk about as they went through the checkout. Darren grabbed things off the shelves he thought would come in handy. Cans of soup, bars of soap, bottles of shampoo, tubs of margarine. Summer topped up the box with tomatoes, carrots and broccoli which she broke off the stalk. She preferred to eat organic but they didn't have the luxury of choice. She backtracked past Darren and grabbed a handful of toothbrushes and some toothpaste.

'Jesus,' said Darren. 'Why d'ya need so many?'

'For me, for the squat and for God.'

Darren grabbed some corn chips and onion and chive dip. He got pissed off when he couldn't find chilli bean or guacamole. Summer found some one-kilo bags of rice.

'What do you reckon?' she asked.

'Got enough.' Darren pulled a roll of gaffer tape from his pocket. A used tissue tumbled out; they both pointedly ignored it. They'd already had that conversation. He folded the box lid closed and bound the edges together with gaffer tape. The way he taped the box made it look like it had just come from a long sea voyage. When he'd finished taping he pulled out some string and bound it around the box in such a way that it ended up making a handle. He wrote a fake name and address on the box with a squeaker and 'By Courier' across the top. Summer picked up two loaves of multi-grain and together they Ari Krishna-ed to the checkout.

'Here we are again,' said Summer brightly to the checkout girl. Darren gave her his best 'wanna-bed-down-with-me?' smile. The checkout girl smiled back.

'Better give me some money,' said Summer. Tactics demanded they make a big deal of paying. Darren handed her five dollars in coins which she carefully counted and passed to the checkout girl.

'Ever thought of just getting up and running away from this place?' asked Summer.

'Only every waking moment,' said the checkout girl.

'Hey, let us know when you do,' said Summer. 'There's plenty of room at the squat. We'll take care of you.'

'Thanks for the offer,' said the checkout girl.

'Don't forget us,' said Darren. 'Have a nice day, what's left of it.'

'Ta,' said the girl and turned to the next customer. She didn't notice that the box Darren was carrying had changed. Why would she? She never expected anyone to walk out with a whole box full of stuff they'd lifted. Didn't care if they did, anyway.

* * *

'You can ditch this. And this.'

Darren hesitated to argue because he'd already caused the squat enough aggro. But Ciaron gave him the shits. She wasn't just a dyke who could do with a good shave, she was also bigger and almost as strong as he was. Nevertheless, he and Summer had gone to too much trouble and taken too many risks.

'Fuck you,' he said and picked the soap and shampoo up off the floor.

'Tested on animals, you effin' moron.'

Everyone in the squat knew that was a no-no, but also understood that what was at stake was good quality shampoo which they desperately needed. Sometimes it didn't hurt to waive principles. They watched with interest and waited. Ciaron snatched the shampoo off Darren and threw it back down onto the floor.

'Get rid of this shit before Thalia comes home.'

Darren bent over and picked them up.

'Listen Ciaron, there's no fuckin' way I'm throwin' this stuff away. If ya want to use it, go ahead. If you don't, then leave it for others.'

'You tellin' me how I should live? You tellin' me it's all right to use this shit? You sayin' it's okay to test products on live animals?'

Summer covered her ears and walked as far away from the argument as possible. She walked through to the common room, which wasn't supposed to be a bedroom but often was, and curled up on a sofa someone had rescued from a council clean-up. Arguments were inevitable but also stupid. You couldn't have so many people living so close together without some arguments, even though Summer couldn't remember arguments ever solving anything. Arguments were negative and people only solved things by being positive. She tried hard to focus on something positive. If only she knew what was wrong with her she could start doing something positive about it. Above all she needed to move on, to get back to basics and do something constructive. She tried to think about her hike through the East Gippsland forests, fifteen of them sharing food, tents and toothbrushes for ten glorious days. They'd held each other's hands and only just managed to link up around the trunk of a massive five-hundred-year-old messmate. They'd sat up at night to spot for powerful owls and possums, and held their breath in the hope of seeing a long-footed potoroo, a leadbeater's possum or a spotted-tailed quoll. Summer had learnt to recognise incense plants and sunshine wattles, bitter peas, showy boronias and the wonderfully named geebungs. People shared the same beliefs, hopes and passions in the forests, and there were never any arguments or drugs, apart from grass and sassafras root. The forests were humbling, majestic, beautiful. People didn't need drugs to feel high. That was a city thing. Summer felt her eyes water and she wanted to cry for what she was missing. She yearned to hit the road but there were too many things holding her down. The hospital wanted her back for the results of her tests. She had Darren to deal with. She needed money but couldn't face the DSS. Everything was ganging up on her. She forced herself to remember the most special place they'd trekked to, an untouched pocket of forest that reached back in time to the break-up of the great southern continent of Gondwanaland. Summer fell in love with Little Potoroo Creek the moment she set eyes on it. She felt its age and unchangedness, its stillness and foreverness, let its immaculate, pristine beauty wash over her. In it she found justification for her chosen path and a shrine to her calling. She carried the shrine in her head and retreated there whenever she couldn't cope. It was where she went when trips turned bad, and in the loneliness of night when she couldn't sleep. It was where she went when she needed to hide. It was also where she went to find God.

'How d'ya put up with that dickhead?'

Ciaron slumped down on the sofa next to Summer's feet. Summer thought Ciaron had become a dyke because she didn't have the sort of looks that attracted guys. She didn't help matters by shaving the sides of her head and wearing her hair like a floppy black mop. When she wore lipstick she wore black, and painted her nails to match. She had a rivet in one earlobe, embossed with the word Levis. Her mother had christened her Ciaron instead of Sharon because she thought the spelling had more class. 'Class my arse!' said Ciaron the moment she was old enough to understand, and watched a parent's hopes shatter. Summer tucked her feet up under her and tried to smile. Even in the gloom the tracks of her tears were easy to spot.

'Oh shit.' Ciaron put her arm around Summer's shoulders and hugged her. 'Arsehole's not worth it, Sum.'

'I agree.' Summer started to laugh. 'Got other problems.'

'Wanna tell?'

'No.'

'Make you feel better.'

'No it won't, but what the hell. I have to get away, go to Gippsland but, you know, everything's trying to stop me going.'

'Like what?'

'Doesn't matter.'

'If it's The Dick, I'll give you the bus fare and a push start. Go with you if you like. Take you on me bike.'

Summer smiled. She knew what that meant. 'I don't think so.' She made no effort to move or make Ciaron take her arm away.

'What's the matter? Aren't I man enough for you?' Ciaron sniggered dismissively, but the question was still loaded.

'Only in one small area.'

'I could always strap one on, you know.'

Summer laughed. There'd been a time when she'd just lobbed in from Sydney and was open to trying anything. She hadn't resisted when Ciaron had seduced her and was exhausted by the time Ciaron had finished. The big girl had known exactly which buttons to press and when to press them, and Summer had never suspected her body was capable of so much sensation. Yet she wasn't satisfied when she should have been, and she didn't need Einstein's help to work out what was missing. Once had been enough, but Ciaron still held out hope.

'Well you should just piss off anyway. If that's what you wanna do.'

'I need money.'

'I could loan you forty dollars.'

Summer thought about it. Forty dollars would just about do it. Toothbrushes, batteries, candles, heavy-duty garbage bags and a flagon of Chestnut Teal sherry. Forty dollars would go a long way, and what it didn't cover she could always steal. She'd also need a bit of money for the road and of course some more rice. Gifts for God. There was a lot to be said for just packing up and running away. Temptation didn't beckon, it grabbed her by the hand. She leant over and gave Ciaron a kiss on her cheek.

'Forty dollars might do it,' she said.

'One condition,' said Ciaron. 'You give dickhead the big A.'

* * *

Summer waited until they were halfway through dinner before telling Darren her news. That was when Darren told her his.

'Why didn't you tell me before?' she said.

'Forgot,' said Darren. 'So what? Doesn't change anything.'

Summer dipped her fork into her vegetable risotto and raised it to her mouth. Once more the squatters had put aside their differences and petty squabbles and become one big happy community. The fact that there was good food and plenty of it always helped. Someone had seized upon the rice and vegetables and added a couple of cans of chicken soup for stock. The result was gluey but tasty, and nobody complained because it was also free. The vegetarians had copied the idea and used vegetable soup. Everyone was welcome to eat as much as they liked and nobody wasted the opportunity. Summer had begun to feel really positive when Darren dropped his bombshell. That was so bloody typical of him.

'The others will only be in it if you do the organising,' said The Dick. 'Nothin' to do with me.'

'Know what you are, dickhead?' said Ciaron. 'A complete arsehole.'

'Fuck off,' said Darren.

Summer should have guessed. If she'd been feeling normal she'd have been ahead of the game and volunteered. Of course the East Gippsland Conservation Group would need money for the blockade. For food and tarpaulins. If she'd gone along to the Friends of the Earth office she would have seen the message for her on the noticeboard and not hesitated. She felt embarrassed that they'd had to ask for her.

'We'll all help you,' said Ciaron. 'Right?'

Summer was showered with offers of illicit access to computers and photocopiers. She started to laugh. One moment she'd broken free and was off to Gippsland, the next she was organising a rave. Nothing ever went the way it was supposed to. At least she was needed. At least she could use her talents and contribute. She was the best organiser, the only person the pros felt safe dealing with.

'First we have to find a venue,' she said. 'See what you guys can come up with. I'll do music, DJ and lights.'

'What about posters?' someone asked.

'Yeah, I'll do the posters.' Summer's posters were legendary.

Ciaron caught her eye and shrugged helplessly. Both knew Summer wouldn't borrow the forty dollars or give The Dick the shove. Not that night anyway. Instead Darren would snuggle up to her and start playing with her perfectly shaped tits, totally unaware of how close he'd come to playing with himself. They both began to laugh.

All around them people were throwing in ideas. It didn't take much to get the squat motivated, just a good cause with a desperate inflexible deadline. Ciaron suggested they go gothic and everybody loved the idea for ten seconds. But gothic was factional and not everybody was into goth clothes and music. They needed mainstream with as little organising as possible. It would have to be a techno rave with some gothic they decided, but Summer knew they'd have to settle for whatever they could get.

* * *

Summer sidled up to the bar near the heater. Jerry's father pointedly ignored her. The young exec had left half a macchiato and a third of a ham and cheese croissant. She turned the cup around and broke off the bit of croissant that had been chewed. The coffee needed more sugar but the croissant tasted fine. Summer had been one of the first up and had braved the shower, but even so most of the new shampoo had gone. Nothing good ever lasted long. She'd washed and scrubbed but had no underwear or clean clothes to put on. It seemed a waste of a wash.

'Thought you were going down to Gippsland.'

'G'day, Jer. Change of plan.'

'Ya coulda come with me to the rave.'

'Sorry. You want to come with me instead?'

'Yeah? Where?'

'Dunno.'

'When?'

'Dunno.'

'I'll be there.'

Summer burst out laughing and Jerry joined in.

'You're bloody hopeless, Sum.'

* * *

Summer knew better than to try and plan her day because something else always came up. She set off for the Friends of the Earth to check the noticeboard and get in touch with EGCGs. The Friends of the Earth let her use the phone to organise things. She also needed some underwear, especially warm underwear and spencers to wear in the forest. She didn't really want to walk into

Woolies and steal stuff because it was too risky, but without money she didn't have a lot of choice. Thinking of underwear made her think of the bras she didn't have and the doctor she had to go back and see. The shadow reached out and found her. How sick was she?

'Summer, please phone home, love Mum.' There were two exes for kisses, and three more increasingly urgent messages from her mother.

Summer read the notices and felt guilty. She hated herself for feeling guilty because she'd done nothing wrong. She'd told her parents right at the start that they'd have to get used to the way she chose to live. The notices always indicated otherwise.

'Summer, please contact Brian or Liz at EGCGs.' There was a date at the top and a phone number at the bottom. The message, like those from her mother, was over two weeks old.

'Hello, Summer, where have you been hiding?'

Mrs Thomas was retired, seventy years old, and totally dedicated to the Friends of the Earth. She gave her time for nothing to help out in their office and shop, and gave all of it.

'Hello, Mrs Thomas.' Summer reached across the counter and gave the old lady a kiss on both cheeks. 'I've been around. You know.'

Mrs Thomas did know. More than any other conservation group, the Friends of the Earth appreciated and valued what the ferals did, and went out of their way to help them. They took messages, provided a noticeboard service, a phone and whatever facilities they could. They even provided recycled paper for posters. What they didn't do was judge or criticise. At any blockade the ferals were the front-line troops, often the ones who were arrested, usually the ones who got beaten up. Mrs Thomas regarded Summer as a displaced feral, a bush baby on holiday who really belonged in the forest.

'Can I make a reverse charges call to Sydney?'

'Good girl. Of course. I was hoping you would. I had a long chat with your mother the other day. I told her I'd look out for you.'

'I've got to ring EGCGs, too.'

'Mum first or no phone.'

Summer laughed. She always felt awkward phoning home and it helped when Mrs Thomas made her feel good. 'I'm trying to get away to see God.'

'Give him my regards when you do,' said Mrs Thomas. 'Now ring your mum before anyone else wants to use the phone.'

'Hi Mum!' Summer made her voice sound like she was an over-excited schoolgirl phoning home from camp.

'Summer, thank God.'

She thought her mum was going to burst into tears. She heard her voice crack and fight for control.

'Where are you?'

'Melbourne.'

'Why didn't you call sooner?'

'I just got your message.'

'How are you?' The million dollar question.

'Good. Really good. How's Dad?' Summer deflected the questions into routine exchanges. She knew her mother wanted to ask her what she was doing, did she have enough to eat, enough clothes, enough money, how she was coping, but Summer also knew she wouldn't like the answers. Beneath it all would be the unspoken accusations about leaving home, not going on to university, throwing away her life. So she asked about her brothers, her cat Smidgy and dog Wilbur. She could've been a schoolgirl at camp, not a sick young woman off to try and save the world in the forests of East Gippsland. In the end she told her mother about the blockade at Little Potoroo Creek, and how much she was looking forward to it. She made it sound like a Girl Guide jamboree. In her heart she knew her mother just wanted to hear her talk, hear her voice, hear that she was well, that she was safe. She hoped her mother wouldn't be too upset when she hung up, but there was absolutely nothing she could do about that.

'When are you coming home?' her mother asked. 'What can I tell your father? When will we see you?'

'I'll try and get up after the blockade,' said Summer. 'Yeah, after the blockade. I'll really try.' All of a sudden she felt her emotions well up inside. She wanted to tell her mother everything, tell her how sick she felt, how scared she was, be a little girl again and go home so Mum could look after her and make everything right.

'We'll look forward to it.'

'Me too. Bye, Mum, love to Dad and everyone. Got to go, other people want to use the phone.' It was a harmless but necessary lie.

'Goodbye, baby. Love you.'

'Love you, too, Mum.'

'Love you.'

'Give Dad a hug for me. Bye.'

'Love you,' said her mother once more and Summer could almost hear the tears rolling down her mother's cheeks. She swallowed the lump swelling in her throat, fought back her own tears and hung up. It wasn't easy. It never was.

* * *

Summer pulled out her notebook and began phoning around. But people who'd helped before were either unavailable or uncooperative. Summer crossed another name off the list. It wasn't easy to get sound gear for nothing. Sound hire was a marginal business at best and nobody wanted to touch charity gigs, especially on a Friday which was one of the nights they made their money. She rang two more numbers but the guys had moved on. There was no point asking if they'd left a forwarding address or phone number. Nobody ever left anything behind except an unpaid rent bill. Normally she'd know where they'd gone, know they were moving before they did themselves. But she hadn't been getting around. The realisation momentarily stunned her. She hadn't been getting around. Hadn't been to the Friends, hadn't been to the Wilderness Society, hadn't been to the Australian Conservation Foundation. Hadn't been out. What had she been doing? How long had she been feeling off?

'G'day Kevin. It's Summer. How're you doing?' Silence. She'd been putting off this call, knowing it would be difficult. She wasn't sure how she'd cope with it. She tried to be positive. You had to be positive to make things happen. Kevin was every woman's dream. Tall, athletic, charming and weird. He was goth before gothic took off, had the whitest skin she'd ever seen and always wore black. His hair was naturally black but he dyed it blacker, had black eyes too, heavy eyebrows, high cheek bones and lips like Val Kilmer's. Colour him up he would have made a great Apache, but for the silver ring through his left nostril and the crucifix tat on his chest. He'd turned his charm on Summer and blown her away. He'd taken her home and she'd stayed three weeks. They'd fallen in love and made love at every opportunity. They'd done it standing up, sitting down, lying down, on the floor, in the bath, on the back of his Honda bike. Summer had never known anything like it. They'd been like Siamese twins joined at the groin. One day she'd realised she'd lost her freedom and independence, walked out of Kevin's flat and hadn't stopped until she'd reached the far north coast two thousand kilometres away. She'd hitched rides with truckies who bought her meals and drinks and gave her amphetamines to try to stop her crying. She'd left Kevin in bed, waiting for her to come back with his coffee. He'd waited two hours, unwilling to believe the impossible. Now Summer held her breath, knowing it wasn't up to her to break the silence.

'No card, no flowers, no phone calls, nothing.'

It was an old joke but at that precise moment it could have been the best one Summer had ever heard. She burst out laughing, heard Kevin start laughing at the other end.

'You okay, babe?'

'Good. Real good. You?'

'Apart from three weeks of my life, never felt better.'

Summer bit her lip. 'Yeah, it was good,' she said eventually.

'No regrets. You probably did the best thing. Are we going to see each other?'

'That depends on your best price,' said Summer and told him what she wanted.

'Where?' asked Kevin.

'Dunno,' said Summer.

'When?'

'Week Friday.'

'Knew it. No worries. I'll get someone to cover for me.'

'You'll do it?'

'Do anything for you, babe, you know that. Just cover my costs.'

'No worries.'

'What do you want?'

'Dorf dorf beedle-eep beedle-eep.'

'Easy. I've got heaps of new stuff. Hey, any chance ... you know ... for old time's sake?'

Summer laughed teasingly. It didn't say yes and it didn't say no, it just left him in hope.

'If you're stuck for a venue,' said Kevin, 'you might try Morrie Mayberry. He's trying to set up a sound stage in an old warehouse in Collingwood. I'll give you his number. He'll want a percentage of the gate.'

Summer took down the number as Kevin read it out. Sure Morrie would want a percentage of the gate, but Summer could beat him down. They'd been friendly a while back and Morrie would do anything for her too. She hung up on Kevin and dialled Morrie. It seemed both former lovers were in good health and she felt relieved about that. She wondered again what the doctor at the hospital would find in her blood. Sure, she'd had other lovers but Kevin went back two years and Morrie at least one. That wasn't sleeping around. No way.

CHAPTER SIX

Dear Editor,

My Friends call Me God. Every morning I wake at Dawn and look out over my Kingdom and see Heaven on this Earth. The Mists peel back like a fluffy blanket from My Bed, roll back over the Ridges and rest momentarily as if impaled on the soaring tops of Giant Messmates. Few Mortal Eyes have seen what I see.

My Forest is dense with the finest Eucalypts in Creation. Mountain Ash, Silvertop Ash, Shining Gums, Grey Gums, Blue Gums, Angophoras and so many more that I fear listing them would test your Patience. Some are so very old The Twelve Apostles could not reach around their Trunks. They have been here for Hundreds of Years and their Ancestors for Millennia. Do you know that all of Victoria's Eucalypts sprang from this Cradle? It's true. East Gippsland was the Ark that bore these trees from the Great Southern Land — Gondwanaland. I take Pride and great Joy in their Existence.

Beneath them in the Understorey, I find Geebungs, another Gift from Gondwanaland. To touch them is to touch the very Origin of this Great Land, to understand the Lesson that we inherit not from our Fathers but borrow from our Children. Everything I have is Theirs and it is my Solemn Duty to hold it in Trust for Them. The Geebungs share the Soil with Wattle and Boronia, Waratah and Olive-Berry, and more. Again, though every Bush and Shrub is Precious and Equal in My Eyes I will not tire you with their many Names.

There is a Stream that runs Silver with the Purest Water, that broadens beyond My Domain and carries to the Pasture Lands below. It sustains Me and My Neighbours. Yes! My Neighbours, for I do not live alone. Sometimes in the quiet of the Evening, after the Sun has gone from My Sky, I catch glimpses of My Neighbours as they come to drink from My Stream.

I have won the Trust of a Family of Long-Footed Potoroos. They drink in My Presence provided I do not move, for they are shy, timid, little Creatures. They may lack the size and numbers of their larger Cousins, the Kangaroo and Wallaby, but are more Precious because of it. They are a Rare Sight now and their Species endangered.

I see Spotted-Tailed Quolls, the last of Victoria's Carnivorous Marsupials, who regard Me with caution. Their Coats are a magnificent brown dotted with ginger and white spots. It is saddening to realise they, too, face Extinction and soon may never be seen again.

Ringtail and Brushtail Possums eat from My Hand though I offer only what they can find for themselves, and their Food is plentiful. I see Gliders some Evenings, and hold My Breath for a glimpse of the Rarest of

Treasures, a Leadbeater's Possum. I have found traces in Hairtubes and believe I have located the dead Grey Gum in which they have made their Nest.

Sometimes on clear, still Nights when the Moon is full I see the Shadow of Death, the mighty Powerful Owl, and its lesser cousins the Sooty and Masked Owls. The tiny Antechinus which shares My Humble Dwelling trembles at their passing. Sometimes I hear Koalas roar and call to their Mates, but all too rarely. It is a Privilege to live among these Creatures, a Joy to know that such Creatures still Exist.

In three months, your Government will begin building a Road into My Paradise. Regional Consolidated Sawmillers will take all of My Trees, turn them into tiny Chips, load them onto Ships and send them off to Japan where they will be made into Pulp. They will take those Trees that fit nicely into their Machines and cut down the rest to rot. This Process is called Clearfelling, but whoever called it that never saw the Slaughtered Trees left behind, nor the blocked and silted Streams. The Habitats of the Animals will all be destroyed. The Food Sources of My Neighbours will all be destroyed. The Animals will all be destroyed. Those lucky enough to survive this Onslaught will then have to survive Fire which is used to clear the Land for the sowing of Plantation Ash. Those few Animals which survive the Fire will be poisoned to stop them eating the Seedlings.

In a few short Months they will turn my Heaven into Hell on Earth. Why do You allow this to happen?

G.O.D.
Little Potoroo Creek
East Gippsland

* * *

'You're gunna have to do something, Miklos, and do it bloody quick.'

'Hell can I do? Ain't as if he's in the phone book.' Miklos thumped the kitchen table. Knives, forks and plates bounced into the air and clattered back down. Cheryl didn't even bother looking up.

'You gotta find him and get the boys to have a word with him.' Bernie Dwight was calling from Melbourne and he didn't like to waste his electoral allowance on electoral matters. 'You gotta shut him up. Greenies have been on all the talkback shows and got a straight hour on ABC radio. Whole bloody hour. Bastards are killin' us. Had the minister on the blower and the bloody Premier. Mate, you gotta do something before they pull the plug on us. They're runnin' scared. Talking about a bloody moratorium.'

'Okay, okay! I'll think of somethin'. Maybe send Arnie and the boys in with semi-automatics. They'll find the prick.'

'Jesus Christ! When will you learn? Think it but don't say it! I don't want to know what it ain't good for me to know. Besides someone could be listening.'

'Piss off, Bernie, there's just Cheryl here.'

Just Cheryl grunted.

Miklos hung up and glared at the phone, then at his wife. 'That freakin' letter in the paper has got us right up shit creek. Why would anyone print shit like that?'

'I think it's really well written for someone whose only other published work was the ten commandments.'

'You read it?'

'Every beautiful word.'

'You tryin' to be funny?'

The *Melbourne Herald* had run the letter intact on the front page beneath the headline: A MESSAGE FROM G.O.D. The accompanying editorial preached the need for tighter government control on the activities of woodchippers, and the need to ensure the conservation of protected and endangered flora and fauna. There were library photos of potoroos and leadbeater's possums. The *Sydney Morning Herald* had done likewise, beneath the headline: G.O.D, WHAT ARE WE DOING? Both papers were smart enough to include the full points so they didn't offend the religious.

'Man's a nutter. What kinda weirdo writes crap like that? That's heresy, blasphemy and bloody undemocratic. Bloody pinko puke.'

Cheryl resisted the temptation to laugh. She watched her husband punch his fist into the palm of his hand in frustration. It occurred to her that, for once, he didn't know what to do, where to go, where to turn. He'd had opposition before, but it had always had a face, something to punch or bulldoze, something to manipulate.

'Why don't you exercise your own democratic right?' she said.

'Whad'ya mean?'

'Write your own letter to the papers. Present your case. Tell them how you feel. It shouldn't be hard to put a few potoroos and possums into perspective when export earnings are at stake. Anyway, who cares about a forest no one ever goes to and hardly anyone will ever see? It shouldn't be hard to justify pulping the lot.'

'Bloody right! Good one, Cheryl!' He gave her a look that, while it fell short of admiration, was certainly headed in that direction. 'I'll do that. Straight after I talk to your stupid brother.'

'Call me if you're coming home in case his stupid sister is mad enough to make dinner.'

'Yeah,' said Miklos and disappeared out the front door. Cheryl picked up the *Melbourne Herald* and re-read it, a slow smile spreading across her face.

'God, you cunning bugger,' she said wistfully.

* * *

'Arnie! Come here!' Miklos found Arnie in the yard, watching logs get fed into the chipping machines, killing time while his truck was unloaded. Arnie could get so fascinated by the process he would stand there all day. His two offsiders stood watching with him. It never ceased to amaze Miklos that none of them had any more ambition than to earn a bit more than they spent on beer, horse racing, their beaten-up utes, and in keeping the missus off their back. Then again, he didn't pay them for their brains.

'Into the office,' he said.

'What'd I do now?'

'Nothin'. Shut your face and listen. Read this.' Miklos threw the paper to him. He knew this was probably the first time in years anyone had asked Arnie to read anything other than the sports pages, and decided to pass the time productively. He stepped out of his office and stood over his secretary.

'Jan, I want you to take down some dictation.'

'What? Now? With Arnie in the office?'

Miklos hadn't exactly hired Jan for her brain either. 'Real dictation. You remember — shorthand?'

'Oh,' she said and giggled.

'I want to send a letter to the papers. Melbourne and Sydney *Heralds* and the *Australian* and the other one.'

'The *Age*?'

'Yeah, you can find their addresses later. Dear Editor,' he began. 'How could you print such a load of crap? If God exists he sure ain't that lamebrain pinko in the forest ... Jesus, Jan, why aren't you taking this down?'

'They won't print that. You've got to write proper.'

Miklos stopped and thought about it. He was a man of action not words and the first to admit it. 'Yeah, maybe you've got a point. Maybe I oughta get Bernie Dwight to help write it. How about some coffee?'

'One or two cups?'

'Coffee for me and you, Nescaff for Arnie. He can't tell the difference.'

'Oh, there's something else — a Mister Townsend rang from the Victorian Association of Forest Product Management. He left a Melbourne number and he wants you to ring him. Says it's urgent.'

'Tell him to get stuffed,' said Miklos. 'Too busy. Arnie! You got past the caption yet?'

'Yeah.'

'What d'ya think?'

'Bastard.'

'We've gotta shut this arsehole up, right? I want you to take some of your mates up into Little Potoroo Creek and sort the prick out.'

'Little Potoroo Creek?'

'Yeah.'

'We'll have to hike in. Take days.'

'You got somethin' better to do?'

'No, boss.'

'Pretend you're going shootin'. Take your crap Chinese assault rifle with you. Better take a tent and some food. Get in there, find that prick and make sure he doesn't write any more freakin' letters. Got it?'

'What does this bloke look like?'

'Flowing robes and a beard. Sandals on his feet. Hell do I know! Get in there. The first bloke ya see will be him. Who else d'ya reckon you'll find up there?'

'Gotcha.'

'Take the Toyota and drive the fire trails as far as ya can. Hike in from there. Don't come back unless ya find him, okay?'

'You want us to shoot him?'

'Nah. Better not. Just give him a lesson. Tell me who ya taking and I'll write ya down as working Diggers Hill in case ya need an alibi. Tell your mates I'll pay their wages and give them a bonus if you're successful. Now get going! And for fuck's sake, don't tell anyone else what ya doin'. Got that?'

'Yep, got that.'

Miklos watched him go. He liked Arnie because he had attributes that counted in his business. Arnie was mean, tough and never knew when to quit. Whenever he got in a fight his mates had to pull him off before someone got killed. Miklos liked to joke that Arnie was a cross between a pit bull and a mallee bull, and almost as smart. But, above all, Arnie was a diehard logger, dog loyal, and family. God knows why being family was important to Miklos, who'd shafted his own father, but it was.

He picked up the phone. 'Bernie? It's me. Cheryl reckons we oughta write a letter of reply. Whad'ya think?'

'Good idea. So bloody good I've already written it. I'll fax it to you as soon as it's printed out so Jan can retype it on Rip, Chip and Ship letterhead. Over your name.'

'How many pages?'

'Five.'

'Christ, that'll take her all morning.'

'Yeah,' said Bernie. He started laughing. 'Great tits, but.'

Miklos laughed for the first time that day.

* * *

Jan was midway through retyping Bernie's letter to the editor when the phone rang. She thought if she left it ringing reception would get the message that she wasn't to be disturbed. Miklos had made it plain he wanted the letter in a hurry and she couldn't be expected to do two things at once.

'Answer the freakin' phone!' The ringing got on Miklos's nerves.

She answered it. 'Mr Bollok's office. Who's calling please?'

'Clyde Townsend for Mr Bollock. I rang earlier on a matter of some urgency.'

'One moment please. Mickey, it's that bloke from Melbourne again.'

'Piss him off.' Miklos hated being called Mickey.

Made him sound like a mouse. Jan was the only person who got away with calling him that.

'Putting you through.'

The phone on Miklos's desk began ringing.

'Jesus Christ, Jan, you deaf?'

'If you don't take his call he'll just keep ringing and I've got this bloody great letter to type.' Her voice rose in pitch and became shrill. Miklos gave in.

'Bollok here.'

'Clyde Townsend from VAFProM, the Victorian Association of Forest Product Management.'

'Never heard of you.'

'I'm not on the Association's staff.'

'So why did ya say you were? Make up ya mind.'

'I'm calling on their behalf. I'm with Weitzler and Hand, a US-based international public relations corporation. My specialty is issue management.'

'What's that when it's at home?'

'The reason for my call. We didn't like what we read in the papers this morning.'

'Well, Mr Issue Management, I didn't care for it much either, but I don't need no fancy consultants to tell me that. What do ya want? I'm busy.'

'What we want, Mr Bollok, is your full cooperation. We want you to take no action in regard to the letter in this morning's papers.'

'Oh, is that right?'

'Correct.'

'Well up yours! I'm not lettin' that bastard get away with what he said. I've sent a letter of ... of ...' He searched his brain for the neat word Bernie had used. Found it and flung it. 'Repudiation!'

'That was not very smart, Mr Bollok. Has the letter gone? If not, please tear it up.'

'Tear it up?'

'Please. Your letter will only serve to keep the issue alive, besides which we've already taken measures on your behalf.'

'Oh, really?'

Clyde Townsend ignored the sarcasm. 'Can you stop the letter?'

'Yes I can. If I want to. Why would I want to?'

'Because your interests are best served by allowing us to kill the issue rather than by prolonging it. '

'Kill it? How?'

'We've threatened every paper that ran the story with a lawsuit. We can't stop them printing readers' letters, but we can attack their editorials for bias and lack of factual basis. We're demanding a retraction or we'll sue for damages amounting to tens of millions of dollars.'

'Holy shit!'

'Holy shit, indeed, Mr Bollok,' said Townsend. 'That's precisely what the respective editors of the *Melbourne Herald* and the *Sydney Morning Herald* are probably saying right now. That is precisely what their managements are probably echoing.'

'You can do that?'

'We've already done it.'

'How about that?'

'So you withdraw your letter?'

'What letter?'

'Exactly. Now, Mr Bollok, we need to talk. You are part of the Victorian timber and woodchip industry, whether you choose to acknowledge it or not. Everything we do affects you and, regrettably, everything you do also affects us. Newspaper pictures of protesters with their faces smashed in does not win us friends or help our cause.'

'Pricks deserved it.'

'That doesn't change anything. Issue management is not about being right or wrong, it's about winning. It's a very delicate business, Mr Bollok, and you have to embrace it or lose.'

'Says who?'

'We do, Mr Bollok. We are experts and you are not. We have experience and you do not. Let me give you an example from the US. Do you smoke?'

'No way, but I don't see what that has to do with woodchips.'

'Why not?'

'Freakin' cancer sticks.'

'That's right. You know that, I know that, in fact the whole world knows that. The carcinogenic properties of cigarettes have been known about for more than thirty years.'

'So?'

'The addictive properties of nicotine and the manipulation of nicotine in cigarettes by cigarette companies have also been known about for more than thirty years.'

'So?'

'So how come cigarette companies are still making cigarettes and selling them?'

'You tell me.'

'Issue management, Mr Bollok. We've managed to suppress the truth for thirty years. Thirty highly profitable years, and the shit's only just hitting the fan now.'

Miklos fell silent. The man was speaking his language. The scale of the manipulation was beginning to dawn on him. 'You did that?'

'Issue management did that, Mr Bollok. It's your most powerful weapon when public interest runs contrary to your private interest. Wherever we encounter unfavourable comment we hit hard, harder than you can believe. We may be in the wrong and our opposition in the right, but who's going to risk losing the farm by taking us on? We practise the public relations version of Einstein's theory of relativity: for every fact we present another, equal and opposing. No one can ever be one hundred per cent certain of their facts beating our facts in court. Who's prepared to take the risk? Do you get the point, Mr Bollok?'

'I'm ahead of you.'

'So you see why it's mutually advantageous for us all to get together and present a united front, speak with one powerful voice? Like the cigarette companies did.'

'Yeah, I can see merit in that. Maybe you and me should have a beer?'

'I'll drive down tomorrow.'

'I'll warn the pub.'

'One more thing. Levies, Mr Bollok, or to be more precise, non-payment.'

'What business is that of yours?'

'Not the levies you pay the government, Mr Bollok, the levies you owe VAFProM.'

'Oh. Those levies.' Miklos chuckled mirthlessly. 'Tell me, Mr Townsend, since you're a smart fella, why should

I pay them? Every single member of your association has been trying to screw me ever since I started up. They opposed my application for a concession. They want me out of business. Why the hell should I fund people who are trying to shaft me?'

'Before my time, Mr Bollok. You won, they lost. You're now a fact of life. They've hired me to ensure they don't lose again.'

'Stuff 'em.'

'You need me and my company does not come cheap. Little Potoroo Creek would make a fine World Heritage Area. It meets at least two criteria. National Parks and Wildlife would love to get their hands on it. If things aren't handled properly, they probably will. Now, it's not compulsory to pay up, Mr Bollok, but if you don't we'll squeeze you out. You and your tin-pot company. You listening? That is my promise to you. I'll bring the account with me.' He hung up.

Miklos stared at the phone. 'Holy shit,' he said.

He heard Jan typing in the background. 'Jan, forget that stupid letter. Bad idea. Get Bernie on the blower then get ready to come in here and take your dictations down. Had a hard day. Got a feelin' it's gunna get harder.'

CHAPTER SEVEN

The alternative sub-culture got hold of Summer's poster and the CIA distributed it faster and more accurately than any commercial organisation ever could have. It went straight to its target group, was read by sympathetic eyes and went straight to sympathetic hearts. The poster was put up in squats, cafés, new age book shops, libraries, music shops, sympathetic health food shops, naturopathy, homeopathy, reiki, herbalist, aromatherapy and colour therapy clinics. Within three hours of the ink drying it was on the internet and every green website, courtesy of someone who knew someone who had access to a scanner and computer. God's message had helped, but everyone knew someone who knew someone who knew Summer, who was a legend, and by then Little Potoroo Creek had become a major cause.

'DORF-FOREST,' her poster screamed, backed by an illustrative style inspired by Beardsley, Tolkien and the not infrequent use of acid. 'A Benefit Rave For Little Potoroo Creek. Go beyond the techno government conspiracy and the capitalist control concoctions that are up your nose, in your veins and on your tongue,' it urged. 'Open your mind to subliminal messages of higher awareness for the strength to fight for the last of this precious land, so that we can live self-sufficiently in an eternity of forest parties in a green world of ecstasy. Time is running out. With everyone's help a positive outcome is inevitable!'

Along with the inferred promise of drugs it gave time, date and location. A line at the bottom said, 'Written and authorised by the CIA — Concerned Individual Activists.' Summer approved of every conservation group, but valued her independence far too highly to belong to any of them. In a moment of insight inspired by an acid tab, she'd hit upon the CIA. Everyone thought it was neat. Others who shared her sentiments regarding any kind of formal organisation leapt at the idea, at the concept of being free to decide who they'd help, when, and if they could be bothered. If the police or ASIO ever wanted to penetrate the CIA they would be condemned to frustration because no organisation, no structure, no hierarchy existed. The CIA didn't exist. It was just an idea supported by a loose assembly of people who offered — or who had access to — all kinds of skills, and who only came together when need be.

In the middle of it all, while Summer was riding high and feeling wanted and more positive than she had for months, a letter arrived for her from the hospital. Somebody found it in the letterbox and put it on the table in the communal room where everybody could see it, read her name, and observe that whatever news was inside came from the hospital. Everyone knew the news would not be good.

On the same afternoon Summer was caught nicking underwear by a security camera in Woolworths. She gave them a false name, Sarah Jenkins, the first name that came into her head, a false address, and told them she was only fifteen and a runaway from home. She told them her parents lived in Ballarat and that she'd run away because her father sexually abused her and her mother had had a breakdown. Summer could easily pass for fifteen when she wanted to, and there was no denying she could look like a runaway. A couple of tears and she had them eating out of her hand. The store security didn't want to involve the police as Summer was legally a juvenile, the items were inexpensive and had been recovered, and her reason for stealing was so pathetically obvious. They let her go with a warning and told her they were obliged to pass on the details to the police. Any further indiscretions, they cautioned, would not be dismissed so lightly.

Summer passed Georgie, Matt and Sky on the way home, busking outside Flinders Street Station. They'd temporarily given away techno and gone country. They stood behind a blow-up stat of the front page of the *Herald* carrying God's letter.

'Rip, rip, woodchip, turn it into paper,' they sang. Summer had to laugh, and when they saw her they burst out laughing themselves. It was blatant opportunism but it worked. The money in their hat was generously salted with one and two dollar pieces. They told her to help herself to the contents, but all she took was the tram fare back to Port Melbourne. She'd intended to scam a ride but one bust for the day was enough.

When she got back to the squat nobody would meet her eyes and she couldn't work out why. Suddenly everyone seemed keen to avoid her, but she was too tired to ask. She just wanted to crash and listen to music and hope somebody would share their dinner with her. Then she found the letter. She just stood looking at it, too scared to pick it up, aware of others around the periphery of her vision, watching her, waiting, wanting to know the worst. She finally snatched it up and almost ran to the part of the old factory where the transients dossed down. She slumped onto a mattress and wished like hell she hadn't given the doctor the squat's address, but he'd been so insistent. She'd promised to come back for the results but her promises hadn't been good enough. Someone ghosted up alongside her. Darren? No, he had no subtlety. If he had something to ask he would've just stood at the door and yelled.

'You okay?'

Summer felt Ciaron's arm slip around her. She collapsed against her.

'I dunno.'

'What does the letter say?'

'Too scared to open it.'

'Want me to?' Ciaron took the envelope from Summer's hand and gently forced the flap. She unfolded the note inside, twisted so that some light fell on the type, and silently read it. If it was bad news she wanted to know so that she could break it gently.

'Fuck!' she said. 'Effin' bastards!' Ciaron heard Summer gasp and realised how her reaction may have been misinterpreted. 'Bloody typical. They scare the crap out of you and tell you nothin'!'

'What's it say?'

'Nothin'! Just says they've got your results back and they want you to come in as soon as possible.'

'As soon as possible?'

'Hell do you expect them to say, Sum? Come when you feel like it? Now shut up and don't interrupt. Dear Miss West, we have the results of your recent blood tests and in your best interests we urge you to contact the hospital as soon as possible. We have taken the liberty of making an appointment for you to see Dr Grainger at 10 am, Wednesday, 15 September. Please phone if the time is unsuitable.'

The clouds gathered over Summer once more and she felt the chill of their shadow. She pressed herself hard against Ciaron, as if seeking protection from her fears. 'Wednesday's tomorrow, isn't it?' she whispered.

'Yeah.'

'Who's Dr Grainger?'

'Isn't he the bloke you saw?'

'No. Oh God, Ciaron.'

'Now look. All this letter means is they've found out why you feel sick, which is why you went to the hospital in the first place. Now they want to do something about it.'

'Might be something serious.'

'Might be something stupid. Could be the clap. Knowin' The Dick it wouldn't bloody surprise me. Could be diabetes or low iron. Could be anything.' She was careful not to use the word she suspected Summer was dreading, the word she was dreading, the word the whole squat was dreading. She tried to make Summer laugh instead. 'Could be mad cow disease.'

'I'm scared,' said Summer.

'As far as I can see there's nothing to be scared of.' But there was and they both knew it. Even so Ciaron might have got away with her words of comfort if Darren hadn't burst in on them.

'Jesus Christ,' he yelled. 'I've just heard. You haven't got AIDS, have you, Sum?'

* * *

Summer didn't want to talk about it but she didn't have any choice. The news had the potential to affect them all. The Dick with Ears had put a name to their fears seconds before Ciaron had nearly put an end to him. He left the squat nursing his injured pride and battered genitals.

'They might give him the edge over me in some departments,' Ciaron had said triumphantly, 'but they're effin' useless in a fight.'

Gloom descended over the squat as the inhabitants tried to remember who'd slept with whom and in what order so they could assess their risk. Summer didn't exactly sleep around but she was hardly celibate. There were nights when everybody was high and having a good time and sex seemed a logical conclusion to the festivities. By squat standards, Summer was hard to get but that didn't mean she hadn't been got. That was the worrying part, the part everyone was trying to remember, when, at the time it might have happened, they could count themselves lucky if they could even remember their own name.

'No way it could be AIDS,' said Lyndal thoughtfully. Everyone looked up from the organic lentil and vegetable stew which had been served over barely cooked brown rice. Some wanted to hear what Lyndal had to say, others to see how everyone else was coping with the meal. Thalia, who'd taken it upon herself to cook the stew out of consideration for the stress everyone was going through, glared back at any eyes that found hers, defying anyone to criticise. 'If it was AIDS, or VD, or anything like that, dickhead Darren would've got a letter too.'

'Hey, that's right!' said Ciaron.

'Depends what address Darren gave,' said Summer, killing the brief flicker of hope. 'Or whether he even gave an address.'

'Prick,' said Ciaron. 'Bloody moron.'

'If it was anything infectious, I'm certain the letter would have mentioned Darren as well.' Thalia liked to think of herself as the mother of the group by virtue of the fact that she was slightly older and a permanent. 'VD clinics do that ... I'm told.'

'Probably right,' said Barry. 'It's cool, Sum. Right, Thal?' Pot made him oblivious to the withering glare Thalia gave him. Nobody else took a blind bit of notice. Everything was cool as far as Barry was concerned.

'How about we change the subject,' said Summer. 'I'm sick of talking about it. It's my problem.'

'Yeah, give her a break,' said Ciaron, protectively. 'It's her problem.'

'Magic Johnson had AIDS and they still let him play basketball,' said Dougie. Anke threw a stale bagel at him.

'Ciaron's right,' said Pete. 'It's Summer's problem, and if it turns out she's really got a problem my friend's a special counsellor.'

'Jesus, Pete!' Lyndal threw her fork at him. It was one of the great ironies that the one resident most at risk of AIDS was the least threatened by Summer.

'It's not AIDS,' said Summer.

'You tell 'em,' said Ciaron.

'I got real sick once,' said Stretch. 'Up in Java.' Stretch was a talented, even gifted guitarist who could be staying in the Southern Cross Hotel one week and the squat the next. Cynics claimed he preferred down to up. He was famous for kickstarting groups on the road to fame, and falling out with them seconds before they achieved it. It was like he was scared of success and hid behind drugs and booze. He was always stoned, or had been stoned so long he always acted that way even when he wasn't. He finished rolling a joint and took a long deep drag before sending it on its rounds. 'Somebody got this idea it would be great to ride mountain ponies around tea plantations. We all went along with it because we had a couple of days between gigs and it was cooler in the mountains than in Jakarta. Never ridden a horse before and those bloody mountain ponies were a dumb place to start. Wore two holes in my bum either side of the one God gave me. They became so badly infected I had to be flown back to Australia. Ended up spending two months on my stomach.' The joint completed its circle and came back to him. He took a long suck on the butt and continued. 'Took months to heal and the bloody scars are forever. Next time we toured I had to get my passport renewed. You know that bit where they ask if you have any identifying scars? I wrote yes. I mean, shit, did I have scars! Know what? Stupid pricks asked me to draw them! So I drew a picture of my arse and mooned an entire government department.'

Summer laughed along with everyone else. It wasn't hard to feel up when people gave you a chance. Others chipped in with stories and the mood began to lighten, until Stretch did a Darren.

'Ever used smack?' he asked Summer.

'No,' she said defensively.

'Never shared needles with nobody?'

'No. Just toothbrushes,' she added ironically for a bit of laugh. Nobody laughed. The whole squat fell silent. Even the CD player paused between tracks. At some stage everybody there had borrowed her toothbrush.

* * *

'Sum ...'

All the lights were out except the one in the toilet. Summer opened her eyes as she felt a hand grab her shoulder and shake it lightly. It was Darren, and he was out of his skull.

'Shove off, Darren!' Ciaron, her friend and protector, had risen like a king cobra from the mattress.

Summer started to sit up but Ciaron knocked Darren's hand away and pushed her gently back down.

'Piss off, dickhead. Didn't you hear me the first time? Summer doesn't want anything to do with you. Ever. Got that?'

'Finally got your way, eh?' He flicked his tongue up and down against his lips.

'Piss off!'

Darren turned away. 'Fuckin' dykes.'

Summer screwed up into a ball, eyes closed, hands covering her ears. She was sick. Sick and scared. And she wasn't a dyke, she just needed a friend.

Thalia woke her with a cup of Nescafé, a clean towel and a used but precious bar of tea-tree soap. The squat had tiptoed around, taking care not to wake her. Ciaron had told them all how long it had taken Summer to finally fall asleep, before she'd had to dash off to the bike showroom where she was part-time dogsbody. Her employer had advertised for a girl Friday, but had changed the job description the instant Ciaron showed up. Dogsbody seemed to fit better.

'It's eight-thirty,' said Thalia. 'I'm just off to work.' She knelt down and gave Summer a lingering hug. 'You'll be right, girl,' she said.

The hug was a signal for the others who had late-starting jobs or lectures to go to. They'd waited, fidgeting and awkward, to give their squatmate a reassuring hug and kiss, mostly out of real affection and concern, but also from feelings of guilt that they'd put their own wellbeing first.

'Take care,' they said. 'Nothing to worry about.' And promptly contradicted their advice by their actions.

'Watch your arse,' said Stretch. 'Dorf dorf.'

Summer laughed. 'You bet. You going to work?'

'Nah,' said Stretch. 'Just going to bed.'

Summer finished her coffee, amazed that Thalia who was strictly vegan had added milk and sugar. She wet herself under the shower, washed her hair with Thalia's tea-tree soap and even thought about cutting off her rat-tails and talons. Stuff it, she thought to herself, she was beginning to think like the others. It was all a question of being positive. She'd be back, stronger and more dedicated. People depended on her and so did Little Potoroo Creek. As she dried herself she regretted the fact that the security camera had denied her a new bra and underwear. She'd cleaned her jeans and t-shirt and was trying to decide what else to wear when Thalia called through the door and told her she had visitors. One of them, Sky, had brought her a clean bra and knickers. Summer wondered how they knew.

'Darren came round this morning,' said Matt.

'We're taking you to the hospital,' said Georgie. 'In a taxi.'

'I can't come,' said Matt. 'Have to go to a job interview or they'll cut off my dole.'

'I remembered how you didn't have any underwear last time you went,' said Sky. 'You can keep them. I've got more at the flat.'

'First I harmonise,' said Gretta. 'Before anyone goes anywhere.' Gretta still pronounced her double-us as vees and mangled sentences, despite the fact that she'd lived the last twenty-five of her forty years no closer to her original home in Essen, Germany than a Melbourne tram could take her.

Summer lay down on her mattress as instructed while Gretta cleared the room, and closed her eyes as she heard Gretta's whispered prayers. She let her body relax. Summer wasn't entirely convinced of the efficacy of harmonising, but believed it did something because she always felt better afterwards. Gretta never laid a finger on her yet Summer knew exactly where her hands were at every moment. She felt their presence as heat as they hovered millimetres above her skin and moved to each of the centres of healing. She felt herself drifting away to the little ferny glade by Little Potoroo Creek where she'd first met God, saw him look straight at her, nod gently and smile lovingly. There wasn't a trace of sadness in his eyes, just pure joy. God knew! God knew she was going to be all right and she wanted to cry out. She must have started because she felt Gretta's hand on her shoulder.

'We are finish now,' she said softly. 'Is good?'

CHAPTER EIGHT

'The rules have changed,' said Clyde Townsend. 'You can't just go around bashing people over the head any more.'

'Still works around here,' said Miklos. A reverential hush had descended over Osbourne's only pub, not that mid-afternoons mid-week were ever much different. Miklos had simply told Macka, the publican, that he needed the lounge bar and to keep everyone else in the saloon and make sure they kept quiet. Everyone else amounted to Cheryl's father, four other alcoholic retirees and three out-of-work loggers competing with one another to see how long they could nurse a beer. They watched the mid-week races from Caulfield, straining to hear the names of the horses and dividends because Macka had turned down the sound. It didn't make much difference. None of them could afford a bet.

'Son, tell Mr Townsend about those two ferals trying to hitch a ride,' said Bernie. 'Nugget did us proud that day.' Nugget — or Police Sergeant Nugent — was the most senior officer in Osbourne's force of three. Miklos had insisted that he sit in, and Nugget had been only too happy to oblige. Sitting in the pub drinking beer beat the hell out of sitting in a patrol car not booking logging trucks for speeding, overloading or defects. The four men sat around a fifties' vintage formica table on vinyl-covered tubular-steel-framed chairs. A newly crowned Queen Elizabeth smiled down upon them through fly-specked glass and a frame that had never been cleaned. A jug of beer sat in the middle of the table; Macka kept it filled.

'Arnie slowed down like he was going to give them ferals a lift, then knocked them flying,' said Miklos. 'Sent one off into the bush, the other went flying up in the air and smashed his head through the ute's windscreen when he came back down.'

'What did you do?' asked Clyde Townsend. They'd sucked him right in.

'Booked one for break and entry,' said Nugget. 'The other for leaving the scene of the crime.'

Miklos and Bernie broke up laughing but the city man just shook his head.

'It's a joke,' said Miklos. 'Can't you recognise a joke?'

Clyde thought he could. He thought he was sitting opposite three.

'Loosen your tie,' urged Bernie. 'Ditch your coat. We're not big on formality around here.'

Clyde ignored him. He wore his dark grey suit and tie for a purpose. They were his uniform and his calling card, proof that he was both different and better than the men around him. He was hard, lean and fit, and when the cock was on the chopper fancied himself in any fight against anyone. But he'd elected to use his brains over his brawn, a decision he'd made when he abandoned a promising career in football in favour of pursuing a university degree. He'd passed without distinction in law and subsequently in business administration. Law firms had ignored him, but the building workers union saw genuine potential. His physique was plain intimidating, and he had an unconscious and disconcerting habit of standing too close to people and invading their personal space. He appeared nerveless and his cold blue eyes rarely blinked. Hollywood wouldn't have hesitated to cast him as a hitman. His voice was strong and deep yet he never raised it. He gave every impression of being a powerful, even violent man, consciously holding his impulses in check. He came across as threatening even when he was asleep. The union thought he'd make a top negotiator.

Some of his negotiating involved busting heads and he quickly gained a reputation as a man you didn't play silly buggers with. He was happy enough with his job until one day his union bosses decided they needed professional help. Their tactics had drawn a pounding from government, business, the media and even from other trade unions. The consultants came in, and gave Clyde Townsend his introduction to the world of public relations. He'd listened spellbound as they expounded the principles of issue management, and he'd dominated question time. Powerful men are always attracted to power, and Clyde saw for the first time the power of media manipulation. Typically, the union ignored the consultants' advice, but the consultants could not ignore the one person who'd understood and championed their cause. They offered Clyde a job. It was the first time they ever saw him smile.

‘We’re dealing with an unpalatable truth,’ said Clyde. ‘We risk trouble the moment we forget it.’

‘Hell you talkin’ about?’ said Miklos.

‘One unpalatable truth, Mr Bollok, is that clearfelling for woodchips destroys native forests and their ecosystems forever. We take flourishing old growth forests and leave behind a barren wasteland.’

‘Bullshit!’ said Miklos. He exploded from his seat. Bernie quietly reached up, put a hand on his shoulder and pushed him back down onto his chair.

‘Hear him out, son,’ said Bernie. ‘I’ve never seen a calendar with pictures of clearfelling.’

‘So what?’ said Miklos. ‘We get rid of a bunch of trees of no use to anyone. Just freakin’ bush. We turn bush into something useful. Woodchips. Any decent trees go to the sawmills. Keep people in jobs, put food on their freakin’ table.’

‘We get rid of old trees of no use to anyone, the understorey, which is also of no use to anyone, and a bunch of useless native animals.’ Clyde continued in the same even voice as if Miklos’s outburst had never happened.

‘Damn right,’ said Miklos.

‘The unpalatable truth is that we take old growth forests and rainforests which support a vast and complex array of trees and plants and annihilate them. The unpalatable truth is that we destroy the habitats of native animals, many of which are rare, protected or endangered. As a result we destroy them as well. We kill cuddly little koalas, kangaroos, wallabies, potoroos, rare possums and gliders, and quolls. We destroy or banish native birds, the parrots, eagles and owls. And we leave behind something that looks like it's been hit by an atomic bomb.'

'Whose freakin' side are you on?' said Miklos.

'Let him speak, Miklos. I can see where he's heading.' Bernie sat fascinated.

'I'll give you a good example,' said Clyde. 'When Harris-Daishowa started up in Eden, they needed a steady supply of timber before anyone had got around to building roads into the forest. So what happened? The loggers took what they could get, and what they could get was in plain view of everyone driving up the Pacific Highway. Once people could see the destruction clearfelling caused, the shit hit the fan. What did we do then? We began the practice of logging forests from the inside out, and were careful to leave a screen of native timbers along roadways so everyone thought there was still a forest behind them. Once people could no longer see what was really going on, the problem largely went away. What we did was hide an unpalatable truth.'

'Everyone knows that,' said Miklos. 'That's how we're going to do Little Potoroo Creek. Build a road in then rip the shit out of it.'

'Then you're beginning to understand issue management,' said Clyde. 'The mistake some of our people make is that they also create screens in their own mind. They hide the unpalatable truth from themselves, and from that point on they are incapable of dealing with it constructively.'

'What do you mean?' asked Bernie.

'Confronted by an unpalatable truth they create an acceptable lie, convince themselves that the lie is the truth, and become passionate about it. When anyone challenges them they can't mount a logical argument so they get irate instead. Say things which haven't been thought through or examined for media impact, or start throwing punches. The acceptable lie is that woodchipping is good for everybody, when the truth is that it's really only good for the companies that engage in it and governments desperate for rural votes.'

'That's crap!' Miklos started to rise from his seat again and once more Bernie's hand had to intervene.

'He's right, son,' said Bernie. 'Lying's my business. I oughta know.'

'Let's see,' said Clyde. 'You would claim that forests are a resource that regenerates. How can they be? We make no attempt to renew the forests we destroy. How could we? How does anyone replace five-hundred-year-old trees? How do we regenerate the understorey? How do we revive extinct animals? We take forests and turn them into single-species plantations, growing only the trees most suited to woodchipping.'

'Still a bloody forest,' said Miklos.

'More than fifty per cent of the time replanting fails,' said Clyde. 'Another unpalatable truth.'

'What about jobs?' said Miklos.

'What jobs?' said Clyde. 'Sawmills are closing down everywhere. You've closed down a dozen yourself. And woodchipping only makes economic sense when it's automated. Another unpalatable truth.'

'So what do you propose?' Bernie asked quietly.

'We continue to present our alternative truth, our acceptable lies, but we never forget the reality of the unpalatable truth. The weaknesses in our arguments are our enemy's strength, and if we ignore our weaknesses we ignore our enemy's strength. How can we defend the indefensible if we can't anticipate what our enemy is going to do? If we are to keep winning we need to hold to a long-term proven strategy with everybody singing the same song, irrespective of provocation. Issue management isn't about right or wrong, it's about winning. Our opponents can claim right is on their side. They have the ammunition but lack the resources to use it powerfully. We've got to make sure things stay that way, and we do that by countering our opponents' every move, by muddying the water, by threats of litigation, and by putting pressure on governments. The truth may not be on our side, but the might of the dollar is. It's a tricky business, one best left to experts in the field.'

'Like yourself.'

'Exactly, Mr Bollok. In East Gippsland alone we're up against the Australian Conservation Foundation, the Wilderness Society, Friends of the Earth, Concerned Residents of East Gippsland, GECO and EGCGs. These people are often highly educated and passionate. On TV they present far more sympathetically than a bunch of loggers hellbent on kicking people's heads in. We have to counter them, and we're doing that very successfully. Have you heard of the Sisters of the Forests?'

'Sounds like another freakin' bunch of greenies.'

'They're supposed to. Except that we set them up and fund them. The Sisters were recruited by us to use as a mouthpiece. We tell them what to say, and what they say is tailored into catchy sound bites. The media love them and so do viewers and readers. By using female actors instead of loggers we've made people sympathetic to our case. You see my point?'

Miklos nodded reluctantly.

'We have many other techniques which I won't go into right now. The point is, clearfell logging is unacceptable and we can't support it by doing other unacceptable things like beating people up. Like forcing people off the road. Like chasing ferals down the main street of Osbourne with chainsaws. You see, I've done my homework. Little Potoroo Creek has the potential to destabilise everything we've achieved and we won't allow that to happen. What's going to happen here may be unpleasant, obstructive and even costly, but we'll win in the end. You'll win in the end. Provided, of course, everyone does exactly as they're told. Have I made myself clear?' Clyde Townsend had reached the business part of his pitch and he didn't want to leave anybody in any doubt as to where they stood. His unwavering eyes fixed on Miklos and he leant forward across the table, so close that he could smell Miklos's breath. 'Do you understand, Mr Bollok?'

'I get your drift.'

'I don't want anybody going after that nutter in the forest. Okay?'

'I hear you.' Miklos didn't flinch. He reckoned he could stare down anybody.

'He's now a national figure and he has the sympathy vote. Hurt him and you hurt our cause, possibly irreparably. We'll find credible ways to discredit him once things have died down. We've got people in DeCaF who'll come out and state unequivocally that they have no evidence of koalas, quolls or long-footed potoroos inhabiting Little Potoroo Creek. They will speak with authority. When the greenies come to mount a blockade, let them. We'll discredit them too. All they do is bring drugs into the area and try to corrupt good clean-living country youth. You with me? Moving them on is Nugget's department. Frankly I wouldn't be surprised if one or two of them were found in possession of illegal substances.'

'You're dead right there,' said Nugget, and helped himself to the beer jug. 'Some of them protesters might be surprised but.'

Clyde Townsend reached into his briefcase and took out an envelope. 'Your account, Mr Bollok.' He tossed it casually onto the table.

Miklos stared at it for a moment. Nobody treated him so disdainfully. He was tempted to rip Clyde's head off his shoulders and shit down his neck, but couldn't work out what was stopping him. He ripped open the envelope. 'Ten fuckin' grand!'

'Quarterly,' said Clyde. 'I'll expect your cheque in the mail tomorrow.'

'And if I decide not to pay?'

'We'll send you broke, Mr Bollok.' Clyde rose from his chair and seemed to ease the leash on his control. He set his legs slightly apart, left foot forward, weight on the balls of his feet. There was no mistaking the message in the stance.

Miklos jumped to his feet. His eyes bulged and fists spasmed. He was barely holding himself in check. 'I don't like you, Mr Townsend,' he said. 'I want you to know that and I warn you never to forget it.'

When Miklos was really angry he stopped swearing and his voice became all the more chilling because of it. Every word fell with the weight of a piledriver. 'I'll pay your account and try things your way. But I expect value for my money. Value, Mr Townsend. One more thing ...' Miklos was a big man but he moved like lightning over short distances. Clyde Townsend was also quick, but in this instance not quick enough. He'd been mentally guarding his chin and his six-pack abdomen and got caught cold when Miklos's hand clamped tightly around his balls. His eyeballs nearly popped as Miklos began squeezing.

'Don't you ever threaten me again, Mr Townsend. Don't think you can come into my town and ... ahhhhhh!' Miklos gasped. He hadn't considered the possibility of a counterstrike. His brain felt like it was about to explode. His eyes bulged. He wanted to throw up.

'Stalemate, Mr Bollok,' said Clyde through gritted teeth. He squeezed harder to make his point. Miklos responded in kind.

'You two keep that up you'll geld each other,' said Bernie. He poured himself another beer.

'Ten bucks on Miklos,' said Nugget loyally.

'Son, you're on,' said Bernie. 'Feel the way that city bastard shakes hands? Log loaders don't grip that hard.'

The two combatants stood toe-to-toe, clutching each other in the Christmas hold, neither one prepared to blink.

'How many kids you got, Mr Townsend?' asked Nugget. 'Wouldn't count on adding to your score.'

'No distractions,' said Bernie. 'Let's keep this fight fair. They reckon they pop like sea grapes when they go.'

Every time one of the combatants tightened his grip the other immediately responded. Both knew it was a game that neither could win.

'Can we agree on one thing, Mr Bollok,' said Clyde Townsend, keeping his voice calm and even despite the fact that his knees wanted to buckle and his brain was frying. 'We've both made our point.'

'We can agree on that, Mr Townsend. Count of three?'

'One ... two ...' said Clyde slowly and deliberately, keeping eye contact the whole time. 'Three.'

Both men kept to the deal.

'That,' said Bernie to Nugget, 'is the best example of a hands-off agreement you'll ever see.'

'I'll expect your cheque in the mail,' said Clyde.

'I'll expect results,' said Miklos.

Clyde Townsend shook hands with Bernie and Nugget. 'Nice meeting you,' he said.

'The pleasure was all ours,' said Bernie.

'Mr Bollok.' Clyde shook hands with Miklos.

'Goodbye, Mr Townsend.'

The three men watched their visitor stride purposefully to the door and out to the car park. Miklos stood and waited until he was certain Clyde Townsend wasn't coming back. He collapsed into his chair and clutched his groin.

'Oh holy shit!' he said. 'Oh sweet Jesus!'

'Want me to get Jan to kiss them better?' said Bernie. He started laughing and couldn't stop.

'Here, drink this,' said Nugget. He handed Miklos a beer filled to the brim. Miklos downed it in one gulp.

'Get me a double Scotch,' he gasped.

'Double Scotch,' yelled Bernie. Out in the saloon ice thudded into glass. He glanced at Miklos. 'And some nuts.'

‘If it’s any consolation,’ said Nugget, who’d drifted over to the window, ‘your mate hasn’t driven off yet. He’s looking down at something. Could be a map, but I don’t think so.’

‘What’re you going to do about Arnie and the boys? Want Nugget to go fetch them?’

‘You kiddin’? That shit-for-brains weirdo’s to blame for this. I hope they shoot his dick off and leave him to bleed to death. Who the hell would know?’ Miklos downed the Scotch.

‘Want me to tell Jan she’s got the night off?’ asked Bernie.

‘Tell her she can have the whole freakin’ week.’

‘What about Cheryl?’ said Nugget.

‘She can have the whole freakin’ year.’

Out in the car park a motor kicked into life and Clyde Townsend’s Ford eased gently out onto the highway. Miklos and Bernie looked at each other and started laughing.

* * *

Arnie liked guns. All the men in his family liked guns; they were about the only things they ever cleaned. Around the time of his tenth birthday his father had a rare win on the races and Arnie got his only decent birthday present. The old Webley air rifle had suffered at least two previous owners but it was still reasonably accurate to ten metres. The first thing Arnie did was add his initials to the stock … then he went out and shot a fat wood pigeon in the bum. The pigeon was Cheryl’s pet; used to flying down for handouts, it was sitting on a branch only two metres above Arnie's head. It looked down at the boy, expecting something nice to eat, and copped a lead enema instead. Cheryl witnessed the murder, belted her brother over the head and hid his new toy for a month. But a love affair had begun and the passion never dulled.

When Arnie was old enough he passed his Webley on to his brother Davo, bought his first real gun and joined a gun club. He shot at targets and clay pigeons with a borrowed shotgun, but that wasn't enough. Every spare moment was spent shooting rats, rabbits, possums, wombats, wallabies and kangaroos, magpies that dive-bombed him in spring, mynahs that buzzed him, and beautiful black currawongs that sang too loudly when he was hungover. He shot ducks in season, crows when he felt like it, and road signs all year round. He particularly liked the road signs that warned motorists of the presence of wildlife: there wasn't a painted koala, kangaroo or wombat for miles around that didn't have a bullet hole through its head. Arnie also liked shooting out the porcelain insulators on power lines, and didn't connect his activities with power cuts in Osbourne or all the phones going out until Miklos explained it to him with a left-right combination that almost broke his jaw.

Arnie had a dead eye when it came to shooting. He demonstrated it one day by shooting the wing mirrors off the school bus while it was taking kids to school. Nugget explained that one to him with another left-right combination that left him deaf in one ear for a week. Arnie didn't enjoy the beatings but he didn't object to them either. He figured for whatever reason he probably deserved them and, besides, pain was no big deal. He could never understand why the people he beat up whimpered, cried and begged him to stop hitting them. He'd chuck a few more punches or stick the boot in to try and help him understand what it was exactly that made blokes carry on like sheilas. That was the only time Arnie consciously tried to improve his mind.

The fact was, Arnie's brain was an evolutionary throwback. Most of it worked fine: his medulla oblongata kept his heart pumping and lungs working and, with a bit of help from his cerebellum, kept his coordination in good shape, which is why he was such a crack shot. His mid-brain — the hearing, seeing, feeling bit — worked especially well, and his forebrain never failed to let him know when he was horny, happy, hungry or thirsty. It was his cerebrum that had failed to climb the evolutionary tree: the part that governed thought, reason and imagination. Arnie was a forebrain man, often acting with the reckless anarchy of a baby, doing whatever he wanted to do without burdening himself with consequences. If he saw something he wanted, he took it. If he needed to break wind he generally did, with no beg pardons. If he was hungry, he ate. And if he wanted to shoot something, he shot it. The walls between his id and his superego were tissue thin, and morality and guilt were alien concepts to him. He liked felling trees and hauling them to the mills, he liked fighting, being with the boys, looking at the nude sheilas in Penthouse and Hustler, and he liked beer. He also liked sheilas who gave him what he wanted and didn't hang around bothering him afterwards. Sometimes the girls weren't equally enthusiastic and his attempts at seduction often fell just shy of rape. In his own way,

Arnie was one of the happiest men alive. But trekking into Little Potoroo Creek didn't make him happy at all.

'Arsehole of the earth,' said Charlie. 'Know what I mean?'

'More like pisshole,' said Wozza.

'You guys finished?' said Arnie. The three of them were holed up inside their A-shaped two-man tent on the only flat piece of ground they'd been able to find. The rain showed no sign of letting up. They were cold, wet, hungry and pissed off. Arnie sat cross-legged, cleaning his Chinese semi-automatic SKS, which didn't need cleaning, and wishing it was an AK-47. Neither Charlie nor Wozza was game to mention Arnie's farting because they figured the glorified pup tent was unlikely to survive an all-in brawl, and they'd left their guns at home to save carrying them.

'Whole bloody country could be in drought and it'd still piss down here,' said Charlie.

'Rainforest,' said Wozza profoundly. 'Needs rain.' He ripped the top off another can.

'You going to drink all the beer now? Don't you want to save some for later?' Arnie was really pissed off. Pissed off at the rain. Pissed off that a day and a half of lugging their eskies and gear through the bush had only just got them to the edge of Little Potoroo Creek. Pissed off that they could only carry four dozen cans. Four dozen over four days for three men didn't bear thinking about. They'd drunk a third of them the first night, a third the second day and now Charlie and Wozza were trying to drink the rest for breakfast. He was duty bound to help them, if only to ensure he got his share, but it was plain bloody stupid. 'Let's get moving,' he said.

'What? In this? Mate, you outta ya head or somethin'?' Charlie turned to Wozza. 'What do you reckon?'

'Madness. Sheer bloody madness. Man needs his head read to go out in that.'

'Bloody hell, Arnie, why don't we just sit here for a coupla days? Tell My Left Bollok we couldn't find the creep. Who's to know?' Charlie nodded at Wozza. 'Two to one against you, mate.'

Arnie scowled. 'Ain't lyin' around here for another coupla days with you arseholes. We gotta job to do. Sooner we get out and fix that prick the better.' He picked up his semi-automatic and rewrapped it in oilskins before zipping it into its carrybag. 'We'll make this our base. Leave everything here. Now move it!'

'Ah shit,' said Charlie. 'What about somethin' to eat first?'

'Help yourself to a can.'

'Pukin' cold stew!'

'No. Pukin' cold beans,' said Arnie. 'Pukin' cold stew's for dinner.'

'How're we gunna recognise this creep even if we find him?' said Wozza. 'Don't even know what he looks like.'

'Miklos said he had long hair and flowing robes,' said Arnie uncertainly.

'Jesus Christ!' said Charlie.

'Yeah, somethin' like that,' said Arnie. He tied the Toyota's keys to the rear tent pole so he wouldn't risk losing them if he slipped over. He edged out of the tent into the rain. 'One thing's for sure — that creep's gunna pay for this.'

The three men spent half the day trying to find God and the other half trying to find the way back to their tent. They'd learnt three things: that Little Potoroo Creek covered enough country to build a decent-sized city on, that the dense undergrowth made every step a battle, and that they had Buckley's chance of finding someone who didn't want to be found.

'Shoulda stayed in the tent,' said Charlie. 'All we're doin' is lettin' the beer get warm.' Just how the beer could get warm in an ambient temperature of five degrees Celsius was a trick of physics he didn't bother to explain.

'Waste of bloody time,' said Wozza. 'Charlie's right. Shoulda stayed in the bloody tent, wherever the hell it is.'

The trouble was, they hadn't bothered looking for landmarks on the way out so there was hardly much point looking for them on the way in.

'Can't be far,' said Arnie. 'We haven't covered much ground.' And they hadn't. But they covered twice as much ground, and wore themselves out, before they laid eyes on their tent again.

'Oh bugger me,' said Arnie. 'He's been here.'

His mates peered inside the flap. God had been there all right. There was a stack of dry firewood in one corner. A rock fireplace had been built up beside the tent flap. Their only saucepan sat on top of it. There was a note attached to the rear tent pole. 'Thanks for the loan of the Toyota,' it said. 'Enjoy your dinner.'

Arnie ripped the air beds back from around the base of the pole. The car keys had gone.

'Bugger me dead!' he said. 'Bastard's taken the bloody keys! Taken the bloody car!'

'Bloody hell!' said Charlie. 'Think he'll bring it back?' Arnie's cerebrum wasn't up to much but Charlie's was almost non-existent.

'Bastard!' said Wozza. 'Oh Jeez, he hasn't taken the beer, has he?' He lunged for the esky and knocked the top off. 'Oh, thank God. Should be ten left. One, two, three ...' Even Charlie looked at Wozza in disbelief.

'Day and a half to walk outta here,' said Charlie, accepting the inevitable. 'Another day on the fire trails. The bastard! What're we gunna do?'

'Catch a cab,' said Arnie. 'What d'ya think? The hell with it, we'll figure it out later. I'm tired and I'm hungry. I need to eat.'

All three turned to look at the saucepan on the little stone fireplace. Arnie reached over and gingerly lifted the lid. It was still slightly warm. He looked inside and saw the contents of all four of the cans of stew they'd carted in. And something else.

'I didn't know cans of stew had mushrooms,' said Arnie.

'They don't,' said Wozza. 'I oughta know 'cause we practically live on them. Only thing me missus knows how to cook.'

'These have got mushrooms in them,' said Arnie.

'Show me,' said Wozza. 'Shit, they look like fresh mushrooms.'

'Oh shit,' said Arnie. 'He wouldn't, would he?'

His two companions looked at him blankly, until the significance slowly dawned on them.

'The bastard,' said Charlie. 'Surely he wouldn't ... nah ... he wouldn't ...' But no matter how he said it he couldn't make it sound convincing.

'What if he did?' said Arnie.

'Nah ...' said Wozza. His stomach rumbled as if to confirm his conviction. 'Maybe ...'

‘Maybe what?’ asked Arnie. The hollow in his stomach felt big enough to park a truck in.

‘Well, he borrowed our car, didn’t he? Maybe this is his way of paying us back. You know — the firewood, fireplace. Guy’s weird. I mean, if he’d meant us harm he woulda taken our beer, wouldn’t he? That’s what I woulda done. Reckon it’s his payback for nickin’ the bloody car.’

‘Reckon Wozza’s right,’ said Charlie. ‘I woulda gone for the beer. Reckon he wanted to make things right, like Wozza said. He saw our cans of stew and, you know, put mushrooms in them because he wanted to make them taste better.’

‘What’s wrong with them how they are?’ asked Wozza.

‘Shut up, Wozza,’ said Arnie. ‘This is serious. Tell you what I reckon. I reckon you can’t entirely trust a bloke who knocks off your wheels. I mean, there’s mushrooms and mushrooms. They could be poisonous. Could be bloody toadstools for all I bloody know. Right?’

‘What’re we gunna do?’ asked Charlie.

Arnie thought for a moment. ‘Got an idea. Gunna have to be scientific. What I reckon is, we heat the stew up and one of us has a go at it. The other two wait and see if anything happens to him.’

‘Like he dies or chucks up or somethin’,’ said Charlie. ‘Who’s goin’ first?’

‘Wozza,’ said Arnie.

‘Fuck you!’ said Wozza. ‘Why me?’

‘Because you eat this shit all the time. If there’s anything wrong with it you’d know straightaway. Only logical.’

'Bugger you.'

'Look,' said Arnie. 'There's ten beers left. That's three each with one left over. Whoever tries the stew first gets the extra beer.'

'That's different,' said Wozza. 'Let's get cooking.'

By the time the stew had heated through the tent was full of the smell of it, and their stomachs rumbled in keen anticipation. Arnie and Charlie couldn't help licking their lips as they watched Wozza tuck in.

'Hey,' said Wozza. 'This is good. This is great. This tastes bloody ripper.' It smelt good too, and in the confines of the tent there was no escaping the fact.

'Bugger it,' said Charlie caving in. 'I'm not waitin'. I'm so bloody hungry I could eat a dirty nappy and come back for the baby.' He grabbed a plate and shovelled stew onto it.

'Hey,' said Arnie. 'Bloody hell! Look how much you took. Put some back!' Charlie flicked a sliver of mushroom back into the saucepan.

'Wozza's right,' said Charlie. 'This is ace.'

Arnie watched them tucking into the stew and licked his lips again. The tent was full of meaty aroma. He could feel its warmth. See its steam rising. There was good food sitting there and all he was doing was looking at it. His stomach rumbled noisily, reminding him of all the bush he'd tramped through with only the two beers he'd had for breakfast to sustain him, and he weakened. All he had in his stomach was gas and some of that leaked out. 'Suppose you're right,' he reasoned. 'If I wanted to dud someone, I woulda gone for the beer as well.'

CHAPTER NINE

The consulting room was tiny, windowless and airless, with an untidy desk that would have cramped a room twice the size. Two prints of wild fowl adorned the only walls free of bookshelves in a futile attempt to create a sense of warmth and humanity.

'Please sit down,' said Dr Grainger. 'Let me tell you right from the start that you're not a well girl.'

Summer felt her world begin to collapse around her. She waited for the verdict, the death sentence, not daring to speak, not wanting to know the worst before it was time to know. She had been expecting to see a man but the doctor was a woman in her early fifties; she looked like she'd spent all of them working thirty-hour shifts. Spectacles hung on a bead chain around her neck, her hair was an almost perfect grey and so badly brushed that it sat across her shoulders like a thatched roof in need of repairs, and she wore jeans, a white blouse buttoned to the neck, and a white coat which hung open.

Dr Grainger put on her glasses, opened a manila folder and forced herself to concentrate on the contents.

Summer thought the doctor looked more worn out and weary than she did.

'How have you been feeling?' Dr Grainger asked suddenly.

'Tired, sick and negative,' said Summer weakly. 'How about you?'

Dr Grainger looked up and smiled. Her smile surprised Summer because it lit up her face. 'Not many patients care how I feel. Tired and overworked, since you ask,' she said. 'But that's a choice I made so I've no one to blame but myself.' Her smile faded and she became businesslike once more. 'Your liver functions indicate chronic active hepatitis, and we've found hepatitis C antibodies.'

'Hepatitis! Is that all?'

'What?' The doctor looked perplexed.

'I thought you were going to tell me I had AIDS or something.'

'No, you don't have AIDS, but I suspect that could be more by good luck than good management.'

But Summer wasn't listening. She didn't have AIDS! The dark cloud that had enveloped her lifted and dispersed. She wanted to burst out laughing. She wanted to rush out and tell Georgie, Gretta and Sky the good news. 'Dorf dorf!' she said, dropped her left shoulder and punched the air with her right fist. 'I can't tell you how relieved I am.'

Dr Grainger sat patiently until she had calmed down.

'Summer, I'm sorry if we led you to think you had AIDS, but hepatitis C isn't something to cheer about.'

'I'm sorry.'

'You and I are going to have a little chat, and you're going to sit there and listen carefully to every word I say.'

Summer sat and listened. The word 'hepatitis' had finally penetrated. 'Is hepatitis C serious?' she asked quietly.

'Yes and no,' said the doctor. 'How about you let me talk for a while. The doctor you first saw, Dr Bowen, included a note in your file to the effect that he thinks you're intelligent, sensible and ... able to be helped.' She stressed the last phrase. 'Dr Bowen doesn't normally make these sort of comments. You obviously made an impression on him.'

'Yeah, I forgot to wear a bra,' Summer said helpfully. She thought Dr Grainger was going to choke. The doctor tried to keep her face straight but her eyes were laughing.

'Summer, please, let me do the talking. Hepatitis has an interesting history. Until recently we only really knew about two kinds of hepatitis: A and B. As our pathologists got cleverer we discovered two other kinds which didn't conform and called them non-A and non-B. Not very helpful. Now we've worked our way through six different kinds from type A to type F, all with varying degrees of infectivity and morbidity.

'Hep C, the one you have, is an interesting customer. We don't know the mortality rates but I can tell you that, to the best of our knowledge, they're very low. We also know it has a very low level of infectivity. Do you know how you get infected, Summer?'

'No.'

'From blood transfusions primarily.'

'I haven't had a blood transfusion.'

'And from needle-stick injury, which isn't how you contracted it.' She looked long and hard at Summer until the young girl looked away. 'How do you think you got it, Summer?'

'I don't know.'

'Think.'

'From my toothbrush? Everybody uses my toothbrush. You'd think they'd get their own, but no. If I leave it in the bathroom everybody cleans their teeth with it. I go through toothbrushes all the time. When I camp out in the forest people always borrow my toothbrush. It's ridiculous.'

'Summer, the probability of contracting hep C through sharing toothbrushes is about on par with a Martian becoming our next prime minister. What else have you shared?'

Summer sat silently.

'Hep C is not communicated through exchange of secretions, which pretty much rules out infection through food or sex. Infection comes through contact with someone else's blood. How could that have happened?'

'I know what you're trying to make me say.'

'Then say it. Prove Dr Bowen right. Prove to me that you're intelligent, sensitive and able to be helped. I'll be quite frank with you, Summer, I'm far too busy to waste my time with someone who will not be helped, or will not help herself. Do you understand what I'm saying?'

'Yes.' Summer sat head bowed.

'There is no medical cure for hep C but the disease can be managed, and managed so well that your own immune system will eventually deal with it. But we need your willing cooperation, we need your commitment and, before we can feel satisfied that we're going to get it, we need you to face up to what you're doing wrong. Now, tell me, are you going to let me help you?'

'Yes.' Her response was barely audible.

'Then let me hear it. Tell me, and look me in the eye when you tell me. What is it — heroin? Look at me, Summer. I see young people like you every day of my life and just about every single one of them lies to me. They lie till they die. They could sit here with the blasted needle hanging out of their arm and they'll still deny using. I can't help those people, Summer. There's nothing I can do for them, and nothing they can do for themselves. And do you know what? They'll never feel well again in their entire lives. They'll always feel run-down, listless, debilitated. Some of them will turn jaundiced. They'll always have a cold or the flu or worse. Is that how you want to live the rest of your life? How many times have you sniffed since you came in here? Hey? Summer, look at me. Look at me! Are you going to let me help you or not?'

'Yes.' Summer wiped tears away with her sleeve. She wished she had a handkerchief, helped herself to tissues from a box on the doctor's desk, and blew her nose loudly. She thought about Kevin and the three weeks she'd spent with him. She'd loved him and trusted him and he'd promised her it would be the best trip she'd ever had. It hadn't been. She'd puked her guts out instead. She'd vowed that she'd never try it again, but she had. With different boyfriends, always unwilling at first, but accepting in the end because everyone else was doing it. She felt mortally ashamed.

'How long?'

'I'm not a user. I'm not! The first time was about two years ago. All it did was make me sick. I've maybe tried it five or six times since then. It always made me sick. People gave it to me. I've never bought a cap or anything.'

'Do you realise how incredibly stupid you are?'

Summer sat silently, the doctor's eyes pinning her to the chair.

'You could've been infected with AIDS. But you knew that, didn't you, and you still went ahead?'

'Yes.'

'What do you normally take?'

'Acid mostly. That's harmless. It just makes you feel good and see things more clearly.'

'Utter rot!' Dr Grainger snorted contemptuously. 'What else?'

'Speed. I always take speed when I go somewhere.'

'What do you mean?'

'Hitching rides. Some of those truckies are real weird.'

Dr Grainger looked at the pale frail eighteen year old in front of her with the purple-red hair and rat-tails entwined with dead parts of a large bird, and wondered how far out the truckies had to be if Summer thought them weird. 'What else?'

'Bit of E. But it's ridiculous what they want for it. Sixty dollars for one tablet! I can get six acid tabs for that.'

The doctor wrote it all down wearily. 'What else?'

'Pot, bit of hash. Sometimes share a snow cone, but not often. Nothing when I'm in the forests.'

'Anything else? Cocaine?'

'Too expensive. That's yuppy stuff.'

'Alcohol?'

'Maybe a beer. Glass of wine.'

Dr Grainger put down her pen, pushed her glasses up and rubbed her eyes wearily. 'Smack, speed, ecstasy, pot, hash. Do you smoke?'

'No. That's really bad for you.'

The smile crept back onto Dr Grainger's face, half amusement, half exasperation. 'Well that's one thing you won't have to give up. Tell me about your diet.'

'Vegetarian. Organic wherever possible.'

'And when organic vegetables are not possible?'

Summer laughed. 'Whatever there is. I try to eat organic because of the pesticides and stuff, but I mostly eat what's going.'

'And what might that be?'

'Whatever people leave. We just hang around cafés and restaurants at lunchtime and wait for people to go. You'd be amazed what people leave. It's gourmet food.'

'So what do you do?' Dr Grainger leant backwards in her chair, as if trying to get away from a thought too awful to contemplate.

'We just sit down and finish what they've left. It's good food and it'd only get thrown away. We get bits of steak and chicken, fish sometimes. Lots of vegetables and rice. It's good.'

'Dear God.' The doctor shook her head. 'Well, I'm not sure I approve of your methods but at least you're getting some protein. That's another point I want to make. Human beings are omnivores, Summer, we eat everything and have done for millennia. Now, I'm going to tell you what you have to do to get back on your feet again, to start feeling well again and keep feeling well. You're going to have to do everything I say, and come and see me at least once a month to make sure you're progressing. Promise?'

'Promise.'

'Firstly, no drugs. Definitely no intravenous drugs and absolutely no sharing needles. No substance abuse of any kind. No speed, no ecstasy, no LSD, no pot, no hash. We've got to give your system a chance to clean itself out. No alcohol at all for a couple of months at least. That's what you can't have. Now I'll tell you what you can have. Red meat, at least twice a week. No ifs, no buts. Fish at least twice a week, and I don't mean fish fingers. By all means eat as much tofu, soya bean and organic vegetables as you like, but not instead of red meat and fish. Okay?'

'Okay.'

Dr Grainger took Summer through the essentials of a balanced diet and warned her of the need to eat regularly, encouraged by the fact that Summer appeared to be listening and taking it all in. 'Good food and rest,' she said. 'That's what you need now. By the way, is there anyone who can look after you for a while until you get your strength back?'

'What do you mean?' asked Summer.

'Parents, perhaps?'

'My parents joined a religious cult up on the north coast of New South Wales. Sold our house and gave them all their money. They're both fruit-loops. I haven't spoken to them for years.' The lie came automatically.

'Pity. What about friends, boyfriends?'

'I'm giving my boyfriend the flick.'

'I see. Well, you've picked a good time because hep C can also suppress your libido.'

'Tell me about it!' said Summer. 'I haven't been hot to trot for ages. All my boyfriend does is play with my breasts. I think he's trying to move them to a new location or something.'

This time Dr Grainger made no attempt to hold back her laughter. 'What about friends?' she asked eventually.

'Got lots of them,' said Summer. 'All over the place.'

'Yes, I suppose you would. Tell all of them your problem and ask for their help. See if someone will give you a bed for a month or two and some decent food. More than anything else you need rest. A good six months of rest. Okay?'

'Okay.'

'By the way, there's no mention here in my notes of what you do.'

'I protest against woodchipping. Join blockades. Other causes too, like cruelty to animals and using animals for testing. Mostly I try to save the forests. I'm about to go to a blockade in East Gippsland. Little Potoroo Creek.'

'I think I read something about that in the *Herald*.'

'Yeah. A message from God. Wasn't it great?'

'Yes, he made his point rather well. But Summer, I think the next few months would be spent more productively saving yourself. That should be your number one priority. There'll be other forests.'

'There's only one Little Potoroo Creek. I've got to go. EGCGs are counting on me.'

Dr Grainger looked steadily at Summer, trying to gauge the parameters of her influence over the young girl. 'Okay, Summer, you can go. So long as you rest up when you get there and do everything else I told you to do. Promise me?'

'I promise.'

'Good girl. I can't give you any medicine for hep C because nothing will help except rest and three good meals a day. I'm counting on you to administer that yourself. I'll give you a shot of vitamins, which you look like you need, and some gamma globulin which will give you ninety per cent protection against hep A and probably boost your resistance all round. I'm tempted to give you a hep B shot as well and tetanus. Are you on medication of any kind?'

'Friends make up herbal remedies.'

'No, we'll have none of them. I don't want you taking any substances of dubious origin. Good food, regular meals and rest, that's all. No drugs. No witches brews. Now, roll up your sleeve while I go get your shots.'

'No worries,' said Summer and did as she was told. No worries. No worries! It was amazing, fantastic, brilliant! She didn't have AIDS and all she needed was good food and rest. The shadow had passed and she felt reborn. There was nothing stopping her, nothing that she couldn't handle. She closed her eyes and all she could see was forest. She kept her eyes shut while Dr Grainger administered one shot after another.

'I want you back here to see me the day you return from the blockade. Promise me?'

'I promise.' Summer ignored Dr Grainger's extended hand and hugged her instead. 'Thanks a mill.'

'Summer.'

Summer stopped at the door and turned around.

'It's none of my business, but how are you going to get to Gippsland?'

'Hitchhike.'

The doctor shook her head helplessly. The girl needed a mother, someone to care for her and give her guidance, and for some reason Dr Grainger was tempted to apply for the job. 'If you have to hitchhike, do it with a friend,' she said lamely. 'Don't hitchhike alone.'

Summer laughed. 'Don't worry, Doc, nothing will happen to me.'

* * *

'It's not AIDS,' said Summer jubilantly, and was immediately smothered in hugs.

'What is it? What they say?' demanded Gretta.

'Hepatitis C. It isn't infectious and all I need is good food and rest.'

'Pifff!' said Gretta. 'I mix you some herbs. I know liver. I know what is good.'

'The doctor said no herbal remedies and definitely no drugs. She said I have to eat lots of fish and red meat.'

'Red meat! Piff!' Gretta looked aghast, and had the backing of Georgie and Sky.

'Red meat's the worst thing you can eat,' said Georgie.

'Matt's made some dahl,' said Sky. 'That's what you need. You don't need a dead animal rotting in your guts.'

'Come,' said Gretta. 'I make you herbs. I know what is good. Come now.'

'Okay,' said Summer.

CHAPTER TEN

Summer took just over two thousand dollars at the rave and cleared thirteen hundred dollars after expenses. The drug and dope dealers took twice that amount and Darren hit them for a cut. That boosted the kitty by two hundred dollars. Summer cleared five dollars dealing acid tabs, even though she could easily have made a couple of hundred. The trouble was, she could always make money for a good cause but had trouble coming to terms with making a profit for herself. She didn't want to make a profit out of friends or people she felt she owed: people who'd let her crash at their flats, bought her meals or even a simple cup of coffee. She'd start talking to people she didn't know, and by the time she'd finished they were friends and she couldn't make a profit out of them either. She didn't give a toss. Jerry had had to get tough with her or she wouldn't even have covered the money she owed the guy who'd given her the sheet of acid to flog. Summer laughed it off.

Kevin, her first true love and blood brother by syringe, hadn't let her down. The music was brilliant, pounding like a hundred jackhammers inside her head, louder than a low-flying squadron of F-18s. The strobe and coloured lights were killers. Everybody had got right into it and the positive vibes gave Summer the charge she'd been missing. The only bad moment was when The Dick stage-dived into the mosh pit and started banging heads. They couldn't get the bouncer to throw him out because he was the bouncer. Weight of numbers eventually told and Darren was carried outside and dumped semi-conscious in the gutter. He was a lot quieter when he came back in.

Summer didn't care if she didn't make the money she needed to go to East Gippsland. She didn't have AIDS, she was going to get well again and, one way or another, she was going to see God. At first people were a bit wary of the acid she offered. She'd forgotten to bring scissors to cut up the little squares so had torn them off instead. The whole thing looked dead dodgy. What made it worse was that she'd bought a plain white sheet of tabs she could draw on and write subliminal messages. She drew a poster of the forest and filled it with animals. She wrote Little Potoroo Creek on every tab along with the exhortation to 'Be there!' Summer hoped that somehow the message would infiltrate into the subconscious of the users via the bloodstream, come to the fore as the acid kicked in, and steer them towards deep and insightful thoughts about saving forests, maybe even convincing them to turn up for the blockade. She probably only succeeded in making the tabs look even dodgier, but at twenty-five dollars a hit, reduced to fifteen dollars, reduced to ten, reduced to 'how much did you say you had?', who could resist?

Jerry resisted, and he watched Summer like a hawk to make sure she didn't sample her merchandise either. Jerry didn't do drugs and he wanted to make sure Summer obeyed her doctor's orders. Of course he had an ulterior motive. This was his chance to wake up alongside Summer and he didn't want her passing out or puking her guts up before he'd had the opportunity to enjoy all the benefits of sharing his bed with her. He saw off Darren who was moping around like a kicked puppy. He saw off Morrie Mayberry, the owner of the warehouse, who was a real slimo. Pale-skinned, black-eyed Kevin caused him a few anxious moments because the guy was just so cool and good-looking. When Kevin kissed Summer they looked like two pythons trying to swallow each other. Summer was electric when Kevin kissed and held her, laughing, bubbling and eating him with her eyes. Jerry hoped like hell he'd have the same effect on her. His heart ached just watching.

Summer dropped a tab when Jerry wasn't looking. She just had to. She was having such a good time it seemed wrong not to finish it with a trip. Jerry guessed but it didn't matter because the trip was good, and he was happy just listening to Summer's running commentary and ridiculous revelations. When he got her back to the duplex he shared with his brother and two other guys, he made her take a shower. He did this by dragging her into the shower with him. It was the first time Summer had ever taken a shower with anyone while she was tripping and she couldn't stop giggling. Jerry got harder than three-unit maths, but he wouldn't let her climb on even though his prick was throbbing so hard it looked like it might launch itself into space.

He dried her, picked her up and dropped her naked and gorgeous onto his bed. He didn't know that Summer's libido was depressed, and she seemed to have forgotten that it was anyway. He lined up his condoms on the dresser, and didn't think half a dozen was overly optimistic.

'Strawberry jam,' said Summer.

'What?'

'Cover me in strawberry jam.'

This was a fantasy Jerry had only ever heard about, but he reckoned he could handle it. He got the jam, a whole pot, and wondered how he'd ever explain the sheets if his flatmates saw them. Summer was giggling and wriggling like a kitten on speed, and licking him all over. He let her, hoped she'd lock onto his aching dick and blow his lights out. But she didn't. He kissed her firmly to shut her up, slipped down to her breasts, licked the jam off her nipples, and worked his tongue down her tummy towards the only forest he was interested in.

'You'll leave snail trails,' said Summer, giggling helplessly.

Jerry refused to let anything put him off, licking with the determination of a kid with a stolen iceblock. He slipped his head between her legs and was encouraged to discover she was already wet and not just with jam. He licked till his tongue ached. Round and around, faster and faster, slowly increasing the pressure. He felt her hands grab the back of his head, guiding, kneading.

'Oh Christ,' said Summer, her voice suddenly husky. 'You been taking lessons from Ciaron or something?'

Jerry ignored her. He wasn't as cool as Kevin or as loose as Darren, but he was Italian. He had a job to do and he did it wonderfully, with all the attention to detail Italians give finicky little motors. He wanted Summer on the cam and motoring. He wanted to take her to the red line and past it. He wanted her in overdrive and revving to the max, wanted to hear her engine scream, wanted her to look at him the way she'd looked at Kevin. Summer arched her back, pushed her crotch hard into his face and grabbed handfuls of his hair. She even crossed her toes.

'Oh God! C'mon, c'mon!' she urged. 'We haven't got all night!'

'Yes we have,' said Jerry, and reached for the first of his condoms.

* * *

Summer woke up feeling warm, contented and absolutely stuffed. Dr Grainger had told her she needed good food and rest but she'd had precious little of the latter. Her weariness was overpowering but she refused to let it get her down. She felt too good, immortal even, and knew there was nothing stopping her from taking off to see God. Well, not much anyway.

The duplex was silent and Summer guessed that Jerry and his flatmates had cleared off to work. She staggered to the toilet, washed her hands, her face and her bottom with someone's face cloth. Her teeth felt furry and there were four toothbrushes to choose from. Unaccustomed luxury. She cleaned her teeth and wiped the toothpaste from her mouth. Sunlight flooded into the kitchen and she headed towards it. There were no clocks to give her a clue whether it was breakfast or lunchtime so she switched on the radio.

She found eggs in the fridge and boiled one, found some white hi-fibre, toasted it and made soldiers with real butter. Summer wasn't used to having food on tap and was blown away by the novelty. She boiled the egg so that it was soft and runny without being watery, and licked the yolk off the fingers of toast as if it were chocolate around an ice-cream. She finished eating and wondered why she hadn't boiled two eggs. There was no doubt about it — her body knew what was needed and wanted more.

The kitchen was surprisingly tidy considering four blokes lived there and used it. More than that, it was clean. Summer was impressed enough to wash her dishes and dry them. The toilet was clean too and there were no hairs blocking the sink in the bathroom basin. She looked through the CDs stored neatly in the stacker, recognised Charly Lownoise, Def FX, Itch-e + Scratch-e, Sisters of Mercy, and Snoop Doggy Dog. There was another stack with names like Elizabeth Schwarzkopf and Jessye Norman, which reminded her of home and her father's passion for opera. There was something else weird about the place: there were no posters anywhere. No stinging exposés of government corruption, no blunt rebukes of capitalist conspiracies, no forest posters. There weren't even any pictures. She thumbed through a pile of magazines on the bookshelves. They were all car, bike or sports mags. No copies of Sista Web, not that she really expected to find any, but no green mags or newsletters either. The place was weird. She decided it would do for another night or two before she hit the road, if things worked out that way.

She forced herself into action. Bed was a good idea, but there were some things that couldn't wait. She had to see Mrs Thomas at Friends and give her the money she'd raised to hold on behalf of EGCGs. She had to go see Georgie and Gretta and figure out how to raise some money without going to the Department of Social Scrutiny again and being humiliated. She felt too good to even think about going to the DSS. She also wanted to get some stuff to give to the squat by way of thanks. She'd come for a week, maybe a fortnight, and wound up staying three months. She owed them and wanted to leave on a note which ensured a warm welcome on her return. Trouble was, Darren, her partner in crime, was no longer her partner and it took at least two of them to scam the supermarkets. She wanted to give the Blackmores shelves a workover for Thalia's sake. The squat's self-appointed mum loved vitamins and naturopathic remedies, and liked dispensing them just as much. Busking seemed the only option and she wished she didn't feel so stuffed.

The radio cut to a newsbreak and Summer heard the name of a girl she knew, a girl who'd stood side by side with her on the blockade in the Tarkine and who'd stayed a couple of nights at the squat. Summer felt a chill and suddenly the day didn't seem quite so cheery. The police had finally identified the murdered hitchhiker. The girl hadn't been much older than she was. Didn't use drugs or anything. All she'd ever wanted to do was save the forests from the woodchippers.

'Christ!' said Summer. 'Now they're killing us.'

* * *

The Friends office was like a morgue. Mrs Thomas was weepy. The noticeboard had already begun filling up with messages of sympathy and rage from people who'd met and befriended the murdered girl. Summer just had to get out of there. Handing over the money should've been a happy occasion and given her a charge. Instead she felt like a balloon-seller at a funeral. She took off the moment Mrs Thomas handed her a receipt.

By the time she was back on the street the sun had taken refuge behind dark gathering clouds and the wind had sprung up. It picked up newspapers and tossed them down the street, sometimes pinning them against lampposts. It took all of Summer's strength not to join them. Either Melbourne was living up to its reputation of delivering four seasons in a single day or it had come out in mourning as well. Summer was still only wearing the short denim skirt and blouse she'd borrowed from Sky for the rave, and the chill cut through them. Her eyes watered mercilessly and the effort of walking into the wind began to wear her down. She was wondering how the hell she'd make it all the way to Georgie and Matt's place in Collingwood when she remembered the five dollars she'd scammed on the acid. But where was it? She slipped her little backpack off her shoulder and rummaged through it. There was her wallet, sketch pad, two Pentels, some tissues, but no money anywhere. Her spirits sank when she realised she'd bundled all the money together and given it to Mrs Thomas. Trams were out because she couldn't dodge paying the fare unless they were crowded. She saw two young guys coming towards her in jackets and ties. They were laughing and carrying on. Summer decided to approach them. You have a problem, you solve it. It was all a question of being positive.

'Hi,' said Summer as brightly as she could. 'Can one of you guys help me?'

'What's your problem?' one of them asked. Both stopped.

'I need the tram fare to Collingwood,' she said.

'Piss off!' said one.

'Get a life,' said the other. They started to walk on.

'Dorf-dorf, dee-it dee-it,' said Summer and laughed. She turned and kept walking, knowing there was just no chance that she could walk all the way to Collingwood, or to the squat in Port Melbourne. She began to feel light-headed and dizzy. Food and rest, the doctor had said. What she was doing didn't feel much like rest. She walked down Latrobe Street, crossed Russell Street, and pointed her nose towards the café by the freight yards. Maybe, just maybe, somebody she knew would be there.

'Excuse me.'

Summer turned and the quick surge of hope died just as quickly. A patrol car had ghosted up beside her. A young cop had his head stuck out the passenger window.

'Are you Sarah Jenkins?'

'Never heard of her,' said Summer. But she had. The name rang bells and she couldn't figure out why.

'You match her description,' said the cop. 'Right down to the purple-red hair and bird's feet. You got any identification?'

'Sure,' said Summer. She took out her wallet and showed them the ID card she'd had made when she was sixteen so she could go and listen to bands in pubs without getting thrown out for being under age. The cop looked from the photo to Summer and back again.

'Where do you live?' he asked.

'Wherever I'm welcome,' said Summer with a laugh. 'Squats, friends, you know. I'm from Sydney.'

'Not from Ballarat?'

The penny dropped for Summer. The supermarket. The name she'd made up and given to store security. Christ! There was a real Sarah Jenkins. 'Don't even know how to spell it,' said Summer.

'No, don't suppose you would,' said the cop. 'Here.' He handed Summer back her ID and a card with a phone number printed on it. 'If you see anyone who answers your description anywhere except in a mirror, ring this number.'

'She in trouble?'

'Runaway. So far just a missing person. Her parents are really upset. Her father's a Chief Inspector. Are you sure you're not her? Save us all a lot of aggro. Can't be too many girls wandering around with bits of dead bird in their hair.'

'That's where you're wrong,' said Summer. 'It's all the rage. Hey, you're not going anywhere near Collingwood, are you?' She started laughing.

'What do you think this is? A bloody cab?'

'How about Flinders Lane, by the freight yards?'

'All right, get in.'

'Great,' said Summer. God had once told her she was born to be liked, and it was true.

* * *

The café was empty but for a couple of couriers. The owner simply pointed to the No Credit sign when Summer asked for tram fare. She figured she'd been there often enough to be recognised and for the owner to know she'd be back. She got the distinct feeling that others less scrupulous had asked before her. A short shapeless woman came out of the kitchen, drying her hands on a towel that looked like it had been used to catch oil leaks from a semitrailer.

'Hey!' she said. Her accent was Southern-Italian peasant. It was harsh and crackled, breaking sometimes to a hoarse whisper. 'You the sick girl?'

'Yeah,' said Summer. 'But don't worry, it's not catchy.'

'Here, you take,' she said. She opened the cash drawer and took out a five dollar note. 'Fife dollar. You take. Go on. You take. No worries, him.' She elbowed her husband aside. 'You pay back next time. Good girl, you.'

'I promise,' said Summer. And at the time she really meant it.

* * *

Matt and Georgie made her keep all the money they earned busking. They played to the rush-hour crowd, then hung around and did a number on the movie and cinema crowd. Even people who couldn't stand techno loved the paradox of techno a cappella. They wound up in a Lebanese restaurant eating felafel and tabouli. Summer disgusted them by ordering a lamb kebab and eating it in front of them. Doctor's orders, she said, and promised not to enjoy it.

By the time they'd finished Summer was exhausted and insisted on catching a cab back to Collingwood. That still left her one hundred and seventeen dollars. Summer crashed down on the sofa tired but contented. She had money, and she didn't have AIDS, and didn't have Darren, and didn't have to go to the DSS. What's more she was on the mend. She was free, and free to hit the road. No sooner had her eyes closed than she heard a truck coming up behind her. The air brakes hissed and she just knew it was going to stop.

CHAPTER ELEVEN

If Miklos had had any idea what was ahead of him he would've stayed in bed. The morning newspaper came wrapped in clingwrap which really pissed him off. His podgy fingers simply weren't capable of finding the edge to unwrap it. He scratched and scraped and swore.

Cheryl sat and watched him from the opposite side of the kitchen table, wondering why God had made men so pathetic. She wondered why he'd made them at all. Surely the Almighty could have come up with a better way of ensuring the survival of the species and keeping lawns mowed. She thought about helping but decided not to. She liked to see Miklos suffer. She wished she'd been in the pub when Clyde Townsend had wrung his balls — that would've been something. The whole town was still talking about it. They called it the Battle of the Bulges, but never in front of Miklos.

'Here, you do it!' snarled Miklos and tossed the paper to her. 'Wipe the stupid grin off your face while you're at it.'

Cheryl rotated the rolled-up paper once, picked at the clingwrap seam and lifted it neatly with a fingernail. She handed it back to him disinterestedly, as if it was the easiest thing in the world to do; for her, it was. Miklos peeled back the wrapper impatiently, tossed it aside and unrolled the newspaper.

'Oh bugger my bloody days!' he said. 'That feral bastard's gone and done it again! Where's Arnie? Where's that moronic brother of yours?'

Cheryl glanced across to see what had upset him this time. A headline caught her eye and brought a genuine smile to her face. G.O.D FACES CALVARY FOR ALL HIS CREATURES it said.

'Ten grand I gave that prick Townsend,' raged Miklos. He threw the paper down onto the table and paced around the kitchen, thumping his fist into his palm. 'I'm gunna crucify him for this.'

'Seems crucifixion's all the rage,' said Cheryl innocently. She was really enjoying herself. She picked up the paper and began reading. They'd reprinted God's letter in full:

Dear Editor,

Any day now I will face my Calvary.

I do not fear Death, but mourn the loss of All that Death will steal from Me. I mourn for all the Things I will never again See or Hear, Touch or Feel. The gentle tinkle of the Bellbird will not carry to the Grave, nor the lonely, haunting Cry of the Powerful Owl. The perfume of Banksia, Wattle and Grevillea will not draw Me to gaze upon their Beauty. The shuffle of Wombat or Potoroo on Forest Floor will not waken Me. The Fingers of Dawn will never again touch Me. Death is insatiable, it truly is.

Yet I give My Life willingly if in giving it there is a chance that the Life of My Forest will be spared. I will not give up My Life easily, but will rail and protest until the End, until My Last Breath is crushed from My Body and my Life Spark extinguished. When the Tractors and Bulldozers come to destroy my Kingdom they must first demolish Me.

What Value can be placed upon one Human Life? Is all Human Life sacred and precious, or does it have a Value in Commerce? Is the loss of one Life against Hundreds of Millions of Woodchip Dollars considered reasonable? Is the loss of two? Is three reasonable or unreasonable? What then is the value of the Life of a single Long-Footed Potoroo? Is one Potoroo expendable? What then an Entire Species? How much is a Koala worth, how much an entire Colony? Does the Spotted-Tailed Quoll have a price on its Head? Is there a Bounty to be paid in Woodchip Dollars? How much is an Entire Ecosystem worth that dates back Millions of Years? Ten million dollars? One hundred million?

It is worth more than My Life, that is for sure.

Little Potoroo Creek has been given a Value quantified in Dollars and Cents and something even more demeaning — Votes. That My Forest and all its Inhabitants can be sacrificed to Careers of such Little Worth and potentially Dire Consequence is one of the lasting Mysteries of the Universe. Will Victoria be worse off if Bernard Dwight is not re-elected? Will Victoria be worse off if our State Government loses Office? Will Victoria be worse off when I cease to exist?

Probably not.

But never doubt this. The loss of Victoria's little Ark of Creation, Little Potoroo Creek, would be a Loss beyond Estimation. Beyond Words. Beyond Forgiveness. Why do you sit by and let this happen?

Yours Sincerely,

G.O.D.

Little Potoroo Creek.

'Here! Gimme that!' Miklos snatched the paper from Cheryl and went storming out of the house. Cheryl watched him go, sat motionless as troubled thoughts tumbled over each other. God's message had reminded her of her obligation to photograph the valley for posterity, and her hesitation in doing so. But more than that, his message had got to her, got her wondering. She recalled the valley as she'd seen it and how God had described it. If there was a paradise on earth, Cheryl thought, God had introduced her to it. How much was Little Potoroo Creek worth? It was easy to picture the torn, broken, plundered wasteland that Miklos would leave behind because she'd seen it all many times before. She raised her head and took in the Miele dishwasher, cooktop, oven, the table and benchtops made from four-hundred-year-old plum pine, the stainless-steel sinks, the parquet floor and all the other trappings that justified her marriage to Miklos. Little Potoroo Creek was certainly worth something, and was certainly worth saving. But it wasn't worth giving up everything she had, giving up the house and the bank account. It wasn't worth going back to living hand to mouth. Nothing was worth that.

* * *

Miklos parked his four-wheel drive and looked to see if Arnie was in his favourite position, watching the chipper swallow logs. He wasn't. That pissed him off even more. The Toyota had been back for two days and still nobody had clapped eyes on Arnie or his deadshit mates. He'd got up one morning to find his Toyota parked neatly out in front of his house. Miklos's first thought was that Arnie had suddenly become considerate and left the Toyota outside rather than bring it up the drive and wake them. When Arnie failed to appear he sent one of the men around to his home. He hadn't appeared there either. Nugget said he'd see what he could do and organised a search. Miklos was starting to feel uneasy. Something was definitely wrong but he hadn't a clue what.

He went straight to his office and put on the coffee. There was a bunch of messages on his desk to ring various newspapers and TV stations. He swept them into the bin. There was no sign of Jan and he knew there wouldn't be for some time. She'd be late in because she was the reason he'd been late home the previous night. He'd needed to know that his bits still worked despite Clyde Townsend's assault on them, and had been relieved to discover they did. Jan had nearly bust them again celebrating. He sat and read God's letter while the coffee infused. His blood boiled along with the water. He thumped the plunger down so hard half of the scalding liquid erupted out through the spout.

'Shit!' said Miklos as it splashed on his wrist. He grabbed a paper towel and tried to take the sting away. He wanted to smash the jug. He wanted to rip up the

Herald. He wanted to break something, wanted to hurt someone. He wished Arnie would walk in so he could thump him for disappearing, thump Jan for being late, thump Townsend for being an arsehole and a liar. Townsend! Miklos remembered his mission and made a grab for the phone. It rang instants before he picked it up.

'Miklos?' said Nugget. Miklos could hear an engine in the background and somebody groaning and realised the cop was on his mobile. 'I've found Arnie and his mates.'

'Yeah? Where? I'll kill the bastard.'

'Maybe you won't have to. He's half dead already.'

'Where are ya?'

'Up the fire trails off Thirsty Creek Road, up towards Potoroo Creek. About an hour away. I've never seen anything like it. All three of them are absolutely rooted. If they were dogs you'd put them down.'

'What happened?'

'Mushrooms.'

'What?'

'It's a long story,' said Nugget. 'And I got a hunch you're not going to like it.'

Miklos listened in growing disbelief. He thumped his desk so hard he launched his coffee into suborbital space.

'They let that feral dickhead steal my Toyota?' he shouted.

'Seen the note myself,' said Nugget. 'Got it in my pocket.'

'They knew he stole my car and they still went ahead and ate the bloody stew?'

'Scraped the pan out with their fingers. Licked their plates clean.'

'Then what?'

'Spraypainted the inside of the tent. Didn't have a bucket so they chucked up on each other. Wozza got the shits and went outside to drop his duds, discovered he was blind and couldn't find his way back. Lay on the ground screaming all night. He started seeing devils and thought possums were trying to steal his nuts. He's had his hands clamped around them ever since we picked him up. The others couldn't help him 'cause they were no better off. Had worms coming out their eyes, wombats eating their toes — you know, that sort of shit. Apparently some of the mushies were of the magic variety. Psychedelic, or something. The blindness was pretty temporary, but it sounds like they were tripping for at least twelve hours.'

Miklos groaned.

'Once they started feeling better they started feeling hungry.'

Miklos braced himself. 'Don't tell me.'

'Yeah. Cold baked beans and beer.'

Miklos closed his eyes.

'Well you can imagine.'

'Yeah, I can imagine,' said Miklos.

'Mate, they've lost kilos! There's nothing left inside 'em! They're hollow, like three farts in an echo chamber. Made 'em strip and wash in a creek because I couldn't stand the stink.'

Miklos thought for a moment. 'Where are you now?'

'Getting near Thirsty Creek Road,' said Nugget.

'They got clothes?'

'Yeah. We took overalls just in case they were soaked.'

'Nugget, I don't think those dipshits deserve a ride. Do you?'

Miklos heard the brakes squeal on the police four-wheel drive just as he hung up. He flopped back in his chair and reached for his coffee but it was long gone. He spotted the cup, lying in a puddle in a far corner. He sat stunned by the sheer audacity and effrontery of the man who called himself God. The bastard had stolen his car and had had the nerve to leave it parked outside his door. The bastard had stolen his car and ... yes! ... used it to come into Osbourne to post his letters to the bloody newspapers. The bastard had walked through his town and stood outside his door, had flaunted his triumph. The man was laughing at him, treating him with contempt, like he was nothing. Miklos stared at the wall in disbelief. People didn't do that sort of thing to him. Nobody did. Not to Miklos Laszlo Bollok.

But apparently one person did.

* * *

'Ten grand,' said Miklos menacingly. He had Clyde Townsend on conference because he didn't trust himself to hold the handset without chucking it through the window. 'I gave you ten grand and you screwed up.'

'You screwed up,' said Clyde Townsend. 'I told you not to go after that guy in the forest. You provided his transport.'

'I screwed up? I'll put that on your headstone,' said Miklos. 'You said you'd warned the papers off.'

'Can't stop them publishing letters to the editor. Did you notice there were no editorials?'

Miklos picked up the *Herald*. Clyde was right. 'What about the Sydney papers?'

'One ran the letter on page three, no editorial. None of the others were game. I guess you could say our message has been received.'

'Still not much for ten grand.'

'Have the press rung?' asked Clyde.

'Have they what!'

'So?'

'So what?'

'Have you talked to them?'

'Ten grand and you want me to do your job?'

'No. If there's one thing you don't do, Miklos, it's talk to the press unless I tell you to. And when you do, I want to hear my words coming out of your mouth. Now, run through what happened out in the forest again.'

Miklos did. Clyde listened without interruption.

'Okay,' Clyde said when he'd finished. 'Here's what we do. You got a sledgehammer?'

'Yeah.'

'Well go wreck your four-wheel drive. Smash all the lights and mudguards.'

'Are you out of your freakin' mind?!' Miklos screamed.

'Make sure you break the windscreen. When you've finished call the local paper and tell them to go take some pictures of it. Tell them God stole your Toyota and smashed it up, okay? Make sure you give them a copy of the note.'

The light came on in Miklos's head. He began to smile. 'Like it,' he said.

'I'll fax you what to say. Next send Arnie and his dipshit mates to the nearest hospital. Private wards if you can get them.'

'Yeah?' said Miklos doubtfully.

'The way I understand it,' said Clyde, 'you sent some of your best men, including your own brother-in-law, into the forest to negotiate with God, right? To see if there were grounds for compromise. What did he do in return? He poisoned your men. Nearly killed them. In fact, if it wasn't for the diligence of Police Sergeant Nugent those poor men could have died. Charges may be laid pending further investigation. Makes you wonder what kind of animal that guy is, doesn't it?'

'Like it, like it,' said Miklos, feeling good for the first time that day. 'What I've been saying all along. Man's a freakin' animal.'

'Tell your local paper to go to the hospital too, okay? I'll make sure the national dailies pick up the story. But remember, we've all got to sing the same song. I'll send a fax telling you exactly what I want you to say, and what I want Arnie to say when the press come calling. Stick to the script. I want Arnie looking like he's at death's door. Reckon he'll be up to it?'

'Oh I guarantee it,' said Miklos. He pounded his fist onto his desk and disconnected. He rang Nugget's mobile. 'Nugget, go back and pick the boys up. Make them put their own clothes back on and take them to the hospital in Orbost.'

'But ...' began Nugget.

‘Don’t argue!’ He could hear Nugget trying to think, wanting to question. He hated it when stupid people tried to think. That’s not what he paid them for. ‘One more thing ...’

‘Yes, Miklos?’

‘Make sure they have another feed of beans.’

* * *

Miklos had built a house for himself and his new bride just on the fringe of Osbourne so he could have a bit of space around him. He didn’t want neighbours, and didn’t bother asking Cheryl whether she did or not. He bought a one-hectare plot without consulting her, and one day a convoy of timber trucks carrying sawn and dressed timbers pulled up and mysteriously lost their loads. When guests admired his house Miklos liked to say it fell off the back of a truck. Its isolation made his backyard the ideal place to carry out Clyde Townsend’s instructions. He drove straight home after hanging up on Nugget. Cheryl met him at the door, paintbrush in hand.

‘What’s up?’ she asked.

‘I need to borrow your car,’ he said.

‘What’s wrong with yours?’

‘It’s about to have an accident. Get me some newspapers.’

Cheryl obliged, even though she hadn’t a clue what he was going on about. She watched fascinated as he spread newspapers over the driveway and drove his Toyota onto them. Her fascination turned to outright laughter when he picked up his sledgehammer and smashed it into a headlight.

'What are you doing?' she asked.

'Issue management,' said Miklos.

'Are you out of your mind?' she said. She thought it was the dumbest thing she'd seen in ages.

Miklos paused and looked at her. He hated it when people laughed at him. Hated it even more when his wife laughed at him.

'Who had my car last?' he said. 'Who stole it from me? Who smashed it up, deliberately and maliciously? That weirdo thinks he's clever, thinks he can shit on me and get away with it. Thinks he's got all them bleedin' heart, pinko newspapers on a string. Well now the world's gunna find out what he's really like. If you had any kinda brain you wouldn't stand there all high and freakin' mighty laughin' at me, you'd be down here helpin'. Don't forget where your bread and butter comes from, sister. Now piss off!'

Cheryl stepped back inside the house and closed the screen door behind her. Miklos was too busy beating metal to hear her walk straight to her studio then out through the front door.

* * *

Miklos didn't waste time admiring his handiwork. He backed the battered Toyota into the carport, gathered up the newspapers with their incriminating piles of paint flakes and shattered glass, rang the *East Gippsland Gazette* and asked to speak to the editor.

James Ferguson, the editor, was the son of a Scottish ship's engineer who'd survived five years and two sinkings in the merchant navy before packing himself and his family off to Australia as soon as the war was over. James took the first bold steps in his chosen career by writing stories for, and ultimately becoming editor of, his university magazine. The *Melbourne Herald* snapped him up on graduation, and over the next thirty years he made a reputation for himself as a journalist of the highest integrity. He had his own columns writing on politics and business, where his intelligence and integrity could unravel the lies and deceits and present an unbiased analysis. His Scottish temperament seemed to make him the ideal man for the job, but he kept longing for and returning to his true love which was reporting world affairs. Unfortunately world news moved further and further back into the body of the newspapers he worked for, and increasingly the stories were run verbatim from foreign news services. Cancer claimed his wife just as his two children left home to make their own way in the world. James retired from the pressure and increasing disappointments of mainstream journalism. The *East Gippsland Gazette* was his retirement present to himself.

James had been mortified when God's story broke in the major metropolitan newspapers. It was a local story, an East Gippsland story, yet he'd been cut out of the loop. James still abided by the principles which had governed his career. He believed he'd always been fair and presented both sides of any issue. He'd given equal space to the arguments of the timber workers and the conservationists. He felt insulted and belittled at being ignored and having his newspaper treated as inconsequential. When Miklos rang, James saw his chance to regain lost ground and score points off the major dailies for failing to do their homework and present both sides of the debate. His elation turned to dismay when he realised his only senior reporter was forty kilometres away in Bonang, covering a dispute between neighbours over septic tank leakage. He thought about grabbing a photographer and covering the story himself, except he didn't have a photographer, and what he did have was a paper to get out. So he sent the only person he had available, a kid not long out of Monash University who shaved more out of hope than need. James had seen peaches with a heavier growth. Still, the kid had a slick way with words, an intelligent cynicism, and owned a camera. He lent the kid his micro-cassette recorder and instructed him to let Miklos do all the talking.

The kid thought his lucky day had come at last. He normally only covered weddings and council meetings, and collected handouts from the Sisters of the Forest, EGCGs, CROEG and other green groups. He could see his story running in the national dailies with his name, Samuel Johnson, on the by-line. He could see himself being plucked out of backwood obscurity and into mainstream journalism, a reporter on a major metropolitan daily. He could scarcely conceal his excitement. This was the big break he needed.

He took his own car, a '56 oval-window VW Beetle, forgetting the witty sticker the East Gippsland Conservation Group had given him which he'd stuck on his back window. He didn't know it was a CIA gem, and it wouldn't have made any difference if he had because he had no idea who or what the CIA was. But he did know who Miklos Bollok was and he should have known better.

He fronted up to the Orbost Hospital, introduced himself to Miklos Bollok and dutifully recorded every word the boss of Rip, Chip and Ship uttered. He tried to interview Arnie and the other two men, but all three were beyond speech. Mushrooms, exposure, exhaustion and the extra serve of beans had all contributed to their inability to communicate. Miklos had contributed as well, shortly before the reporter had arrived, letting a couple of well-placed right rips to the body express his general displeasure with their performance. Samuel could take photos though, and he made sure they were beauties. He got Miklos to prop the patients up and shot them from below with side light bounced up from the bottom of the stainless-steel bedpans held below their chins. He put the Polaroid back on his camera and took a couple of shots to show Miklos the effect.

'Christ,' said Miklos. 'Glad you didn't do my wedding photos. Though hang on, when I think about the pictures of my wife you might have.' He laughed. He liked the shots of Arnie — they reminded him of promos for old Hammer horror movies. 'Let's see what you can do with my four-wheel drive,' he said. He told the kid to follow him home.

'Hey,' said Samuel when he saw Miklos's Toyota, 'whoever did this sure didn't miss.'

'It was a malicious and vindictive act,' said Miklos. 'You still running that tape recorder? Make sure you get that bit.'

Samuel took the micro-cassette from his top pocket and switched it on. 'Malicious and vindictive act,' he said solemnly.

‘And unprovoked,’ said Miklos, departing only slightly from Clyde’s script. ‘Time everybody woke up to what that weirdo who calls himself God is really about. You got a copy of the note he wrote?’

‘Yup.’

‘You wanna shoot from below? You wanna reflector? Gotta have somethin’ around here looks like a bedpan.’ He heard a snigger come from the shadows inside the back verandah. Cheryl was sitting there on the swing chair, wearing the smug superior grin he hated. ‘What’s up with you?’ he said.

‘Nothing,’ said Cheryl. ‘Just been admiring your friend’s car.’

‘Don’t need reflectors,’ said Samuel. ‘This late afternoon light is perfect. It’ll make every dent look like the Grand Canyon.’

Miklos turned his attention back to the business at hand. ‘Like it,’ he said. He really did, and he really liked the kid. ‘You oughta watch how this kid works,’ he told Cheryl. ‘You might learn somethin’.’

He watched the kid dip and squat his way around the Toyota, taking wide shots and close-ups. Miklos thought the shot of the mangled headlight dangling by its wires was pretty neat. ‘I’ll walk you to your car,’ he said. He put his arm around the kid and even held his car door open for him. He was smiling as the kid took off down the driveway. Only then did he see the sticker on the Beetle’s back window. ‘My Left Bollok Has No Right!’ it said. ‘Save Little Potoroo Creek.’

CHAPTER TWELVE

Three hundred kilometres away to the west, Summer stood by the side of the Princes Highway trying to thumb a lift. She'd meant to leave in the morning but, as usual, things hadn't turned out that way.

She'd woken early and gone busking with Georgie, Matt and Sky because they were broke and it seemed only fair to help them out. By the time she got back to Collingwood, put a new fire-red rinse through her hair and took the herbal medicine Gretta had brewed for her, lunch had beckoned. They wouldn't hear of her leaving on an empty stomach.

She'd gone straight from Collingwood to a discount health food shop, spent thirty dollars on pills and potions for Thalia, and taken them around to the squat. She found Barry trying to fish out a foreign object somebody had tried to flush down the loo, thanked him for letting her stay and said goodbye. 'Cool, man,' he'd said. Summer didn't hang around to see what the foreign object was. She could guess what it would be anyway, and wondered which one of the girls had been lazy. She'd woken Stretch to say goodbye to him, left a farewell note for the rest of the residents to find, and collected her few possessions. Her life fitted neatly into her little backpack and shoulder bag. Her final stop was a transport café near the Princes Highway where she bought some speed and a Coke. Experience had taught her that hitching at night could be dodgy if she didn't stay alert.

A cop car cruised up to her and stopped. She thought they were going to warn her about hitchhiking, thought they were part of the conspiracy to stop protesters turning up at the blockade, thought they were going to hassle her. She half expected to be searched for drugs.

'Are you Sarah Jenkins?' said the woman cop passenger. Summer laughed and showed her ID.

'You answer the description,' said the cop, not convinced.

'Then change the description,' said Summer. 'This is the second time I've been asked.'

The cops snorted and drove away. Summer watched them go and let a growing feeling of elation wash over her. She was free at last, free to stick out her thumb and go see God. She had seventy-two dollars left in her pocket to buy warm underwear, toothbrushes, garbage bags, candles, batteries, rice and a flagon of Chestnut Teal sherry. God would welcome her with open arms. Leaving wasn't always easy but this time it had been plain bloody ridiculous.

PART TWO

MOURN TILL DAWN

CHAPTER THIRTEEN

For some reason the currawongs had decided it was their day to sing. The sounds of their eisteddfod echoed across the valley and all God's creatures listened. They had little choice. God sat cross-legged on the floor of his cave, naked but for his Swiss army knife slung on a leather thong around his neck. He worked paste in a bowl like a mother mixing cocoa for her kids, grinding and stirring until he was certain there were no lumps. He added water to the paste, drop by tiny drop, swished it around and stirred it until it became an ochre-coloured slurry. His shoulders and neck stiffened and his heart beat faster at the prospect of bridging millennia. He put the bowl down by his side, joined his palms together and let them rest limply in his lap. His eyelids fluttered, drooped, met with the lower lids, parted and hovered above them, millimetres apart. God visualised the task ahead, and held the image in his mind until he felt calm descend. There was nothing unusual about what he was trying to do, nothing extraordinary, nothing unique. Mankind had been doing it since the dawn of time. He raised his arms high above his head, inhaling as he did so, and let the backs of his hands rest against each other. He exhaled slowly as he lowered them. He repeated the exercise three times before he was satisfied. Nothing extraordinary, nothing unique, he told himself. All the same he had to smile.

God picked up the bowl and stood. He gave the muddy water one final swirl to reassure himself that the solids had dissolved and weren't just held in suspension. He took a deep breath, raised the bowl to his mouth and filled his cheeks with the liquid. His eyes turned to the space on the wall above the carefully chiselled inscription. He placed his right palm against the wall, spread his fingers and began to spray the ochre liquid from his mouth. One pause for breath and a refill and the job was finished. He stood back, admired his stencilled handprints upon the cave wall and grinned foolishly. His mark looked childish compared to the ghostly imprints surrounding it, but they had the advantage of age. Their ancient artists had lived thousands of years earlier.

'I wish we could have shaken hands,' said God's inscription. 'This is the best I can do. Thank you for your company. Thank you for looking after My Forest. Goodbye.' God had chiselled his initials and the date underneath.

He rinsed the ochre off his hands in his wash bowl, emptied both bowls and dried them, and tucked them in his pack. Only one job remained. He reached up and unhooked the rolled-up tarpaulin he used to cover the entrance to his cave. It was time to leave home, this home at any rate. God had two more homes in caves tucked away in other reaches of the valley, and a treehouse which was his summer home and favourite. But he had needs, and the needs dictated that he kept on the move, never staying more than two months in any one place. He had a need to fetch water, to collect firewood, to gather food, and for a toilet tucked away at each location. No matter how careful he was, no matter how lightly he trod, no matter how many detours he took, he couldn't help leaving trails. If anyone came looking for him, trails would point to his whereabouts as clearly as a street sign.

God had other homes too, built high in trees, straddling the projected route of the road the Department of Conservation and Forestry were about to build to let loggers into Little Potoroo Creek. He'd built the treehouses with stealth, hiding them from the eyes of visiting surveyors and local bush fire brigade members who, curiously, lit more fires than they ever put out. He only used these homes when he was working, a week or two at a time, saving them up against the day they could help him save his forest.

God tied a rope to both ends of his tarpaulin and pulled it tight so that the tarp bent like a bow. He threw it over one shoulder and his rucksack over the other where it joined company with his rolled-up mattress. He kept his arms free so he could hang bags of rice, oats, flour and lentils around his neck and festoon his body with his cooking pots and water flagon. His frame was strong and sparse, rippling with muscle and sinew. It needed to be. He turned to look one last time at the home he was leaving. The normal course of rotation meant he wouldn't be back for six months or more, and he had to face the prospect that he might never return at all. This cave was a good winter home, dry and warm, and he'd grown to appreciate it when the southerlies had come roaring in, dumping snow. But before next winter the bulldozers would come. He felt the weight of his load and tensed his muscles. He knew he was strong, had always been strong, but was he strong enough to stop bulldozers? Only time would tell. He turned away and began to stride out for the escarpment high on the western perimeter of the valley, the site of his next cave home. Of all his homes, the next had by far the most spectacular views. It was also his largest and he needed the extra room. The note in his bush letterbox had told him to expect company.

God was a man like any other. Once upon a time he'd captained his school's first fifteen and first eleven. Many believed he could have gone on to represent his country in either cricket or rugby. But for the demands of both sports he would have been dux as well. He was pipped at the post by an Asian swot who'd never held a ball in his hand, never been on a date and never made anyone laugh. Everybody expected great things from God. Nobody ever thought for a second that at the age of thirty-eight he'd be a feral recluse, living in a cave, dependent on handouts.

He met a beautiful young woman while at university and married her shortly after graduation. She had a brilliant legal mind and a fierce determination to succeed. The top law firms had courted her and fought over her. He took his degree in engineering and joined BHP as a project analyst. His job took him all over the country and then all over the world. He didn't see as much of his new wife as he should have.

Even so they got by, and there was no doubt that they loved each other. They only ever argued about one thing — starting a family. God wanted children, she wanted a career. One night, while the debate raged and the jury was out, she fell pregnant as they kissed and made up. The first child, a boy, was followed by another eighteen months later. His wife had decided that if she was going to have kids she'd have them all at once, get them over and done with so she could return to her true calling. Her priorities never wavered: she was a lawyer first and mother second. She wasn't the stuff doting mothers are made of and thought God would share the responsibilities of raising a family. They'd even begun to interview nannies. Then God was sent up to New Guinea, then over to Chile. He was away for months. Even when he came home he was never home. He worked into the small hours of the morning, catching up on paperwork and writing reports. He thought he was doing the best thing by his family, providing a nice home and security. His wife thought otherwise.

He woke up one morning to find he'd provided nothing his wife considered worth keeping. She filed for divorce and moved to Sydney with a man his children learnt to call daddy. He pleaded with her, told her he'd give up his job, told her he'd do anything to keep her and the kids. He told her his doubts about the rightness of what he was doing, told her about Ok Tedi and Escondida. Told her he was having second thoughts. She told him to get lost.

God had learnt how to drink spirits in the mining towns and camps; now he put his learning to good use. He didn't contact a solicitor to represent him in the divorce and turned up at the hearing motherless drunk, tearful and incoherent. His wife had no difficulty gaining custody of his children and control over the bulk of their joint assets. When he finally fell apart BHP covered the bills his medical fund didn't as doctors set about trying to put Humpty together again. He wound up in a clinic surrounded by native bush in the Dandenongs, listening to bellbirds and lyre birds, hand-feeding rosellas and lorikeets, and existing on a diet of psychotropics and antidepressants.

On his discharge from the clinic his friends at BHP rented an apartment for him in South Yarra and began the process of nursing him back into his chosen profession. The trouble was, it wasn't his chosen profession any more. God looked at the ruins of his marriage, the wreck of his life and the landscapes he'd had a hand in destroying, and decided to start all over again. Like the Khmer Rouge he turned his clock back to year zero, then threw it away altogether. He left his apartment one morning and never looked back. He made his way to the Princes Highway and hitched a ride on a truck heading east. He wanted to go as far away from civilisation as he could, wanted to find an ancient untouched world where there were no people. Choosing a destination was easy. He just looked at a map of Victoria and headed for a part with few roads. He found one small part that had no roads at all.

Little Potoroo Creek was one of the few surviving pockets of pristine rainforest. While it rained on most days it didn't rain every day. On the day God decided to shift house it didn't rain at all. Instead the sky cleared to brilliant cobalt, as though celebrating the arrival of spring. The sun burnt so fiercely it could have been heralding the arrival of summer instead. When that thought crossed God's mind he actually stopped in his tracks to digest it. A smile spread across his face. By the time he reached his new residence the morning had gone forever and sweat soaked his shirt. He'd drunk a full flagon of water along the way and the tightening in his calf muscles warned of cramp. Liquid could hold off cramp for a while but it was salt his body lacked.

God's last act in making his goodbyes to civilisation had been to transfer one thousand six hundred and twenty-three dollars and fifty-seven cents to the East Gippsland Conservation Group. It was all he had left in the world after paying for his tarpaulin, ground sheet, stuffed mattress, blankets, radio, kettle, pots and pans. He had no idea what else he'd need, realising that he'd have to become a feral to learn how to live like one. He left his money with EGCGs so that he could draw on it for provisions as they were needed. Even though his needs were basic, his funds had long since been exhausted and he'd come to rely on the kindness of others. EGCGs and other green groups provided him with eight-kilo bags of Thai rice and sacks of oatmeal, lentils and flour which they bought in bulk for the sake of economy. They gave him soap, batteries, candles and matches, but never enough, no matter how frugally he used them. Kind souls donated old clothing and lent him books. One had given him the Swiss army knife which was his constant companion. The green groups provided him with food and essentials and in return he helped their cause. Sometimes they supplemented their gifts with bags of fruit and vegetables which were in season and cheap. Sometimes they forgot he also needed salt and God hated to ask. They didn't understand his request for Chestnut Teal sherry either and usually forgot that as well. Sometimes they also forgot he needed cooking oil. They were the things he missed most: his salt, his oil and his sherry. Nobody except Summer understood about the sherry. It wasn't just a luxury but confirmation of his triumph over his demons. He'd asked her to explain it to EGCGs but she must have forgotten.

God fixed his tarpaulin to the hooks he'd set into the roof at the mouth of the cave many years earlier, and climbed up the grey gum that helped hide the entrance so he could string the aerial for his radio. They were the two most important jobs. The cave was just a cave until he hung up his tarpaulin, and he was nowhere without his radio. Feral cats had used the cave in his absence and he examined the broken bones and the contents of their faeces before sweeping them out with the dying head of a broken branch. The cats had dined well and it broke his heart to see the remains of the rat-like antechinus, glider possums and clumps of ginger and cream fur which suggested the demise of a spotted-tailed quoll. There were also rabbit remains but no traces of anything that might have come from a potoroo. God finished sweeping, unpacked, suspended his bags of food from hooks set into the ceiling of the cave so animals couldn't raid them, then sat and prepared his snares.

God told himself it wasn't vengeance but conservation of endangered species. He believed man had interfered with the balance of nature and, as a member of that species, he was duty-bound to make amends. He could rationalise his action a hundred different ways without acknowledging the one justification that put urgency into his work: feral cats were an important source of protein.

Everyone automatically assumed God was a vegetarian. He often was, but by necessity not by choice. God trapped rabbits as well, but baulked at eating fox. When he had a craving for fish he used parts of the carcasses of the animals he'd trapped to attract and catch eels in the streams. He boiled them until they became gelatinous and ate them with rice. Other times he dried or smoked them. Sometimes he attracted yabbies, and the spiky crustaceans were the greatest treat of all. But mostly he ate mushrooms and rice.

He rebuilt the stones for his fireplace, gathered firewood and set off for a nearby stream to catch some yabbies to supplement his dinner and to use as bait for the feral cat. He'd never known a cat that could resist fresh yabby tails. They didn't need them because there was plenty of other food about, and must have been suspicious. But the smell of yabby tails was seductive and feral cats were no more immune than their city cousins to that affliction called curiosity. It took him an hour and a half to catch the ten yabbies he needed: six for himself and four for the cat. He waited for evening before setting the trap because he didn't want kookaburras, crows, currawongs or any other birds tempted by the bait. He was glad to finally make it back to his new home with his catch and his refilled flagon of water.

While his rice slowly steamed he cooked the yabbies, removed their tails and put them to one side. He added a handful of finely chopped mushrooms to the yabby heads and bodies to make stock, and tossed in a pinch of crushed peppergum leaves. He wished he had salt, fervently wished for it. But, more than anything, he wished he had sherry. A drop in the cooking and a drop in a cup, just the one and never a chaser. He tipped his rice into a bowl, removed the yabby shells from the stock, tossed in the tails for a few seconds to warm through, and poured the sauce over the rice. He threw a few more sticks onto the fire to take the chill from the cave, turned on his radio and began to eat his dinner. He ate slowly, like a Buddhist monk, appreciative of every mouthful. The ABC played Beethoven's Pastorale. God sat cross-legged, motionless but for the slow rhythmic movement of his jaws and the occasional transport of food to mouth.

God was in his heaven and peace descended upon the earth.

* * *

Night also fell on Orbost, and James Ferguson had a job to do which gave him no pleasure. The locals claimed he'd only ever made one decision in his life, and that was to sit on the fence. That wasn't fair. James Ferguson's fault was that he stubbornly held to the principles of old-style journalism, believing it was his role to present facts and let his readers make up their own minds as to the rights and wrongs of any issue. Only in his editorial did he express opinions, and then went out of his way to present both sides of the argument. Unlike Rupert Murdoch he failed to understand that readers expect their newspapers to think for them and tell them which side to take. The people of East Gippsland were no different from those held in the thrall of the city tabloids. They didn't want reason but reinforcement of their prejudices. Yet James battled on to educate and enlighten, steadfast in his beliefs and policy of neutrality.

Miklos's phone call had shaken him. The boss of Rip, Chip and Ship had powerful friends who advertised in his paper. The day they ceased placing ads was the day he went out of business. Miklos had demanded his young reporter's head on a plate and James had no choice but to deliver it. The young man had been foolish and, worse, he'd broken the golden rule of impartiality. James didn't need his young cadet to write up the story of the poisoning or the trashing of Miklos's car because a press release containing Miklos's statements had come by fax. A phone call to Police Sergeant Nugent had confirmed the basic facts. James had written the story himself and only needed Samuel's photographs. He felt sorry for the lad because he liked to think of his employees as family, and young Samuel had shown promise. He couldn't help wondering what on earth had possessed the kid to do something so stupid.

Samuel burst through the door like a man obsessed, which is exactly what he was. He was driven by the prospect of escape, a job going places and, ultimately, fame. He'd written the copy in his mind during the drive back from Osbourne and had it word perfect. The headline loomed large and pithy. UNGODLY VENGEANCE! it shrieked. 'God Rebuffs Peace Deal With Poisoned Chalice,' trumpeted the sub-head. He knew exactly which photos he'd use before the film was even processed. At that moment he was immortal. Life was wonderful, his occupation enthralling, and the *East*

Gippsland Gazette was a place he'd remember fondly in his memoirs. Samuel burst through the door ready to hit his keyboard, anticipating compliments from an approving editor who'd read his copy as he keyed it in, anticipating the long-awaited call from a talent-spotting editor at the *Age* or the *Herald*. About the only thing he wasn't anticipating was the sack.

He listened dumbfounded as James Ferguson pompously lectured him on the principles of impartiality, the qualities that distinguished journalists from hacks, and relieved him of his micro-cassette, film and his job. Samuel went out and spent a large portion of his severance pay getting paralytically drunk for only the seventeenth time in his life. How would he get a job on a major newspaper when he'd just been fired from one as piss-anty as the *East Gippsland Gazette*?

James Ferguson took the call from the publican just as his presses began to roll for the following morning's edition. He drove straight to the pub, picked Samuel up off the floor and carted him home to the room his ex-cadet rented above the saddlery shop. He desperately wanted to have second thoughts but knew he couldn't afford them. Samuel's photos were first-rate. He apologised to the unconscious boy in the hope that it would ease his guilt, but it didn't. When he returned to his home he was still sufficiently upset to add two Mogadons to his nightcap tumbler of Bell's whisky.

The radio alarm clock woke James with the six o'clock news, just as the *East Gippsland Gazette* was hitting the street. He thought he was still dreaming when he heard the name of his paper mentioned as the source of the story, knew he wasn't dreaming when he heard

Miklos Bollok live on a phone interview. He was dressed and in his car inside two minutes. When he burst into his office all he could hear was the sound of phones ringing. He lifted the handset on line one and discovered he was on ABC Radio. It was his moment of revenge on the national dailies, his moment of reinstatement, one which he knew would continue all day, yet he was burdened by two pressing concerns. How had the story got out so quickly? And, even more urgently, why hadn't he stopped to have a pee?

* * *

When James took Samuel home from the pub and dropped him onto his bed, he forgot to do the boy one last favour — to turn off his alarm clock. It woke Samuel at six o'clock as it had been programmed to do, as if he still had a job to go to. The boy stirred, and groaned as his brain struggled to come to terms with the distinct possibility that during the night someone had hammered tent pegs through his eyes, through his skull, through his pillow and through his mattress. He tried to move but the flash of scorching pain left him scarcely daring to breathe. His tongue was swollen, parched and cracked like a dry river bed. Sound penetrated his brain but barely registered. Yet, through it all, he somehow heard the *East Gippsland Gazette* mentioned, then Miklos Bollok and the man who called himself God. It registered and for one lightning second he thought his moment of fame had come. He sat up so quickly that the blood drained from his head and he almost passed out. The pain hit him about the same time as the realisation that he had no job, no future and nowhere to go. He collapsed sobbing back onto his bed.

No job. No future. Nowhere to go.

He heard a familiar voice and risked opening his eyes. For a moment he thought the voice was in his room, come to bring both pardon and reprieve. It came as a shock to realise his old boss was speaking on the radio. He forced himself to sit up. His boss was speaking and in the background he could hear phones ringing incessantly. James needed help and he was in a position to provide it. In the single most courageous act of his life to date, Samuel dragged himself out of bed, stood under a cold shower for fifteen seconds, and was into his clothes before he was even dry. A helping hand in the hour of need had to count for something, maybe even a second chance.

Samuel went to the office via the pub so he could pick up his car. If the cops had risen as early and breathalysed him on the way to the newspaper office, they would have locked him up and thrown away his licence for life. He staggered up the stairs, head pounding, heart bursting, pushed open the door and picked up the nearest phone.

'*East Gippsland Gazette*,' he said, and let the caller do the talking. 'Mr Ferguson will ring you back the moment he has finished his present call,' he said, and repeated the number he was given. He picked up phone after phone, taking down numbers, professional to the last.

'Hold the fort,' said James. 'I'm busting for a pee.'

Samuel held the fort, the phone, the edge of his desk and, by the narrowest margin, a grip on his consciousness. He handed a slip of paper to his editor as he passed by on the way back to his office. 'Radio 3AK, then 3DB, then 2UE, Sydney. Keep them brief. I've got half a dozen more.'

'There's the paper,' said James. 'There's the story. You covered it, lad, you take the calls.'

This was the moment Samuel had dreamt of throughout his brief career, but he'd always imagined he'd be sober and articulate when it arrived. He soon realised that the radio interviewers were reading from the same copy he had in front of him, and that they preferred the sound of their own voice to his. It made things easier. He managed to fall back on his training and make radio a visual medium by conjuring up pictures his listeners could readily imagine. He also managed to put himself squarely at the centre of the story. He'd actually interviewed Arnie and the boys in hospital and could confirm their life-threatening condition. 'They looked to me like they'd been run down by a booze truck, but not before they'd drunk all the contents,' he said with feeling. He'd also spoken to Miklos Bollok and seen the damaged car. 'Picture a beer can after an elephant has tap-danced on it,' he said. Samuel could see his one-liners being picked up and quoted by both newspaper and TV. Someone, somewhere, might spot his talent and throw him a lifeline.

* * *

God woke with the dawn and rolled up his tarpaulin. It had rained in the night and clouds sat skewered on the tops of trees. He shivered in the early chill but still held hopes that the day would bring Summer. If not, it would still bring her closer and that was something to be grateful for. Her joy and optimism fed his soul, and she was one of very few mortals in whose company he felt comfortable. She'd shared his mattress too, and he'd found himself crying silent tears he couldn't explain and refused even to try. She'd laughed and sung to him, and he'd loved her even more. She'd chirped incessantly like a hungry lorikeet, a happy tinkling sound, bubbling with enthusiasm and discovery. When she went away she left behind a hole as deep and as wide as the valley he lived in, but one which he accepted as inevitable. He refused to look back because he never looked back. The past was gone and regrets changed nothing. Love came and love went, and it was best to know that in advance so that pain never again regained dominion. He allowed himself to look forward because the future was only today in the making, and that was something he was comfortable with. Summer was coming, and the day was all the better for it. The note had promised this and he'd confirmed the promise the night he posted his second letters. He'd had to borrow envelopes and stamps from Liz, the woman at EGCGs who mothered and worried about him even though she was years younger.

He put a cup of oatmeal on to boil and stirred in a spoonful of precious honey. There'd be no milk or salt, but food was food and didn't always have to taste good. But oatmeal without anything was like penance and he couldn't recall his sin. A kookaburra on the grey gum outside his doorway burst into laughter and he immediately joined in. Another day had dawned, another precious day in the life of his forest, and that was cause for joy. Then God turned on his radio and discovered he was a pariah.

He sat and listened to Miklos Bollok speaking words that came from another man's mouth. He heard how he'd deliberately and maliciously poisoned Rip, Chip and Ship's emissaries, how he'd deliberately and vindictively stolen and destroyed Miklos's Toyota Landcruiser, heard his pleas to save Little Potoroo Creek dismissed and discredited as the ramblings of a troubled mind. He heard Miklos read the note he'd left in the tent. 'Enjoy your dinner,' read Miklos. 'It was intended to be their last supper,' he ad-libbed.

God heard a carefully orchestrated succession of listeners phone in and accuse him of prowling the streets of Osbourne by night, terrifying mothers and children, and old women who lived alone. He heard loggers talk about the concealed marijuana plantations they'd found in the forests, and the shadowy figure who sold drugs to their children outside the school gates. He heard Miklos read from the transcript of his divorce proceedings, when the judge had described him as 'an alcoholic incapable of caring for himself let alone the welfare of his wife and children'. He heard a man who claimed to be a psychiatrist state that Mr G.O.D exhibited classic indications of schizophrenia, citing the use of capitals in his letters as evidence. He heard a spokesman for the clinic in the Dandenongs confirm that he had been a patient. He heard Liz's voice raised in strident protest, heard the sob in her throat, heard her frustration and anger, and knew it would be of no use to him at all. Anger was impotent in the face of hard evidence. His mistake had been to leave a note.

He was surprised at how swiftly and comprehensively the forces of destruction had countered and discredited him. Their campaign was as thorough as it was unexpected. He'd taken the high ground and they'd lynched him upon it in the name of the unholy trinity. God the thief, poisoner and vandal, God the dealer of drugs to children, God the nutter who was a danger to the community.

He sat and pressed his palms together, let them fall limply into his lap. His eyelids drooped, met with his lower lids, parted and hovered millimetres above. He inhaled long and steadily, exhaled the tension from his body. He tried to visualise the timelessness of his valley but calm was a long time coming.

* * *

There is more than one way to skin a cat and God had tried most of them. He cleaned his knife and carried the stripped carcass back to his cave where he began to make stew, hands busy to distract and occupy a troubled mind. Without refrigeration cooked meat kept longer than fresh. He cut the flesh into long thin strips which, when boiled, would fit easily through the neck of a flagon bottle. He'd discovered that food also kept longer and tasted better if he stored it in glass. He wished he had potatoes to add to the stew but all his attempts at growing vegetables had ended as a bonanza for the other forest inhabitants. When the time came, he'd make dumplings and eat the cat more as a thick soup than a stew, stretching it with lentils and mushrooms so that it spread over several meals. All the stew lacked was salt, pepper and a splash of Chestnut Teal.

Unless Summer came.

Unless Summer came bearing gifts.

But would she come now that he was a pariah? Would anyone come to man the blockade? He thought he'd done what was right, thought he'd win sympathy for the cause, but all his efforts had rebounded on him. He stared over the forest canopy to the opposite side of the valley and wondered how much he'd contributed to its destruction. Don't look back, don't look back, he told himself. There was still his village in the treetops and his tripods. All he needed was troops to man them, and the dedicated would still come. He'd lost a battle, not the war. Years earlier he'd surrendered one home weakly and pathetically, had joined the blockade in '94 and spilt blood for Ellery Creek. It hadn't been enough. God had surrendered too much and refused to surrender any more. He'd do something to make amends. He'd do something. His palms touched automatically and fell limply into his lap. His radio sat silent and he missed it terribly.

* * *

The phones eventually stopped ringing. Samuel looked up and was surprised to discover the rest of the staff had come in while he was talking. The girls who did the classifieds, the designers who did the page make-ups on their computers, the two women who ran the advertising department, Mrs Watson who manned the switchboard, and Glynnis the senior reporter. They all smiled sympathetically when they caught his eye.

'In my office,' said James. Samuel meekly did as asked. 'Why did you come in?'

‘Heard you on the radio. Sounded like you needed help.’

‘I did. It was good of you to come and I appreciate it.’ The old editor peered closely at Samuel over his reading glasses. ‘How do you feel, lad?’

‘Sick, hungover and lost.’

‘I can give you Disprin for the first two afflictions.’

‘But can you give me my job back?’ Samuel was surprised to hear the yearning in his voice. What had been a stepping stone had suddenly become a rock he desperately needed to cling to. James turned away from him and shuffled some papers on his desk.

‘Lad, if it was up to me I wouldn’t have taken your job away in the first place. I can’t fight the likes of Miklos Bollok.’

‘Could you ring him?’

‘I can’t see that it would do any good.’ James turned back to the boy, a glimmer of hope in his eyes. ‘However, if you were to drive up to Osbourne and apologise, and if Mr Bollok were to accept your apology, then that would be a different matter. Let me know how you get on.’

‘Thanks,’ said Samuel. He left the office clinging to that slender hope.

* * *

‘Is Mr Bollok in, please?’ said Samuel.

‘No. Mr Bollok is at the mill,’ said Cheryl. ‘You’re the reporter, aren’t you?’

Samuel’s brain still wasn’t functioning properly. Of course Miklos would be at the mill, yet he’d driven to his home. He looked up into Cheryl's face, saw kindness in it and a hint of amusement. 'Ex-reporter,' he said.

'Oh?'

'I got fired. I've come to apologise to Mr Bollok to see if I can get my job back.'

'Want to tell me about it? I've got some fresh coffee on.'

Samuel followed Cheryl inside, glancing through doorways as he went. The rooms all gave an impression of space and it took him a moment to realise why. It wasn't so much the furniture he saw but the furniture he didn't see. There was nothing that was surplus to requirements. The dining room had a large ten-seater dining table and ten chairs, nothing else. Bedrooms had a bed and built-ins, nothing else. What furniture he saw was classical, conservative and good quality. He found he was looking at a house that had no soul.

'Nice house,' he said.

'Came with the husband,' said Cheryl.

The only decoration was provided by forest landscapes and every room seemed to have at least one.

'Local artist?' asked Samuel.

'Very,' said Cheryl without elaborating.

'Ahhh …' said Samuel. The door to Cheryl's studio was open and he could see the unfinished canvases leaning against the walls and the landscape upon the easel. His eyes took in the reference photos pinned to the frames, the camera bag with Nikon, lenses and boxes of Fuji film. 'I should have guessed. They're very good.'

'Are they?' said Cheryl humourlessly.

'I think so,' said Samuel. He decided to change the subject to one he was more comfortable with. 'Why Fuji?'

'Best daylight film. Colours are more accurate, providing the film's processed properly.'

'Who does your prints? They're fantastic.'

'A woman in Bairnsdale, Heather McKeown. She's worked in all the major labs in Melbourne and done a lot of work for commercial photographers. Gave it up when her husband retired.' She led the way into the kitchen. 'Now, sit down and tell me your story.'

Samuel sat down at the kitchen table and told his tale. Cheryl listened sympathetically and gave him two more Disprins and a Berocca to chase down the coffee.

'I wish there was some way I could help,' said Cheryl. 'But Miklos is very black and white. You're either one hundred per cent for him or he'll jump on you. I'm not sure apologising will do you much good. He's not in the habit of picking up people he's jumped on.'

Samuel smiled. He had a feeling he wasn't the only one in the room Miklos had jumped on. He wanted to say something but couldn't begin to think what. 'Thanks for the coffee and friendly shoulder,' he said instead. 'I'd better go. I have to try anyway. I've got no choice.'

'There is one small way you could improve your chances,' said Cheryl as she saw Samuel to the door. 'You could take the sticker off your back window for a start.'

* * *

'My name's Samuel Johnson. I'd like to see Mr Bollok, please.'

'What about?' said Jan.

'I've come to apologise. I'm from the *East Gippsland Gazette*.' He felt like a naughty boy waiting outside the headmaster's study, only he couldn't remember any of the headmaster's staff having such amazing tits.

'Hang on,' said Jan. She punched Miklos's internal number. Samuel could hear the phone ringing through the wall not two metres away. 'There's a Sam somebody from the *Gazette* wants to see you. Says he's come to apologise.'

The door to the office swung open before Jan had time to hang up the phone. Miklos Bollok filled the doorway.

'Mr Bollok, I've come to apologise for the sticker on the back of my car,' Samuel began earnestly. 'It was unprofessional, thoughtless ...'

'Has Ferguson fired you?' Miklos cut in.

'Yes, however ...'

'Good,' said Miklos. He slammed the door shut in Samuel's face.

Samuel drove to the pub, realising he needed to get some food inside him before he attempted the drive back to Orbost. He figured he may as well have a drink because the Disprins weren't working and he had nothing else to do. He sat in the main bar nursing a beer while he waited for his grilled chops, fried eggs and sausages. His stomach rumbled in anticipation of the fat hit. There were five other blokes in the bar, regulars who'd haunted the pub so long they'd grown into the shape of the chairs they sat on. Samuel's spirits sank further just looking at them. He wished he'd gone to a café instead. He couldn't help feeling he was looking at his own future. The barman plonked his meal down on the table in front of him.

'You're the reporter bloke, aren't ya?' he asked.

'Yeah,' said Samuel. Sometimes it was better to lie than explain.

'You did the pictures of My Left Bollok's car, didn't ya?'

'Yeah.'

'Saw them in the paper this morning. Bloody bewdy. Those bruises came out real good.'

'Bruises?' said Samuel. 'Don't you mean dents?' His curiosity wasn't aroused, he just thought the barman was trying to be clever. A couple of the old lags up at the bar sniggered.

'Nah, bruises,' said the barman with a broad wink aimed at his audience of five. 'You know, you get a bump one day and it takes two more for it to show.' He roared with laughter and his audience laughed with him. Samuel was halfway through swallowing an overcooked piece of lamb chop before he realised what the barman was saying.

* * *

'He set you up and he's using you!'

'Prove it!'

The two women outside James Ferguson's office winced and looked grimly at each other. They were the only other people left in the office, both answering the phone and taking down late classified ads. They were used to shouting and screaming at home, but it was the first time they'd heard it in the office.

'He suckered us both!' insisted Samuel. 'Think about it.'

James did. Doubts had been gnawing away at him all day. How had his story been picked up in Melbourne and Sydney before the *Gazette* had even hit the streets? Who were all the people who claimed to have seen God prowling around Osbourne frightening old ladies and selling dope to kids? When God's letters had started appearing in the dailies, he'd even driven to Osbourne himself to try to find somebody who knew God or had seen him. Nobody had a clue except Liz and her husband Brian at EGCGs. They'd admitted to knowing who God was, but had refused to provide any information about him except to say he was gentle, sensitive and a recluse who was entitled to his privacy. He didn't sound much like the archetypal drug dealer. Something else worried James. God had gone straight to the major dailies; why hadn't Miklos? Why did he go through the *Gazette*? James felt a sickness invade his stomach and a loosening in his bowels. It was one thing to deceive a regional, another thing altogether to deliberately deceive a major daily.

'I talked to more than twenty radio stations,' said James. 'Went out live on most of them.'

'I would have talked to at least ten,' said Samuel.

'I spoke to the *Age*, *Melbourne Herald*, *Sydney Morning Herald*, *Daily Telegraph* ...' James wrung his hands in despair. 'They know me, they know I have principles. They accepted every word I said on the strength of my reputation. Channel Nine sent a film crew down and I did a segment on *The Midday Show* while you were in Osbourne. They trust me, you see?'

'I know,' said Samuel. 'I've got nothing to lose. You've got everything. If some other reporter finds out the truth, they'll have you for dinner and spit you out afterwards.'

'Aye, I know. But finding proof is not going to be easy.'

'Give me my job back and I'll find it.'

'You know I can't do that. But come back with proof and you can have your job and a salary increase.'

'Will you cover my expenses then? The old VW won't run on air.'

'I suppose so.' James called Mrs Watson in and instructed her to give Samuel a cheque for one week's wages. 'Strictly freelance, understand. But feel free to use our facilities if you need them.' He ushered Samuel out of his office. 'Now go home and take a shower. You're beginning to smell like a real reporter.'

CHAPTER FOURTEEN

The night nurse woke Summer at six o'clock with a steaming mug of tea and the promise of bacon and eggs so long as she got a move on. A patient had conveniently died the previous day, which had meant there was a bed for her and she hadn't had to sleep on the storeroom floor. Summer hadn't done too badly on her first night's hitchhiking. A truck delivering heavy machinery had picked her up and taken her all the way through to Sale, which was just over halfway. The part-Maori driver was going on to Eden but had stopped at Sale to visit a girlfriend. He was thirty years old, thirty kilos overweight and his taste in music was thirty years out of date. He was a John Rowles fan and made Summer sing along with him. On the tenth rendition of 'Cheryl Moana Marie', Summer asked to be dropped off at the next town. The driver laughed, apologised and switched to John Denver. They drove the rest of the way via West Virginia and the Rocky Mountains. The driver reckoned it was the most enjoyable trip he'd done in ages.

By the time they reached Sale everything was closed. Everything except the back door of the Sevenoaks Nursing Home. One thing Summer knew was that nursing homes always had food and always threw away more than they consumed. Old folks ordered meals out of habit but often hardly touched them. Summer was only too happy to help dispose of the waste. When she knocked on the door a familiar face opened it. Summer had been there before and the night nurse was an old friend. On one occasion when Summer had called in, the staff had been decimated by flu and she'd volunteered to work half the day in the kitchen without pay and the other half reading and chatting to patients. The old folks thought she was weird. When she told them her story they thought she'd come from Mars. Yet they succumbed to her charm and understood about the forests and her mission to save them. She had their sympathy and best wishes. People on death's doorstep have a very clear appreciation of the value of life, and have no trouble applying it to all living things.

Summer knew she had to get moving before the day supervisors came. They were the people who made the rules and therefore felt obliged to enforce them. Her presence smacked of a breach in security or, at very least, poor practice. It was important she didn't spoil things for others who also relied on the nursing home's generosity.

'How are you going to get to Orbost?' asked the night nurse as she passed Summer a plate of bacon and eggs ordered by the deceased patient.

'Hitch,' said Summer.

'Locals won't touch you,' said the nurse. 'Unless it's to sort you out. More mills have closed and feelings are running pretty high. A lot of people are hanging out for the pulpmill to give them new jobs and that's dependent on logging Little Potoroo Creek.'

'No one will hurt me,' said Summer. 'This hep C's made me look too fragile, like I'd break if they touched me.' She started laughing but the nurse wouldn't be drawn.

'Wouldn't be too sure of that,' she said insistently. 'If someone does get you, you won't be able to count on help from the police. Those blokes have to live here. They know where their loyalties belong.'

'I'll be all right,' said Summer. 'It's all a matter of being positive.'

'We'll see,' said the nurse. 'If you're not careful you'll end up like poor old Mrs Owens. That's one thing I'm positive about.' Her face suddenly lit up and she grabbed Summer's arm. 'Hang on,' she said. 'I've just had an idea, and I'm sure Mrs Owens won't mind at all.' She picked up the phone and dialled.

* * *

'You a relative?' asked the driver.

'Of Mrs Owens?' said Summer. 'No. Never met her. Wish I had so I could say thanks.'

'What do you mean?'

'Last night I slept in her bed. This morning I ate her breakfast.' She started laughing. 'De-dit,' she sang, 'de-dit, de-dit, dorf dorf dorf.'

'You're crazy,' said the driver. 'No one sings in a hearse.'

When they pulled up in the middle of Orbost's main street the people looked at one another to see who'd died. Sometimes it wasn't always easy to tell. Some of the older men spotted the coffin in the back and took their hats off in respect. When Summer got out and blew the driver a kiss, hats went back on in an instant and lips drew tight or curled in disgust. As Summer gathered her bag and tossed the strap over her shoulder, two young blokes who'd been trying to decide between a slab of VB and Carlton Draught stepped in front of her, blocking her path.

'Where d'ya think you're goin'?' said one of them. Everyone in earshot stopped to listen.

'Piss off back where ya came from,' said the other.

'Excuse me,' said Summer and tried unsuccessfully to push past them. She looked up into the eyes of the bigger of the two men.

'Piss off. We don't want ya here,' he said.

'Suits me,' said Summer. 'I don't plan to stay a second longer than I have to. Now excuse me, I have to do some shopping.'

'You're not listenin',' said the big man's mate. 'We don't want ya money and we don't want you. Just piss off back to where you came from.'

'Or what?' said Summer. 'You're going to beat me up in the main street with all these people watching? Just because I want to go shopping?'

'Shaddup slut, we can do what we like and nobody here will see a thing. Understand?'

'Well go ahead,' said Summer. 'Hit me.'

The two men looked at each other uncertainly.

'Oh, there is one thing you should know before you start throwing punches. Look at me. I'm sick. You can see I'm sick. Know why? I've got AIDS. I've got AIDS and I bleed real easy. You lay one finger on me and I'll bleed all over you. You understand me?' She pushed the smaller of the men in the chest and he nearly tripped trying to get out of her way. Summer started walking and walked on all the way down to Woolworths without anyone trying to stop her. The locals stood by and watched her, mothers pushed their kids into shop doorways as if she was a vampire striding their streets with blood dripping from her teeth. She wanted to laugh so badly tears came to her eyes.

* * *

The night nurse had been right. Summer stood on the edge of Orbost laden down with her purchases but lifts were hard to come by. Plenty of cars and utes slowed down, but that was only so the occupants could spit or hurl abuse at her. Summer knew that she had to expect some hostility in a timber town but the extent of the abuse stunned her. It hadn't been as bad when she'd attended the blockade a year earlier. One group of women stopped and blamed her for the closure of the sawmills and for their husbands being out of work. Summer knew better than to try and argue, and listened to their familiar litany of deprivation. There was no money for clothes, no money to pay bills and barely enough to put food on the table for the family. And she was to blame.

Summer began to worry as the hours passed and the sun sank lower. She didn't want to be alone on the open road in hostile territory at night. She longed to hear the sound of a twenty-six wheeler, to hear the hiss of the air brakes as the rig slowed to pick her up, but the only big trucks that passed carried logs or logging machinery. They would've run her over sooner than give her a lift. She thought about walking back into town and asking the police to let her sleep in the lock-up, but that wasn't always a smart move. They'd probably tell her to piss off or charge her with something. She heard a car slow down and prepared herself for another tirade. An old Mazda ute with jacked-up suspension pulled up in front of her. Her blood froze when she found herself staring at the barrel of a shotgun pushed through the passenger window. Two cattle-dog-kelpie crosses snarled and barked at her from the tray. Summer didn't know which scared her more.

'If ya still here in ten minutes I'm gunna feed ya to me dogs. Ya got that?'

The sun had dipped below the tops of the trees and Summer could barely make out the shape of the person inside the cab. Somehow that made it even more frightening.

'Get across the road and piss off back where ya come from. Don't come back. Ever. Understand?'

Summer nodded.

'Ya got ten minutes. Better get on ya knees and pray for a ride.' The two dogs had their front paws on the sides of the ute and were straining to get at her, saliva foaming at their mouths. They jerked back as the driver dropped the clutch. The ute did a U-turn and sped off.

Summer didn't know what to do, whether to run back into town and ask the police for protection, or what. She could see no point in standing on the other side of the road. If people wouldn't pick her up heading out of town, why would they pick her up heading in? The minutes ticked by and for the first time in years Summer wished she had a watch. Every time she heard a car coming her heart jumped into her mouth. She waited anxiously, heard another car coming and stared down the road. It looked like a four-wheel drive of some kind, and behind it another car. No! Not a car. A ute. The ute! Summer had to do something. She stepped out into the middle of the road and forced the four-wheel drive to stop. She almost cried with relief when she saw the driver was a woman.

'Help me, please!' she said.

'What's the matter?' said the driver.

'The guy in the ute behind just threatened to shoot me and feed me to his dogs.'

'Bit tough on the dogs,' said the woman. 'You better get in.'

As the four-wheel drive took off Summer looked behind and saw the ute turn around and head back into Orbost. She started to shake. 'It was just like that old movie, you know, *Easy Rider*.'

'Don't know it,' said the driver. 'You the girl with AIDS?'

'I'm the girl who said she had AIDS,' corrected Summer. 'I was born skinny.'

'Good one,' said the woman and started to laugh. 'You've got half the town locking up their kids. You okay?'

'I'll be okay in a minute.' Summer took another glance over her shoulder to make sure no one was following. She folded her arms in front of her and pulled them tight to stop herself from shaking. 'That was scary.'

'You're safe with me,' said the woman. 'Where are you heading?'

'Osbourne,' said Summer.

'Good choice,' said the woman. 'Nice friendly town. Not quite as friendly as Orbost though. What's your name?'

'Summer.'

'Pretty. I suppose you've come for the blockade?'

'Yeah. I've got nothing against logging except when they destroy old growth forests and native habitats. The woodchippers could all be using plantation timber now if they'd started replanting right at the beginning.'

'You may have a point.'

'Have you ever spent time out in the forest?'

'Yeah.'

'Lived in it?'

'Yeah. Sort of.'

'Don't you think it's beautiful?'

'Yeah. As a matter of fact I do.'

'Don't you think it's worth saving?'

The woman hesitated, then said softly, 'Yeah, I don't doubt that it is.'

'Then come out to the blockade with us. It'll be great. Everybody in the same situation believing in the same thing, high on the cause. It's great.' Summer never missed a chance to recruit.

'I don't think my husband would appreciate that.' The woman smiled grimly. 'He'd say I was biting the hand that fed me.'

'Oh. I suppose he's a logger,' said Summer.

'Yeah, I suppose he is.' The woman turned and looked Summer squarely in the eye. 'My husband is Miklos Bollok.'

'Oh shit,' said Summer.

'Oh shit, indeed,' said Cheryl and started to laugh.

'Did you read God's letters?' asked Summer.

'Of course.'

'What did you think?'

Cheryl grinned slyly. 'I thought they were beautiful. I even told Miklos they were beautiful.'

'What did he say?'

'I don't think my husband knows what beautiful is.'

Summer laughed. 'God's beautiful. He's the most gentle caring man I've ever met. The only thing he cares about is the forest and its inhabitants. You ought to meet him.'

'Oh I've met him.'

'What!' Summer nearly jumped through her seatbelt in surprise.

'A while back. I gave him a ride along the fire trails. He introduced himself and told me all about his kingdom.'

Summer stared at Cheryl open-mouthed, waited for more.

'I thought my eyes were open until he showed me how to see. Even Miklos concedes my painting has improved out of sight.'

'God does that to you,' said Summer. 'He helps me get my head straight.'

'He helps you get your head straight?' said Cheryl. 'Red hair, rat-tails with bits of — what is it, owl? — stuck in them is straight?'

'Yeah,' Summer laughed. 'All that's just superficial. Talking to God is like communing with Sai Baba. It's a kind of spiritual thing, a sort of refocusing on what's really important. He makes you feel good and see things more clearly.'

'Love and tolerance. Peace to all men.'

'Right on,' said Summer.

'Yeah, well there are a few people who'd disagree with you there. They don't think God's about love and tolerance at all. They think he's a psycho dope-pushing perv.'

'What? That's crazy! You've read his letters!'

'Yeah.' Cheryl looked down and picked up the *Gazette* from the top of the console between them. 'I've read his letters, but have you read this morning's paper?'

Summer read, anger and outrage building by the second. She couldn't understand how anybody could say such terrible things about God. Her anger turned to tears of frustration when Cheryl told her about the radio phone-ins.

'It's a carefully orchestrated campaign to discredit your friend,' Cheryl explained. 'They call it issue management. They've got the resources to make people believe anything they want them to believe. God doesn't stand a chance.' She looked at the upset girl alongside her, felt an overpowering urge to put an arm around her and comfort her. It staggered her that she'd want to do that. She'd always believed that ferals were just ratbag troublemakers zombied out on dope, with morals that would shame an alley cat. She'd never thought to question the belief instilled in every country dweller that they were just dole bludgers down from the city because they were bored and had nothing better to do. But Summer was clearly intelligent and articulate, and her only crime appeared to be that she dressed strangely and believed passionately enough in saving forests and wildlife to want to do something about it.

'You know him,' Summer sobbed. 'You've met him. Do you think he'd do any of that stuff?'

'I know he didn't,' Cheryl said bitterly, and repeated it as if she was spitting out something sour.

* * *

Cheryl dropped Summer off at EGCGs so no one else would have the chance to shove a shotgun in her face. That was the stupid sort of thing Arnie would do. She didn't think the guy in the jacked-up ute would have carried out his threat, but wouldn't have bet on it. If the guy had been drunk, anything could have happened. She drove on home and parked in the driveway by her back door. She got out and started unloading her shopping from the rear, unaware of the figure creeping towards her in the shadows of the bushes. A hand grabbed her arm. She screamed.

'Shhhhh!' said Samuel. 'It's okay! It's only me, Samuel Johnson the reporter.'

'Oh Jesus ... don't you ever do that to me again!'

'I'm sorry,' said Samuel.

'What the hell do you think you're doing?'

'I need to talk to you.'

'Do you know the risk you're taking coming here at night? You got a death wish? What if Miklos came home and found you here?'

'I need your help,' said Samuel. 'You're my only hope of getting my job back.'

'Miklos didn't accept your apology?'

'My apology was fine. It's me he has a problem with.'

'I don't know how I can help you,' said Cheryl. She looked down the road for any signs of headlights. There were none.

'I think you can,' said Samuel. 'You know as well as I do who really damaged your husband's car. Miklos did it himself, didn't he?'

'I don't know what you're talking about.' Cheryl flushed bright red and was grateful that it was too dark for Samuel to see.

'You know exactly what I'm talking about.'

'No! Go away. I can't help you.'

'Can't or won't?'

'What's the difference?' she snapped.

'Not much,' said Samuel bitterly. 'I know Miklos smashed up the car himself, but unless I can prove it I'm out of a job. And if I'm out of a job in a tinpot place like Orbost, I'm out of a job everywhere. So it's not just a job I'm talking about. It's my entire career. My entire life.' He peered into the gloom, trying to read Cheryl's face. He noticed she'd made no attempt to move away. 'Will you help me, please?' he asked softly. 'I'm begging you. Please?'

'No,' she said.

CHAPTER FIFTEEN

Bernie Dwight was in his element. The TV camera was right in his face and he'd mastered the art of staring it down.

'What the people of Victoria have got to understand is that we're not dealing with serious conservationists down in East Gippsland,' he said. 'We're dealing with the lunatic fringe. Dole bludgers with nothing better to do, drug users and people just looking for trouble.'

Clyde Townsend had rehearsed him in front of a camera, using one of his PR people to make sure he hit all the buzz words and kept his argument succinct. The trick, Clyde claimed, was to polarise themselves as the goodies and the greenies as the baddies.

'It is ludicrous to suggest that East Gippsland has any areas of unspoilt forest left. Good heavens, it's been logged for a hundred years. A hundred years!' Bernie had to fight hard not to smile. He'd always engaged in repetition instinctively and now he understood why. As Clyde had said, 'You're sweet, sweet, sweet, if you repeat, repeat, repeat'. So he repeated. 'For a hundred years people have been going into the forests with their saws and taking timber to build homes and furniture. They've been taking timber since bullocks were used to pull the logs out. How can the forests be untouched?'

'How would you describe the condition of the forests now?' asked the host.

'I'd have to say degraded. You can't log forests for one hundred years without their becoming degraded. The best thing we can do is strip out all the rubbish that remains and replant with quality timbers. Renew the resource.'

'But don't the forests still provide essential habitats for endangered species like the spotted-tailed quoll and the potoroo?'

'What spotted-tailed quolls, what potoroos? Has anyone seen one lately? Have you? I haven't. Nobody I know has either. I have a report here from the Department of Conservation and Forestry that casts serious doubts on the presence of any endangered species in the areas of East Gippsland we're talking about, especially Little Potoroo Creek. There have been no authenticated sightings of quolls or potoroos for more than twenty years. Twenty years! People who tell you otherwise are living in the past. I'm concerned with the future, and a good future too, for the people of Tathra Valley and the whole of East Gippsland.'

'You're saying there are no protected or endangered species at all at Little Potoroo Creek?'

'Well now, that's a large area of land and it's impossible to say with absolute certainty. There may be the odd animal there, but it's a bit like the Tasmanian Tiger. Nobody's seen one for fifty years! Is that a good reason not to go ahead with reforestation? Is that a good reason to leave worthless land to just sit and rot when it could be used productively? I think the people of East Gippsland deserve better than that. I believe they have a right to jobs, to security and to a future. I'll be pressing this government to release all the remaining forest land in East Gippsland to logging. All of it! The people of East Gippsland need it. The people of Victoria need it. The country needs it.'

'Thank you very much,' said the host.

'Thank you,' said Bernie.

'That was Bernie Dwight, the independent member for Tathra Valley. Now something special. The story of the cat that stopped three lanes of a six-lane highway when the fire brigade was called to rescue it from a tree. On the other side of this break.'

'How'd I do?' said Bernie.

'Born to it,' said Clyde Townsend. 'Now we'd better get the transcript and the DeCaF report to the morning papers, and get you over to Channel Seven. Heard from Miklos?'

'Yeah. He's got the Toyota in the body shop. Nine News sent a chopper down to do shots of the wreck but they were half an hour too late. It had already been stripped.'

'Probably best.'

'Probably? Son, you could see the hammer marks!'

'Yeah, but who swung the hammer? Who rang the bell?'

'Bugger me, Clyde. That sounded almost like a joke.'

'Why not?' said Clyde. 'We've got the rabbits on the run. We won't stop until we've got all of East Gippsland divided into logging coups, and made Miklos Bollok the High Priest of issue management.'

* * *

Lobbyists from the Wilderness Society and the Australian Conservation Foundation went into damage control. They prowled the corridors of State Parliament and sent faxes to the Premier, every minister and every elected member. They believed they had Bernie Dwight nailed on facts. They tendered reports of recent sightings of rare, protected and endangered species, sent dated photos of specimens that had been trapped and released, sent photos of hair caught in hairtubes set high in trees with hollows. They believed they had hard evidence that Little Potoroo Creek supported colonies of koalas which were genetically distinct from every other colony in Victoria, that it supported many of Victoria's few remaining quolls, potoroos and leadbeater's possums. They showed photos of rare and endangered trees, shrubs and plants complete with the dates they were taken. They prepared an argument which portrayed Little Potoroo Creek and the whole of Tathra Heights as being of high conservation value. They mentioned World Heritage Listing, which fell under the auspices of the Federal Government, as a thinly-veiled threat. They found a hundred ways to waste their time.

Against their argument was contrary evidence from DeCaF, and a swing in voter sentiment away from the greenies who poisoned hard-working loggers, stole cars and peddled drugs to kids right outside the school gates. The government did what every elected government did once it suited their purposes: they listened to their constituents, ignored the lobbyists and filed their faxes in the rubbish bin. Truth was no counter to sentiment and they knew exactly what happened to politicians who thought otherwise. They lost. And, anyway, greenies gave them the shits. Any chance to stick the boot in was seized with glee.

In desperation the Australian Conservation Foundation made a plea to every green group with an interest in Little Potoroo Creek for reports on all the field studies they'd conducted on the area's flora and fauna. In desperation the other green groups — who often fought each other as bitterly as they fought the timber groups — provided them.

Friends of the Earth and other grass-roots green organisations did their best to rally support for the Little Potoroo Creek blockade. Georgie and Sky drew up a poster, and a CIA with contacts in Corporate Boardroom Australia — a company which specialised in corporate presentations — scanned it on computer and tizzed it up with fancy art direction and lots of drawings of cute and cuddly marsupials. Someone else got five hundred A3 copies run off by a mate who worked in a colour copy shop. He just waited till the owners went home and made a donation on their behalf. The posters looked great and the CIA machine got them put up everywhere that mattered.

'God Needs You at Little Potoroo Creek,' screamed the headline. 'Don't be fooled by the lies and media-multinational-government conspiracy!' screamed the sub-head. 'Only direct action can save Little Potoroo Creek. Only YOU can save the potoroo. Only YOU can save the spotted-tailed quoll! Join the Blockade. BYO tent, sleeping gear, eating utensils. Organic food provided.'

No one suggested the poster was quite in Summer class, but nevertheless it was pretty good. Everyone thought the sign-off was a ripper: 'Do you believe God's word or a load of Bollok's?' it said. The only problem was, the poster didn't work and neither did the urgings by the various green groups. Little Potoroo Creek had a smell about it, and nobody wanted to travel three hundred kilometres to get cold, wet and their arse kicked.

* * *

'We gotta do something,' said The Dick with Ears. He looked helplessly around the squat. Faces flickered back at him by candlelight. The electricity company had worked out how the squatters were stealing their power and had cut them off. The lack of electric light added to the gloom.

'Like what?' said Ciaron. 'You keep saying we've got to do something, and we all know we've got to do something. Just saying we have to do something is no effing help.'

'Bickering isn't going to help either,' said Sky.

'Anybody got any ideas?' said Darren.

'If anybody had they would've said something, dickhead.'

Darren looked at Ciaron but refused to be drawn. This was the side of Darren the squat didn't see enough of, the boyish part of him that sucked in the women.

'Anyone got any ideas?' said Sky supportively.

Stretch burst out laughing. They'd been going around in circles for half an hour, all good intentions and no ideas. Like a couple of bands he'd been in trying to write songs. He picked up his guitar and started strumming country. 'Maybe we need a jingle. You know something like: "Don't turn our forests green into porno magazines, don't turn our ash and gums into sheets for wiping bums ..."'

'Pure Willie Nelson,' said Barry. He sucked on a joint and passed it to Stretch.

'Shouldn't make fun of people trying to help,' said Thalia.

'What're we going to do?' said Lyndal helplessly. 'Plenty of guys say they're going but you can tell they're not. There's no enthusiasm.'

'Know what you mean,' said Georgie. 'Everyone's given up. It's like we're beaten already. If only Summer was here.'

Georgie, Matt, Sky and Gretta had joined forces with the squat to try to figure out what they could do to help. It wasn't just a forest that needed help, it was a friend. It was Summer and her friend God.

'Maybe we should march,' said Gretta. 'March on State Parliament.'

'Worked for Hitler,' said Stretch.

'Maybe not,' said Matt. 'But at least it was a suggestion. Anyone else got any ideas?'

'We could have a parade,' said Pete. 'Paint trucks green and make floats with papier-mâché trees which we could ceremonially chop down outside Flinders Street Station. Some of my friends from the gym could be the loggers. We could dress them in loin cloths so they look primal.'

'And wouldn't you love that,' said Dougie contemptuously.

'At least I had an idea,' said Pete. 'Don't remember you having one.'

'Dougie doesn't need ideas, he has a basketball,' said Stretch.

'You guys aren't helping,' said The Dick.

'Christ, this is like a wake,' said Matt.

'If we're gunna have a wake,' said Stretch, 'let's at least make it professional. Who's going out for the piss?'

'Shut up,' said Thalia. 'This is serious.'

'Hang on,' said Darren. 'I've got an idea.'

'God help us,' said Ciaron.

'A wake's a good idea. I reckon everyone wants to do something but they just think that going down to East Gippsland's a waste of time. I mean, you know — we go down there, the media's going to make us look like troublemakers, and whatever we do'll be wrong.'

'So what do you suggest?' asked Matt.

'We protest in Melbourne. Maybe see if people up in Sydney will hold a protest too.'

'Stand around waving placards? We're going to have to do better than that,' said Thalia.

'Yeah, and we've gotta do something original, something the media can't grab hold of and use against us,' said Matt. 'We've gotta think like Gandhi.'

'Yeah, I know. Let me finish,' said The Dick. 'Like Stretch said, if we're gunna have a wake we oughta make it professional. We oughta have a wake for Little Potoroo Creek. A night of mourning. Not a wake so much as an all-night vigil. A peaceful sit-in by candlelight outside State Parliament.'

Everyone looked at Darren in stunned silence. It didn't take much imagination to picture a sea of candles flowing from the steps of Parliament House and spilling down into the streets outside. It was the sort of idea Summer might have had. No one expected it from The Dick.

'A night of mourning,' said Thalia, in awe of the prospect.

'Reckon we'd get thousands,' said Darren. 'Do it from eight at night until six in the morning so we don't block rush-hour traffic and lose support. Can you imagine it?'

They could.

'Is good idea,' said Gretta. 'Is very good idea.'

'He had to have one sooner or later,' said Ciaron. She wondered if Sky was just excited or moving in on Darren now that Summer had moved out. She couldn't begin to understand what Sky saw in him.

'What'll we call it?' asked Thalia. 'Light a candle for God?'

'Nah. Better keep God out of it,' said Matt.

'How about, light a candle for the last potoroo?' said Sky.

'Yeah! Then we can do all sorts of extensions,' said Lyndal. 'You know, light a candle for the last powerful owl, light a candle for the last Victorian rainforest. We could go on forever.'

'Yeah, but we gotta have focus,' said Darren. 'All the big banners and posters should focus on the potoroo because, at the end of the day, we're talking about Little Potoroo Creek. I reckon I know what it should be.' He stood and held his arms wide as if holding up a banner. He moved his head slowly from side to side as if reading it. 'Mourn till Dawn!' he said. 'Light a Candle for the Last Potoroo.'

'Brilliant!' said Matt.

'You're having a big night,' said Ciaron grudgingly.

'I'll get started on the posters,' said Georgie. 'We should aim for next Friday night so people can sleep in Saturday.'

'I'll go down to Friends first thing,' said Matt.

'I'll go to the Wilderness Society,' said Lyndal.

'Me and Sky'll go get some bagels,' said Darren.

'Sky needs to help Georgie,' said Ciaron. 'I'll take you on me bike.' For the second time that night the squat fell stunned motherless silent.

* * *

A good idea is obvious to all, so obvious it makes people wonder why they didn't think of it themselves. By noon the next day, Mourn till Dawn had the full and active support of all the green groups. They began organising speakers, music, theatre and dance groups, and tried to find someone who could supply them with a minimum of ten thousand candles on the cheap. Concerned Individual Activists printed and distributed the poster and put it up on the internet. By evening the newspapers, radio and TV channels were beginning to show interest. God was yesterday's news; Mourn till Dawn was tomorrow's. And it promised great visuals and public outpourings of emotion.

High in his office on Collins Street Clyde Townsend heard about the candlelit vigil and smiled. The greens were fighting back and their response was just cute enough to draw a good crowd and attract media attention. It wasn't good enough to beat them, but it would make life interesting and justify fees. The first thing he had to do was control his side's response and put a negative spin on the event. He called in his secretary.

'I want a media brief to go to all the usual people and especially those idiots Bernie Dwight and Miklos Bollok. Get some of the PR writers to do me some good lines for sound bites. Something like: "Friday night of chaos. Greens blockade traffic". Tell them to play up the traffic problems, then the problems of litter. You know: "Traffic stalls in sitters' litter". Or "Squatters Squalor!" — that sort of thing. Get photos of young mums with kids pointing to a pile of used needles in the gutter. They'll know where to get them from. Tell them I need the lines in a hurry, two hours at the most. Got it? Great.'

He reached over, grabbed the phone and punched Bernie's quick-dial number. 'Bernie? Clyde. Heard about the candlelight sit-in? Good. Say nothing. Make no comment. Don't do any interviews. Just stay shut up till I've got you some decent lines so we can turn the protest back onto the greens. We only get one hit and we've got to get it right. Okay? Ring you in two hours.'

He dialled Miklos to give him the same message but got Jan instead. He groaned. Jan was living proof of his theory that a woman's brain was inversely proportionate to the size of her breasts. Miklos wasn't available, she told him.

'Tell him I called,' said Clyde. 'Ask him to ring me as soon as he gets in.'

'Okay,' said Jan and hung up. She would have made a note on the message pad if she hadn't dropped her emery board and got distracted.

CHAPTER SIXTEEN

The morning sky was threatening to clear as Cheryl loaded her overnight bag, sleeping bag, esky, thermos, camping gas cooker and lamp into the back of her Toyota. She put her camera equipment in the front footwell. Miklos had shown his usual lack of interest when she'd told him she intended to stay out in the forest overnight so she could take photos by dawn light.

'Make sure you lock your car,' was all he said. 'There's some thievin' bastards out there.' He didn't even ask where she was going or when she was due back, assumed she'd call him on her mobile if she got bogged. He drove off in the company's Holden ute, which he'd commandeered while his four-wheel drive was out of action.

Cheryl tried to calm her nerves. She tried to convince herself that she was going up to the plateau simply to fulfill an obligation. She failed miserably. At least she was getting away, away from pressures that were begining to build, pressures she didn't entirely understand. Away from the desperate young reporter who made her feel guilty. Away from her beautiful home which she loved and felt guilty for loving. Away from the guilt she felt at having nice things and for no longer being poor. She needed a break from her life and the guilt that was closing in on her everywhere she turned. Even the young hitchhiker, however unintentionally, had managed to twist the knife. Once again she wished Miklos would let her have a dog so she'd at least have a few moments of uncritical love to look forward to each day.

The phone rang as she closed and locked the back door. She thought briefly about unlocking it but decided it was probably the reporter chasing her again. She felt sorry for him, but if he expected her to sacrifice her home, lifestyle and marriage for the sake of his fledgling career he was playing with himself. He had a much better chance of finding another job than she had of finding another wealthy husband. Samuel was providing the impetus for her taking off up to Little Potoroo Creek, but really it was Summer who'd planted the idea.

'Don't you think it's worth saving?' she'd asked. Cheryl did, and she was going to save Little Potoroo Creek the only way she could — on film and canvas. That, she decided, was the best she could do. But even as she eased the Landcruiser down the drive and out onto the road she knew that wasn't really why she was going.

Overnight rain had left a greasy slick on the fire trails, but nothing Cheryl couldn't handle. It just slowed her down and gave her time to get her thoughts together. A fox broke cover onto the trail ahead of her, paused and watched her approach. It made Cheryl smile. If Arnie had been in the car with her he would have shot the fox on sight, turned it into a colander with his Chinese semi-automatic. But then there'd have been no way the fox would have presented itself as a stationary target in the first place. She wondered how it knew she was unarmed. The rocky ground offered plenty of traction so she allowed the car to slow and stop. She reached down for her camera and finished off the film inside. The fox lifted its head, held its pose eye-balling the camera, then casually sauntered off as if satisfied with the audition. Cheryl burst out laughing and felt good for the first time in a very long while.

She didn't stop again until she'd reached a clearing on the plateau above Little Potoroo Creek. By then the sun had broken free of the clouds and had well and truly begun its descent. She plucked up her courage and wandered over to the lip of the plateau, gazed down over the valley. She'd forgotten how big it was and immediately felt foolish. Relief and disappointment vied for ascendancy. God could be anywhere, days even weeks away, in any one of the smaller valleys, under any of the overhangs, in any of the myriad tiny glades. Near or far, she had no hope of finding him, and he no reason to look for her. She returned to her car, poured herself a coffee, made a ham sandwich, unfolded her canvas chair and let the warmth of the fading sun wash over her. All she had to do was what she'd come to do, what had brought her up onto the Heights in the first place. As she checked her camera and cleaned her lens with her puffer she listened to the forest drowsing. There were no staccato calls from the currawongs, no melodious magpies, no madcap games of tag from lorikeets, no cooing from pigeons, no shy chatter of rosellas. When she listened very carefully she could hear bees somewhere, investigating spring blossoms, and a gentle trickling of water. Five miles overhead a jet soundlessly left a feathery trail across the sky. Her eyes grew heavy and, despite the fact that she'd just finished a coffee, she slowly dozed off.

The cold woke her. The sun had retreated behind clouds and a light breeze had come in from the south-west. She pulled on her quilted jacket and took her compass out of the pocket. Experience had taught her the value of finding camera positions in the evening so that she didn't waste precious time racing around when the dawn light was at its best. She looked for the spot where the sun was most likely to set to help her calculate where it was most likely to rise, checked her compass, and set up the tripod. The position she chose gave her the option of shooting wide, with gums framing the outer edges of the shot, or using a long lens to shoot right down into the valley as the light brightened and lit upon the walls of the escarpment. She clipped on her five-hundred-mil lens and peered through the camera to focus. She tried to picture the shot, imagining where the morning mists would be and how thick. She was concentrating so hard it took her a moment or two to realise what she was looking at, who she was looking at. Her stomach tightened and felt suddenly hollow. The distant figure waved to her and smiled. He began to climb towards her. She held her breath, not knowing whether to run away or stay put. It seemed to take an eternity but he finally stood alongside her.

'Hi,' she said weakly.

'Shhhh ...' he said. 'Listen.' He turned his back to her and stared off down into the valley.

Cheryl listened, but didn't know what she was listening for, and couldn't concentrate either. Her knees felt wobbly.

It was a sensation that didn't come easily or often. She hadn't moved from the time she'd spotted him, hadn't moved a centimetre as he'd slowly made his way up the hill towards her, often disappearing from sight for minutes at a time. Just seeing him was enough to unsettle her. Seeing him in a dress was plain disturbing. He wore a patched and darned sweater over the top, and his bare legs sprouted from sockless boots. The dress was a ludicrous floral print. He looked like a hillbilly in drag and didn't seem to care a damn. She had no idea what to say to him or whether explanations were even necessary. She wondered if he knew about Miklos's car and all the accusations levelled against him, and whether it was her duty to tell him. He hit her with his smile and her brain seized.

'Hear it?' he asked.

'No,' she whispered.

'Listen,' he said. 'There!'

Cheryl closed her eyes to concentrate and strained to hear. Her mind refused to be still and all she could hear was the pounding of her heart and the rush and surge of her blood. Why had she come? Why did she feel so helpless, so foolish? Why was he wearing his mother's clothes? Trees murmured as they shook their heads, and dried bracken fronds scratched and rasped. Butcherbirds warned off mynahs. Then she heard it, a far-off cough. 'Koala,' she said.

'Big Boy,' said God. His voice was dreamy and seemed as distant as the cough. 'He always wakes up cranky.' He turned around to look at Cheryl and his face lit up once more. 'Welcome to my kingdom,' he said.

Cheryl went weak at the knees. 'I've come to take the photos,' she said lamely. 'At dawn.'

'It's good that someone does. Before it's all gone. My kingdom is too beautiful to be forgotten. I can show you a better place to put your camera. I will take you to my rock. It has the best morning views in my valley. Yes, you must come with me.'

'God ... whatever your name is ... do you know who I am?'

'Yes,' said God simply. 'You're Cheryl Bollok. Your husband owns Regional Consolidated Sawmillers. He wants to turn my forest into woodchips and kill all my animals and plants.'

'Yes,' said Cheryl. All her guilt came hurtling back and she felt mortally ashamed.

'I'm Godfrey,' said God. 'Godfrey Owen Dutton. But people call me by my initials. I'm not really God, you know, and this isn't really my kingdom.'

'Doesn't it worry you that I'm married to Miklos?'

'No.' He looked intently at her for a moment. 'You love the forest, that's all that matters. Come.'

Cheryl stood and watched as God took her bag, sleeping bag, esky, camping gas cooker and lamp from the back of the Toyota. She made no effort to stop him. God was taking her to his home and that was what she'd wanted all along.

'Bring your camera,' he said and began to walk away.

Cheryl did as she was told, then, remembering Miklos's parting words, pointed her key towards the Toyota and pressed the button. In the stillness the click of the doors locking was embarrassingly loud.

God laughed.

* * *

Freshly laundered clothes lay on rocks in the sun around the entrance to God's cave. Cheryl had to step over them to see inside. She took note of the cave's neatness and order, the bacon and egg plant and white tea tree standing in one flagon and the sprigs of flowering wattle in another. A fire smouldered gently in a little rock hearth.

'Looks like you're expecting company,' she said.

'Yes,' he said.

'I think I know who. She arrived last night. I gave her a lift into Osbourne and dropped her off at EGCGs. Summer said she was coming to see you.' God showed no surprise that Cheryl knew Summer and that he was expecting her.

'When I heard your car I thought it was bringing her,' he said.

'Are you disappointed?'

'No. Summer will still come. In the meantime you are here, and I am pleased that you are. Would you like to meet my neighbours?'

'Yes, I would.'

'It would take me two weeks to introduce you to all of them. They are very shy. Do you have batteries?'

'I have a Dolphin torch,' said Cheryl.

'Good,' said God. 'Now we must hurry.'

God took her down into his valley through the gathering dusk. There was no pathway that she could see, yet he seemed to be following one. She could hear a stream babbling nearby, but it was hidden among a screen of ferns and undergrowth. The gums and ash did their best to filter out what little light remained in the day. The pathway grew so steep and rocky that Cheryl had to concentrate on every step so she didn't slip. Up ahead of her God quietly sat down on a rock and motioned for her to sit alongside him. The rock offered ample room for one bottom but barely enough for two. Cheryl had no choice but to squeeze up close to him. He smiled and took her hand in his. Nothing in the world could have stopped her blushing. She discovered she was sitting five metres or so above a stream where it tipped over into a miniature waterfall. Despite the gloom she could see that still ponds had formed in the rocks above the fall. Clearly this was where God expected his neighbours to appear. She went to swish away the tiny insects flitting around them, but God shook his head to discourage her. Instead she sat motionless, letting them land on her neck and wrists, and suffered their bites. She wished she'd thought to put on some Rid, groaned silently when she realised she hadn't packed her Stingoes to stop the bites itching later. The insects landed all over God too, but he seemed not to notice. She sat perfectly still, staring into the gathering dark until she felt the muscles in her legs begin to ache and threaten to cramp up. Her bottom was beginning to object as well. Second thoughts weren't far away when she felt God squeeze her hand and saw him nod ever so slightly towards the stream beneath them. She followed his gaze but saw nothing, and wondered how anybody could see anything in the gathering gloom. But God apparently had, and if he had, so could she. She looked hard at the area where she'd seen the still pools and gradually they took on form. She concentrated on them now that she knew what she was looking at and suddenly saw something. Movement! Her heart began to pound although she had no idea why. She concentrated on the movement, saw more, and gradually began to discern a shape. It was small and obviously timid, had a small head and what appeared to be miniature radar dishes for ears. She stared and stared, willing her eyes to pierce the gloom, and finally saw what few people have ever seen, what DeCaF denied existed, and what was suddenly as precious as the rarest of diamonds. Cheryl Bollok found herself staring at her first long-footed potoroo.

The potoroo didn't stay long, slipping back into the bush as quietly as it had come. Cheryl felt free to breathe at last and slowly exhaled.

'My God,' she said unthinkingly, 'it was so beautiful. So fragile and delicate.'

'There were three.'

'Three!'

'Parents and offspring. The mother and child were about two metres further upstream.'

'Why didn't you tell me? Why didn't you use the torch?'

'The torch would scare them away. They might never come back.'

'So why bring it?'

'For you,' said God. 'So you don't trip in the dark on the way back. Here.' He handed her the torch. 'Shine it at my feet and follow in my footsteps.'

She laughed. 'You've no idea how much this would please my old Sunday school teacher. At last I'm walking in the footsteps of God.' She expected him to laugh with her but he didn't.

They stopped twice on the climb back up to the cave, once to listen to the mournful cry of a powerful owl, and then to gather some black bracken. On both occasions Cheryl was grateful for the rest. By the time they reached the cave she was exhausted. It only dawned on her then that there were no chairs or table in the cave, nowhere to sit except on the floor or on God's stuffed mattress. She wished she was fitter, blamed herself for not keeping up her morning walks, and eyed God's mattress longingly. Her back and legs ached and she felt light-headed. She slumped against the cave wall for support, and turned to see what God was doing. He still wore the dress but now it was tucked into black tracksuit pants.

He'd lit her camping lamp and begun sorting through her esky. She'd made a chicken casserole which she'd intended to heat up for her dinner, brought tea bags, coffee, sugar and milk, half a dozen slices of bread, some sliced ham, two tomatoes, two Mars bars, two one-litre bottles of mineral water, and two tiny salt and pepper shakers. God took everything out of the esky, put the lid back on and lay Cheryl's sleeping bag across the top.

'Come and sit down,' he said. 'It's time for the news.'

Cheryl sat on top of the esky and listened to the ABC while God squatted Aboriginal fashion in front of her gas ring and began to make dinner. The Arabs were bombing the Israelis, the Irish were bombing the British, the Afghans were bombing each other, and Shane Warne was bombing unfortunate batsmen with his leg-breaks. There was no mention of God, Little Potoroo Creek or candlelight vigils. A recording of John Williams's Seville Concert took over as the casserole displaced the rice on the single gas burner. God began cutting up mushrooms to add to the casserole.

'My brother still hasn't recovered from the mushrooms you cooked for him,' said Cheryl. 'He was the one with the rifle. Every time he looks like getting better Miklos slips him a couple of laxatives in case a reporter comes to interview him. He might have stopped now that they're no longer in the news.'

'It's good to have salt and pepper,' said God. 'And coffee with milk and sugar.'

Cheryl smiled. 'What more could anyone ask for?' she said softly.

'Sherry,' said God. 'Chestnut Teal. Just the one.'

* * *

God poured the crushed black bracken roots over the back of Cheryl's hands and the back of her neck. She lay on her stomach on God's mattress and waited for the itching to subside as he had promised it would. The radio played Pachelbel's Canon and the flickering candles cast monstrous shadows. It was all Cheryl could do not to fall asleep. Dinner by lamp and candlelight, coffee afterwards beneath the stars, with God quietly identifying the various calls of bird, possum and glider. His hands began to search out and massage the muscles in her back to ease away the aches and the tension in her shoulders. She didn't object when he slipped his hands beneath her windcheater and shirt, or when he undid her bra. She let God undress her and relaxed while his healing hands went about their business. She felt special, blessed, privileged. The muscles in her buttocks tensed involuntarily at his touch, but relaxed just as quickly. She had no doubt that she would share God's mattress, just as he would share the warmth of her sleeping bag, opened and spread like an eiderdown quilt. It seemed quite logical, totally natural and the right thing to do.

'Turn over,' he said, and she did without embarrassment. He leant down and kissed her gently on her lips, lingering there before resuming his massage. But things had changed. The hands that cupped and caressed her breasts had become those of a lover not a masseur, and her whole being focussed upon them. She closed her eyes. God would soon discover that she was already wet, but that didn't matter. Nothing mattered. Nothing mattered but the progress of his hands. He whispered to her but she was far too distracted to hear. His hands passed over her waist, her hips and down the vee of her lower abdomen across muscles drawn tight in anticipation. An upwelling of love surged through her and brought tears to her eyes which she made no attempt to hide. She wanted him then and there, wanted him more than she'd ever wanted anyone or anything, but didn't dare speak in case she broke the spell. She gasped as God slipped between her thighs and entered her, opening her eyes at the moment of giving to preserve it forever. At the end of the night they would wake together and he would take her to his rock to capture the sun's ascent over Little Potoroo Creek. Cheryl was happier in God's cave than she'd ever been in the house that Miklos built.

* * *

Cheryl drove slowly back down the fire trails with God sitting alongside her, wanting with all her heart to stay, but knowing she had no choice but to go. Miklos was expecting her, and God was expecting Summer. That was the way things were and no amount of wishing on Cheryl's part could change it. God had hitched a ride with her so that he could meet Summer on her way up. But for a while, for one long wonderful night, God had belonged to her and she to him. Every moment scrolled in front of her to be relived and cherished.

That morning he'd squatted naked in front of a pot of water, washed his body, trimmed his beard, scrubbed his fingernails and borrowed her toothbrush so he could clean his teeth. She'd told him to keep it and threw in her toothpaste and soap. Cheryl hadn't needed her artist's eye to frame up her photos. Dawn had crept into the valley, slowly colouring the monochrome and heating the mist so that it could begin its ascent through the trees. It clung to some, relinquished its hold on others, and sometimes streamed upwards in thermal currents. There hadn't been enough light for the long lenses but it hadn't mattered. She'd stood on God's rock like a conductor before a full symphony orchestra and filled her camera with beauty. She'd played with filters, timed exposures, and fiddled with focus, but mostly she'd just let the vista speak for itself and her camera do its job. She tried to imagine what Heather would do with her prints.

God had made porridge for breakfast, salted it, sugared it and trickled milk around the edges of the bowls. He'd savoured every mouthful and so had she. She told him to keep the salt, pepper, sugar and milk as well. Together they'd listened to the news from a world which had become too sophisticated for its own good, and to which Cheryl reluctantly had to return.

She started as God placed his hand lightly over hers on the steering wheel.

'Next time I'll show you a spotted-tailed quoll,' he said. 'But you'll have to stay longer.'

'I'd like that,' she said and smiled.

'Could you bring some sherry with you?'

'No problem. Chestnut Teal.'

'And batteries. I always need batteries.'

'No worries.'

'First we have to stop the logging.'

Cheryl stopped smiling and glanced sharply at God, but he wasn't putting pressure on her or hinting that she should use her influence with Miklos. There was no hidden agenda; it was simply a statement of fact. First they had to stop the logging or there'd be no Little Potoroo Creek, no quolls, and no need for Chestnut Teal sherry or batteries. There'd be no shy and shadowy potoroos. No shy and lovely God either.

'Do you think it would help if I wrote another letter and told everybody about my family of potoroos? I don't think many people know enough about potoroos. Do you think that would help?'

'Maybe,' said Cheryl doubtfully. 'You listen to the radio. You must know what Miklos has done to you.'

'That was yesterday,' said God. 'I never look back.'

'Others aren't so kind.'

'What about the photographs you took of my kingdom? Do you think it would help if you sent your photos to the newspapers?'

'No,' said Cheryl. 'I don't think that would help at all.'

* * *

They spotted the little Suzuki as they dipped over the crest of a hill. It was battling up towards them in low ratio, its little motor whirring like an overwrought sewing machine. Cheryl recognised it immediately. It was usually parked outside EGCGs.

'Summer is coming,' said God.

Cheryl swung the Toyota around so that it came to a halt sideways on the slope. 'I suppose we should say our goodbyes now,' she said. 'Thank you for taking me into your home and for showing me your potoroos.' She felt suddenly embarrassed. 'Thank you for ... everything.'

Her words were stilted and hopelessly inadequate. She hadn't yet allowed herself to admit quite how she felt about him, but whatever it was felt a whole lot more than she'd managed to say. The dream had ended, the moment she'd been dreading had finally come, and it was time for a reality check. She was Cheryl Bollok, wife of Miklos Bollok the destroyer of forests and enemy of all creatures great and small. No amount of wishing could change that.

God took her hand in his and she found herself crumbling before the sunrise of his smile. His eyes were wrinkled, full of warmth and affection and Cheryl dreaded to think what else.

'Always be my friend,' God said. 'Always be my friend.'

'Always be mine,' said Cheryl. 'Please.'

Cheryl watched Summer rush into the arms that had recently held her, and was immediately aware of an emptiness inside her. She envied Summer's youth, her looks, her unselfconscious enthusiasm, and wondered what Summer's reaction would be to her presence. Jealousy? Anger?

Liz from EGCGs held the Suzuki's door open so that a second passenger could climb out from the back seat. Cheryl's heart sank as she recognised him.

'G'day, Mrs Bollok,' said Samuel.

'How're you going, Samuel? What brings you here?'

'I went to interview Liz, met Summer, and seized the opportunity to interview God.'

'It won't do you any good, you know.'

'It will when I find out what really happened to Miklos's Toyota. According to Summer, you told her you knew God didn't do the damage. Want to change your mind and tell me?'

'We've had this conversation before.'

'Hi Cheryl!'

Cheryl spun around at the sound of Summer's greeting, grateful for the distraction. She was unprepared for the hug and kiss that followed. Summer made her feel like a long-lost and much-loved friend.

'Great to see you! What are you doing up here?' Summer asked breathlessly.

'I came up to take dawn photos of Little Potoroo Creek.'

'Did God take you to his rock?'

'Yes.'

'Isn't it fantastic?'

Cheryl started laughing. The young woman didn't have a possessive bone in her body. God was Summer's friend just as he was her friend. It was impossible not to get caught up in her enthusiasm.

'Did you stay in his cave?'

'Yes.'

'Did he wear his dress?'

'Yes.'

'Isn't he amazing? Somebody used it to wrap up some plates they gave him, and it didn't occur to him to throw it away or use it as rags. To him it's clothing so he wears it.' Summer burst out laughing again.

'Took me by surprise, I must admit.'

'I bet. But he must like you or he wouldn't have come near.'

Cheryl reddened. 'Like I said, we're old friends.'

'Have you met Liz?'

'We know each other by sight.' Cheryl held out her hand to the woman approaching her. Liz's arm was around God and she pulled it free to shake hands. 'Nice to meet you at last, Liz,' said Cheryl.

'Likewise,' said Liz.

'Now there's something I never expected to see,' said Samuel. 'Where's my camera?'

'Anything you can do to stop Miklos logging the Creek?' asked Liz hopefully.

'You know Miklos,' said Cheryl. 'It would take an act of parliament to stop him, and even then you couldn't be sure.'

Liz laughed. 'I had to ask.'

'If there was something I could do, I'd do it,' said Cheryl.

'She would,' said Summer.

'There is and she won't,' said Samuel. 'Unfortunately Cheryl has a wife's loyalty to her husband. You have to credit her with that. A lot of people will pay a terrible price for her loyalty but, at the end of the day, you have to respect it.'

'Yes, you do,' said God. 'Loyalty is one of the finest things there is.'

* * *

Guilt was Cheryl's only companion for the rest of the journey down the fire trails. She knew damn well she wasn't keeping silent out of loyalty to Miklos but out of selfishness, in defence of her home and possessions. A lot of people would pay a terrible price so that she'd never have to scrimp and save again, never have to work again, never wash dishes again, never boil mud and bark-stained work clothes in the copper, never hose down mud-encrusted work boots. God, Summer and Liz would lose their valley, the animals would lose their lives, Samuel would lose his job, and the world would be a far poorer place, all because of her silence, her loyalty to herself. Rain began to splatter on her windscreen and distort her vision. For a moment she thought it was tears.

Then there was Miklos. She knew about Jan and Miklos's ways. She'd married him with her eyes wide open. Now, for the first time since their wedding, she'd shared a bed with another man. What did that make her? It had seemed so right and natural at the time, but the time had passed. She'd slept with another man and that was a cold hard fact. Not just another man either, but Miklos's enemy. It was hard to think of that lovely man with the heart-melting smile as anyone's enemy, but that was what he was. He'd given her love when her whole lonely soul ached to be loved, valued her when no one else did, and given her the uncritical affection she craved. He was kind, sensitive and compassionate — everything that Miklos was not — yet he was also her enemy.

It didn't seem right. As she agonised an idea occurred to her. There was one thing she could do to repay God for his kindness. She couldn't save the forest, but perhaps she could save the man.

CHAPTER SEVENTEEN

Miklos was not happy. It was drizzling a bit but not enough to stop work. The mill was ticking over, logs were flowing in regularly from Diggers Hill, everyone had a job to do and was doing it. Except him. He sat upright at his desk, gripping the edges so hard his knuckles turned white. He had anger, energy and opportunity, and nothing to do except strain against the leash Clyde had strung around his neck. They'd kicked the opposition's arse and had them on the run, but nobody was chasing. If this was a battle and if he was a general, he would've poured all his troops and armour through the breach and the war would've been fought and won. Instead he had to sit back and twiddle his thumbs, and let the enemy regroup. He was at the front, Clyde and Bernie were in Melbourne. What the hell would they know? Nothing was going right. He rang Bernie on the private line in his South Yarra apartment.

'This better be important,' said Bernie. Miklos could hear girls giggling in the background, giving Bernie his morning workout.

‘Bugger my days,’ said Miklos. ‘Am I the only one who gives a shit what’s happening down here?’

‘What’s the matter, son? Jan flying the flag?’ More titters in the background.

‘Mate, we gotta get started on the road. Now! Before the bloody greenies get their shit back together.’

‘I told you I’d speak to DeCaF and I have.’

‘So when are they starting?’

‘Beginning of November, when they always said they’d start.’

‘Bloody hell! Why waste three weeks? Why not start now?’

‘Because they’re a bureaucracy. They’ve done surveys of the weather patterns and concluded that it’s too wet to start before November.’

‘That’s bullshit.’

‘No, son, that’s bureaucracy.’

‘It always pisses down in November.’

‘Son, it’s a rainforest. It pisses down all the time. That’s why they’re called rainforests.’

‘Hell Bernie, they’ll hardly get started before it’s time to knock off for Christmas.’

‘Yeah. Life’s crook. Now, son, go find Jan or go get pissed and give both of us a chance to make things a little less crook for a while, because there’s nothing else we can do. Okay?’

‘What if I start on the road?’

‘You’d be wasting your money and mine. But if that’s going to make you happy, go ahead. But speak to Clyde Townsend first. Now, I’ve got some unfinished pleasure to do.’ Bernie hung up amid giggles and shrieks.

'Shit!' said Miklos. He slammed the phone back onto its cradle. If there was one person in the world he didn't want to talk to it was Clyde Townsend. He switched on the radio and hunted down a Melbourne station to catch the eight a.m. news, hoping Clyde had figured out another angle to shaft the greenies. The news said nothing that interested him. Whatever Clyde Townsend was doing was no more constructive than what Bernie was doing. Mr Issue Management had let his story die. He was about to switch off when the station returned to its regular talk-back program. The DJ began raving about the Mourn till Dawn protest. Miklos listened, stunned, as he was referred to as rapacious, and East Gippsland's answer to Attila the Hun. He heard ferals hailed as latterday heroes, nice boys and girls from all walks of life who risked injury, abuse and freezing cold weather so there'd be a wilderness left for all Victorians to enjoy. The DJ made them sound like front-line troops from a Boy Scouts' jamboree, sacrificing themselves for the good of the nation. The radio station had put themselves up as a sponsor for Mourn till Dawn, and were rallying people to the cause with promises of free candles, coffee and pizza pockets. Miklos listened in disbelief. The DJ promised a live phone interview from England with the world famous conservationist David Bellamy, who'd offered to fly out and address the rally. In the meantime the station invited callers to ring in with their views. Miklos grabbed the phone and punched in the numbers as the DJ read them out. He'd give them bloody views all right. He'd make the air waves sizzle. Just as he made connection his brain kicked back into action and he hung up. He dialled Clyde Townsend instead.

'You bastard!' he screamed into the phone. 'I've just been listening to the radio. The 3NL Mourn till Dawn protest. Light a candle for the last potoroo. Hell's going on and what the hell are you doin' about it?'

'Good morning, Miklos,' said Clyde. 'I'm doing exactly what we should be doing. So relax. Everything is under control.'

'Control, my arse.'

'Miklos, you have to understand that one of the great joys of coming up against fragmented amateurish organisations is that they keep making fundamental mistakes.'

'Yeah? Don't sound like much of a mistake from where I'm standing.'

'You might think kids turn up at blockades simply to annoy the hell out of you, and because they're unemployed layabouts with nothing better to do. That's not the case. They have what they like to refer to as a social conscience, and their social conscience demands that they do something whenever they perceive something wrong is being done.'

'Get on with it.'

'That essentially is it. Tell me, would you rather ten thousand kids appeased their collective consciences on the streets of Melbourne or down on your doorstep?'

'What?'

'Think it through. Why should they go all the way to East Gippsland, risk getting cold, wet and arrested, when the organisers have made it possible for them to protest in comfort outside Parliament House where there are coffee shops, plenty of places to eat, good music and entertainment, and portaloos? We let them get all the protesting out of their system up here, out of the way. Understand?'

'Doesn't sound so bad when you put it that way.'

'If they hadn't come up with the idea I probably would have myself.'

'You said ten thousand people. The government's gunna take notice if ten thousand people suddenly squat on their doorstep.'

'Ten thousand is probably a generous figure, but I like to deal in worst case scenarios. 3NL is a low-rating station with a tendency to hitch itself to any cause that might get it noticed or bring it some notoriety. A couple of months back it was the Moscow Circus because of its mistreatment of animals. And don't worry about the government. They're used to this kind of thing. They'll nominate someone as spokesman, reinforce the fact that Little Potoroo Creek has been logged for a hundred years, even though only the surrounding land has, and repeat DeCaF findings that it supports no endangered or protected species, even though it does. You see, Miklos, every time they open their mouth we get another chance to put our message across. It's simply a question of being persistent and keeping our message consistent. What is truth but the lie told most often with the most conviction and frequency? Talk to Bernie Dwight. He's proved something of a revelation. He has a genuine talent for disinformation and sticks religiously to the script. You should be proud of him.'

'Stuff Bernie. The bottom line is, you reckon we'll come out of this okay.'

'No, we'll come out of this stronger. We're hitting them from all sides. If you look through the morning paper you'll see that the transport minister has damned the rally as irresponsible for blocking traffic, and a couple of city councillors are having a shot at the organisers on the basis of all the litter and rubbish they'll leave behind. We're not sitting on our hands here.'

'Okay, I'll get off the phone and let you do your stuff. Nice to know somebody's doing something. Hey, what if I send my boys in to start clearing the way for DeCaF?'

'What do you mean?'

'You know, start clearing where the road goes through. Give DeCaF a flying start.'

'No,' said Clyde. His voice turned icy. 'Jump the gun and the conservationists will think all their birthdays have come at once. They'll have photographers in there within five minutes of you firing up your saws. Why would you want to do something so bloody stupid?'

'Wise up Clyde, we've got the pricks on the run. Why not hit 'em where it hurts before they get organised?'

'Because it gives them ammunition to hit back, and that could hurt even more. The answer's no, Miklos, and I can't make it any plainer than that.'

'You know something, Townsend? I don't like you any more than I did when I met you. You'd give a dead dingo the shits. Fair dinkum.' Miklos slammed down the phone. He pounded his fists together in sheer frustration. What was he supposed to do? Just sit by and wait? There was as much chance of Arnie helping little old ladies across the road. Miklos grabbed his coat and stormed out of his office.

Without a load on the back the Holden ute went like a pig in mud, with the arse end forever trying to overtake the front. But he figured it would get him to the site of the Little Potoroo Creek road with a bit of stroking. He had no real reason to go there, other than a need to do something and the belief that just walking along its projected path and imagining all the trees down and the roadway bulldozed would help make him feel better. It had crossed his mind to take Jan along with him, but as much as he liked the idea of a bang in the bush, he didn't like the idea of Jan twittering away alongside him.

Thirsty Creek Road was unsealed but quite driveable, even though it was badly corrugated and trucks had carved deep furrows into it. Rain had gathered in the ruts and Miklos had to steer around them to avoid getting bogged, but it was child's play for an ex-truckie. He was starting to relax and enjoy using his old skills when he saw the four figures up ahead of him. They wore garbage bags for raincoats, shoes instead of boots, carried rucksacks and bedrolls, had pasty white skin and looked like they'd never done a decent day's work in their life. He didn't need to see the earrings or the greasy technicoloured hair or smell the body odour to know what he was looking at. He recognised them in an instant. One of the protesters stuck his thumb out for a lift. Nugget's story came to mind and Miklos thought briefly about driving over the lot of them. Instead he put his boot down and timed it so that he hit a puddle just as he passed by them. A brown wave rose and engulfed the hitchhikers. If they'd had surfboards they could have ridden it all the way back to Melbourne. Miklos had to laugh when he looked in the rearview mirror and saw the havoc he'd caused. The two-fingered salutes only made him laugh more.

'Here's mud in your eye,' he said out loud. He felt good. At last he was doing something constructive. His good humour lasted almost forty minutes. He enjoyed driving through what appeared to be forest, knowing full well there was nothing behind the screen of trees. Miklos liked to think his chips were satisfying the Japanese obsession with porno magazines and comics. Every time he passed a service road leading into the wasted land beyond the fringe he couldn't help a self-satisfied smile. It was all his doing and he was proud of it. His good humour might have lasted longer than the forty minutes except he came to the end of the road where the new road was to begin and discovered someone else had got there before him. 'Bastards,' he said.

His windshield wipers weren't up to much, but there wasn't a lot to see. Two drab-coloured tents, a tarp, a couple of old Jap rice-burners, an old VW Beetle, smoke from a fire made with damp wood that seemed too heavy to rise and lay trapped in the undergrowth instead, and three banners strung above what he supposed was intended as the rallying point. A couple of people wearing garbo bags ducked out from under a tarpaulin and watched him approach. He wished he had a shotgun with him, wished he had Arnie with him. If nothing else, he could shoot out the banners. 'My Left Bollok Has No Right!' Oh yeah? 'Save Little Potoroo Creek!' 'Say No To Woodchipping!' As he drove closer two more figures emerged from the tents and then another two. Four he could handle but six would be pushing it. He wanted to do something constructive but couldn't work out what.

'Stay calm,' Clyde Townsend had said. 'Take no action. Ignore them, endure them, but do nothing they can use against you later.' Yeah? Well that was okay for Clyde to say, but he wasn't where the action was. He didn't have people shitting in his nest. Miklos flicked the wheel sideways and pulled on the handbrake. The ute shuddered to a stop sideways across the road so he could take a good look through the open side window without the distortion of rain smears and mud. He sneered. The ferals had come to save the bush but were too scared to go into it. They'd pitched their tents on the very edge of the scrub, on the only reasonably clear ground. He wondered what would happen if he sideswiped the tents and decided to find out. He couldn't see them hanging around in the rain without shelter. If he couldn't hook up on the guy ropes then at least he could do a few wheelies on the remaining open ground and churn up the surface. If that was to be their rallying point, let them rally in mud.

He punched the shift into first gear, revved and dropped the clutch. He drove straight at the tents and enjoyed watching the campers scatter. He swung the wheel and hit the first tent's ropes side on, rode over them, collapsed the tent but failed to hook up. He charged at the second tent, drove over the leading guy ropes and collapsed it. This time he was luckier and the forward rope hooked around the bent coathanger that acted as the ute's radio aerial. Miklos had visions of dragging the shredded tent all the way back to Osbourne as a trophy. But it was too big and heavy and it ripped the coathanger out of the aerial socket.

'Bastards!' said Miklos. He gunned the throttle and started doing wheelies, blipped the pedal to keep the rear end in check and fed in heaps of opposite lock. He knew he had to keep the revs up and keep moving or he'd bog down. He glanced out the open side window to gloat and saw one of the blokes shooting away with a camera. Miklos gave him the two-fingered salute, but as he turned back to see where he was going he got a sickening feeling that he knew who the photographer was. He wasn't bothering to use bedpans as reflectors this time, but Miklos had no doubt that Samuel was picking up clean crisp shots, and couldn't help wondering what Clyde Townsend would make of them. Instinctively he backed off the accelerator and let the ute slide to a halt. He was out of the door and after the camera almost before anybody realised what was happening. Almost.

Samuel turned and made a dash for the scrub, yelling to the protesters to help. He didn't need to ask. There were three men and two women just waiting for the chance to get even. They must have thought their prayers had been answered. The first mud ball hit Miklos full in the kisser before he'd gone five metres, the second before he'd had a chance to cover up.

'Fuck!' he screamed. Suddenly five against one seemed like reasonable odds. Nobody threw mud balls at Miklos Laszlo Bollok and lived. He decided to make a fight of it. Another mud ball hit him, and another which was more rock than mud. It took him squarely between the eyes, made him stop and blink. As his sight cleared he realised the opposition had picked up pieces of dead branches which they held like clubs, and one even had a small tomahawk. Miklos saw all he needed to see; he dashed back to the ute. They chased him.

He leapt into the seat, gave the idling motor a bootful and dropped the clutch. The ute lurched, slid, and started digging into the churned-up mud. The tomahawk crashed down on his bonnet and split the metal.

'Farrrrrk!' yelled Miklos. He rocked the ute forward, slammed into reverse and coaxed it backwards out of the ruts he'd dug. A hunk of firewood crashed down on the cabin. Another shattered the rear window. But the ute was moving and Miklos knew exactly what to do. He zigged left, then zagged back right with handfuls of lock and executed a textbook J-turn. As the bonnet swung around so that it faced home, he whipped the shift into first and gunned it. Thirty-two minutes later he encountered the protesters he'd splashed on the way in. They saw him coming and were ready. The first rock took out his windscreen, the second nearly took off his head.

* * *

'Anyone says anything they're dead!' Miklos strode down the corridor to his office, slamming the door behind him. The rain had combined the mud with the blood which oozed from a split over his left eye. Glass pebbles from the shattered windscreen fell from his hair and crunched beneath his boots. Jan rose wide-eyed from her desk and followed him into his office. One of the perks of ownership was that Miklos had his own private bathroom and shower. He ripped off his clothes, turned the taps on full bore and stood under the shower. Jan joined him moments later.

'Not now!' he snarled. 'Get dressed. Get Arnie. Get on the CB and get everyone into the pub at five o'clock. Get going!'

It was the first time he'd used the office shower without Jan or one of her predecessors to scrub his back and other bits, but desperate times demanded desperate measures. He pulled his stomach in, bent forward and glanced down at the water pooling around his feet. It still ran red with blood. He touched the cut over his eye and examined his fingers. There was a little bit of blood but not enough to justify the red swirls streaming around his feet and down the plug hole. He lifted one foot to swish the water away and felt a sharp sting. The source of the blood became immediately apparent: he'd trodden on the glass which had washed out of his hair.

'Freakin' bastards!' he said. Miklos hated coming second in any confrontation, but he had to admit he'd lost the first round in spades. Dingoes would give up bothering sheep before he lost another.

* * *

As soon as Samuel saw the Ford ute blocking the road he thought he might be in trouble. When he saw Arnie leaning against the tray, nursing his Chinese semi-automatic, he knew he was. He slowed down, stopped. Arnie was smiling; Samuel took that as a good sign.

'G'day Arnie,' he said hopefully. 'How're ya going?'

'Good mate, real good.'

'Still shitting through the eye of a needle?'

'Nah mate, all fixed.'

'What can I do for you?'

'Kind of ya to ask.' Arnie pushed away from the ute and leaned into the driver's window of Samuel's VW. 'Good picher ya took of me, mate. Made me look like shit. Now I'm gunna make you look like shit, only it won't just be in any picher.' He pushed his head further into the car. Samuel shrank back in fear.

'Jesus, Arnie, I didn't mean any offence. I was just doing what Miklos wanted.'

'Fair enough,' said Arnie. 'Most of us do that. The only thing that's gunna save ya now is if ya keep doin' what Miklos wants.'

'What's he want?' asked Samuel eagerly.

'Ya took pichers you shouldna taken. Miklos doesn't like people goin' around takin' his picher without permission. He wants ya to give the film to me. He doesn't care if I have to smash ya face in or shoot ya balls off to get it.' He grabbed Samuel by the shirtfront and lifted him off his seat. 'Do me a favour and tell me to get stuffed.'

'No! No! You can have them!' Samuel screamed.

'Smart thinkin',' said Arnie. He gave Samuel's shirt a final tug, which popped buttons, and let go. 'Disappointin' but smart.'

'Film's still in the camera,' sobbed Samuel. 'I'll have to unload.'

'Do that,' said Arnie. 'Then we'll both unload.' He patted the magazine on his rifle.

* * *

Hard Yakka reigned supreme in the pub. If the makers ever had doubts as to the popularity of their indestructible workwear, all they had to do was visit any timber town. The pants were legends. You washed them like you washed your dog: two or three times a year and only when they smelt. You didn't take them off so much as climb out of them, and they didn't lie down until you pushed them over. Some loggers reckoned they were so tough they took the edge off their chainsaws when they got careless. The timber workers liked them because they were the only things in the world as tough as they were.

All the workers from the mill and office were in the pub, every logger, every log loader, every log trucker, and so was Nugget and his two constables. They all liked to think they came for the free beer Miklos put on, but the truth was they came because they didn't dare do otherwise. If they weren't actually on Miklos's payroll, they still depended on him for their living one way or another. If Miklos didn't remind them of the fact, Arnie would.

'I asked you here tonight,' said Miklos, 'because I thought you might be able to help me.' Everybody looked at the scarlet weal above his left eye that Doc Richards had just put nine stitches in, and briefly felt pity for the poor bastard who'd caused it. Miklos's views on punishment weren't a million miles away from those of Islamic extremists.

'You all know about the blockade and what to expect. The first bunch of doped-out, dole-bludgin' dickheads has already arrived, and we can expect plenty more. Normally we'd bang a few heads, run a few cars off the road, and generally give 'em the kinda welcome they don't easy forget. Right?'

'Yeah, right!' The rabble guessed they were there to be roused and so allowed themselves to be.

'Wrong.' Miklos glared around the room. 'Nothin' would please me more if they all head-butted bullets. Nothin' would please me more if their cars all climbed trees, the faster the better. Nothin' would please me more if every poxy one of them went tits-up or pissed off back to Melbourne with a set of boot irons up his arse.'

‘Yeah!’ said Wozza.

‘Shuddup!’ said Miklos. ‘Unfortunately, Big Brother in Melbourne has decided to tell us what we can and cannot do. They call it issue management. We can’t do anything the opposition can use against us, especially if there’s a photographer lurking around — and let me tell you, there is! So no punch-ups. No chasing ferals with chainsaws. No tell-tale bruises. Understand?’

‘Shit, Miklos,’ said Arnie. ‘That’s not fair.’

‘No, it ain’t fair. But you gotta admit, the blokes in Melbourne have done a good job of pullin’ the rug on that feral out in Little Potoroo Creek. They’ve made him look a total mug. That won us a lot of support. Now they’ve got the greenies holding a protest in Melbourne so they won’t have to come down here and protest. What they’re doin’ seems to be workin’ so it would be stupid of us to stuff things up. We’re gunna have to be patient and turn the other cheek.’

Nobody could believe what they were hearing. A silence descended over the pub. They figured the greenies would open a mill in competition before Miklos went non-violent on them.

‘On the other hand,’ said Miklos, to a collective sigh of relief, ‘some things don’t show bruises. For example, there are some banners up there that the wind could easily blow down. Some tents that could easily collapse in a decent shower. I wouldn’t like to be camped up there without a tent. They don’t appear to have any dunnies up there either. I reckon it would be worth Bob’s shit wagon takin’ a run up there. Deliverin’ not collectin’.’ Bob ran the night soil truck, pumping out septic tanks.

'Another thing. Some of the vehicles them troublemakers are comin' down in have got shockin' tyres. I don't reckon they should be allowed back on the road. What d'ya reckon?'

'No way!' People started getting in the mood, laughing and cheering. This was the Miklos they knew.

'Wouldn't surprise me either if they were all carryin' drugs. Whad'ya reckon, Nugget?'

'I'd be derelict in my duty if I failed to search each and every one of them,' said Nugget smugly. 'And the good-lookin' ones twice.'

'I'll leave it to you,' said Miklos above the laughter. 'But remember what I said — no bruises!'

'No bruises!' echoed the gathering.

'No photographs.'

'No photographs!'

'Now get into it,' said Miklos. 'In half an hour you start buyin' your own.'

He stood down, satisfied with his performance. Half an hour's good guzzling would prime them all for a decent piss-up. After that, he reckoned the new arrivals could expect visitors.

CHAPTER EIGHTEEN

Samuel parked his Beetle behind the *East Gippsland Gazette* office and clumped heavily up the stairs, beaten, dispirited and still shaking from his brush with Arnie. He staggered to what had once been his desk and slumped down. James was busy doing the final make-up for the front page of Thursday morning's edition while Mrs Watson took last-minute classifieds over the phone, even though the deadline had closed two hours earlier. Samuel pushed his chair back and covered his face with his hands as he imagined real reporters did when the world became too much. His week had begun well. He'd coaxed an interview from Liz, then from a feral who'd organised fundraisers for the blockade, and finally from God himself. The interview with God was a first and an exclusive. James had suggested he write them up as background stories and offered to send them to his contacts at the *Herald* and *Age*. When he'd discovered the first protesters setting up camp he thought his luck had really changed. He could hardly believe his good fortune when Miklos Bollok did his demolition job on the tents, and realised then with blinding clarity that all the interviews in the world didn't rate a fart in a thunderstorm when a real story came along. For a few brief moments all his dreams and aspirations had revived. He'd thought his story would even make the six o'clock TV news. Then along came Arnie, and for the second time he'd had his scoop whipped away from him. Sometimes life really sucked.

'Get your story?'

Samuel looked up to find James Ferguson standing over him.

'Nothing more on Miklos's Toyota, but a story just as damaging.'

'Go on.'

'No proof. I had it, close-ups in glorious living colour, but it was taken away from me.' He paused and the memory brought a quaver back into his voice. 'At gun point.'

James stared hard at the boy, pulled up a chair and sat down. 'Out with it, lad. If you're serious, you'd better start talking.'

Samuel began talking and James listened, his outrage and indignation growing by the second.

'That does it!' he said when Samuel had finished. 'I'm going to ring Mr Almighty Miklos Bollok right this instant. And the police! He'll think twice before he ever pulls a stunt like that on one of my reporters again.'

'Save it,' said Samuel. 'I'm not one of your reporters and you have no proof. Without proof you have no story. It's Arnie's testimony versus mine. The testimony of the guys at the blockade will count for nothing because both Miklos and Arnie will have alibis. No proof, no story. The advice you gave me applies equally to you. Miklos would just laugh at you.'

'I won't let him get away with it!'

'You have no choice. Sooner or later our day will come, and we have no alternative but to wait until it does.'

'The lad's right,' said Mrs Watson, who'd pulled the plug on all incoming calls so she could listen in. 'That Miklos Bollok is a nasty piece of work, if you ask me. Even if you still had them photos you'd have to think twice before you printed them. A lot of people wouldn't thank you for doing that, no my word they wouldn't.'

'See?' said Samuel. 'Mother knows best.'

'Oh dear,' said Mrs Watson, 'I forgot. This envelope arrived for you in the mail.' She climbed down off her chair and handed it to Samuel. 'Never know, might be something important. Might cheer you up.'

'Thanks, Mrs Watson.' Samuel didn't bother to open the envelope, just let it fall onto his desk.

'You had no luck with Mrs Bollok?' asked James.

'She knows Miklos smashed up his own car, knows God is innocent, but won't admit a thing. She's loyal to her husband. She has everything to lose and nothing to gain by blabbing. Who can blame her?'

'I thought there was an outside chance she'd tell you,' said James. 'A woman scorned and all that. I don't envy her the life she leads. I got your stories off by the way, but nobody's keen to lead the charge on the rehabilitation of God. Unless something dramatic happens, the papers don't want to know about him.'

'What about the piece on Summer?'

‘They’re holding it for the time being. Encouraging, but more likely a delayed rejection. I thought it was good myself, mind.’

‘I think I’ll go home. Let you put your paper to bed. Maybe call into the pub.’ Samuel dragged himself to his feet.

‘I’ll drop by later and have one with you. Don’t forget your parcel.’ James turned and wandered back into his office. Mrs Watson took another classified, swearing it would be the last. Samuel picked up the envelope and looked idly at the postmark. Osbourne. He felt the package, the hard tapered cylinder inside. He ripped the envelope open, caught the roll of thirty-five-mil film as it tumbled out.

‘James!’ he yelled. ‘Oh please God, please, please!’

There was no note, no hint as to the identity of the sender, nothing except the roll of forty ASA Fuji film — the same brand he’d seen in Cheryl’s camera case.

* * *

‘Mrs Watson,’ yelled James. ‘Get me Ted Shehadie over in Bairnsdale. Not at the shop, at his home.’ He turned back to Samuel. ‘Lad, I’ll give you seventy-five minutes to get to Bairnsdale and get a print off the neg. If I don’t hear from you within an hour and a half I’m going to run the presses. Take my mobile and dictate your story to Mrs Watson on the way in case we’ve just got lucky. I want the story of Miklos driving over the tents, but sit on Arnie taking the film off you at gun point. Without proof they can accuse us of a beat-up and I’ll not allow anything that questions our credibility or detracts from the story. I'll give you the front, back and inside covers, and save space for my editorial which I'll start writing as soon as I put the rest of the paper to bed. We'll do the whole thing as a wrap-around. Now get going!'

'Mr Shehadie on the phone,' said Mrs Watson. She beamed, loving every second of the drama. James snatched up a phone.

'Ted? Hope I haven't interrupted your dinner but this is important. I need you to open up shop and process a roll of thirty-five-mil. Lad's on the way with it. What? So change the bloody chemicals! I don't care what it costs! And Ted, you only get one chance. Make sure everything's working before you put my film through. Okay? Owe you one.' He hung up. 'Now, Mrs Watson ...'

'Everything is under control, Mr Ferguson. I'll just do a spot of dustin' while I wait for the lad to call.'

'Better call one of the designers in to work the Mac. And call Glynnis as well. Get her in to help.' Glynnis was his most senior reporter, a part-timer and grazier's wife who was a diehard National Party supporter. But she was a pro, valued her job and understood his insistence on objectivity. She was good for a headline and could help sub-edit Samuel's copy. The phone rang and he heard Mrs Watson answer and start taking down copy. Years of recording classifieds over the phone had made her particularly adept at dictation. James shook his head and wondered why he hadn't thought of using her to take copy over the phone before. He settled down to his page make-up.

'Dirty Tricks Exposed,' he wrote, then changed his mind. 'Caught in the Act!' Better, he thought. He decided to run four photos on the front page with a box in the middle into which he relegated 'Dirty Tricks Exposed!' That was much more tabloid, much more sensational, and as far from his normal style of journalism as he'd ever dared venture. He added a flash across the corner: 'An *East Gippsland Gazette* Exclusive!' It would be exclusive too, until he'd emailed and faxed every newspaper, TV channel and radio station in the country. 'G.O.D. Accusations Exposed as Load of Bolloks!' he blazed across the inside page. He was behaving precisely like the new-wave, sensation-seeking journos he despised, and loving every minute of it. His fiendish and entirely uncharacteristic laugh startled Mrs Watson and momentarily broke her concentration. Miklos Bollok had used him, callously abused his trust, and put him in a position where all the respect and credibility he'd built up over his working life was in jeopardy. He wrote with malice and delighted in it.

* * *

Shehadie Grove was the sort of shop that attracts tourists like footballers to free beer. It had fishing and surfing gear, racks of swimming costumes, beachwear, caps and sun visors, tourist t-shirts, thongs, Aboriginal artifacts, postcards and paperbacks, and every women's magazine available. Part of the premises was devoted to a pharmacy, most of which was occupied by sun-care products and insect repellents. The part Samuel was interested in was the one-hour photo lab tucked in the corner. It was ninety-six kilometres from Orbost and still the closest. His '56 VW was designed to run flat out all day, but flat out in the old Beetle was still only one hundred and ten kilometres an hour, half that on hills and even slower in the rain with six-volt wipers. Samuel pulled up outside Shehadie Grove and sighed with relief when he saw all the lights on.

'Hello, son,' said Ted when Samuel walked in. 'What's all the fuss about then?'

'G'day, Mr Shehadie,' said Samuel. He handed over the roll of film. 'Take care, there's a lot riding on that piece of film. God's integrity, Mr Ferguson's reputation, my career, my life and the future of Little Potoroo Creek.'

'That all,' said Ted. 'Thought it might be something important. I'll give you a yell when I'm running the prints. Now shove off and make yourself a coffee.' There was a café at the back of Shehadie Grove as well.

Samuel found the filter jug, boiled some water and sat back to let the grounds infuse. He was absolutely certain he knew what the photos would show. He couldn't for the life of him understand why Cheryl had taken them. What had been her reason, her intention? Was she starting to gravitate towards the green cause? Whatever the answer, he knew he'd still have to protect her as a source. She hadn't sent the film anonymously without good reason. He poured his coffee and sipped.

'Just about ready,' called Ted. 'By the time you've made me a coffee I will be. Black and two if you don't mind.'

Samuel poured another coffee and was staggered to see how much his hands were shaking. He kept the level well shy of the lip of the cup so it wouldn't spill while he was carrying it. 'Here you are,' he said.

'Bloody low tide,' said Ted. 'It doesn't cost any more to fill the cup, you know. Particularly considering it's free.'

'Sorry,' said Samuel. He craned his neck to see the first photo emerge from the printer. He found himself staring into the eyes of a fox. 'Oh shit!' he said. More photos followed. Fox looking at camera, fox looking left, fox looking right, fox standing, fox trotting ... 'Oh God!' said Samuel. He almost sobbed.

'The last shots come out first,' said Ted. 'Looked like there was something different on the other end when I checked the neg.'

Fox with mouth open. Fox out of focus. Blank. Miklos Bollok swinging a sledgehammer and belting the daylights out of his Toyota's bonnet.

'Eu-bloody-reka! Thank you God!' shouted Samuel. The film was slow and the light levels low, and the photographer had used a long lens which had soaked up more light. But the shot was sharp enough and no one who knew Miklos Bollok could fail to recognise him.

'Bloody hell,' said Ted. 'Bloody, bloody, bloody hell,' he said as more prints emerged. Samuel grabbed them.

'You darling!' he said. 'You beauty!' Every shot had a piece of branch or leaves soft in the foreground. Whoever took the photos wanted to make sure Miklos didn't know about it. They were classic spy photos, like the ones paparazzi took of royalty having their toes sucked, and they were meant to look that way. The message wasn't lost on him.

'You don't mind, do you, if I never processed these shots? In fact, you don't mind if I never saw them before in my life.' Ted turned to Samuel and he wasn't smiling. 'Tell bloody James Ferguson thank you very much. Tell him I won't send a bill. I don't want anything tying me to this. Now get outta here.'

* * *

'Can I get you another Scotch?' said Miklos. When Cheryl had furnished the lounge she'd ordered two button-back Chesterfields in black leather, the kind a man could sink right back into and feel at home.

'Sure,' said Cheryl.

'Nice to have a night home for a change,' said Miklos.

'You can get tired of them after a while,' said Cheryl.

'Don't start,' Miklos warned. He'd wanted a bar in the lounge but Cheryl had forced him to settle for a cocktail cabinet, a chrome and mahogany extravagance which had originally been built for an ocean liner.

'What are you doing home?' Cheryl was watching NYPD Blue. She turned to face Miklos when the commercials came on.

'Fancied a barbecue.'

'Sure.'

'And a nice friendly chat with my wife.'

'Well, we've had the barbecue.'

Miklos laughed. 'You don't waste words, do you? You've got more balls than any man I've ever met, with the exception of my father. It's one of the few things I like about you. Truth is, there are some protesters set up camp on the site of the new road. Some of the boys have decided to go and make them welcome. Nothing to do with me, of course, and best I know nothing about it.'

'Ah,' said Cheryl. 'I'm your alibi.'

'Here's your Scotch.'

'Ta. Nice to be useful for a change.'

'Thing about you, Cheryl, people might look sideways at me but they trust you absolutely.' He flopped back down on his Chesterfield. 'How are the boys?'

'Our boys? I'll tell you if you can tell me how old they'll be on their next birthday. By the way, do you know when their birthdays are?'

'Cheryl, I'm trying to be nice. Why do you always want to spoil things?'

* * *

Arnie led the charge to the protesters' camp. The line of utes and four-wheel drives stretched back three hundred metres, connected by headlight beams of glowing drizzle. Bob's night cart brought up the rear. Some of the loggers ran shotgun on the backs of the utes, hanging onto the roll bars and playing silly buggers with the spotlights they used for spotting roos. All the talk in the pub about flanking manoeuvres and taking the camp by surprise had died the moment they'd staggered out into the car park. From then on it was a race, with Arnie's younger brother Davo threatening to shoot any hoon who tried to overtake them. They could've been poachers after ivory, Ku Klux Klan members after the sons and daughters of slavery, or a bunch of bikies after trouble. But whatever was going through their minds wasted its time making the journey. When they reached the camp site it was empty. There was no one there to terrorise, nothing to destroy. No protesters, no banners, no tents, no cars with tyres to shoot holes in.

'Hell's this?' said Arnie and skidded to a stop. Other utes slid to a halt alongside him. Roo lights played over the abandoned camp site and surrounding bushes. 'Bastards!'

'What're we gunna do now?' asked Davo.

'Nothin' to bloody do,' said Arnie.

'What're we gunna shoot?'

'Nothin' to bloody shoot.'

'Bastards have gorn,' said Wozza. 'Buggered off.' He was standing on the back of Charley's ute. 'Anyone bring any beer?'

'Not enough,' said someone.

'May as well go back to the pub,' said Arnie.

'Hey,' said Bob. He got out of his truck and staggered up to Arnie's window. 'What am I gunna do with all the stuff in my truck?'

'Bob,' said Arnie. 'Do what I'm gunna do. Get the shit outta here.'

* * *

Back in the forest the protesters breathed a collective sigh of relief that they'd stumbled across God's treehouses. They could have been bigger and they could have been drier, but nobody was complaining. They couldn't have been safer.

'Thank God,' they said.

* * *

The presses started to roll; Samuel could feel the vibration through the floor. It matched the state of his nerves. Nothing else in his entire life could equal the excitement of this night.

'Get yourself around this.' James handed Samuel a beer and passed another on to Glynnis. 'Here's to you, lad. I'm proud of you. You've done really well. And thank you, Glynnis. Do you think we'll make a reporter of him?'

'I think he's made one of himself, apart from the odd split infinitive and misrelated participle. Know how many years I worked before I got a by-line? Don't ask.' Glynnis yawned. 'Do you two mind if I leave you to bathe in your glory? I've got a feeling it'll be an early start tomorrow and I need my beauty sleep.' She put her beer down with the bottle still half-full. 'You do know what you've let yourselves in for, don't you?'

'Aye,' said James. 'And I wouldn't miss it for quids. I've buried my head in the sand for far too long. Goodnight and thanks.'

'Same goes for me,' said Samuel.

'It's really going to hit the fan, you know.' Glynnis paused at the doorway. 'If I were you and I had to choose what colour suit to wear in the morning, I'd think very seriously about wearing brown.'

CHAPTER NINETEEN

Ciaron prowled around the squat looking for someone or something to hit. The Dick with Ears had taken Sky and gone to scam some pies. He'd heard about a mum and dad bakery that gave away pies with broken cases to anyone needy who came to their back door. She wasn't even cheered to hear that they also made vego pies, because they probably loaded the pastry with lard and cooked the vegies in chicken or beef stock. But what really gave her the shits was that Darren had slipped effortlessly from Summer to Sky and hardly taken the time to do his fly up in between. Summer had given The Dick the flick, but Ciaron still thought Darren should've had a period of abstinence. She missed Summer, missed having her around. Ciaron didn't make friends easily, particularly with young attractive women who could see beyond her sexuality and accept her without fuss. She wanted to do something for Summer, she wanted to make sure that Mourn till Dawn was a runaway success.

Every lunch break and every day after work she rode around to all the green groups and cafés, revving people up. She organised squads of people to ring talk-back radio, and even rang a couple of stations herself. She harangued the squat. What Summer achieved by charm Ciaron set out to achieve her way, by threat. She rang diehard greenie Peter Garrett, lead singer and front man for Midnight Oil, who promised to come and perform. She made Stretch ring his musician mates and extract similar promises from them. It pissed her off that dickhead Darren wasn't doing more to help. He'd had the idea then retired, as if he'd made his contribution. But, despite all her efforts, there was an odium still attached to Little Potoroo Creek because of God's alleged indiscretion. Nothing was going as well as she'd hoped. She needed a miracle and she knew it.

Sky and The Dick breezed in with a box of broken lukewarm pies, carrying on as if they'd just unravelled the mystery of the universe. Ciaron sighed. Deep down The Dick was unbelievably shallow. She gave up and joined the stampede. At least pies made a change from bagels. The squat settled down to supper, evenly divided over whether they'd get two thousand or ten thousand people to the following night's vigil.

'There ain't no buzz,' said Stretch. 'Need a buzz or ya just pissin' in the wind.'

'Depends who you talk to,' said Lyndal.

'Too many people are uncommitted,' said Thalia. 'Two thousand's still not bad.'

'It's the rain,' said Sky. 'Depends on whether it stops raining.'

'Still reckon we'll get ten thousand,' said Lyndal.

'Don't bet on it,' said Stretch. 'Ain't much fun holdin' a candle when you're freezin' ya arse off in a puddle.'

‘It’s gotta work,’ said Ciaron grimly. She stuffed a potato and spinach pie into her mouth and crushed it. ‘Someone’s gunna pay if it doesn’t.’ She glared at Darren. ‘Summer’s countin’ on us.’

* * *

Miklos woke early, at peace with the world. Arnie had rung from the pub to tell him the protesters had all moved on, and Cheryl had obliged when he’d called her up off the bench and made love to her for the first time in more than a year. One of the ironies of their relationship was that they still shared a double bed, but neither had seen fit to change the arrangement. Married people slept in double beds; that was the way it was. Miklos had slept like a baby and could sleep no more. There was no interruption to Cheryl’s snoring as he eased himself out of bed and crept through to the kitchen to make coffee. He thought about switching on the radio but five-thirty was too early for anything interesting to be on. He wandered out onto the front verandah while his coffee infused to see if the *East Gippsland Gazette* had arrived. Typical, he thought. The one day he’d got up early the paper was late. It was also too early for the *Age*. At least the clouds had moved on and it had stopped raining.

Miklos hated having nothing to do. If he’d been stuck on a desert island with no one to push around and nothing to organise, he wouldn’t have hesitated to take the one-way swim. At least it would’ve given him something to do. He heard a car drive past while he sipped his coffee, and waited for the thud of newspaper on drive. It never came. Someone else was up and off for an early start.

Miklos decided to do likewise. He drained his coffee cup, stood, stretched, yawned and farted, rubbed his belly and took a step towards the shower. The phone rang. He grabbed it quickly before it had a chance to wake Cheryl, wondering who the hell had the nerve to ring him so early.

'Miklos Bollok,' he snarled. 'Hell you want?'

Miklos listened, his jaw dropped, his face turned white then flushed crimson. His picture was all over the front pages of the *Herald* and the *Age*. Smashing up his car. Would he like to make a comment? 'No I fuckin' wouldn't!' he screamed. He slammed the phone down and immediately realised his mistake. It began ringing again straightaway. He grabbed the cord and ripped the plug out from the wall. It still rang in the hall. He raced out of the kitchen and ripped the hall phone's plug out from the wall as well. He stood shaking with rage, not knowing what to do or what to say. A picture of him smashing up the Toyota was on the front pages of the *Age* and the *Herald*? Oh God! He raced back into the kitchen and switched on the radio for the six o'clock news. He was the lead story.

'Shit!' he yelled. 'I'll have someone's guts for this! I'll kill 'em!'

'What's the problem?' Cheryl called sleepily. For once words failed him. He heard a car pass and a dull thud. One of the papers had arrived. He raced out the front and picked it up off the drive. He tried to rip it open to read it but, as always, was frustrated by the clingwrap.

'Arrghhhhhh!' he said. His podgy fingers searched and scratched but couldn't find the seam. 'Cheryl!' he yelled, and raced back inside. He threw the paper at her. 'Open it and see for yourself! Stuff me, I'll have someone's balls for this!'

Cheryl blanched. She'd never seen Miklos so angry. Her fingers quickly located the edge of the wrap and she picked at it. As soon as she had enough to start unwrapping Miklos snatched the paper from her.

'Oh holy shit!' he said.

CAUGHT IN THE ACT! the headline screamed in the biggest type he'd ever seen the *East Gippsland Gazette* use. But what rivetted his attention were the four incriminating photos. 'Dirty tricks exposed!' screamed the sub-head. 'Special investigator's report inside' screamed the amended corner flash.

'What's up? What's happened?' said Cheryl. The alarm in her voice was genuine.

'Wait!' snapped Miklos. He opened up the wrap-around cover for the rest of the bad news. It was all there. He reeled under blow after blow. His accusations against God. More pictures. His trashing of the camp site with a picture of the eye-witness reporter. In another column God demanded an apology and a pledge to abandon woodchipping at Little Potoroo Creek. An editorial sermonised about abuse of the media. A small article at the bottom of the page caught his eye: 'Gazette pays $5000 for photos'. He slumped down on the bed, feeling sick and betrayed. Cheryl took the paper from him and stared at the photos.

'Ouch!' she said.

'What do you think?' he asked.

'Professional job,' said Cheryl. 'Long lens, low light, every shot sharp. Whoever took these was hiding in the scrub out by the letterbox.'

'Was it you?' Miklos looked steadily at her.

'I'm not that good,' said Cheryl evenly. She mustered all of her inner strength and stared back at him. 'Besides, as I recall you were giving me heaps at the time for not helping.'

'Might be right.'

'Am right. This time you're *my* alibi.' The longer she looked at the photos the more secure she felt. She'd done a far better job than she'd ever hoped.

'Shit! Okay, if it wasn't you, then who?'

'Can't you guess? It's not that hard, Miklos,' said Cheryl softly.

'Whad'ya mean?'

'Figure it out. Nobody just happened to be passing on the off-chance that you'd beat the crap out of your car and then blame it on God. Nobody in the world is that lucky or that smart.'

'Go on.' Miklos could see where she was heading but needed to hear the suspicions voiced.

'Who knew what you were going to do? Who did you discuss it with? Look at these photos, Miklos, they're pro and whoever took them made sure he wouldn't be spotted. Someone set you up.'

Miklos's jaw tightened, then relaxed. 'You know something, Cheryl? I oughta talk to you more often.' He began to smile, but it was a smile calculated to freeze blood. 'Got to admire that Clyde Townsend,' he said. 'Not only has he stitched me up, he conned me into giving him ten grand for the privilege. The man's got balls, give him that.' His jaw tightened again and his face hardened. 'But I'll have 'em on a plate come dinner time.'

As soon as Miklos reached his office he rang Arnie and told him to take his ute, his rifle and the company mobile phone and head for Melbourne. Then he rang Bernie Dwight.

'This better be important,' said Bernie, his voice heavy with sleep.

'Bernie,' said Miklos, 'if you've got someone in your bed, piss 'em off now.'

'Hang on,' said Bernie. Miklos heard some muffled complaints, heard a woman swear, then Bernie's voice came back clear. 'What's the problem, son?'

'Your mate Clyde Townsend. Seen the morning papers? No, you wouldn't have. Your mate has stitched me up better than Anthony Squires.' Miklos wasn't swearing and Bernie recognised this as a bad sign. 'They're all over the front page. Glorious pictures, in colour no less, of a certain person beating the crap out of his Toyota. Ring any bells with you?'

'You're kiddin'!'

'No Bernie, I'm not. When I took the hammer to the car someone was already hiding in the bushes out front with a long lens on his camera. Who told him to be there? Who was the only person apart from myself who knew what I was going to do? You guessed! The same person who told me — no, ordered me — to do it.'

'You sure about that?'

'Oh yeah, I'm sure. Cheryl knew nothing until I started swinging the hammer. She was on the back porch watching me.'

'Couldn't there be some other explanation?'

'Wake up Bernie! We've been done over by an expert. Figure it out. Who does Clyde really represent? The Victorian Association of Forest Product Management? They're just a lobby group for our competitors. They must be pissing themselves laughing. Rip, Chip and Ship's making things too hot for them so they send their boy down to sort us out. Sell us on all that issue management bullshit, suck us in, set us up, then kick our arse.'

'You might be right, Miklos, but if you are the man's a bloody genius. I never got the slightest suspicion.'

'Bernie, you're a politician. When you think you're being screwed, what's the first thing you do?'

'Look to see who stands to benefit.'

'Exactly.'

'You might be right. Bastard sure had me fooled. What're you going to do?'

'I'm gunna put Townsend through the chipper.'

'For real, I mean.'

'I am for real.'

'Tell you what. I've learnt a bit about this issue management business in the last couple of days. You deal with Townsend, I'll talk to the media. Obviously we won't get out of this smelling like roses, but I reckon if I thought about it I could figure out some way to lessen the damage. Don't you talk to anyone, okay.'

'You're startin' to sound just like Townsend.'

'Right now maybe, but I got a feeling that pretty soon he's going to sound more like Tiny Tim.'

* * *

The phone rang the instant Miklos hung up. He snatched the handset back up off the cradle. 'You deaf or stupid? I told you no calls!'

'It's Mr Townsend and he insists!' Jan spat back.

Miklos took a deep breath and exhaled. 'Okay, put him through.'

'You could say sorry, you know. Doesn't cost nothing!' She put Clyde through.

'Miklos?'

Miklos took his time responding. There was urgency and even anger in Clyde's voice. He hadn't rung to gloat but to deny. Didn't matter much either way. 'Well, well, if it isn't the ten thousand dollar man.'

'What the hell's going on? I've been trying to reach you since six o'clock.'

Miklos smiled. 'Spare me, Clyde, we both know what's going on. You've done me like a dinner. Others have tried but you're the only one who's ever pulled it off. I'm man enough to acknowledge that.'

'What the hell are you talking about?'

'Cut the bullshit, Townsend! You think I don't know you and your mates are laughing your tits off?' Miklos had intended to stay calm but he couldn't keep the menace out of his voice. 'You're cute, sunshine, real cute. Come down here sellin' issue management and all the time I'm the issue. I'm the one who's being managed!'

'That's bullshit!'

'No one else knew, ya stupid prick! Only you and me. And I know I didn't take no photos.'

'Miklos, I swear you've got it all wrong!'

'No mate, you're the one that's got it all wrong.' Miklos's voice died away until it was little more than a whisper. 'You're the one who's gunna spend the rest of his life lookin' over his shoulder.'

'Miklos, for Christ's sake! I'm coming down.'

'Don't bother.' Miklos started laughing. It was the most chilling sound Clyde Townsend had ever heard.

* * *

Clyde Townsend slumped back in his chair and stared blank-eyed at the phone. He cancelled all his morning's meetings and set about trying to plan a counter initiative. After an hour and a half his secretary brought him a coffee, but nothing registered. His mind was a whirl of pinballing thoughts and ideas, careening off walls and cannoning off each other. Nothing would hold still long enough to be examined, judged useful or discarded. In desperation he grabbed his thought organisation pad, a device he'd discovered and adopted at a management skills seminar. He tore off three pages, wrote 'Damage' on the first, 'Control' on the second and 'Miklos Bollok' on the third. He was about to fill in the squares on the first page when he turned to the third. Miklos Bollok wasn't just a name, he was a threat, one he knew he couldn't afford to take lightly or delay neutralising. Under 'Negatives' he wrote: 'violent, vengeful, vindictive, bully, amoral, ruthless, powerful, arrogant, determined, driven', and figured he'd written as much as he needed. His hands shook as he grabbed his phone. 'Get me Security,' he said. 'Then get me Bernie Dwight.'

Clyde organised a guard on his apartment and his car, and two burly ex-SAS bodyguards to sit outside his office and accompany him on his travels. He turned back to his Miklos organisation sheet. Under 'Positives' he wrote: 'street smart, intelligent, greedy, pragmatic', underlined 'greedy' and 'pragmatic' and realised that both attributes combined provided grounds for negotiation. It never ceased to amaze him how forgiving pragmatic people could become once the greed button had been pushed hard enough. He applied the disciplines he'd learnt at the seminar: cover the negatives but focus on the positives. That, his instructor had said, was the only way to achieve 'The Objective'. He wrote 'Pacify Bollok and regain control' as his objective. His phone rang.

'Mr Dwight on his mobile,' his secretary said and demonstrated why he paid her so well. 'Digital. Safe from intercepts.'

Clyde smiled. At last the ball had bounced his way. 'Bernie. Where have you been? We need to talk.'

'Better be good,' said Bernie.

Clyde didn't hold back. He gave his side of the story and protested his innocence. His performance was all the more convincing for the fact that, for once, he was telling the truth. 'We've got to get together to handle this thing,' he urged. 'I've got a couple of ideas. In return I want you to try and hose Miklos down.'

'I'm not convinced,' said Bernie. 'But I'll hear you out. Then I'll decide what to do about Miklos.'

Within ten minutes they had their argument sorted out. Whether Clyde was innocent or not was irrelevant. At least Bernie had something plausible to say to the media. Clyde hung up. He was in the middle of addressing the 'Damage' sheet when his phone rang once more. It was a leading radio station after a comment for the 'News at Noon'. Clyde always took calls from the media, always welcomed the opportunity to put his spin on an issue and negate anyone else's, but this was a call he could easily have done without. He could tell immediately by the interviewer's bluntness that the interview would be hostile.

'We understand you represent the Victorian Association of Forest Product Management,' said the interviewer.

'On occasions,' said Clyde.

'Your speciality is issue management.'

'I'm not overly familiar with the term issue management. My business is corporate public relations, that's the area in which I give advice.'

'Are you currently giving advice to Regional Consolidated Sawmillers?'

'Among others.'

'Was it your idea to trash the Toyota four-wheel drive?'

Clyde laughed. He was in the position every PR person dreaded of having to lie publicly. 'That's hardly the domain of corporate public relations.'

'That's not an answer.'

'Oh, I think it's answer enough.' Clyde was sweating but still managed to laugh. 'Your question is clearly ridiculous.'

'So you categorically deny advising Miklos Bollok to beat up his own car?'

'What is this? An exercise in the "do you beat your wife" school of journalism?'

'Yes or no, Mr Townsend.'

'Do I beat my wife? No I don't.'

'Did you advise Mr Bollok to destroy his own car? Yes or no?'

'That is not within the province of corporate PR,' said Clyde. 'How many times do I have to tell you? How can I be any clearer?' He hoped fervently his lie wouldn't come home to haunt him. 'What you have here is a clear case of someone who has been wronged simply trying to make sure that everyone gets to hear about it. Fact: the man who calls himself God poisoned three of Mr Bollok's employees. Fact: he stole their car — Mr Bollok's car. Fact: he wrote to the newspapers and made outrageous and wrongful assertions about the presence of protected and endangered flora and fauna in an area over which Mr Bollok has a logging concession in a deliberate attempt to mislead and deny Mr Bollok his right to conduct his lawful business. Those are the facts. Mr Bollok is the wronged party. There is no question but that he went too far in his attempts to bring the issue to public attention. He was both foolish and naive, and doubtless he will apologise for his actions. But I stress they were the actions of a man who has himself been victim of a campaign to discredit him. If Mr Bollok is guilty of anything, it is only of gilding the lily in his attempts to defend himself.'

'Thank you, Mr Townsend. By the way, the words "gilding the lily" were used moments ago by Mr Bernie Dwight, the independent member for Tathra Valley, when we interviewed him. I would suggest this issue is being well and truly managed. Thank you for speaking to us.'

Clyde stared at the phone, pressed a button and got through to his secretary. 'You tape that? Okay, give me playback.'

'Before I do I've got an urgent call on hold.'

Clyde heard the tension in his secretary's voice and wondered what new disaster had occurred.

'I think you should take it,' she said.

'Put it through.' He closed his eyes wearily and listened. 'Townsend here.'

'Mr Townsend, Security. Someone has just fired a high velocity round through your apartment window.'

Clyde groaned, reached across his desk for the Miklos Bollok sheet and wrote another word under 'Negatives'.

'Arnie,' it said.

* * *

Summer had hoped to spend a week in the cave, recuperating and enjoying God, tramping through the bush and getting reacquainted with all the animals, but the morning radio news changed everything. She screamed and grabbed hold of God's arm. His spoon of porridge was en route to his mouth and spilled over his beard. By the time they'd heard the news right through and listened to Samuel and James Ferguson on talk-back, the porridge had set as hard as concrete. Samuel played the intrepid investigative reporter while James took the high ground on media manipulation. If Rip, Chip and Ship had been a public company its shares would have plummeted. Outraged listeners phoned in with comments and pledged their support for Little Potoroo Creek. Summer and God heard about the candlelight vigil for the first time.

'Mourn till Dawn!' said Summer. 'That's brilliant! Bet the squat's behind it. Bet Stretch came up with the idea!' She raved on and on, trying to guess how many people would turn out, and filled the cave with her joy. God sat quietly, felt his excitement rise and dared to let his hopes rise with it until it got too much. He rose, stepped outside into the morning light, squatted and slipped into meditation. Summer switched off the radio and turned her attention back to breakfast. Despite the fact that the night before she and God had shared a piece of steak she'd bought in Orbost, she still felt hungry. She'd never eaten so well in her life nor felt so hungry. Her body was healing and demanded food to fuel the process. The porridge in her bowl had set like lava and looked about as appetising. She found God's rice, boiled a cupful, threw in a handful of chopped mushrooms at the last minute and a pinch of salt. It wasn't much but it was about as complicated as Summer's culinary skills ever got. She distributed the rice evenly over two plates and gave God a wake-up call by trying to rip away the porridge plastered to his chin.

'Mushroom risotto,' she said optimistically.

God winced then smiled slowly. Sometimes it took him a while to get back up to speed after meditation, especially when he was interrupted. He sat up and ate his rice and let his thoughts follow their course. Summer still prattled away, filling the cave with words and laughter, but none of it penetrated. Things had changed and there was the future to consider, the future of the forest and the animals. 'Time to go,' he said eventually. Summer had no idea what he was talking about until he started packing up the tarpaulin.

'No!' she cried. 'I just got here!'

'Yes,' he said sadly. He thought of the days they'd planned roaming the valley, seeking out their neighbours; the beautiful nights when he gave her a massage and she gave him her body in return; the mornings when the kookaburras gave up rather than try to compete with her laughter. 'They'll all come now and we need to be ready.'

'No!' said Summer. She needed rest, needed time out from the cause, needed desperately to reacquaint herself with the forest and with God, to wander aimlessly and timelessly through the bush as she'd dreamt of doing during the long winter nights in the squat. 'No!' she urged. 'Just five more days. Three! Okay two. Just one more! One more won't make any difference!'

God slowly climbed the gum outside the cave to retrieve his aerial.

When they reached the lip of the escarpment God paused and turned to look back over his valley, over the tops of trees burnished with new growth and the hopes of spring. Summer was startled to see tears first brighten then flow from his eyes. She could do nothing but throw her arms around him and his bundles and hold onto him as tightly as she could. His feet seemed to grow roots and tie him deeply to the soil, immobile and immoveable. She felt guilty for her tears and her tantrum. God didn't want to leave any more than she did, but he accepted the need to make sacrifices. His selflessness made her feel ashamed.

Summer had no idea how long they stood there, and it didn't matter anyway. This was no time for haste. God was leaving the promised land and going into a battle from which he might never return, nor have anything to return to. Summer held onto him with all her strength. Leaving was a real bastard, sometimes.

* * *

Opinion was divided over whether ten or twenty thousand people turned out to light a candle for the last potoroo. A sea of flickering light flowed along Spring Street, and down every street between Collins and Lonsdale Streets. Melbourne hadn't seen a protest like it since the days of the Vietnam War. Radio 3NL played host and broadcast the proceedings live. The TV channels covered it for their news. Every green group sent a speaker and sold candles to raise money for the cause. Band after band gave time and talent to entertain the crowd. Matt, Georgie, Sky and Stretch revived the blow-ups of God's letters and worked the alleys and side streets, singing 'Rip, rip, woodchip' till they were hoarse, and filled their guitar case with money for the blockade. Thalia and Lyndal joined in with a street theatre group, one of many on the night, acting out impassioned and heavily symbolic little plays, while passing the hat around for donations. Midnight Oil's Peter Garrett introduced Ciaron to the crowd and the misfit was cheered for the first time in her life. She took the microphone in a glare of TV lights, terrifyingly aware of the thousands of people awaiting her words of wisdom.

'Come to the blockade,' she said. She looked around belligerently at the flickering sea of upturned faces. 'Otherwise you may as well just shove your candle up your arse.'

CHAPTER TWENTY

It took God and Summer a day and a morning to reach the Little Potoroo Creek road site. Brian and Liz from EGCGs had got there before them and were preparing for an invasion. Already more than sixty protesters had found their way to the blockade. The success of Mourn till Dawn suggested that hundreds — if not thousands — more were likely to follow up on Ciaron's salutary advice. Brian and Liz had put the first arrivals to work digging out latrines away from the camp and the nearby Thirsty Creek so that it wouldn't be polluted by run-off. Others strung up tarpaulins, pegged ground sheets, and set up the camp kitchen. The first truckload of organic vegetables — paid for by Summer's rave — had just arrived, and sacks of potatoes, carrots, onions, cabbages, beans, cauliflower and zucchinis sat on the ground alongside a mountain of pumpkins, waiting to be put away and stored. Summer had every right to feel elated but instead she slumped to the ground alongside the vegetables, utterly exhausted.

'Summer!'

A girl she recognised from a north-coast blockade came running towards her. They'd shared a truck together on the journey back south. Other voices called out and she recognised faces from other blockades and demonstrations, from fundraising raves, from lonely highways, from various squats and communes — all of them running towards her. This was normally the moment she loved most, the renewal of old friendships and the beginning of the bonding that would help see them through the hard times ahead. But the fire trails, the load she was forced to carry and God's relentless pace had left her drained of everything except her smile. She staggered to her feet in time to meet the first embrace. Rest and good food the doctor had said, and right then she was in urgent need of both.

'Hi!' she said. 'Hi!' Her face lit up as she greeted friends she hadn't seen since Tasmania or the blockade at Sellers Road. She looked around for God to introduce him, but he'd already slipped away. Her excitement had buoyed her up and got her back on her feet, but excitement also needs energy to draw upon and Summer's reserves were exhausted. Too many people were talking at once, too many people telling her things, too many people wanting her attention. She felt a stirring in her stomach sweep upwards like a summer willy-willy and closed her eyes. A guy she'd met during the forest embassy protest in Canberra caught her as her knees buckled.

'Christ! You all right, Summer?' He gently lowered her to the ground. The sky above her closed out in a ring of anxious faces.

'Get Liz!' somebody shouted.

‘It’s okay, I’m here.’ Liz pushed through the crowd and knelt down beside the unconscious girl. ‘Okay everybody, the best thing you can do right now is go back to whatever it is you should be doing. We’ve got to get all the food put away in case any of the town thugs come. This protest will be over before it starts if we’ve got nothing to eat. Okay?’ Summer’s friends dispersed reluctantly.

Summer opened her eyes and looked around unsteadily.

‘What happened?’ she said.

‘You tell me. You fainted.’

‘I feel sick.’

‘Just lie still.’

‘I feel stuffed, Liz. Don’t know when I’ve ever felt more stuffed in my life.’

‘You came down with God, right?’ said Liz. ‘He just passed me on the way to the treehouses. No g’day, no hello, no acknowledgement.’

‘He’s not in a talking mood,’ said Summer.

‘Any stops for rest?’

‘We camped overnight.’

‘Big deal. And force marched the rest. Tell him about your hepatitis?’

‘Yes.’

Liz shook her head helplessly. ‘He’s hopeless sometimes. He’s gone to set up one of the treehouses. Doubtless he knows exactly which one he wants, which one fits his tarpaulin, which one his mattress fits in. He’s done a great job of preparation — the treehouses saved the first arrivals when the locals got nasty one night — and he’s prepared tripods as well which only need putting up. He did it all himself, God knows when.’

'Man on a mission,' said Summer. She struggled to sit up. 'He just ignored me when I said I needed to rest.'

'He didn't mean to hurt you,' said Liz softly. 'Probably couldn't help himself. Unlike you and me, and most other people for that matter, God can only handle one issue at a time. It's not his fault, it's the only way he can get by. To do one thing he has to shut out everything else or he can't cope. That's one of the reasons people like us are attracted to him. When we're with him he doesn't just give us his attention, he gives us all of his attention. Think about that. That's the highest compliment anyone can pay you, but it has its down side. When something more important comes along, you've got to be prepared to stand aside. God's on a mission, you said that yourself, and until his mission's completed you're going to have to leave him be.'

'What do you mean?'

'He doesn't need you right now. You'll be more use to us down here, rallying the troops. Leave him be. God knows exactly what he needs to do and how to do it. He doesn't need your help or mine. If he needs something he'll come and get it. Let him go, and in the meantime we'll get you fed and rested.' Liz looked critically at Summer, took note of her pale clammy skin and obvious exhaustion. 'It mightn't be a bad idea if you came back to Osbourne with Brian and me for a couple of days.'

'I'd rather stay here.'

'Summer, nothing's going to happen for a week, and when it does you'll know all about it. We want you fit and strong. What's a day or two?'

'I'll tell God.' Summer struggled to get back up. Liz gently but firmly prevented her.

'No, I'll tell him. You stay put. I'll bring you back some water.'

Summer watched Liz stride off and fought back tears. The camp site was already throbbing with activity and soon it would be bustling with hundreds and possibly even thousands of activists. This was what she'd been looking forward to all through winter when it had been so hard to feel good about anything. The thought of leaving so soon after arriving, and leaving God behind, brought bitter disappointment. Yet she didn't have the strength to fight. There's no cure, Dr Grainger had said, except rest, good food and time. Summer didn't need a degree to work out she'd pushed too hard too soon and was paying the penalty with a relapse.

'You okay?' Summer's friend from the north-coast blockade had come back to check on her.

'Liz wants me to spend a couple of days at her place to rest up.'

'Place to be,' said her friend. 'Can you imagine all those poor bunnies on the road between here and Melbourne? Hundreds of them fighting for the same lift. You wouldn't swap places for quids.'

Summer had been through it all before, the boredom and desperation, the hunger and thirst, stuck between towns on desolate highways, accepting rides she'd normally wave on. But that was all part of life on the road. On other days one ride would take you right to where you wanted to go. She loved being on the road, loved the freedom. 'Yes I would,' she said.

CHAPTER TWENTY-ONE

'That's all your radio plays, is it? Friggin' country.'

'You don't like it you can get out and walk.' The truckie looked across at the girl he'd just picked up. She was slim but had strong shoulders, like she could have been a swimmer. Her hair was cut short with blonde streaks and she had the sort of pouting lips he liked.

'Thinkin' about it,' she said.

'Stuff you, sister. Look at these pricks here.' They roared past a couple of guys with bedrolls and backpacks, trying to thumb a ride. 'Coulda picked up a hundred hitchhikers today.'

'Not if you told 'em you were gunna play country for the next four hundred ks.'

'Okay. Find another station. But none of that head-bangin' shit. What's ya name anyway?'

'My name? Let's see, what day is it? Ronnie, today I'm Ronnie.' She leant forward and pressed a button on the radio. Somebody was singing a saccharine cover of a Cat Stevens classic. She hit another button, scored Genesis and sat back.

‘Ronnie,’ said the truckie. ‘Strange name for a girl. What’s it short for? Veronica?’

‘Ronald,’ said Ronnie.

‘Come off it,’ said the truckie.

‘My old man wanted a boy,’ said Ronnie. She twisted out of her seatbelt and pulled her sweater off over her head. The truckie stole a quick glance sideways to watch. She wore a light tight-fitting jumper beneath. He tried to work out if she was wearing a bra. ‘Bastard was pissed off when I was born without a cock.’

‘Hey, watch your language,’ he said.

‘Yeah? And you watch the friggin’ road.’

The driver pretended not to hear. Ronnie decided he was a bloke she’d have to watch. There was something furtive and plain unpleasant about him. All the vibes she was getting were bad.

‘Where you going anyway?’

‘Told you. East Gippsland. Orbost.’

‘These other blokes hitchin’, they all goin’ to the same place?’

‘Probably.’ She told the driver all about the blockade.

‘You one of them ferals?’

‘No, I’m one of them activists.’

‘Suppose you lot sleep around a bit.’

‘Sure,’ said Ronnie. ‘Sometimes I sleep up around Ballina way, sometimes down around the Tarkine in Tasmania, now I’m going to sleep around East Gippsland.’ She decided the driver was definitely worth watching. Right on sunset they passed two more hitchhikers waiting by a truck stop just outside of Morwell.

Sky and The Dick watched the truck roar past.

* * *

Ciaron woke with a hangover you could photograph and wished she'd done hash instead of booze. The squat was deathly quiet and dark which was unusual for a Saturday afternoon. It took her a moment to realise that her fellow residents were still sleeping off the candlelight vigil, had already shot through to East Gippsland, or were off somewhere else. She pulled on her jeans and boots and staggered over to the light switch. It was on but the power was off. She fumbled her way to the bathroom, stale beer slopping from side to side in her gut, sat on a wet seat and cursed. Some of the guys had simply aimed into the darkness and hoped for the best. She lurched through to the kitchen, where weak light filtered through a rippled glass window, and searched for something to eat, some bread or cold pasta, anything to soak up the beer still inside her. Somebody had left some Weet-Bix in a packet in the cupboard. She took four, poured cold water over them in the absence of milk, and sprinkled some sugar over them in the absence of honey. It tasted terrible but did the trick. Above all she needed a caffeine hit, but there was no electricity to heat the water. She opened the drawer where they kept candles to get some light so she could collect her things, but somebody had donated them to the previous night's festivities. That did it.

Ciaron kept her bike in a shed in the yard at the back of the squat, chained to an old truck wheel she'd nicked from a wrecking yard. She forced the back door open and wedged it as wide as it would go. She had to work the handlebars a bit to get them through the doorway but after that it was plain sailing. Her Kawasaki was no superbike, but at 350cc was no motor scooter either. When she kickstarted it the four casuals still asleep in the squat woke up in a hurry. God knows what they thought when Ciaron blasted past them with her headlight on full beam. She rode past the bathroom and kitchen, past the partitioned-off rooms where Thalia, Barry and the other permanents slept, and down the half-dozen steps to the semi-permanents' room. Someone threw a shoe at her but she took no notice. She swung the handlebars around so that the headlights lit the one and only wardrobe and turned off the motor.

'Fuck you, Ciaron!' someone yelled, but someone else laughed. Ciaron took no notice of either.

She dropped her jeans and climbed into her leathers, packed her carryall with undies, sweaters, t-shirts and jeans, and bungie-strapped it onto her carrier along with her sleeping bag. What else? She searched along the side of her mattress for her toothbrush and soap but some needy arsehole had got there first. Her hat. Ciaron had an old Akubra which she'd picked up at a second-hand shop and kept hidden on top of the wardrobe. She reached up half-heartedly, knowing that the odds of it still being there were roughly equal to her winning the Australian motorcycle grand prix. When her hand brushed it she felt simultaneously delighted and affronted that nobody had thought it worth stealing. She dusted it down by bashing it against her thigh. What the hell was wrong with it, she wondered? Her fellow squatmates weren't normally so choosy. Something else was missing and she couldn't figure out what. Then she remembered. Stretch. She'd promised to give Stretch a lift. She went back up the steps to the secluded corner where Stretch liked to doss down and felt around. There was no one there. In the back of her mind there were fuzzy images of Stretch linking up with some of his old musician mates and giving the ganja a solid workout. Probably be days before he came back down for a landing.

Ciaron kicked the bike back into life and walked it up the stairs, flicking it in and out of gear. She rode out the way she'd come, stopping briefly to slam the back door shut. Only then did it occur to her to check her wallet for money. A ten, a five, a twenty and — miracle of all miracles — a fifty! Eighty-five bucks. She'd never woken with a hangover and money in her life. But then, after her little speech in front of the crowd and the TV cameras, there had been no shortage of people clamouring to buy her a beer.

She roared out of the yard and pointed her front wheel towards East Gippsland. Allowing for breaks for coffee and a pee, she still reckoned she could do it in a bit over four hours. She stopped by the side of the road after just thirty minutes, threw up a disgusting slurry of Weet-Bix and stale beer, burped like a real bloke, threw her leg back over her bike and felt a helluva lot better. That was the one problem with a full face helmet. You had to stop if you wanted to puke.

* * *

Georgie, Matt and Gretta had intended to split up because the chance of anybody stopping to pick up three hitchhikers at once was more remote than McDonald's opening at Mawson Station. But an old couple who liked fishing and had a shack down at Mallacoota stopped to pick them up in their old Holden Kingswood. It meant that the three of them had to sit in the back with their packs on their lap, but that was something they could put up with. The old bloke was a talker and when he talked the speedo, which should've been sitting on a hundred, slipped back below seventy. Even so, they still would have made good time if the old bloke hadn't mentioned his back, and if Gretta hadn't insisted that he stop so she could harmonise him. He pulled off the road into a parking area and lay down on the grass. The old fisherman thought it was fantastic, thought it was Christmas, went on and on about how he could sense where her hands were by the heat. He drove his wife nuts.

'I've got a bad back too, you know,' she complained. 'And arthritis in me hip.'

Gretta insisted on harmonising her as well.

* * *

Lyndal and Austrian Anke accepted a ride through to Warragul with a bloke going home to visit his folks for the weekend. He did the right thing and dropped them off on the exit side of town, but it didn't take Lyndal long to realise the mistake they'd made. Anyone driving further on with space for hitchhikers had already picked up someone. They'd passed countless hitchhikers on the way, some in pairs, some trying it alone, and had even waved in joking triumph to those they'd recognised. Now the shoe was on the other foot and they were the ones being waved at.

Lyndal had never had much trouble hitchhiking before. Being a girl she presented no threat to the driver, and had quite often been picked up by women who'd never consider stopping for a man. She was also good-looking, a factor which had won her a few rides. Anke was also an experienced hitchhiker and every bit as attractive as Lyndal. She had dark hair and an olive complexion where Lyndal was fair, and had the novelty of being Austrian. She'd hitchhiked across from Western Australia and had been to all the interesting places along the way that Lyndal had only dreamt of visiting.

They sat on their packs and waited for their luck to change, filling in the time by exchanging experiences. Lyndal heard a car decelerate and felt briefly hopeful, until she heard the slick racing double-shuffle through the gears and the crackle of the exhaust. She didn't need to look up to know the local boys were on the make.

'Hey, you wanna ride?'

There were four guys, none of whom topped twenty, crammed into a V8 Torana. Just where the girls were supposed to fit was an issue they hadn't bothered to address. It was easy to be rude but Lyndal could see they were just out for fun.

'G'day! How're ya doing?' she said.

'You wanna come back to Chook's place?' asked the front passenger eagerly. 'We got plenty of dope.'

'Next time,' said Lyndal, still smiling. 'We've got to keep moving. Unless you guys are going to East Gippsland you're no use to us.'

'Ja,' said Anke. 'Piss off so ve can get lift.'

The guys burst out laughing at her accent, obviously thinking it was put on. 'See ya,' called the driver. 'We prefer blondes anyway.' He dropped the clutch and burnt rubber as they roared off.

‘Just kids,’ said Anke.

‘I counted three empty cars and a truck go past while we were talking to them,’ said Lyndal. ‘Bloody morons.’

They sat and watched more cars go by, getting more depressed by the minute. Lyndal stood up when she saw a ute slowing down and stuck out her thumb. There was just one bloke in it and plenty of room alongside for two girls. She flashed her most charming smile. She didn’t realise what was happening when the man flicked his arm out the driver’s window. She was concentrating on making eye contact and failed to see the beer can hurtling towards her until the last instant. She tried to bring her hands up but it was too late. The lip of the half-filled can thudded into her left eyebrow and split it open like a knee through worn jeans. She screamed and dropped to the ground.

‘Animal!’ yelled Anke. She crossed her left arm across her body and gave the continental salute with rigid right forearm and index finger.

But Arnie only laughed and hit the gas. He never missed. Lyndal was his second victim for the day and he had another six pack to go.

* * *

The Dick with Ears was seriously pissed off. They’d stood on the same spot for three hours and done nothing but watch cars and trucks go past. It looked like they’d never get a lift. Whenever he’d hitched with Summer and the lifts stopped coming, she always did something outrageous. Sometimes she just stepped out into the middle of the road and flagged cars down. A lot of people were affronted and some told her to get stuffed, but she also got a lot of lifts that way. Sometimes she stood outside petrol stations and put the hard word on people as they were leaving. Summer was always so high and good-natured, even when people turned her down, that nobody really turned sour on her. She got a lot of lifts that way too. The trouble was Darren wasn't hitching with Summer but with Sky, and all she did was moan about her headache and her tiredness. The Dick was tired as well, but Sky was almost out on her feet. She was relying on him when he was used to relying on Summer.

He wished they hadn't partied on so long, then stayed to help clean up the litter. When someone had suggested breakfast at the café in Little Swanston Street they'd automatically tagged along. When someone else suggested heading straight down to the blockade, they'd thought that was a good idea too. By the time they'd collected their things from the squat and made their way to the Princes Highway it was well past lunchtime. They were tired before they'd even started and still had four hundred kilometres ahead of them. The Dick realised he had to do something. When a Commodore filled up with gas he stepped in front of it as it was leaving.

'Out the bloody way,' said the driver. He jammed his hand on the horn and left it there. The Dick stepped aside. He tried the same trick on a woman in a Pajero. She was more polite but the result was the same. Darren thought he'd struck gold with the sixth car, a Ford Falcon with a florid middle-aged driver and a woman alongside who seemed to be asleep.

'Take youse ta Sale,' said the driver. 'S'where we're goin'.'

The way the driver spoke made Darren think he'd had a stroke, but he wasn't about to ask for his medical record. Sky was pitiful in her gratitude as she climbed into the back and pulled on her seatbelt. Darren put both backpacks on the seat between them and buckled up. Sky dropped off to sleep immediately. The Dick had a rude awakening seconds later when the driver pulled out onto the road right in front of a Nissan Patrol. The driver of the Nissan slammed on his brakes, hammered the horn and still had to swerve over the centre line to miss them. Darren could hardly believe it when his driver gave no sign of even having noticed.

'Name's Mike, but call me Lucky,' he said.

'Darren,' said The Dick. 'She's Sky.' He figured he knew why people called him Lucky.

'Bettin' man?' asked Lucky.

'What?' said Darren.

'Gee-gees, you know, 'orses?'

'Nah,' said Darren. 'You?'

'Where we been, eh. Flebbington.' Lucky turned around to see if Darren understood and smiled. He didn't seem to want to turn back. Darren watched in horror as the Ford started to veer across the road.

'Jesus!' he said.

Lucky turned around and corrected, totally unfazed. 'Big day,' he said. 'Bloody ripper, atcherly.' He started to tell Darren about the winners they'd backed, but Darren wasn't listening. He couldn't drag his eyes away from the road in front of them. Every time a car approached the opposite way he held his breath, sighed with relief every time they passed by safely, and steadily grew more and more angry.

'Want me to drive?' said Darren.

'Piss off! Whassa matter? You're bad as she is. Nag, nag, nag. Too mush ta drink, she says. Huh! Lookit it. Fasa sleep. Bloody snorin' its head off before! Too mush ta drink, she says. She's the one snorin' not me.' Right on cue his wife snored like someone ripping canvas. 'Listen to it!'

Darren watched the speedo climb past eighty, past ninety, past one hundred and head off into the twilight zone. The old pisspot in front had stopped talking and seemed to be watching where they were going. The Dick was about to relax a little when he noticed Lucky's chin drop onto his chest and the car head back across the centre line. The bastard had fallen asleep! He leapt up and reached between the two front seats. He grabbed the steering wheel just as the driver's hands slipped off it. He pulled it hard left to get them back on their own side of the road. Up ahead an oncoming car was flashing its lights. His elbow whacked Lucky across his ear.

'Fuck ya doing?' asked Lucky.

'Ya fell asleep ya dumb bastard!' said Darren. 'Pull over!'

'Get fucked!'

'Pull over, shithead,' snarled Darren. He grabbed a handful of Lucky's thinning hair and pulled it back as hard as he could. With his other hand he tried to steer.

'Aghhhhhh …' said Lucky. 'Fuck off!' The oncoming car whizzed past, horn blaring.

Darren pulled harder. 'Hit the brakes or I'll rip your fuckin' head off!'

'Fuck off!'

Darren yanked his hair hard enough to lift Lucky's bum off the seat.

'Okay!' he screamed.

'Wassat?' asked his wife.

'What's happening?' asked Sky.

'Fuckin' scalped me,' moaned Lucky.

Darren guided the Ford to a halt by the side of the road. He leapt out and raced around to the driver's side, opened the door and pulled the key out of the ignition. 'You stupid bastard!' he yelled. He grabbed the front of Lucky's coat and tried to drag him out of the car.

'Dun hit me! Dun hit me!' screamed Lucky. He covered his face with his hands. 'Ya fuckin' scalped me!'

'You stupid bastard!'

'Whaddya doing? Whaddya doing to him?' screamed Lucky's wife.

Sky started crying.

Darren brought his fist down hard on the roof of the Ford. It left a dent the size of a football but made him feel better.

'Fuckin' shut up! All of ya!' He glared at Lucky, his wife and then at Sky. They all shut up instantly and stared fearfully at him. 'Right!' he said. 'I'm gunna drive. Anyone wanna argue?'

'No,' said Lucky. He still had his hands up shielding his face.

'No,' said his wife.

'What the hell's got into you?' said Sky tearfully.

Darren helped Lucky into the back seat, slammed the door on him and climbed into the front. 'Now I don't want to hear a sound from any of ya. Understand?'

'Can I sit in the front with you?' said Sky.

'No,' said Darren. He glared at her. Sky's tits were as good as Summer's but that was where all comparisons ended.

* * *

The police in Warragul were sympathetic but there wasn't much they could do except offer Lyndal and Anke a lecture on the dangers of hitchhiking and give them a lift around to the local hospital. Neither of the girls had taken the ute's licence number, or knew what make it was. They even disagreed on the colour. Lyndal let the duty nurse put eight stitches in her eyebrow, swallowed two Panadeine Fortes, then asked if they could sleep the night there. The nurse said no but managed to scrounge two dinners for them. The roast beef was overcooked, grey and smothered in packet gravy, the cabbage was stewed and cold, and the mashed potato had the same consistency as plasticine. Doubtless it looked impressive on the nutritionist's charts. The two girls cleaned their plates anyway and wandered back onto the highway, knowing that no trucks ran on Saturday night, and the only traffic they were likely to see would be local. They'd just about resigned themselves to sleeping in the bush when light misty rain started to fall. It was the kind of rain that took its time but ultimately saturated everything. They walked back to a petrol station that had a diner attached, ordered two coffees, and wondered if anyone would mind if they nursed them for the next eight hours or so.

* * *

'Got a boyfriend?' asked the truckie.

'Heaps,' said Ronnie.

'What's he look like?'

'What do they look like? Well, for a start they're all big blokes, bigger than you. All gun freaks. One's in the army, the SAS. One's a detective in the vice squad. He's married and I'm one of his vices. He reckons he's going to leave his wife sometime soon within the next fifty years. One plays football for Hawthorn. Used to play in the local comp up at Ballarat. He's sat on the bench twice and his life's ambition is to make Hawthorn's starting line-up. Then there's the South Melbourne cricket team, but they're not in season yet. What about you? Got a girl in every town you pass?'

'Don't need to. Get all I need pickin' up hitchhikers.' He turned to leer at her. Ronnie met his stare without flinching.

'Well ya dipped out here.'

'Dunno about that.'

'Well let me explain it to you. In simple words. I'm bullshitting about my boyfriends. I'm a dyke.'

'What?'

'I'm a dyke. I like women. I lied about all those guys, especially the South Melbourne cricket team. It's actually the South Melbourne netball team.'

'Bullshit!' said the driver. He turned and glared at her. Took one hand off the wheel and waved a fist in her face. 'Don't give me that shit.'

'Get your fist out of my face.'

'You know the rules, lady. Nobody rides for free.'

'Fine. Let me out.'

'No way. You've had your ride. Now you gotta pay up.'

'No friggin' way!'

He reached over with his left hand to grab her by the back of her neck. She twisted free.

'C'mon, ya bitch, what's one more screw to you? A ride for a ride. That's the deal.'

'Fuck off!'

The back of his hand crashed into the side of her face. 'I told you before. Watch your language.' The truck had started to weave and he needed both hands to bring it back under control. Once the truck had steadied he took one hand off the wheel to unbutton his fly. 'Let you off with a blow job.'

'Just let me off.' Ronnie knew she was in trouble and fished desperately in her bag for something — anything — that she could use to protect herself. All she could think of was the girl who'd been murdered; she didn't want to end up like her.

'No worries. Soon as you've paid for the ride. Be glad to get rid of ya.' He pulled his dick out and stroked it. 'Ya can do it hard or ya can do it easy. What do ya want?'

'Easy,' said Ronnie hastily. She rubbed the side of her face where his backhander had caught her.

'Smart girl,' he said. 'Now, ya got nice lips. Let's see what they can do with this.'

'Okay,' she said. 'Okay. You want a blow job, I'll give you a blow job.'

'Show us ya tits first, I wanna see ya tits.'

Ronnie pulled up her sweater. One of the driver's questions was instantly answered: Ronnie wasn't wearing a bra. He reached across and squeezed her breasts like he was tooting an old-fashioned car horn.

'Nice ones! Now do it!' He leant back to give her room. Ronnie smiled and wet her lips teasingly with her tongue. 'Do it, you bitch!' he said.

'Keep your eyes on the road,' she said. 'Unless you want to die head on with a hard on.'

'Come on!' he said.

She reached across him, lowered her head over the target, then looked up teasingly at him.

'Get on with it!' he snarled.

'Eyes on the road,' she said. As soon as he looked back at the road she whipped her arm up and fired the can of insect repellent she'd taken from her pack. It blasted him point blank in the eyes. He screamed and tried to grab her but she was too quick. The truck lurched, started to fishtail. The driver fought blindly for control.

'Fuckin' bitch!'

'You're on the wrong side of the road!' Ronnie screamed.

He pulled the wheel left, corrected, pulled left again, making lightning corrections in a desperate effort to dissipate the pendulum effect. The truck lurched crazily.

'Stupid bitch! Stupid bitch!' screamed the driver.

'Oh shit!' said Ronnie.

* * *

Ciaron was about to pass the truck when it started weaving. She backed right off when it crossed the centre line. The load was trying to steer the truck and it seemed inevitable that the whole rig would roll or jackknife. Against all odds the driver pulled his rear wheels back into line with the front ones and gently coaxed his rig back over the centre line and onto the left side of the highway. The truck braked erratically onto the shoulder and lurched to a stop. Ciaron pulled up behind it in case the driver was sick and needed help. She was about to kill her headlight when the passenger side door opened and a backpack flew out. A girl tried to follow it but she was grabbed and pulled back. Ciaron had seen enough. She jumped off her bike, raced around to the driver's side and ripped the door open. She damn near ripped it off its hinges. The makers built them tough for truckies, but not for fire-breathing dykes on bikes with a pathological hatred of rapists. The cab light was on and the girl inside was bleeding from the nose and mouth. The truckie had his back to her so Ciaron did the only thing she knew which was guaranteed to get his attention. She made a grab for his nuts, and was gratified to find his fly already gaping wide and his dick standing up invitingly. She grabbed it and ripped it towards her as if she was pulling the starting rope on a Victa lawnmower. The driver gasped and spun around. Ciaron's helmet met his head mid-turn in a deafening Liverpool kiss that The Dick would've been proud of. She dragged the driver out of the cab and onto the road. Her boot crashed into his jaw, smashed into his nose, thudded into his ribs, ground into his hips. She saved her most vicious kick for his balls. The driver didn't even groan. He'd long since lost consciousness.

Ciaron stopped kicking when her legs got tired and dragged the limp form onto the grass verge. The girl was on her hands and knees vomiting, her top torn and modesty a minor issue.

'C'mon,' said Ciaron. 'We gotta get outta here. Clean you up down the road. Here, put your sweater on.'

'What about him?'

'Who gives a shit?'

The girl did as she was told and followed Ciaron to the bike. Ciaron tied her pack on, threw her leg over, and nodded for the girl to do the same. The girl wrapped her arms around her and hung on for dear life as the bike roared off. Ciaron was impressed. The girl had taken a helluva beating but there were no tears or complaints. The wind from the slipstream must have been freezing her tits off but she made no attempt to ask her to slow down. It was also clear she'd been on the back of a bike before. Ciaron was doubly impressed.

She rode on to Bairnsdale, pulled in at the all-night service station and rode straight up to the toilet. The girl looked a bit surprised when Ciaron followed her into the ladies, laughed when she took off her helmet.

'Stuff me,' she said.

'Did ya think I was a bloke?' said Ciaron.

'Funny that,' said Ronnie. She glanced at herself in the mirror, did a doubletake, then took a long hard look. Blood streaked her face, dribbled from her nose and mouth and one eye was making a valiant attempt to close over. 'Glad you came along,' she said. 'I think the guy was about to throw a shitty.'

'What happened?'

'He wanted a blow job. A ride for a ride is how he put it. I figured the price was too high.' She took off her sweater and handed it to Ciaron, pulled the tattered remains of her top over her head and threw it in the paper towel bin. She didn't bother sticking the plug in the sink because it was more of a mess than she was. She splashed water over her face and arms, wet a paper towel and began to clean up. Ciaron couldn't help staring and had to force herself to turn away from the girl's nakedness. 'What's the matter?' said Ronnie.

'I'll go order some coffees,' she said. It seemed unfair to take advantage of the girl after what she'd been through. She might have thought twice about stripping down if she knew her rescuer was a lesbian. Ciaron stole another look as the girl turned back to the sink and began splashing more water over her face. The resemblance was absolutely uncanny. Face was a little fuller and her shoulders broader and stronger, but she had the same colouring, same sort of hacked-about hair with rat-tails, same perky boobs and bottom. 'By the way, what's your name?'

'Well it ain't Ronnie,' said Ronnie.

'Okay,' said Ciaron. 'Then I won't call you Ronnie.' She hung the girl's sweater on the toilet door and went out into the night.

* * *

Summer fell into bed with one of Liz's no-frills spaghetti bologneses filling every inch of her stomach, and wondered how God was coping, wondered if he'd come down out of his tree for dinner. Part of her wanted to worry about him and miss him, but her need for sleep was overpowering. She slept through the banging on the front door at eleven o'clock that night, and again at three in the morning. Years of sleeping in squats had taught her how to sleep through anything. She awoke around dawn, feeling wrecked and more exhausted than she had the night before, and realised she'd be going nowhere for a few days. She could feel the old familiar cloud settling around her and tried desperately to shrug it off. This was a minor setback and nothing to get depressed about. Like a child saying prayers, she began by counting her blessings. She didn't have AIDS. Her body was healing itself. Mourn till Dawn had been a huge success and activists were descending upon the blockade like pushers on a rave. They'd get the turnout they'd hoped for, one that could tip the balance and save Little Potoroo Creek. She had every reason to feel positive. 'Dee-wit, dee-wit, biddle oooh, biddle oooh, dorf dorf,' she sang weakly.

Her legs carried her unsteadily and unwillingly to the bathroom. She didn't so much sit on the toilet as drop onto it. She washed her hands and face in cold water, dried them on the nearest towel and borrowed a toothbrush. She felt a little better, but above all she just wanted to crawl back into bed. She was tiptoeing past Liz and Brian's bedroom when she heard the sound of snoring coming from the office downstairs. There was only one person in the world she knew who snored like that. It took most of her remaining strength, and both hands on the bannister, to make her way down the stairs towards the noise. The office had sleeping bags spread all over the floor. Late arrivals with nowhere else to go. Alongside one was a familiar helmet and set of leathers.

'Ciaron?' she said. The snoring stopped and a voice muffled with sleep groaned. 'Ciaron?' she repeated, her excitement growing. A tired face rose from the other end of the sleeping bag.

'Hi, Sum,' said Ciaron sleepily. 'Hey, there's someone here you gotta meet. Sarah Jenkins. Name mean anything to ya?'

CHAPTER TWENTY-TWO

Miklos Bollok parked his battered Holden ute on the side of the highway, near the junction where Thirsty Creek Road ran off towards Little Potoroo Creek. He sat and watched for an hour until the Sunday morning sun made sitting in the car uncomfortable. He turned around to drive back home. He'd seen what he'd come to see: a steady stream of dole bludgers and dropouts taking the turn-off towards the blockade. Some rode motorbikes, some came in cars, but most were on foot, looking tired and dishevelled but seeming in good spirits. He found it hard to believe that such a motley assortment of misfits could ankle-tap his ambitions. Yet none of his boys were out hassling them, letting them know they weren't welcome, and there was no Nugget searching them for drugs. Miklos didn't need a lesson in issue management to realise why. He'd let his side down and the whole town resented him for it. It was okay for him to cheat, lie and pull dirty tricks so long as he didn't get caught. His cleverness made them all feel clever. But when he got caught, they shared his guilt and ridicule.

Miklos had let them down and he knew they needed time to get over the humiliation before they'd kick arse again with any kind of enthusiasm.

Instead of driving home he decided to head for his office. It wasn't just that he liked to remind himself of his achievements, which he did, but he believed he thought better in his office than he did at home. His chair groaned as he dropped his weight onto it, complained again as he pushed it back so he could swing his legs up onto his desk. Things had gone off the rails a bit but he saw no reason to panic. The important thing was not to make any more mistakes.

Sending Arnie to Melbourne hadn't been quite the smart idea it had seemed at the time. When Bernie had pressed him to whistle Arnie home, he made it sound like he was doing Bernie a favour, but he'd already made up his mind to recall Arnie anyway. Arnie had made his point and managed to give Townsend a message only the terminally stupid could ignore. The more immediate issue was what to do about the protesters. He looked up at his *Playboy* calendar. Work wasn't due to begin on the new road for a week at best, and even then there was no guarantee that DeCaF would get their act together. A week, maybe two. He studied his feet and tried to imagine what Clyde Townsend would do. What could he do that wouldn't backfire on him?

It slowly began to dawn on him that the smartest thing to do was to do nothing. One week sitting on your bum in a forest was a long time to do nothing, and it began to occur to him that it would feel even longer for the freaky kids down from the city. No clubs, no pubs, no drugs, no TV, no videos, nothing but boring trees, shitty weather and shitty food. He'd heard about the truck with its mountain of pumpkins and assorted vegetables and couldn't imagine that satisfying anybody. As far as he was concerned, vegetables were just something people stuck on the side of the plate to make the meal seem bigger. What if there was no meal to go with them? It suddenly seemed a good thing that the town had gone cold on him. Yeah, he was suddenly sure it was. There was nothing worse than getting set for a fight and then not having anyone to fight against. Let the protesters get bored, let them get dispirited, let them start drifting away back to Melbourne or wherever they came from. Let the media lose interest. Then, when everyone was busy looking elsewhere, he could make his move. He'd had to face blockades before and knew exactly what to expect. He smiled and wished he'd had the foresight to pick up Jan on his way in to the office. A little dictation would add the final brightener to his morning. He knew blockades, and also knew they were nothing that forty or fifty hard men with chainsaws couldn't handle.

Given the right moment.

Given the opportunity.

He smashed his fist into the palm of his hand and laughed out loud. His laughter was so loud he almost didn't hear the knock on his door.

'G'day,' said Bernie. 'Son, we need to talk.'

'Mr Bollok,' said Clyde Townsend cautiously.

'Jeez, Bernie, I'm gettin' worried about the company you keep.'

'Maybe you should be more worried about the company you keep,' said Bernie. 'You gunna stand there with your guts blockin' the door or ya gunna let us in?'

'This better be good, Bernie.' Miklos stood aside to let Bernie and Clyde Townsend past. Bernie went straight to the fridge, pulled out three cans of Carlton Draught and tossed one each to Miklos and Clyde.

'You're an ungrateful bastard,' said Bernie amiably. 'Been driving all bloody morning to get here, hanging out for a beer every bloody kilometre. Did I stop? Didn't even think about it.' He drained his can and hit the fridge for another. 'Left behind two of the sweetest things you ever laid eyes on in my bed, almost untouched. Things I do for you, and you never appreciate it.'

'Did I ask you to come here?' said Miklos.

'Ahhhh …' said Bernie. 'Fair point.'

'I asked him,' said Clyde.

'Why aren't I surprised?' said Miklos. 'Bernie, get your man another beer and one for me while you're at it. Now, tell me why I should be pleased to see you.'

'That business with the photos was nothing to do with me,' said Clyde.

'You drove all the way to tell me that?'

'Hear him out, son,' said Bernie. 'He knows Arnie put a bullet through his window, knows Arnie could shoot a pimple off a rat's bum from a hundred metres at night in the rain, and he knows he's not the flavour of the month down here. So why would he stick his neck out if he wasn't tellin' the truth?'

'I'm listening.'

'I had nothing to do with the photos,' said Clyde. 'But I know who took them.'

'Who?' Miklos's eyes hardened.

'Figure it out,' said Clyde. 'I didn't even know you'd sent Arnie after that weirdo in the bush, I didn't know he'd stolen your car, and I certainly didn't arrange for him to poison your men. In fact, I didn't know anything until you rang and told me, which is also when I advised you on what course of action to take. How long was it after you hung up on me that you took the hammer to your car. One hour? Maybe two?'

'Maybe two,' said Miklos grudgingly.

'How could I get a photographer down to Osbourne in two hours? Where would I send him? You hadn't even told me where your Toyota was or where you intended to smash it up. You could have done it in the yard, out in the bush, anywhere! Right?'

'Get to the point!'

'Point is, who knew what you were doing? Who saw you? I knew, you knew, but who else?'

'We know she's got the camera and we know she knows how to use it,' said Bernie.

'And she was on the freakin' back step watchin' me!' said Miklos.

'And she thought what you were doing was normal?' snapped Clyde.

'No fuckin' way! Bitch laughed, had a go at me.'

'She laughed at you and you just ignored her?'

'No way! Told her to remember what paid the grocery bill. Told her to piss off.'

'And did she?'

'Yeah!' Miklos stopped, closed his eyes and saw Cheryl get up and walk indoors. He stared at his beer, downed the dregs, then stared out of the window. Clyde let the silence hang.

'She's got the camera, got the knowhow and you gave her a motive,' said Bernie eventually. 'You pissed her off.'

'Yeah, but why send the photos to the *Gazette*? She's not stupid.'

'You tell us. Maybe she's pissed off at you. Maybe she thinks you're spending too much time with Jan. Who knows?'

Miklos caught the beer that Bernie threw at him. 'Makes sense that she did it — first person I thought of — but what I don't understand is why. Leave it with me.' His voice hardened. 'I'll get to the truth.'

'Meanwhile, can we talk about the other business at hand?' asked Clyde.

'Sure. Why not?' Miklos seemed relieved to move the conversation along. 'I think I've got things under control.'

'How?'

'Issue management, Mr Townsend, issue management. Piece of cake once you get the hang of it. Dunno why you think it makes you so bloody special. Town's gone off me temporarily, but I think I can use that to my advantage. Now, you listen to me for a change.' Miklos told them about his plan to bore the protesters into leaving, but deliberately left out any mention of the chainsaw hit squad follow-up.

'Not bad,' said Clyde. 'But I'd be tempted to take the opposing point of view.'

'What do you mean?' asked Miklos.

'The town needs you and needs you fighting their cause. More than anything else they want you back in control. Fact is, they'd rather love you than hate you. You're the only thing that stands between them and nothing. You go down, they go down with you. You succeed, they succeed. On the whole, most people would rather succeed.'

'What are you suggesting?'

'Your plan to bore the protesters into leaving might only result in boring your town into acquiescence. Once you accept the protesters, or even appear to accept them, the town will accept them too. They're frightened people and they'll take the line of least resistance unless someone stands up to lead them and tell them otherwise.' Townsend looked Miklos squarely in the eye. 'I think it's time you gave those drug-using, dropout, dole-bludging protesters something to think about. For once I think your instinctive recourse to violence is justified. We just have to keep the violence within reasonable bounds.'

'Like what?' said Miklos, clearly warming to the prospect.

'No rapes, no maiming, no mutilation, no killing. Basically, no injuries that would make a good photograph.'

'Been there before,' said Miklos.

'One other thing,' said Clyde. 'In my experience, boring protesters out of forests isn't very effective. They generally spend the time building fortifications, dozer pits, tripods, etc. They grow stronger while you grow weaker. Now, let me ask you this, how do you plan to rally the town?'

'Maybe take a few boys on a tripod-cutting expedition. Maybe take the night cart and dump a load of crap on their doorstep. If the smell doesn't shift them the flies will.'

'Sounds like Arnie and his mates. That's not enough. Those boys are thugs. It won't hurt if they do a bit of harassing on the side, but they're not representative of the town, the decent folk whose livelihood is threatened. You have to motivate the town.'

‘What do you have in mind?’ said Miklos.

‘There’s nothing like a nasty act of sabotage to bring people together. I mean, you know better than I do that felling trees is a dangerous business. Imagine if some of those protesters started spiking trees, and imagine if you sent some of your men to chop those same trees down, and imagine if one of the chainsaws happened to strike one of the spikes ...’

‘Jesus Christ!’ said Bernie. ‘You can’t be serious! Bloke could rip his bloody arm off. Could lose a bloody leg!’

‘Oh, he’s serious,’ said Miklos grimly. ‘He’s serious all right. Man’s a freakin’ gold-plated genius.’

* * *

Cheryl took her time driving home from Bairnsdale. She’d known her shots of Little Potoroo Creek were good but Heather McKeown had been bowled over.

‘Like Olegas Truchanas’s shots of the Franklin,’ she’d said. ‘Like Peter Dombrovskis’s.’ Cheryl had glowed. The two men were her heroes, and their photographs had alerted Australia to the spectacular beauty of Tasmania’s south-west wilderness areas. In fact Heather had been so impressed she’d taken the negative up to Melbourne to her ex-employers, and used their facilities so she could do the prints justice. She’d cropped and blown up different shots and pleaded with Cheryl to do limited editions and sell them through a Melbourne gallery where she had contacts. But Cheryl had other plans. Although she intended to frame and hang some of Heather’s prints — they were too good to hide in drawers — what she wanted to do more than anything else was paint a memorial to Little Potoroo Creek. To commit to oils what was shortly to be ripped into woodchips. She wanted to do it for posterity, but mostly she wanted to do it for God, to preserve something of the wilderness he loved. She honestly believed that on that magical morning, standing on God's rock, she'd captured the spirit and soul of Little Potoroo Creek on film. She also believed — which was the really exciting part — that she could translate it onto canvas. She couldn't stop smiling. It seemed that all the years of clicking shutters and dabbing away with her brushes had merely been her apprenticeship, her preparation for the project that lay ahead of her. Cheryl was convinced that at last she'd found her purpose in life.

She was mildly surprised when she turned into her drive and saw the Holden ute parked in the garage. Miklos usually liked to spend Sunday mornings drinking with the boys and the afternoons making Jan earn her keep. If Miklos was home he'd want a barbecue, and Cheryl's first thoughts were whether or not she'd taken any meat out of the freezer. She wanted to show him the prints Heather had done and tell him what she intended to do, but just as quickly realised that Miklos would do nothing more than nod politely. He just wasn't interested in her work. She parked her car halfway down the drive so she could enter by the front door and drop her prints off in her studio. She opened the front door and her heart stopped.

She stepped over the smashed frames and torn canvases, the flakes of plaster and wallpaper where the plugs supporting the pictures had been torn from the wall. Her blood ran cold. How had Miklos found out? She peered into the lounge, saw more piles of shattered wood and canvas and immediately knew what sort of devastation she'd find in her studio. She bent over quickly to slip the film box containing Heather's prints beneath one of the Chesterfield sofas. That done, all that was left to save was her marriage, her right to continue living in the comfort of Miklos's home, her freedom to keep painting, and perhaps even her life itself.

She had to fight the urge to turn and run, to hop in her car and drive and keep driving until she was beyond Miklos's reach. But that would mean giving up and losing more than she could bear to lose, even though an enraged Miklos was more terrifying than Pol Pot and his teenage torturers. Cheryl was more frightened than she'd ever believed she could be. When she was younger a drunken Arnie had been scary enough, but he didn't even come close to a sober Miklos. One glance into her studio confirmed her fears. She could cope with the destruction of her paintings, but every damaged negative represented images and records of long-gone forests that were lost forever. The senseless pointless destruction horrified and enraged her and in her rising anger she found the courage to continue down the hall, to face her accuser and her punishment. She found Miklos sitting at the kitchen table, playing with her Nikon. Her camera box with its array of lenses sat on the table alongside.

'Why?' she asked.

Miklos smiled, raised his hand and smashed her camera down hard on the edge of the table. The body split open and spilt its innards.

'Attack is the best form of defence, eh Cheryl? You come in here and ask me why?' He picked up her five-hundred-mil lens and smashed it. Then, one after another, worked his way through her camera case until every lens was reduced to glass crystals and scrap metal.

'You didn't answer me,' said Cheryl.

'Now that is interesting,' said Miklos. 'Every question deserves an answer, right? That the point you're making? So let me ask you a question, Cheryl, and make sure you answer it truthfully because I'm in no mood to be fucked around. Understand?'

'Yes. Was that your question?'

'Oh, you're good, Cheryl. There's not one man at the mill who wouldn't be shittin' his pants right now, but look at you. So cool. I admire that. No Cheryl, that wasn't my question. This is my question.' Miklos rose from his chair like a striking cobra and clamped a mighty hand around her jaw. He squeezed hard and increased the pressure until he saw tears roll from Cheryl's eyes. 'Why, Cheryl, why? Tell me why, you ungrateful bitch!' His last squeeze nearly popped her jaw out.

'Arrghhh ...' said Cheryl.

'Take your time,' said Miklos.

'Arrghhh ...'

'I heard you the first time.'

'Urrgh ... oh ... oh ...' Cheryl couldn't help herself; she began to sob. She'd never felt pain so intense and was convinced her jaw had been reduced to the same state as her camera and lenses.

'Come on, come on,' said Miklos. 'Don't make me lose my patience.' He faked another grab at Cheryl's jaw. She screamed.

'See!' said Miklos. 'It's workin'. You might think your jaw's broken, but believe me it isn't. It's still workin'. Now use it! Answer my fuckin' question! Why'd ya do it?'

'Oo wha . . .?'

'Do what? Is that what you said? Do fuckin' what! I don't believe you can be so fuckin' stupid!' He smashed both fists into her ears simultaneously. Cheryl dropped in a heap. 'Maybe you didn't hear the question. Maybe that'll help your concentration. Tell me! Why'd ya do it!'

'Ooo wha ...!'

'Stupid, fuckin' stupid!' His boot slammed into her shoulder and sent her flying across the floor. 'I never took you to be stupid, Cheryl. Now answer the question before I get angry! Why'd ya take the photos? Why'd ya send them to the papers? Answer me!'

Cheryl wasn't stupid. She realised she had nothing to gain and everything to lose by admitting her guilt. There had to be doubt in Miklos's mind, maybe only a shred, but that was all she had going for her. Either way she knew she was going to cop a hiding like she'd never had before, not from her father, not from Arnie. The one reassuring thing was that wounds healed eventually, and eventually — as long as she held out — things would one day return to normal.

'Wan me,' she managed to say.

'What's that? Wasn't you? Is that what you said? Wrong answer.' His boot thudded into her ribs. Cheryl gasped and curled up into a ball. She squeezed her eyes tightly together to stop the tears and tried hard to think of her beautiful prints of Little Potoroo Creek, her reason for living, her reason for not giving in. Sooner or later she knew Miklos would knock her unconscious and she'd get some respite. Until then she had nothing but pain to look forward to.

* * *

It was the cold rather than the pain that woke Cheryl, but the pain wasn't long coming. Her body was battered from the beating and stiff from lying on the hard kitchen floor. She concentrated on finding ways to breathe that didn't hurt. Down the hallway her antique grandfather clock chimed in the darkness, declaring it two in the morning. She tried to push herself up onto her elbows but the pain drove her back down. There wasn't a place on her body that didn't screech in agony. She lay unmoving, realising she had to accustom herself to the pain before trying again. She had to get to the toilet, had to wash off the dried blood which cracked and pulled every time she tried to move, had to find a more comfortable place to lie down. Around two-thirty she heard the ute pull into the drive, heard the car door slam, the back door open, and Miklos's boots on the hardwood floor as he strode past her. She heard him fart and urinate, and the duration of his pee hammering into the pool in the bottom of the toilet told her where he'd been and what he'd been doing since he'd tired of beating her. He belched long and loud, and Cheryl imagined she could smell the alcohol on his breath. She wondered if he'd left Jan in the same condition he'd left her. She heard the bed groan as he threw himself upon it without bothering to undress.

Cheryl gritted her teeth when she realised what she had to do and the pain she'd have to endure. She pushed herself up onto her elbows, gasped but didn't cry out.

The garage seemed a light year away, a journey far beyond her capabilities, but what choice did she have?

Miklos was deep in alcoholic sleep when the chainsaw ripped into life centimetres away from his right ear. He forced his eyes open and woke up to confront a nightmare. He screamed in fear for the first time in his life.

'You bathted ...!' said Cheryl.

'No!' Miklos brought his hands up to protect his head.

Cheryl revved the chainsaw, swung it in an arc and chopped it down hard across his legs.

'Arrrghhh!' screamed Miklos. He tried to get away, feet and hands scrabbling across the mattress, tangling in the sheets. It took five or six endless mind-shredding seconds before he realised there was no blood and no pain, just the weight of the chainsaw across his legs and the heat and vibrations from its screaming motor. 'Jesus, Cheryl! Oh sweet Jesus!'

Cheryl pushed the kill button and the chainsaw stuttered into silence. She let it fall onto the floor.

'Juth two things, Miklos. You lithin to me and lithin good. One, it wathn't me. Two, if you ever hit me again I'll leave the chain on and do you for real. Now move over, you bathted, you're on my thide.'

Miklos moved and Cheryl eased herself painfully into bed alongside him. She passed out immediately. Miklos spent the rest of the night staring up at the ceiling. It took forever for the pins and needles in his legs to fade.

PART THREE

A THRILL LIKE SEX

CHAPTER TWENTY-THREE

Summer slept for three days, her sleep interrupted only by meals and her daily shower, which Liz insisted upon. Despite her frustration at being unable to take part in the preparations for the blockade, she couldn't help feeling a growing sense of excitement. Every day the old Roneo machine in the office below her bedroom pumped out leaflets with maps of the blockade sites, pointing out the kitchen, eating area, toilet sites, bathing areas, rubbish sites and recycling bins. They came complete with instructions on toilet protocol — toilets must be used on all occasions — and washing protocol, aimed at eliminating the run-off of soap and shampoos into the stream. The reverse side of the leaflet urged restraint once the confrontation began, and gave advice on what to do in the event of arrest and who to contact for legal assistance should the arrest progress to prosecution. According to Liz they'd already distributed a thousand and run off an additional five hundred. She feared even that would not suffice. Summer was ecstatic. It was hard to believe that as little as a week earlier they'd been worried that nobody would turn up.

The first inkling Summer got that things were slipping off the rails came on the evening of the third day when she crept downstairs to watch the news on TV. She was hoping to see something about Little Potoroo Creek and in that respect wasn't disappointed. But what she saw wasn't what she'd wanted to see.

Storekeepers from Osbourne to Orbost complained to reporters about an epidemic of shoplifting and pointed the finger squarely at the protesters. They told of gangs moving in on supermarkets, some causing a distraction while others stripped shelves. Publicans complained bitterly of missing slabs of beer; residents of missing chooks and eggs and plundered vegetable gardens. She heard Police Sergeant Nugent say that in his opinion the thefts were a deliberate and well-thought-out operation planned by the organisers of the blockade.

'That's bullshit!' said Summer. 'They say the same thing every time there's a blockade and the media always fall for it.'

'This time they might have some justification,' said Liz quietly.

'This protest has attracted a lot of people,' added her husband Brian. 'Unfortunately they're not all the kind we'd ideally like to attract.'

'We didn't expect so many people to turn up,' said Liz. 'Since Sunday we've been really struggling to feed everybody. We've got the truck running daily with loads of vegetables, but you know as well as I do that they have to be organic or we'll lose a third of our people — the ones we desperately don't want to lose. Organic doesn't come cheap. In the meantime some of our troops are making their own arrangements, and that includes raiding supermarkets. Others claim they're living off the land, and they're not too particular whose land they're living off. So yeah, we've got a problem and we're handing the PR initiative to Rip, Chip and Ship on a plate.'

'Can't we do something?' asked Summer.

'We're doing everything we can. Friends, CROEG, GECO, everybody is helping but we'll end up having to feed, shelter and control more than fifteen hundred. With a few more tarpaulins we might be able to shelter and feed everyone, but I doubt we'll be able to control them.'

'We've got a bunch of skinheads down from Canberra,' interrupted Brian. 'They turned up with slabs of beer, which they probably didn't pay for, and immediately proceeded to drink. Things got pretty testy for a while.'

'Skinheads?' said Summer incredulously. 'What do those Nazis want?'

'I don't think they've had a sudden conversion to the cause,' said Liz. 'In fact it's pretty clear they've just come down for a fight. We're hoping they run out of beer and patience and just shove off back to Canberra.'

'We've also got some pretty freaky people down from the New South Wales north coast who've set themselves up as guardians of all indigenous species,' said Brian. 'I've forgotten what they call themselves but they seem to eat a lot of mushrooms and chew a lot of sassafras root, and link hands around trees and chant. Seems they're asking forgiveness from the spirits of the animals and trees for the destruction wrought by their fellow human beings. I don't know which way they'll jump when the confrontation begins.'

'I think I know them,' said Summer. 'They call themselves the Guardians of Nature, or something like that. I was on a blockade with them up near Lismore. They seem freaky but basically they're okay. The women are more extreme than the blokes. Up north the union trucked in some timber workers from all around the region and the women attacked them as they were getting off the trucks. Screaming and spitting, trying to claw the blokes' eyes out. Christ! I'd never seen anything like it, although those dumb feminists in Canberra who pissed on the politicians' shoes came pretty close.'

'Great,' said Liz.

'I might be able to talk to them,' said Summer. 'They know me. We've linked hands.'

'You're kidding,' said Brian.

'No,' said Summer. 'You have to try everything. Get them on their own territory and they're really nice people, really gentle. I lived with them for a week or so.'

'You're not going anywhere,' said Liz. 'Not yet. Look at you.'

'I'm fine.'

'You're sick.'

'She won't get any worse just talking to them,' said Brian. 'It's worth taking a risk to see if we can get them to fall into line. If Summer has a problem I'll drive her home.'

'Then it's agreed,' said Summer. 'I'll get Darren to have a word with the skinheads too. Might know some of them.' Summer could see an excuse to rejoin the blockade and that was all she wanted to do.

'How do you get on with Aborigines?' asked Liz.

'Great,' said Summer.

'Yeah, well we've had a few of them drop in as well. They seem intelligent, dedicated and well organised. Too well organised for comfort. I think we need to remind them that we all have to follow the same script and remember what we're here for. We don't want the blockade to be hijacked by any special interest groups. If you're going to solve two potential problems why not wear yourself out completely and solve three?'

'No worries,' said Summer. 'I'll talk to them as well.'

* * *

'Oh wow!' said Summer as Liz drove her up to the blockade site. The projected path of the new road bristled with tripods, and teams of skinheads were erecting more among the trees in a last line of defence. They were all naked to the waist, wore jeans and boots, and were so uniform in appearance they could have been new recruits in boot camp. Everywhere she looked there were camp sites and tarps, and the blockade bustled with a familiar air of expectation, optimism and chaos. Brian, who'd driven on ahead with the extra leaflets, came over to meet them.

'How's it going?' asked Liz.

'Not bad,' said Brian. 'The skinheads wanted to erect their tripods in front of everyone else's so that they wouldn't miss out on any violence should there be any, but I managed to persuade them that people were the first line of defence not barricades, guaranteed them a place in the front row when the opposition arrived, and convinced them to build their tripods as a last line of defence, a final bulwark in the event of a retreat.'

'Well done!' said Liz.

'The Guardians have built humpies and are walking around insisting that their way is the right and natural way, and that everyone should pull down their tarpaulins and build humpies too. In the meantime the Aborigines, who invented humpies, have pitched tents and told the Guardians to bugger off.'

'Situation normal,' said Liz. 'Any more arrivals?'

'Heaps. I've got some of our people taking them aside in groups of twenty or so and telling them what to expect and what to do. We're talking tactics and the importance of winning the PR battle, but everyone seems to have their own ideas on what constitutes a successful protest, peaceful or otherwise, GECO particularly.'

'Let me talk to them,' said Summer.

'You've got enough talking to do,' said Liz. 'C'mon, let's start with our humpy dumpties.'

'One other thing,' said Brian.

'What?'

'I think the honeymoon's over. Three separate groups of newcomers have been worked over. Nothing real serious, just bloody noses and bruises. But I think it's a sign that things are about to get rough.'

'It was too good to last,' said Liz. 'Anything I can do?'

'No. A bit of first aid and hero worship and they'll be right. Any more incidents and we might have to consider providing protection, though that would probably only make matters worse. Any sign of the vegie truck?'

'It's on its way. That's all I know. Apparently coming straight from the markets.' Liz sighed. She could see another stressful day looming. She didn't know how she'd cope if the vegie truck failed to show. 'Is that all?'

'For now.' Brian turned to Summer. 'You take it easy, and come and get me the moment you start feeling tired. Okay?'

'Yep,' said Summer. 'Do-wit do-wit, dorf dorf.' She followed Liz into the bush. Liz stopped to check on a briefing being handed out by a blockade veteran.

'You've got to buddy up,' he said to the new arrivals. 'Stay apart but keep an eye on each other. If one of you is arrested, the other has to withdraw immediately and gather up his or her partner's things. There is no point in both of you getting arrested. Someone has to stay free to safeguard the other's interests, which can mean alerting me, Liz or Brian to the arrest so that we can provide legal help if necessary, and also to help us account for everybody. We need to know if somebody goes missing, especially if there's no satisfactory explanation for their absence. People have been taken away and beaten senseless at other blockades, some women have been assaulted. So we don't want any heroes. One of you gets arrested, the other withdraws. That clear?' Heads nodded in assent. The same advice was being handed out all over the blockade site.

'Hey, Simon!' said Summer to one of the new arrivals.

'Hi, Summer! How are you?' Simon was about twenty and built like his dad owned a gym.

'Great,' said Summer. 'I'll catch you later.'

'Anyone here you don't know?' asked Liz as she led Summer away down the track to their meeting with the Guardians.

'Lots,' said Summer. 'But I'll soon fix that.'

Liz snorted but had no doubt that Summer wasn't joking. They had no trouble finding the Guardians and their bark and brush humpies. Liz claimed later that she could have found them blindfolded by smell alone. Part of the way the Guardians identified with the animals they were dedicated to saving was by not washing so that they eventually smelt like them. Liz and Summer were met by a man in his forties wearing ancient King Gee shorts, work boots without laces and a rough hand-knitted woollen vest. His whiskers and hair were matted into foul dreadlocks that had gone years without the touch of razor or shampoo, and his skin was darkened almost black both through exposure to the sun and a substantial accumulation of dirt. Liz wasn't keen to get any closer.

'Sister Summer!' said the Guardian and rushed forward.

'Rainfather!' said Summer and threw herself into his bear hug. Rainfather's face creased into a broad smile.

'This is Liz, the organiser,' said Summer.

'How do you do?' said Liz and made no move to step any closer. She was trying to figure out a way to breathe without inhaling, like Bill Clinton managed to do with his joints. 'Why don't I leave you two to it? Summer, come and find me when you're ready. Don't stay too long because there's a lot we have to do.'

Liz turned and walked a few steps away before she allowed herself to take another breath. It was almost beyond her comprehension that any human being could smell so feral, and she couldn't understand why Summer hadn't been overcome by fumes when he hugged her. Nevertheless she had to smile despite her revulsion. If anyone could talk sense to them it was

Summer. Liz had never known anyone be so uncritical in her affection for others.

'The bush opens wide to admit you and all creatures of the bush greet you as their sister and saviour,' said Rainfather.

'Yeah, I know,' said Summer. 'Where is everybody? Where's Earthmother? Who's come down with you?'

'Everyone who could be spared. Some remained behind to protect our community and care for the young, but most have answered the call. Our family has grown, Sister Summer. Many more brothers and sisters are returning to the life of their forebears. They've gone forth, spreading our message and inviting others to join us and adopt the old ways.'

'Cool,' said Summer. 'But if you want to save the forest here and all the animals, and if you want me to help, we need to talk. Before we do that I want all of you to meet a close friend of mine, someone who knows every creature and every leaf in Little Potoroo Creek by name.' She paused dramatically. 'Rainfather, I want you to meet God.'

The matted thicket that represented Rainfather's eyebrows jumped a notch.

* * *

'Next,' said Summer.

Liz looked up, startled. She was sitting at a table in the admin area, playing quartermaster with supplies. 'Finished already?'

'Yeah, I just said my piece and left them in God's hands.'

'Very smart.'

'You should see them, Liz. They're sitting around God like children around a kindergarten storyteller, hanging on his every word. Of course God's in his element. I bet he's the first person they've ever met who has actually seen a long-footed potoroo or spotted-tailed quoll in the wild. I just hope he remembers to tell them what I told him to say. I reckon they'll do whatever he asks.'

Liz started laughing. 'Do you know your greatest strength, Summer? People can't help underestimating you.'

'You've told me that before. Now where's Darren? I need him to talk to the skinheads.'

'He's helping Brian put up a tarp for the newcomers. God help us if any more show up. Have you any idea how much rice we've got through, how many tonnes of vegetables, or how many tanks of fresh water?'

'No,' said Summer. 'The more the merrier.'

'It won't be so merry if that blasted truck doesn't turn up.'

'Relax, Liz, you've got to stay positive! If you're really worried send people out to collect bunya nuts and bracken fern roots. See you later.' She took off and left Liz wondering how anyone could imagine she could feed fifteen hundred people on bunya nuts and fern roots. EGCGs — with help from their friends — provided cartons of fruit for breakfast, soup for lunch, and did their best to put vegetables and rice or vegetables and potato out for dinner and make it as appetising as possible. It was a healthy enough diet as long as nobody tried to live on it for too long.

Summer found Darren drinking some of Liz's precious tank water under the new tarp. 'Hi,' she said. 'Where's Sky?'

'Dunno. With Matt and Georgie digging new dunnies, or helping Gretta manage her patients.'

'Patients? What are you talking about?'

'Gretta's set up shop dispensing herbal remedies and harmonising anybody stupid enough to lie still for two seconds.'

Summer had to laugh at the image.

'Hey Sum?'

'Yeah? What?'

'You want to buddy up?'

'What about Sky?'

'She can buddy up with Gretta.'

'Like to,' said Summer, 'but I'm already buddied up with God.'

'With God?'

'Yeah. Might not come off. You know what he's like.'

'Tell him to piss off and buddy up with me.'

'I'll talk to him,' said Summer. She had no intention of pissing God off but was smart enough not to piss Darren off either when she needed him to do a favour. 'You do something for me, I'll do something for you.'

'Okay. What do you want?'

Summer told him.

'Sure, no worries,' said Darren. 'They're a bunch of pussies. You want to come and introduce me?'

'My pleasure,' said Summer.

* * *

'Next,' said Summer.

'Don't tell me,' said Liz.

'Yeah, they welcomed The Dick like a long-lost brother. Apparently a couple of them had seen him in action in a mosh pit at a club in Belconnen. Darren brained about six blokes including the bouncer. Knocked him out cold. That counts with those guys. He's talking, they're listening. Can't ask for much more than that.'

'What about our Aboriginal brothers and sisters?'

'I'm on my way. Have you seen Ciaron anywhere?'

'More delegation?'

'No, I just want to catch up.'

'Can't help you. She's hanging around with other bikies. She could be helping out in the kitchen, chopping up what's left of the pumpkins. She spent most of yesterday there with that Sarah girl.'

'Ta.'

'By the way, Brian reckons that Ciaron is actually a boy's name and pronounced Kieran not Sharon. He reckons the female version is Ciara pronounced Kiera.'

'Makes you wonder, doesn't it?' said Summer. 'Maybe her mum had it right all along.'

* * *

'Dorf-dorf,' said Summer. 'Nice camp.' She flashed her famous smile. Some of the Aborigines were trying to rev up a fire they'd lit and weren't meeting with a lot of success. A man around thirty got up off his haunches to greet her. He was the eldest and clearly the leader.

'G'day. Need some meths, eh. I'm Bobby.'

'I'm Summer.'

'G'day, Summer. Hey, I know you. I've seen you before. Don't you do that techno stuff? I've seen you up in Melbourne, out Fitzroy way. Had some other guys with you.'

'Dorf dorf,' said Summer.

'Do you want a sausage? We're trying to get a barbecue going. Gotta cook the lot before they go off.'

'No, thanks,' said Summer. 'I'm sort of vegetarian.' She looked around at the curious dark faces watching her. They all seemed friendly enough. 'Wouldn't mind sitting down and talking for a bit though.'

Bobby stepped back and looked at her. His eyes narrowed. 'This is an official visit?'

Summer laughed. 'Yeah, sort of, but not really. I'm not very good when things get official. I'm helping out Liz and Brian. They asked me to talk to you about your intentions.'

'Right now we intend to do nothing except eat these sausages. You ought to have one too. They were so cheap they can't have much meat in them.'

'Okay,' said Summer. She sat down. 'Where are you from?'

'All over,' said Bobby. 'All over Gippsland. We represent the original owners. Our people have lived and hunted in Gippsland for over forty thousand years. This is our land. White people have got no right to be here, no right to cut down our trees, no right to kill our animals.'

'Right on!' said Bobby's mates.

'Yeah, I know what you mean,' said Summer. 'Your forefathers left their handprints in a cave a friend of mine lives in.' She laughed, but secretly had to accept that Liz's worst fears had been realised. Her new friends intended to split the focus of the blockade and capitalise on the media attention. Being young, black and articulate they'd have no trouble attracting the cameras. Bobby had the assurance of someone who'd done it all before. 'Have you guys met God?' she asked. 'You should. For the past ten years he's been acting as your caretaker.'

* * *

'How'd you go?' asked Liz.

'Not good.'

'You look terrible. I think we'd better get you home.'

'The sausage wasn't cooked properly.'

'What sausage?'

'They wanted me to stay for lunch. You know how they like to share. I'll be okay if I can throw up again. '

'Again? Forget it. You're going home right now. Stay here while I go get Brian. You can tell him what the problem is in the car.'

* * *

'I think they're going to Mabo us,' said Summer. She swallowed hard. Brian's old but loved diesel Peugeot had tackled too many bush trails and loose metal roads and its shock absorbers had all but given up. 'They're going to make a land claim and divert the media attention to their cause. I spotted a couple of women painting banners. Land rights stuff.'

'Shit!' said Brian. 'I'd better have a word with them.'

'Yeah, you'd better. I've asked God to talk to them but he's useless at anything political. He's probably on their side anyway.'

'It's just a stunt, you know,' said Brian. 'They haven't got a dog's show of making a successful claim. How can they show continuous occupation when nobody but God has lived up in Potoroo Creek for the past two hundred years?'

'Yeah, but don't dismiss them. Their claim could buy us time.'

'Doubtful,' said Brian. 'Not with this State government. But I'll give them a fair hearing and ask that they do the same for me. If they really care about the land they'll have to accept that a united front is the best option. If I thought for a second they had a hope of succeeding I'd be the first to back them — hell I'd back anyone to save Little Potoroo Creek. Bloody hell! You okay?'

'Stop the car!'

'Oh shit! Wind down the window.'

Summer did, and emptied her stomach down the side of the car door.

Brian brought the old Peugeot to a belated halt. 'We should have left you at home,' he said. 'I'm really sorry.'

'Rack off,' said Summer. Her face had taken on a greenish hue and was bathed in sweat. 'It's just that bloody sausage. I've had my best day in ages.' She opened the car door and threw up once more.

* * *

Jerry differed from the protesters who'd descended upon the blockade in a number of important respects. He had a regular job which he enjoyed, a regular wage, money in his pocket, and he was only down for the week, which was all the time his father and mother had agreed he could have off. They would have let him take a month if he'd been going anywhere else. He spotted the café sign and pulled his Ducati over to the side of Orbost's main street. He propped his bike on its stand and took off his gloves and helmet.

The café proprietor watched the bikie stroll in and wondered if it was his turn to be done over. He clenched his fists beneath the counter. He was overweight and out of condition but a helluva lot bigger than the kid, which he figured evened things up.

'What do you want?' he said.

'I'd kill for a double long black,' said Jerry evenly. 'And a hot meat pie. What kind of coffee have you got? Lavazza?'

'Lavazza? No. Vittorio.'

'Vittorio's fine,' said Jerry. 'Just don't hold back. I like it strong.'

'Strong, long and black.' The proprietor began to relax. 'You down for the blockade?'

'Sort of.'

'Well, when you get there tell your mates we've had enough of their thieving. Next bloke that tries anything is going to get his head kicked in.'

'Sounds fair.'

'Sounds fair? The whole bloody lot of ya oughta have your heads kicked in.'

'Hey, keep me out of this,' said Jerry. He held up his hands in mock surrender. 'I've only come down to see my girlfriend.'

'She one of them protesters?'

'Sure is.'

'Ever thought of getting a new girlfriend?' The proprietor handed Jerry his coffee. 'There you go. Thick as sump oil. Kill a brown dog.'

Jerry took an enquiring sip. 'Not bad. But I make better.' He laughed and set his coffee down on one of the formica tables. Someone had left a copy of the *Gazette* on his chair so he picked it up and began to read. The proprietor brought him his freshly heated pie and plonked it down on a plate in front of him.

'Ta,' said Jerry. He didn't notice the two guys in the jacked-up ute park behind his bike and watch him through the window. His pie was so hot he'd downed a second coffee long before he finished eating it. The bill came to four dollars fifty and Jerry paid with a five.

'Keep the change,' he said to the bemused proprietor, pulled on his helmet and strolled casually out into the sun.

CHAPTER TWENTY-FOUR

Instead of acting immediately on Clyde Townsend's advice, Miklos waited until the town had become so disenchanted with the pilfering and constant stream of scruffy smelly protesters that they were ready to reconsider his role. He called another after-work meeting in the pub to talk to his employees, contractors and anyone else who cared to listen. He noticed quite a few shop owners in the crowd, some people who'd come in from outlying properties, and others who'd driven up from Orbost. Maybe they weren't yet ready to embrace him but at least they were considering opening their arms.

Miklos knew he had to do more than get Arnie to assemble a few thugs and punch a few heads. That would happen anyway, it was unavoidable. He had to do what all great leaders did in times of crisis. He had to capture their imaginations. One by one he told them the little schemes he'd concocted to disrupt the blockade, schemes that were easy to implement yet effective, and not only appealed both to his audience's desire to hit back but to their sense of humour. They laughed and cheered and slapped him on the back, and went off to spread the news. Miklos was back.

The next morning when he rolled up to his office he felt as if he had his life back under control. He felt so good he was considering calling Jan in for some dawn-breaking dictation. His private line rang and his first thought was that it was Cheryl checking in. He'd sent her up to a private clinic in Melbourne to have her wounds licked by professionals and bridges made for her missing teeth. He'd also told her to buy a new camera and lenses in a rare act of contrition, but the truth was she would've bought them anyway. He picked up the phone. 'Cheryl?' he said.

'Clyde Townsend.'

'Hang on a minute.' Miklos put down the phone and opened the door to his office. 'Jan, go powder your nose or something.'

'I'm busy.'

'Jan, I'm asking you nicely. Go powder your nose.'

Jan stopped typing and rose immediately. She knew exactly what came after being asked nicely and it usually left bruises. 'It'll be your fault if this letter misses the post!' she snapped.

Miklos watched her go, wondering how God could have put so much into her breasts and so little into her brain, closed his door and picked up the phone. 'Just told Jan to piss off. Hard to know who to trust these days. Told you about Cheryl, didn't I? God only knows who took those shots. All I know for sure is who didn't. Maybe somebody was just passing by and got lucky after all. Makes you wonder who though. Now, what can I do for you?'

'Did you get those spikes I sent you?'

'Jesus, not on an open line.'

'It's my direct line. It doesn't go through the board. I rang your direct line and you told me you'd got rid of Jan.'

'All the freakin' same.'

'Did you get them or not?'

'Yeah, I got them.'

'Right,' said Townsend. 'You're clear to use them. I've sent some guys down to join the blockade. They rang on their mobile — they've arrived and they've pitched their tent using identical spikes to the ones I sent you as tent pegs. Okay? Just so Nugget doesn't spend all day looking for evidence, the tent is bright orange, like survival gear, and has khaki trim around the entrance, the poles and guy ropes. To use my guys' words, it sticks out like Pamela Anderson's tits.'

'Nice one,' said Miklos. 'But I don't count on lettin' Nugget or anyone in on this.'

'Do you have a plan?'

'Depends on who knows what's going on. What about your happy campers?'

'Their instructions were simply to join the blockade, pitch their tent, use the tent pegs provided and bugger off when I tell them to. That's all they know, and they know better than to ask questions. They're completely reliable. It's how they make their living.'

'Pitchin' tents?'

'Dirty tricks,' said Townsend patiently. 'Now, who's the player from your team?'

'The one person in this world I trust completely.'

'What do you mean?'

'Think it through. No witnesses.'

Townsend went silent for a moment. 'Where?' he asked cautiously.

'Really only one place it can be. Diggers Hill. We're logging it right now and it's the closest site to the blockade.'

'Who's the victim?'

'Luck of the draw.'

'You're kidding!'

'You amaze me, Townsend. For a moment there I thought I detected a note of concern, thought you'd slipped back into the human race. You better be careful you don't go soft and lose your touch.'

'Just thought you might have singled out one of Arnie's mates, someone older, or some bloke with no wife or kids.'

'Yeah, but imagine if he's a battler with kids and a mortgage. Imagine if it's a real tear-jerkin' made-for-TV tragedy. Town wouldn't stand for that. Reckon the rest of Australia wouldn't either.'

'You're a ruthless bastard, Miklos.'

'Takes one to know one.'

'Let me know when you make your move.'

'Sure.'

'With any kind of luck it might not be necessary.'

'Sure.'

'Just make sure your perpetrator has a water-tight alibi.'

'Dunno about water-tight,' said Miklos, 'but she's definitely tight. I'll vouch for that.' He was laughing as he hung up.

* * *

Wozza stood on the forecourt of the Ampol service station, cleaning the windshields and topping up the radiators of cars when they pulled in for gas. If it was a woman driver he even put the gas in for them after politely enquiring what flavour they wanted — leaded, unleaded or premium. The locals thought it a hoot and razzed him mercilessly. Wozza didn't care. He was enjoying himself and the locals were all in on the joke. Charlie was busy doing the same thing at the Shell further on down the road.

Miklos's original plan had been to slip sugar cubes into the tanks of protesters' cars if they stopped for petrol, but the service station owners wouldn't have a bar of it, arguing that either they or the petrol company would have to cough up for the cost of cleaning out their fuel systems. Miklos had spent all his life around trucks and soon found a solution.

Wozza looked up as a battered old Datsun 200B carrying five squashed protesters rattled onto the forecourt. 'G'day,' he said amiably. 'Like me to do your windshield and check your oil and water?'

'Yeah, be great,' said the driver. 'Where's the dunny?'

'Round the back,' said Wozza. 'Both of them,' he added when he saw two girls get out with the other two passengers. Wozza shook his head as he watched the protesters race off to the toilets, the girls crouched over as if they were trying to run with their legs crossed.

'Chuck ten dollars worth of super in for us?' shouted the driver, almost as an afterthought.

'No worries,' said Wozza. He punched in ten bucks and let the pump get on with the job. It was so bloody easy, that was the beauty of the whole idea. He opened the bonnet, took his Stanley knife out of his pocket and cut three-quarters of the way through the fan belt. For good measure he took a nick out of the bottom of one of the radiator hoses. He splashed water everywhere when he washed the windshield so their suspicions wouldn't be aroused by any telltale puddles.

'Thanks, mate,' said the driver breathlessly. 'Who do I pay?'

'The office,' said Wozza. 'Have a nice day.' He wandered off to greet the next car.

* * *

Arnie sat in his ute on the south side of Orbost eating a Big Mac. Davo, his clone of a brother, sat beside him eating a sausage and egg McMuffin. The breakfast menu had finished two hours earlier but the manager knew better than to argue and had personally made the McMuffin up for him. The franchisee had once tried to explain how McDonald's worked and why Davo couldn't have sausage and egg McMuffins any time of the day or night. Davo had simply jumped the counter and explained how he worked.

Arnie and Davo had got up early and spent the morning cruising the highway. Arnie thought it was time Davo learnt the subtleties of working for Miklos. Two lots of hitchhikers had flagged them down and they'd given them a workover for their cheek. Their last victim had pulled his Corolla over to the side of the road with a motor which had suddenly dropped all its coolant and overheated. The driver had waved Arnie down to see if he'd go for help. Help wasn't what Arnie and Davo gave him. The two girls also travelling in the Corolla screamed so much Arnie had to bang their heads together to shut them up. Davo thought that was so funny he banged their heads together too, to show how well his on-the-job training was going. In truth Davo could have made the girls scream just by looking at them. Arnie had broken his nose at some stage and Davo hadn't bothered getting it fixed. He had the same casual attitude towards cuts and gashes and, as a result, his face looked like it had been zipped together.

But all that was just a sideshow to the main event. Miklos had chosen their target for them and even nominated their weapon. Arnie and Davo had nearly pissed themselves laughing when Miklos had told them what he wanted them to do, and so had everyone else who'd been privy to the conversation. So the two brothers sat, ate their burgers, and kept their eyes on their rearview mirrors.

* * *

Nugget and his two constables had set up a road block by the turn-off to Thirsty Creek Road and stopped any cars they regarded as suspicious. They'd got one protester for driving without a current licence, one for driving an unregistered vehicle, issued two defect notices, breathalysed every driver but no one had come even close to the limit, searched unsuccessfully for drugs, and taken a feisty seventeen-year-old girl down to the station for calling them pigs. Nugget knew there was no point in charging her with abuse because no judge in Australia would convict her. A test case had already ruled the use of the word 'pigs' as regrettable but acceptable and part of the vernacular. He'd just wanted to get the girl alone so he could clip her around the ears a bit and teach her some manners. When she'd cried and threatened to charge him with assault he'd simply pointed out that it was her word against his and she'd be wasting her time. He'd clipped her again to make sure she understood and gone back out on patrol.

* * *

Summer had her head back against the headrest and her eyes closed when Brian spotted the first broken-down car, a Mazda 323 with its bonnet up. He stopped alongside to see if he could help.

'What's the problem?' he asked.

'Done my fan belt,' said the driver. 'Light came on on the dash but I thought we were just overheating a bit. I didn't realise we'd also lost the generator, so now the battery's flat as well.'

'I'll see if I can get a tow truck.'

'Man, we don't have money for that. If you give me a lift into town I'll take the battery, get it recharged and see if I can scrounge a secondhand fan belt.'

'What about your friends?'

'How far away is the blockade?'

'Five or six ks.'

'They can leg it.'

'Mightn't be a bad idea if they stayed put and kept an eye on your car.' Brian looked closely at the passengers for the first time and realised that two of the three were girls. He didn't fancy their chances against Arnie and his mates. 'No, you're right. Better if they walked on. Grab your battery and hop in.'

Two kilometres down the road they came across a cooked Camira. Brian stopped once more. He leant out his window.

'Fan belt?'

'Yeah,' said the driver. 'How'd you guess? Must've come off somewhere back down the road. Motor's overheated and split a couple of hoses as well.'

'Let me have a look,' said Brian. The motor was steaming but he could still get close enough to see that both major hoses leading into and from the radiator had been neatly sliced. 'You've been sabotaged,' he said, 'and more than likely he has as well.' He pointed to the back of his car and the bloke sitting there with a battery on his knee. 'I'll take you into town. Your passengers can start walking. The blockade's about seven ks up the road. If I get the chance I'll come back and give them a lift, but a wise man wouldn't count on it.'

'A lot of bad luck going around,' said Summer as the newest victim climbed into the back, clutching the two radiator hoses that needed replacing.

'Luck's got nothing to do with it,' said Brian. 'Where did you two stop last?'

'The Ampol back down on the highway,' said one.

'The Shell,' said the other.

'Figures,' said Brian. 'I'll drop you off at the local garage. Stick together and don't go wandering off. If you get hungry or thirsty, go to the café on the main street but stay clear of the pub. If you go there you'll just get your head kicked in. I'm going to take a run down to the highway to see if there's anyone else in strife.'

'I'm coming with you,' said Summer.

Brian sensed it was pointless to argue. He dropped off his two passengers and set off with Summer towards the Princes Highway. They'd hardly gone two kilometres before they spotted another car with a plume of steam rising from its engine compartment. Brian drove past with barely a glance.

'What are you doing?' asked Summer. 'They needed help.'

'I've got a feeling they won't be the only ones, and it's too late to worry about them. The damage has already been done. We've got a bigger problem to take care of.' The road straightened and levelled out. Brian pushed up to one hundred and twenty.

'What problem?' asked Summer.

'The vegie truck,' said Brian. 'We've got to get to it before they do.'

* * *

'Half serves,' said Liz. 'And no more fruit.' She ignored the grumbles from the gathered protesters. 'I know a lot of you have been working hard but we have to save something for dinner in case the vegie truck's broken down. Sorry, but there's nothing I can do. If any of you have brought any food with you can I ask you to eat that instead?' Not many people moved. Most of the blockade veterans had brought food with them, as had the vegans and groups like the Guardians, but their food was only meant to supplement what was provided. The majority of protesters had brought nothing but their passion. Liz rolled her eyes. Even at half serves she'd need a loaves and fishes miracle to feed everyone come dinnertime.

'We want some meat,' said one of the skinheads belligerently.

'Yeah!' said his brothers. 'Meat!'

'Can't help you there,' said Liz evenly. 'We provide what we can. If you want anything else you have to provide it yourself.'

'We're fuckin' sick of eatin' vego crap,' called another. 'We want some real food.'

'Fair enough,' said Liz. 'But I still can't help you.' She turned and walked away. Crap or otherwise she didn't see any skinheads giving up their place in the food lines. Part of her wished they would because that would leave more food for the rest of them. But a mob of hungry skinheads wasn't worth thinking about. Sooner or later they'd take their anger out on somebody and that was the last thing she needed. She glanced hopefully towards the dirt road to Osbourne but all she could see were more weary protesters straggling in on foot. More mouths to feed. Away to her right the Aboriginal group were hanging the first of their banners. 'Aboriginal Land Rights!' proclaimed one, 'Hands Off Our Land!' said another. The black, red and yellow Aboriginal flag hung from every nearby tree. Liz sighed. She wondered if they had any sausages to give to the skinheads. They wouldn't know or care if they were off or not.

'Hey Liz.'

She turned around and saw Ciaron and Sarah Jenkins coming towards her. 'What's the problem?'

‘Something weird’s going on,’ said Sarah. ‘Those two blokes in the show-home tent, something fishy about them.’

‘Go on,’ said Liz, secretly wishing they’d just go away.

‘They came in an old Kombi right,’ cut in Ciaron. ‘They talk a good act and you’d swear they’d lay down their lives to save a single tree. If you listen to them you’d swear they’d been to every effin’ blockade that’s ever been held.’

‘So?’

‘No one’s ever seen them before,’ said Sarah.

‘And veterans don’t show up with brand new tents, portable barbecues and a camping gas ring. They don’t barbecue steak and make bacon and eggs each morning,’ said Ciaron doggedly.

‘Two blokes,’ said Liz. ‘Have you thought that through?’

‘Yeah,’ said Ciaron and laughed. ‘First thing we thought of. We set Pete onto them thinking we might be doing them and Pete a favour. They called him a faggot and told him to piss off.’

‘Some nights they drive into town for dinner,’ said Sarah. ‘Pardon me for being a cop’s daughter but I snuck a look around their tent. One of them brought a bottle of Jim Beam, the other a bottle of vodka. They keep ice and mixers in their esky. Don’t sound like green activists to me.’

‘They keep walking off by themselves up the trail towards Little Potoroo Creek as well,’ said Ciaron.

‘Bush walks?’ said Liz hopefully.

‘Mobile phones,’ said Sarah. ‘We followed them. They’ve got to get high to get a signal.’

'Must be digital. My analogue works well enough down here. What do you want me to do?' said Liz. 'Send Brian over to talk to them?'

'Thought we'd send The Dick,' said Ciaron. 'Thought we'd square it with you first.'

'No,' said Liz. 'So far they've done nothing wrong. All you've got are suspicions. But keep an eye on them and keep me informed. Okay?'

'Okay,' said Ciaron. 'But you'll regret it.'

* * *

'In business,' said Arnie. He fired up the motor and eased out onto the highway behind the vegie truck. There was no way they could've mistaken it. 'Save Little Potoroo Creek' stickers were plastered all over the cab and tailgate. They followed it through Orbost, as Miklos had insisted, and returned the sly grins from the locals.

'Let the locals see ya,' Miklos had said. 'Let 'em in on your joke and make 'em feel part of it.'

Arnie sat patiently behind the truck until it turned off the highway towards Osbourne, then pulled in front of it and forced it to stop. Davo leapt from the cab and ripped the truck driver's door open. The driver took one look at Davo and panicked.

'You!' Davo snarled. 'You're coming with me.' He grabbed the front of the driver's shirt and pulled violently.

'Seatbelt!' screamed the driver.

'Details,' said Arnie to his younger brother. 'You gotta pay attention to details.'

'Undo it,' said Davo. He waited for the click then wrenched the driver out onto the road.

‘Arrghh!’ said the driver as he crunched into the ground. He clutched his shoulder in pain. ‘Why did ya do that for? I was getting out!’

Arnie shook his head despairingly and hopped into the driver’s place. A young woman cowered against the passenger door. She was actually whimpering and that gave Arnie a buzz.

‘Good afternoon,’ he said. ‘Don’t do anything to spoil it, will ya?’ He engaged gear and followed Davo off the road and down a fire trail. He didn’t have to see Bob’s truck to know Bob was in position waiting for him. Bob had probably been waiting as long as they had, with the spring sun scorching down on his tanker. That had also been Miklos’s idea.

‘Phew,’ said Arnie, as he pulled up by the night cart. He turned to his passenger and leered at her. ‘You haven’t done anything nasty in your knickers, have ya?’

* * *

Jerry was aware of the Mazda ute in his mirrors but it was far enough behind for him not to give it any thought. Once he turned off the highway towards Osbourne it closed the gap. Jerry thought about speeding up but was right on the legal limit. He decided to let it pass him. He figured the driver was either in a hurry or didn’t like following motorbikes. A lot of people didn’t. He eased back on the throttle as the ute pulled out to overtake, glanced sideways when it dawned on him that it was taking a long time to go past. At first he didn’t realise the thing pointing at him through the passenger window was a shotgun, but hit his brakes the instant he did. He heard the bang, felt his bike heel over and his front tyre and wheel crumple beneath him. He didn't hear the laughter that followed. It was drowned out by the sound of his helmet slamming into the hard top and his bike cartwheeling over the top of him.

* * *

Wozza was beginning to get bored when he spotted the jacked-up ute grind onto the forecourt. He strolled over to meet it. A couple of local louts from Orbost were in the cab, grinning like idiots, and Wozza just had to tell them the score. The Datto had been his fifth victim and he'd just chalked up another. He'd done three fan belts, two major radiator hoses, and put self-tapping screws in the tyres of one car when the driver had asked him to check their pressures. He'd really enjoyed himself for a while and wondered if Charlie had enjoyed himself too. He leant on the passenger door sill out of reach of the mongrel snapping on the tray.

'G'day,' said Wozza. 'What's up?'

'Just saw Charlie. He says it's time to clear out. Came to tell ya.'

'Fair enough,' said Wozza. He heard a toot, turned and waved farewell to a departing Sigma. 'They won't get far. Done their fan belt. Put a few holes in the plumbing as well.' He showed them his Stanley knife.

'That's nuffin',' said the ute's passenger. He lifted the blanket on his lap and showed Wozza his shotgun. 'We shot a motorbike.'

* * *

Brian and Summer spotted pairs of despondent protesters walking or sitting by the side of the road, trying in vain to thumb a lift from the locals. They passed three abandoned cars and an overloaded Kombi which had stopped to pick up two more desperate hitchhikers.

'Miklos's boys have been busy,' said Brian bitterly. Summer didn't answer. A couple of cars had stopped up ahead and their occupants were clustered around something on the ground. They were trying to flag them down.

'Looks like an accident,' she said.

Brian slowed and pulled onto the gravel shoulder. One of the protesters was at his window before the car had come to a halt.

'Mate, we need an ambulance,' said the protester. 'Bloke's come off his bike.'

'Let's have a look,' said Brian. 'Stay here,' he said to Summer, but she was already halfway out of the door. A group of angry protesters were examining Jerry's bike. Summer thought she recognised what was left of it and panic took over.

'Jerry!' she screamed. She raced over to the figure in leathers that was being propped up by two girls. Rightly or wrongly they'd taken off his helmet and Summer's suspicions were confirmed. 'Jerry!'

Jerry responded to her voice and managed a sickly smile. 'Sum?'

'Is he all right?' she asked anxiously.

'He was out cold when we got here,' said one of the girls. 'Been complaining of dizziness.'

'Says his right arm and shoulder hurts,' said the other girl. 'And he's left the tips of two fingers in his gloves.'

'Jerry, what are you doing here?' said Summer.

'Came to see you.' His voice was thick and slurred. Summer immediately regretted forcing him to speak.

'Anyone know what happened?' she asked.

'Not hard to work out,' said one of the guys holding the bike and told her. Summer listened open-mouthed.

'Well, well, here come the cavalry,' said Brian. A police patrol car had swung into view up ahead of them; it seemed to prop and pull to the left as if the driver wanted to do a U-turn. 'Nugget's got himself in the wrong place at the wrong time. Now he'll have to do a report.'

'Bugger the report! Tell him to radio for an ambulance,' said Summer.

Brian walked out onto the road to meet the patrol car which stopped right in the middle, straddling the centre line. Belatedly it began to flash its lights.

'What's up?' said Nugget.

'Bloke's come off his motorbike,' said Brian. 'Some of Miklos's boys got a little too enthusiastic and blasted his front wheel off with a shotgun.'

'Any witnesses?' asked Nugget quickly.

'No.'

'So let's not go jumping to conclusions,' said Nugget. He reluctantly got out of the car. 'Could be any number of reasons why he fell off. Happens all the time.'

'Nugget,' said Brian patiently, 'his wheel's been shot off. The tyres are full of shotgun pellets.'

'So you say.'

'Nugget! Look at the bloody bike. Take a good look at what your mate Miklos is up to!'

'I'll conduct the investigation as I see fit, in my own time and in my own way. Now bugger off!' Nugget refused to look at the bike or at Brian. He silently cursed the witless bastards who'd dropped him into this predicament. Miklos would go ballistic. 'How's the bloke that fell off?'

'He didn't fall, Nugget, and he needs an ambulance.'

'Ambulance will take ages.' Nugget's eyes lit up. He could see an avenue for escape opening up and went for it. 'The best thing we can do is take him straight to hospital in the patrol car. He looks okay to move.'

'Oh no you don't, you bastard!' Brian grabbed Nugget by the shoulder. 'You stay here and do an accident report. I want to see how you explain away the shotgun pellets in the tyres. I'll take the lad to hospital.'

'Constable!' called Nugget. 'Come and give me a hand. As for you, Brian, one more word out of you and I'll arrest you for interfering with an officer in the execution of his duties. And get your hand off me before I also charge you with assault.'

'Anyone got a camera!' said Brian. 'We need photos. We need photos now!' Nobody stepped forward. Cameras weren't a priority among protesters. 'For God's sake!' said Brian. 'Somebody must have a camera!'

'Let's go,' said Nugget. He and the constable gingerly lifted Jerry and carried him over to the patrol car where they propped him up on the back seat.

'I'm coming with you,' said Summer.

'Bullshit,' said Nugget.

'She comes or I don't go,' said Jerry. His voice was as thick as butter but Nugget had no trouble comprehending.

'Get in,' he snarled. 'Constable, did you get a look at the bike?'

'No, Sergeant.'

'Good work,' said Nugget, relaxing at last. 'Neither did I.'

Brian watched the patrol car roar off, lights flashing and siren braying. Just as it disappeared around the bend the vegie truck laboured into view. Brian sighed, thankful for small mercies. He stood in the middle of the road so he could flag it down and warn the occupants about what was going on. Behind him he heard the driver of the first car that had stopped to help Jerry talking to the driver of the car behind him.

'Your Sigma got aircon?' he heard one driver say.

'No, why?' said the other.

Brian braced himself. He knew why. The puddles under the second car wouldn't be condensation from an airconditioning compressor but coolant from a punctured hose. The vegie truck began tooting its horn and flashing its lights. Brian's shoulders slumped.

The truck rolled passed him and onto the grass verge. Brian looked on in stunned horror while everyone around him recoiled and blocked their noses. A thick cloud of flies instantly descended on the load. The vegies had been split and hacked apart, and raw sewage had been pumped over them.

CHAPTER TWENTY-FIVE

When Joseph Weiss began studying law at university he fully expected to follow in the footsteps of his father, elder brother and elder sister, to graduate with honours and prizes and move on to a glittering and illustrious career. His family were mildly surprised when he began to show an interest in conservation and do volunteer legal work for the Australian Conservation Foundation. They dismissed his interest as an adolescent concern for social issues, an infection to which students seemed especially prone. As graduation drew close, two directors of the ACF and the solitary Victorian Green senator took the gifted law student to lunch and made him a proposition which, by their own admission, he had to be mad to accept. The pay was lousy, the hours unlimited and prospects non-existent.

'Just give us five years of your life,' they begged. 'What you do after that you do with our blessing and gratitude.'

'Will I make a difference?' he asked.

'We'll give you every chance,' they replied.

‘Then five years it is,’ said Joseph.

The Foundation kept their word by giving him Little Potoroo Creek. Joseph’s job was to assemble facts, develop arguments, and prepare briefs for higher-profile advocates to use in the courts and for lobbyists to use in the corridors of power. The Foundation differed from other green groups in that while they supported blockades as part of the spectrum of campaign activities, they didn’t run or organise them themselves. They believed they served the interests of conservationists best by putting pressure on governments to legislate adequate environmental safeguards, and by ensuring the law was followed to the letter.

The backroom role suited Joseph just fine. He had no urge to shine or make his mark other than through the quality of the material he prepared, believing his time would come soon enough once he’d completed his mission. He combed through the Foundation’s files until they were as familiar to him as his own face in the mirror, and he inhabited legal libraries until he was on similar terms with past rulings, judgements and precedents. He devoted every waking hour to making certain that everything he did was thoroughly researched and properly attributed. He was a driven man, but his commitment to conservation was not his only motivation. Joseph believed it was time his family gave thanks for their good fortune by putting something substantial and lasting back into the community. His family made money, occasionally they even made news, but he was the one who was going to make a difference.

Right from the beginning, Joseph realised that saving Tathra Heights and Little Potoroo Creek was precisely the sort of challenge he was looking for. He'd be preserving an untouched wilderness and all its protected and endangered species for future generations and scientific study. He passionately believed that winning the battle against the woodchippers would make a difference from which the whole country would benefit, and committed himself to the task body and soul. He devoured the field studies provided by all the green groups, and petitioned the Department of Conservation and Forestry for access to their files under the Freedom of Information Act. His request was denied on the grounds that the information he sought was the subject of on-going cabinet discussion and therefore quarantined. That convinced Joseph they had something to hide and spurred him on even more.

As usual the Foundation was under-funded and under-resourced and Joseph found himself running out of time and ammunition. Although the weight of evidence from the field studies pointed to the existence in the area of a genetically unique koala colony, along with colonies of leadbeater's possums, long-footed potoroos, spotted-tailed quolls, and flora so rare it sent visiting international conservationists into raptures, the studies had been conducted on an ad hoc basis, with neither thorough documentation nor adherence to normal protocols. It was the work of enthusiasts rather than scientists, and that made it vulnerable to counter argument by DeCaF. No matter how he structured his material, he knew he'd be hard-pressed to get a judge to grant anything more than a temporary injunction preventing work on the access road, and that he'd be lucky to get even that.

Joseph didn't give in to despair, because he couldn't afford the luxury, and continued to press DeCaF for information. When the phone rang it was a rude and unwelcome intrusion.

'Weiss,' he said. 'Make it good and make it quick.'

'Your receptionist said you were the person looking after Little Potoroo Creek.' The voice was hesitant, almost frightened.

'Yes, how can I help you?' Joseph was interested but not enough to quell his impatience. Chances were the voice on the phone belonged to some little old lady somewhere who'd saved up bits from her pension and wanted to make a donation.

'I have some inside information which you might find useful.'

'Might or will?'

'Will.'

'I'm listening.'

'I need to meet you.'

'I'm very busy. How do I know you won't be wasting my time?'

'Your time won't be wasted I can assure you.'

'Can you prove that?'

'Can I trust you to be discreet, Mr Weiss?'

'Can you trust me? Can I trust you? Listen, I'll tell you something I've never told a soul before. I like country music. I love Emmylou Harris and Willie Nelson. Dolly Parton's singing makes me cry. There you go. I've bared my soul. I'm a corny old-fashioned dreamer bordering on manic depressive. What more do you want?' Joseph heard a mirthless laugh from the other end of the phone.

'Oh, I think I can beat that, Mr Weiss.' The phone went silent.

'Go on,' said Joseph. He heard someone draw in a deep breath, as if they were about to plunge into a swimming pool before taking the usual precaution of learning how to swim.

'I'm Cheryl Bollok,' said the voice quietly. 'My husband is Miklos Bollok. Name mean anything to you?'

'Oh my God!' Joseph Weiss was suddenly acutely interested.

'I'm counting on your discretion, Mr Weiss. Your absolute discretion.'

'You've got it! Absolutely! Oh God, where are you? Where can we meet?'

'You tell me. Not your office and nowhere public.'

'My flat in half an hour.' He gave Cheryl his address in South Caulfield and hung up to catch his breath. 'Holy shit!' he said in an outburst so unexpected and atypical that every person in the crowded office momentarily stopped working. He stood, grabbed his car keys and yelled to the receptionist. 'I'm going out,' he told her. 'Take messages.'

'You all right?' she asked anxiously. 'You've gone all pale.'

'No, I'm hysterical! But don't touch me! If I wake up now it could be catastrophic.' Joseph raced out the door. He made it to his flat with five minutes to spare and spent the time picking up stray socks, shoes, coffee mugs and wine glasses. Joseph never drank beer but had an encyclopaedic knowledge of cheap Victorian and South Australian red wine. He gathered up his notes and stacked his reference books in piles on the floor. His last act before the doorbell rang was to clean out his filter coffee jug. He was surprised to note that his hands were shaking.

'Come on up,' he said, and pressed the button that opened the ground floor security door. He took a final look around at the chaos and wondered what had possessed him to invite Cheryl Bollok to his flat and not to some discreet café. Nowhere public, he reminded himself. That had left him little choice. He opened his front door the moment he heard footsteps in the corridor and ushered her inside.

'Come in, come in,' he said nervously. 'Can I make you a coffee?'

'That would be nice.'

'Consider it done.'

'One moment,' said Cheryl. 'Before you do, so we both fully appreciate the nature of the game we're playing…' She walked over to the window and took off her dark glasses and scarf.

'Oh dear God!' said Joseph.

'You may recall seeing some photos of Miklos beating up his four-wheel drive. He did this to me because he thought I'd taken them.'

'Looks like he used you for practice.'

'Not pretty, is it. Five broken teeth, dislocated jaw, cracked cheek bone, two broken ribs and that's just for starters.'

'Was it you … did you take the photos?'

'Miklos doesn't think so, not any more.'

'So he did this to you just on suspicion?'

'Exactly. You're beginning to understand the nature of the man we're dealing with.' Cheryl looked Joseph straight in the eyes and her face hardened, turned wintery. 'My life is in your hands, Mr Weiss. Whatever you do from now on, and whoever you talk to, please bear that in mind.'

Joseph stood silently for a moment while he absorbed the ramifications. He took both her hands gently, smiled ruefully when she winced. 'Please come and sit down, Mrs Bollok.'

He led her to his sofa. It was only as she sat that he realised the brittleness of her facade. Both her hands had begun to shake and her eyes no longer met his. He guessed that she was trying to conceal tears or maybe pain. 'Please, put your mind at rest. I'm a qualified lawyer. A lot of people might scoff at that but I happen to take my responsibilities very seriously, and at the head of those responsibilities is client confidentiality. I'd join Yasser Arafat and the PLO before I'd commit any breach.' He smiled, and was gratified to see Cheryl respond. 'I'll get the coffee.'

His mind was whirling as he turned away. What did she have to tell him that justified her taking such risks? What were her motives? Was it simply a desire for revenge, to get even? Joseph couldn't recall ever feeling so excited. He sensed Cheryl was a strong woman, in character as well as physically, and couldn't begin to imagine what she'd been through. He glanced over his shoulder when he heard her get up and go looking for the bathroom. Gone to plaster over the cracks in the facade, he thought bitterly. He turned the hot tap on with such force it splashed back over his shirt. When he returned with the coffee, Cheryl was waiting quietly on the sofa, legs crossed and hands clasped together on her knee, her composure regained.

‘No sugar, no milk,’ she said before he had a chance to ask. ‘I know you’re busy and I have to get back to the clinic, so do you mind if we get straight into it?’

‘One last question before we do,’ said Joseph. ‘What is your present relationship with your husband?’

‘Same as it’s always been.’ She smiled slightly when she noticed Joseph’s confusion. ‘Miklos needed a wife and so I became his wife and mother to our kids. I doubt that he ever loved me and I’m certain that I never loved him. But I do love his house. It’s not much of a deal, I admit, but it was the best available to me. I consider myself lucky. Now, can we continue?’

‘By all means.’

‘The environmental impact study on Little Potoroo Creek was a sham. No field studies were done for fear that the findings could prove prejudicial. The two men assigned to the job were so overworked they had no time to do anything but write their paper based on prior selectively edited reports. They were given the job for the simple reason that they didn’t have time to do it. I overheard Miklos and Bernie Dwight laughing about it. However, one of the men became a bit concerned at the outright dishonesty and started to go all waffly with his observations and conclusions. Sections of his report were rewritten without his knowledge or consent before the study was released. Apparently the man was outraged. The department offered to promote him and his partner on the unspoken condition that they keep their mouths shut. His partner accepted but he didn’t.

‘Out of the blue he gets an offer of a job from TasIndus — the company that chops down more trees in

Tasmania than anyone else — to run their department which manages the wildlife conservation areas within their concessions. The salary's two and half times what he's getting from DeCaF, they throw in a company car and relocation expenses, private medical insurance and private schooling for his kids. Of course he jumps at it. Who wouldn't? He does the hitherto unthinkable and resigns from his job for life. By now he'll have discovered that his new job is nothing but a sham. He'll be on the outer and his family ostracised by his so-called workmates. TasIndus will do all they can to force his voluntary resignation, but if that fails they'll abolish his department and make him redundant. You see how it works? The department can't fire him so they get someone to hire him who can. Result? DeCaF gets rid of a troublemaker.'

'I'm familiar with the practice. Do you have the man's name?'

'No, but you do. It's on the report. Ring DeCaF and whichever one has left is your man. I doubt you'll have trouble finding him, or getting him to sign a statutory declaration.'

'That would be fantastic,' said Joseph. 'Maybe stupendous, even.' He couldn't help himself and began laughing. 'Mrs Bollok, I don't know what to say ...'

'I haven't finished. Little Potoroo Creek deserves World Heritage Listing or at very least to be declared a national park. Take a look at these photographs.' Cheryl opened the box she'd brought with her and, one by one, showed him Heather's prints.

Joseph sat stunned, in awe of the majesty of the landscapes. 'This is Little Potoroo Creek?' he whispered.

'It's the most beautiful place I've ever seen. There are long-footed potoroos there because I've seen them. God took me to see them.'

'The bloke who wrote to the papers?'

'Yes. He's promised to show me some leadbeater's possums as well. He's found three small colonies.'

'These photographs are beautiful, Mrs Bollok. Did you take them?'

'Yes.'

'They're magnificent, right up there with Olegas Truchanas.'

'You're not the first to say that.'

'Can we have them? Can we use them?'

Cheryl bit her bottom lip. 'I want to paint them. I want to do that more than anything in this world. If you publish them and Miklos sees them, that'll be the end. I'll never be able to go anywhere near them.'

'Mrs Bollok, each of these photographs is worth a thousand pages of any submission we make to have Little Potoroo Creek declared a national park. We have nothing that comes even close to them. These can do as much for us as Olegas Truchanas's and Peter Dombrovskis's photos did to save the Franklin. We need them. If we're successful, you'll be able to photograph Little Potoroo Creek any time you like. Imagine four photos like this one taken from the same spot a season apart? Imagine painting that as a series!'

'You want a lot, Mr Weiss, you really do.'

'Mrs Bollok, when you decided to bring these photos with you, you did so because you fully appreciated their value to us. You must have considered the possibility that we'd want to use them. You must also consider the possibility that you want us to use them.'

Cheryl bowed her head. Everything Joseph Weiss said rang true. In her heart she'd known all along that he'd want her to surrender her photos, and she'd accepted the risk. Joseph's enthusiatic expansion upon her theme cushioned the loss but it still cut to her soul.

'Well?'

'Keep them.' She stood to leave.

'Mrs Bollok, once again I don't know how we'll ever thank you.'

'Just win, Mr Weiss. Just win.'

'Can I get you a taxi?'

'I have a car and driver. It's the least Miklos could do, don't you think?' She smiled thinly.

'Let me see you to the door.'

'Can you guarantee we'll win?'

'No. I'd be lying if I said otherwise. But the information you've given me dramatically improves our chances.'

'Then there is one more thing,' said Cheryl.

Joseph couldn't imagine what else there could be.

'This information may come in handy, used with discretion at the right moment. You know who Bernie Dwight is of course?'

'Of course.'

'I understand he has quite a taste for young women. Not just young women, but really young women. Do you follow?'

'What are you suggesting?' Joseph couldn't help showing his distaste. 'The Foundation doesn't engage in blackmail, Mrs Bollok, and neither do I.'

'Sometimes, in serving a higher cause, it becomes necessary to get your hands dirty.' She turned on him. 'Sometimes you have to fight fire with fire. Sometimes you have to give up what people have no right to ask. If Miklos had pictures of you buggering little boys do you think for one second he'd hesitate to use them?' Her sudden viciousness caught Joseph by surprise. 'Hire a private detective. Get photos and names and keep them in your file. You may never need them, but then again you might. You'd be amazed at how reasonable and accommodating Bernie Dwight can be, given the right persuasion. If we lose Little Potoroo Creek because of your preciousness, it'll be on your head!' She slammed the door behind her.

Joseph stared at the back of the door. The intensity of her outburst had left him speechless. She'd just accused him of buggering little boys and of being precious, and he hotly denied his guilt on both counts. Or had she? No. He drew a deep breath and tried to become the cool and calculating lawyer he imagined himself to be. She was the one taking all the risks, she was the one who'd suddenly brought the unattainable within reach. She was the one who was cool and calculating. All she wanted was for him to be prepared to make the same level of sacrifice that she had, and to use all the means at his disposal. The kick in the pants was to make sure he did. Joseph let Cheryl put some distance between her and himself while he collected his thoughts, then raced downstairs to his own car. He had phone calls to make, leads to pursue, and a deadline that was fast slipping away. 'God bless you, Cheryl Bollok!' he shouted out loud as he ran an amber light.

His first call was to DeCaF to get the name of the man he was after. Maurice Connolly. Joseph hoped he was the stuff of heroes despite his unpromising christian name. The second and third calls were to TasIndus to locate him. Maurice Connolly turned out to be a mouse of a man, so beaten down and paranoid that he feared his phone was being tapped. Joseph's fourth call was to book a late flight to Hobart for a clandestine meeting. He made his fifth call out of a sense of obligation, told the private detective what he required, and made arrangements to fund the exercise personally. If the business with Bernie Dwight backfired he wanted the Foundation exempted from his indiscretion.

He made his sixth call to Liz at EGCGs, but had to make do with leaving a message on her answerphone. He chose his words carefully, not wishing to give rise to false hope or to reveal his hand. He wished her every success with the blockade and made his request. Work on the road was scheduled to begin in just three days and Joseph needed time. He needed the blockade to hold out for at least a week, and maybe even for as long as a month, while he prepared a water-tight case. He used the word 'imperative' and knew Liz would pick up on it.

* * *

The locals reckoned they could hear the droning of the flies above the groaning of the truck as it followed Brian's car back into Orbost, executed a cumbersome U-turn and parked right outside the post office in the town's main street. People came out of shops to see what the appalling smell was and promptly wished they hadn't. Pedestrians retreated as fast as their legs could carry them with handkerchiefs clamped to their noses. Dogs slunk away, head down, their tails between their legs, lest they be blamed. Flies swarmed as thick as a blanket over the foul load.

Brian made certain both of the truck's doors were securely locked, sent the driver and passenger two hundred metres up the road to the café where Jerry had stopped for coffee, walked into the post office and asked for five dollars worth of change for the public phone. He hadn't a clue what to do with the load of polluted vegetables. He couldn't leave it at the local tip and it went against everything he believed in to just dump it in the bush somewhere. Ideally he would have liked to dump it on Miklos's front doorstep, at his mill or in the car park of Osbourne's pub, but realised that the satisfaction it would give him would only be temporary, and would be massively outweighed by the consequences. So he rang the local council and made the disposal of the polluted vegetables their problem. He told the horrified town clerk where the truck was parked and asked her to ring him back when she had a solution.

He rang the bakery and asked the manager to save all the unsold bread and returns for him. The manager baulked, claiming that to do so would identify him as a blockade sympathiser and alienate his customers. Brian told him about the truck and where it was parked and made his cooperation a condition of its removal. The manager promptly agreed that he'd be acting in his customers' best interests by agreeing to Brian's request. The leftover bread was only destined for piggeries anyway, he said, and claimed that was about all it was fit for.

Next he rang the Orbost police station and told them about Jerry's accident. He informed them that the *Gazette* was on the way with a photographer, and if the police wished to emerge with a shred of integrity intact they'd be wise to get to the scene, interview witnesses and make a report. He rang James Ferguson and told him not just about the accident but about the various acts of sabotage. James laughed out loud when Brian told him where he'd parked the truck. He promised to dispatch both of his reporters immediately.

Brian brushed a fly off his cheek in disgust, knowing full well what it had just been paddling in. He rang Liz on her mobile and told her everything that had happened, and asked her to organise transport to pick up the stranded protesters.

'How are we going to feed everyone?' she asked.

'I think I can get enough food to get by. I've organised a raid on the bakery for their leftover bread, and I'll buy up every roadside produce stall within ten miles of Osbourne.'

'Will they sell to you?'

'Ever known anybody around here to turn down a dollar?' Brian hunched over the phone and wished, for once, that vandals had bombed the glass in the phone booth. He could hear people shouting and looking for him. 'It won't be organic, and I hate the thought of giving our money to the local farmers, but I reckon they'll hate selling their produce to us just as much. But those bastards never turn their back on a buck. They'll sell me all they've got. I'll have to hire a trailer to carry everything.'

'The good news is you won't have to buy for the skinheads,' said Liz.

'Why?' asked Brian warily.

'The bad news is they decided they wanted meat for a change and went out and clubbed a couple of sheep to death.'

'Dear God!'

'They're skinning and butchering them right now. Well, half of them are. The other half of them are fighting off the animal rights brigade and the militant vegos. It's one big bloody picnic here and I mean bloody. Can you believe they used an axe to cut the sheep up into bits small enough to barbecue? It's just sickening.'

'What are they using for a barbecue plate?'

'A door off that old Datsun someone abandoned down the road. Maybe the rust adds flavour.'

'Anything I can do?'

'Not a bloody thing. Just get food for the rest of us.'

When Liz asked about Jerry and Summer, Brian remembered the call he still had to make. The moment he hung up to look for the number of the Bairnsdale Community Hospital the pay phone began ringing. It was the town clerk and she had a solution. Brian told her where to find the driver and hung up before she went into details. He'd never known the council to respond to anything so quickly, but then they'd probably never had so many angry desperate ratepayers ringing and abusing them before. He smiled grimly as he dialled the hospital number.

The nurse was reluctant to release any information on the basis that the immediate family had not yet been informed. When pressed she conceded that Jerry seemed to have escaped injury apart from bruising, gravel burn and the damage to his fingers, but was being kept under observation because of suspected concussion. 'He was lucky,' she said. 'He didn't hit anything. If he'd hit a tree or a lamppost he'd be an organ donor.' She told him they'd admitted Summer as well with what they thought was food poisoning. Brian hung up. At least he wouldn't have to drive to Bairnsdale to collect Summer, not for a day or so anyway. Hospital was the perfect place for her. When he walked back out onto the street he found an angry mob surrounding the truck, albeit at a distance.

'Jesus, Brian! What the hell are you playing at? Get that stinkin' heap outta here!'

Brian recognised the shopkeeper who'd called out, a man he was normally on good terms with. 'Don't you get it?' he replied. 'This is Miklos's idea of a joke. Thought he'd want me to share it with you.' He hopped into his car and drove off through a chorus of abuse. He had a trailer to hire, bread to pick up, vegetables to buy and, afterwards, a rightfully angry mob of protesters to hose down. Certain elements would demand revenge. Sometimes it was tempting to seek immediate revenge, but Brian knew there was only one kind of revenge that mattered. Saving Little Potoroo Creek would be their revenge, and as fine a revenge as anyone could want.

* * *

Clyde Townsend hung up the phone for the second to last time that day and sat back in his chair, well satisfied. The Gippsland Aboriginal people had lodged a claim for title over Little Potoroo Creek on the basis of continuous occupation, but he'd been expecting it and his legal team had prepared an impressive, thoroughly documented counter argument. The Aboriginal people's case was flimsy and relied more on rhetoric and the suspect memory of elders than facts. Even allowing for the vagaries of judicial rulings Clyde was confident his team could blow any land claim out of court, an opinion adamantly held by his QC. He flicked his TV on in time to see an interview with Bernie Dwight, which he'd orchestrated and which had been recorded earlier in the afternoon.

'Fifteen hundred protesters,' said Bernie in mock alarm. 'You'd be lucky to count five hundred even if you counted everyone twice.' He laughed on cue as he'd been instructed. 'I've been there, and all I saw were the same familiar faces, the same ratbag bunch of dole bludgers you see at every blockade, people who won't rest until they've brought every decent hard-working Australian down to their level. I'll be generous and say there's two hundred of them, but certainly no more.'

'What about Aboriginal protesters?' asked the interviewer. 'I understand they've set up camp there.'

'Beg your pardon,' said Bernie. 'There have been no Aborigines living around Little Potoroo Creek for more than two hundred years, since before Captain Cook first set foot on this continent, and I'm here to tell you there are no Aborigines camped there now.'

'Are you certain about that?'

'Absolutely,' said Bernie with conviction. 'They wouldn't even know where to find the place.' He laughed at his own cleverness and leant in confidentially towards the camera. 'I promise you, the only black butts down there are trees.' He roared with laughter, as if the line was something he'd just come up with and not had fed to him by one of Clyde's writers.

Clyde pressed the off button. Bernie was the best puppet he'd ever had: he always stuck to the script and never tried to introduce an original thought of his own. He was the perfect mouthpiece. Clyde savoured the moment. The Aboriginal issue was as good as dead and Bernie had managed to convey to the world — and especially the media — that the Little Potoroo Creek blockade was poorly attended and of no news value whatsoever. Nevertheless he made his final call to Bernie to remind him to put pressure on DeCaF to begin work on the access road on Monday as scheduled, and to ensure they made no announcement of the commencement of work. Truth could rarely be suppressed entirely, but it could be contained until it no longer had value, provided they took full advantage in the interim. They had to get the road underway and the blockade crushed, and the sooner the better in both instances. Clyde glowed with satisfaction. He had the opposition on the run and, without the prying eyes of TV cameras, Miklos would soon crush the protest. The spiked trees were the ace up his sleeve. Clyde firmly believed that issue management was the most powerful tool ever invented by man, and at that moment he felt his power was unlimited. It gave him a thrill which was almost as intense as sex.

CHAPTER TWENTY-SIX

The three DeCaF lowloaders pulled into Osbourne at dusk on Saturday. They arrived in convoy in a blatant show of strength, passing by the front of the pub amid a roar of straining diesels and blasts from air brakes. The bar emptied as drinkers poured out onto the verandahs and into the car park to watch the procession. They stood silently, almost in awe and trepidation, as if the lowloaders were carrying tanks to a battle front rather than three huge brutish Caterpillar bulldozers. The trucks drove through the town and out onto Thirsty Creek Road where they pulled up onto the shoulder and parked nose to tail. They were followed minutes later by two cherry pickers which turned into the pub car park and pulled up around the back.

'Bloody bewdy!' said Arnie.

'Yeah,' said Miklos. 'Bernie's done real good. I figured we'd get two mid-size dozers and instead we've got three heavies. And two cherry pickers, not one.' The bulldozers weren't quite to the scale Miklos had grown up watching rip tonnes of ore from the earth to ship off to Japan, but they were still intimidatingly large. The crowd had begun to drift back to the bar but Miklos made no attempt to join them. 'Tell Davo to take my Toyota and go pick up the blokes in the lowloaders. You better go as well in your ute. If the Cat operators came in the trucks as well there'll be six to pick up. Go make them feel welcome. Tell them to come and see me when they've checked in.'

As Miklos turned to go back inside a jacked-up ute pulled into the car park, windscreen wipers working. He stared into its headlights and saw the telltale streaks. The lowloaders had brought more than bulldozers with them, they'd also brought rain. Miklos cursed but found it hard to get angry. DeCaF had got their act together and were ready to begin on schedule, and they'd thrown an impressive amount of weight into the battle. That was all that mattered. He turned back into the pub. Macka had told him about the bookings, how DeCaF had taken every room he had available, and Nugget had told him about the police contingent due at Osbourne's one and only motel on Sunday. But bookings were easily made and just as easily cancelled and Miklos was reluctant to believe anyone was coming until they actually arrived.

'Jesus, Miklos,' said Macka. 'Is that a smile on your face?'

'Nah, just the look of a thirsty man.'

The publican poured a schooner of draught which disappeared inside Miklos's massive fist and then down his throat. Macka poured a second without asking. Miklos still looked thirsty.

'Macka, I want to make these DeCaF blokes feel welcome.' Miklos paused while he emptied half his glass in a single gulp. 'I'll pay for their drinks till midnight Sunday. Come Monday they buy their own, unless I say otherwise. Oh yeah, and they don't buy for anyone else, okay?'

'Okay,' said Macka. 'Here they come. Want to tell them yourself?'

'G'day,' said Miklos. He held out a massive hand in greeting. 'Welcome to Osbourne.' He proceeded to tell them just how welcome they were and, in doing so, began the process of buying their unswerving support. The DeCaF men hit the bar as one. 'What's the rush?' said Miklos. 'I said you've got till midnight Sunday.'

'Yeah,' said one of the dozer operators. 'Not a second to waste.'

Miklos laughed. He liked being among big men who handled heavy equipment and really knew how to drink. He could feel himself begin to relax and the sensation startled him. He'd almost forgotten what it felt like to relax and couldn't recall when he'd last felt that way. He laughed again for no particular reason, downed the rest of his schooner and fronted the bar for another. Other drinkers picked up on his mood and the hum of conversation rose to a boisterous roar. Arnie started telling the newcomers how he'd dumped raw sewage over the vegie truck — he had their rapt attention. Two morons up from Orbost told how they'd shot the front wheel off a motorbike at seventy ks. Wozza and Charlie waited impatiently to impress with their heroics. Miklos smiled, as contented as any man could be. The war stories were an important part of priming the troops for battle, and that was how he saw the impending confrontation. He had every reason to smile because his side had all the big guns, he led with strength and he had the law — if not right — on his side. But a good leader pays as much attention to defence as offence and doesn't relax until he is certain his troops and equipment are secure. Miklos banged his empty glass down on the bar to get Macka's attention and looked for Wozza and Davo.

His mistake was to think they were all the defence he needed.

* * *

By Sunday morning every person at the blockade had heard about the bulldozers and estimates of their size grew by the hour. Protesters gathered under every awning out of the rain and discussed the new development. Brian wandered from gathering to gathering, becoming increasingly concerned at the change of mood that had come over the blockade. There should have been a growing sense of excitement now that the waiting was almost over and an impatience to engage the enemy. But instead Brian sensed an undercurrent of nervousness. No one was leading war chants. No one was shouting, 'What do we want?' and no one was answering. No one was painting signs or rehearsing symbolic little plays for the benefit of the TV cameras. Even the skinheads and Guardians had stopped baiting each other and become disconcertingly quiet. He knew he had to do something to put the new threat into perspective or the blockade was already as good as over. He spotted Ciaron with the mob from the squat and waved them over.

'I need your help desperately,' he said. 'Get as many people as you can and join me out front in five.'

'What's wrong?' said Ciaron.

'Look around you,' said Brian. 'Use your eyes. Nothing's happened and already everyone's running scared.'

'Effin' wimps,' said Ciaron.

'Can't you do what you have to do under the tarp?' said The Dick. 'Bloody rainin' out front.'

'See what I mean?' said Ciaron. 'Effin' wimps! Leave it to me.'

Brian had to smile as Ciaron started hauling every person she knew to their feet. The Dick got into the swing of things and laid into the skinheads. Gretta went off to the humpies to speak to the Guardians. They'd discovered common ground in their interest in native medicines and herbs and Gretta had introduced them to the practice of harmonising. Stretch propped his guitar up against one of the tarp posts and sauntered over to Brian.

'What's up?' he asked.

Brian told him.

'You haven't got the voice for it,' said Stretch. 'Leave it to a pro.' He collected his guitar and wandered out in front of the tarps behind the last line of tripods. He ignored the rain and started to strum a song of defiance he'd written at a blockade in Tasmania, only this time he sang it with a lisp. 'Move over bulldozer, you don't frighten me,' he sang. 'Move over bulldozer, I'm tied up to this tree ...' He had the attention of everybody up front and the people behind pressed forward to see what was going on and share the joke. Stretch started to mince and sound wimpish and nobody had the slightest doubt who or what he was singing about. Nervousness began to give way to embarrassment. Stretch saw Ciaron and her troops squeeze to the front and abruptly ended his song. 'Hey! You!' he yelled. 'Save Little Potoroo!'

'Hey! You!' screamed Ciaron and the troops. 'Save Little Potoroo!'

'Hey! You!' Stretch cupped his ear as if to hear better.

'Save Little Potoroo!' The response trebled in volume as others joined in.

'Hey! You!'

'Save Little Potoroo!'

'Are we scared?'

'No!'

'I said, are we scared?'

'NO!' The roar scattered birds from trees a kilometre away. They whirled and swooped, adding their indignant cries to the chorus.

'What're we gunna do?'

'Kick arse!'

'What're we gunna do?'

'KICK ARSE!' The Guardians shook their fists and the skinheads screamed so violently spittle dribbled down their chins. 'KICK ARSE!' they screamed. 'KICK ARSE! KICK ARSE! KICK ARSE!'

Stretch let them shout themselves hoarse then held up both hands for silence. 'Now shut up and listen to the man. He's gunna tell ya how to handle these jerks!' Stretch had got the crowd going and they applauded wildly as Brian walked out front to address them. He copied Stretch and raised his arms for silence.

'Let's get things in perspective,' he said. 'Did anyone expect them to try to move us with their bare hands?'

'No!'

'Did anyone expect them to try to move us without using bulldozers?'

'No!'

'So okay, they've brought in three. Big deal. Look out front here, look how narrow the road is. See? It doesn't matter how many bulldozers they bring because they can only use one at a time! There's not enough room to use two let alone three!' Brian paused to let the laughter die down. 'It doesn't matter how big or how small the bulldozers are. Fact is, even a little one can pull down a tripod.' Once again he paused and then raised his voice. 'But no bulldozer, no matter how big, can pull down a tripod while someone's sitting on it!'

'Yeah!' shouted the protesters.

'No cherry picker ever made can reach over fifteen hundred angry people to pluck the sitters off the tripods either!'

'Yeah!'

'No bulldozer operator can drive his machine while people are chained to it!'

'Yeah!'

'No bulldozer operator can drive his machine over a road already occupied by protesters!'

'Yeah!'

'No police force in this country can clear a path through us when we are determined we will not be moved!'

'Yeah!'

'Anyway,' said Brian, 'by the time we finish digging wide trenches out front there, those bulldozers will be lucky if they go anywhere!'

'Yeah!'

'So give me volunteers. I want pits and mounds, pits and mounds! You know what to do! Get shovels and get digging!' Brian stood back and watched the stampede. The protesters started stripping off clothes and racing to get shovels.

'Good on yer,' said Stretch. 'You're a natural.'

'Bullshit. You're a helluva act to follow.' Despite his denials Brian felt he had done well and it showed in his smile.

'It won't work.'

Brian spun around, his smile fading. God had ghosted up behind him.

'It won't work,' God repeated.

'I know,' said Brian. 'But at least they're doing something positive, something they think is constructive. At least they've stopped worrying about the bulldozers.'

'It's not enough,' said God. 'We must take an eye for an eye.'

'Sure,' said Brian. 'First find the eye.' He turned away. Sometimes God gave him the shits. Half an hour earlier the protesters had been quaking in their boots, now they were ready to kick arse. So what if the trenches didn't do anything? At least the troops had something to focus on and pour their energies into. Brian knew damn well that once they'd been dug deep enough and become sloppy in the rain, the kids would start playing silly buggers. They'd treat the pits like a kindergarten playground. Slide in it, roll in it, wallow in it. Mud wrestlers would have nothing on them. Brian was sure God also knew what would happen. But the thought occurred to him that maybe God also knew something he didn't and had a plan. An eye for eye, God had said, and he wasn't the kind who said things lightly. Brian opened his mouth to speak but God had already gone.

'He went thataway,' said Stretch, pointing back towards the treehouses. 'I'm gunna get my guitar out of the rain before the strings rust.' He sauntered away. Brian turned his attention back to the job at hand. Up ahead of him, in front of the tripods, he could already see dirt flying off shovels in the wrong direction. God's assessment was right, but Brian still had to perpetuate an illusion of usefulness.

'Hold it! Hold it!' he yelled. 'The bulldozers have to cross the pits first not the mounds. If you build the mounds in front, they'll just bulldoze them back into the pits and we'll have achieved nothing. Okay? Get the order right. Pit mound, pit mound. And leave room for the vegie truck to get through.'

The rain intensified as the wind gusted and he shivered. He couldn't see the enthusiasm for digging trenches lasting. Already the diggers were finding the going hard: the rocky ground was difficult to penetrate and the soil heavy and gluey. Volunteers were already complaining about sods sticking to their shovels. He had to accept that the soil was too full of rocks and gravel for there to be any mud baths or slides, and wondered how the hell everyone was going to fill in the rest of the day. Some would sit around and try to get high by chewing sassafras roots or smoking carefully hoarded joints. Some would go on kitchen detail, and others would use the time to repair holes in clothes or make more signs to wave in front of the cameras. But that would still leave a lot of bored restless people of differing views with time on their hands, and Brian was well aware that it was a combination which often led to fights. He found himself half wishing that Arnie and his mates would show up for a pre-confrontation skirmish, a preliminary to the main bout to unite the factions against the common enemy, or that the skinheads in the four-wheel drive riding shotgun on the vegie truck would turn up with a load of beer in the back. Not enough so anyone got pissed and caused trouble, but enough to create a diversion. Anything to create a diversion!

He heard a sudden shout and looked up in time to see one end of a banner strung between two gums break free in the wind. He shrugged despondently and shivered. Some people weren't fit to tie their own shoelaces. As he headed back to shelter he noticed tarpaulins and tents beginning to sag under the weight of the rain, and some of the Guardians abandoning their saturated humpies for drier accommodation. Others had moved into their cars and lay curled up on seats. He hoped that Liz would think to bring him some dry clothes on the way back from picking up Summer and Jerry from Bairnsdale.

* * *

Miklos held court in the saloon bar of the pub, surrounded by the DeCaF crew and his own inner circle of thugs. The pub had closed officially at twelve the night before but they'd kept drinking through till four in the morning, had split up to grab a couple of hours of sleep, and risen to a greasy country breakfast of fried eggs, chops, steaks, sausages and bacon before getting back into the beer.

'You boys sure know how to drink,' said Arnie as Macka brought another fistful of jugs.

'Head hurtin'?' asked one of the Cat operators known as The Bear.

'Arnie doesn't get hangovers,' said Miklos. 'No brain, no pain.'

Arnie smirked stupidly. He liked the idea of not feeling pain and didn't see Miklos's comment as an insult. It wouldn't have made any difference if he had. Miklos let conversation follow its own course until he figured the Cat operators were sufficiently lubricated by his generosity to be malleable. 'So,' he began innocently, 'only one of you blokes has done a blockade before?'

'S'right,' said The Bear. 'Just me.'

'It seems to me you blokes can handle things two ways. You can come down here and do everything the cops let you do, have a nice East Gippsland holiday with free food and accommodation and lots of free booze thrown in, or you can do what you were sent here to do, get the job done, and earn yourselves a bit of a tax-free bonus as an expression of our gratitude.'

'How much?' asked The Bear.

'Depends,' said Miklos.

'What do ya want us to do?'

'Just get the job done, son. Sometimes that means goin' the extra yard, not quite stoppin' when the cops say stop, and goin' again before the cops say go. Y'see, those dole-bludging ferals out there think all they have to do is lie down on the road in front of you and they've got you by the balls.'

'Ya want us to run them over?' asked The Bear.

'Nah, but I like the way you're thinkin',' said Miklos. He laughed, which cued Arnie and the boys to join in. 'Nah,' said Miklos. 'Not even Nugget would stand for that. Can't see the world would be any poorer if you squashed a few of them bastards but the media would do us like dinners.'

'Then what?' asked one of The Bear's associates.

'Simple,' said Miklos. 'We let the cops clear the protesters out of the way and you fill the space with your bulldozer the moment it's clear. You've got to think like you're in the army. The instant we break their defences we have to seize the advantage. The cops'll try and stop you because right in front of you will be these bloody great tripods made of logs and standin' anything up to ten metres high. They'll have some stinkin' feral strapped to the top of them defyin' you to knock them down. At that point you can give in and come back here and enjoy your happy holiday. They win, you lose, we lose. Or you can have an accident.' Miklos sat back and poured himself a beer. The Cat operators followed suit but Miklos could see them thinking.

'What sorta accident?' asked The Bear.

'It's a funny thing,' said Miklos, 'but most people haven't a clue how ya drive those things. All they see is the size and the sheer weight of metal. You know — and I know because I've operated them — that they're more manoeuvrable than the family car. But most people don't know that. Nugget doesn't know that, and even if you told him he wouldn't believe it. Right, Nugget?'

‘Right there,’ said Nugget. ‘I don’t believe it. And I think it might be wise if I went for a snake’s hiss before ya tell me anythin’ else I won’t believe.’

‘Smart thinkin’,’ said Miklos. ‘Now listen close.’ He leant in towards the Cat operators and told them what he required.

‘No worries,’ said The Bear. ‘Bastard of a left track keeps lockin’ and skiddin’ on me. Got a friggin’ mind of its own.’ He laughed. ‘What sorta bonus were ya talkin’ about?’

‘We’ll discuss that later,’ said Miklos. ‘In private. Don’t want my blokes thinkin’ they’re hard done by. Now, have I told you about the treehouses? No? Well, tune in.’ Miklos told them about the treehouses and the interconnecting walkways. ‘There’ll be ferals crawlin’ all over them,’ he said. ‘Any of you blokes ever been fruit pickin’?’ No one had. ‘Well, there’s a couple of ways of doing it — the hard way and the smart way. The hard way is to pick all the fruit one by one. It takes forever and costs heaps. The smart way is to shake the trunk so all the ripe fruit falls down to the ground where you just pick it up and put it straight into boxes. We gotta shift them the smart way.’

‘Dunno ’bout that,’ said The Bear. ‘Them ferals fall to the ground you’ll be puttin’ them straight into boxes as well. Cops ain’t gunna like that. Media ain’t gunna like that much either.’

‘The trick,’ said Miklos patiently, ‘is to persuade them to come down of their own accord. Look, they’ll have seen the tripods go. They’ll have seen that the cops have lost control. They’ll be so scared there’ll be brown rain fallin’ before you can even get near them. You gotta make them believe that nothing's gunna stop you. Not the cops, nothin'. You gotta act like you're hittin' the trees hard. You know and I know that you can just drive straight through any tree in your way. I also know that if you want you can just shake the dew off a single leaf. It's your call. It's your equipment and you blokes know what you're doin'. How hard you shake the trees is your business. All I'm interested in is results. When you hit those trees just think you're hittin' me, and you're not just shakin' stupid ferals out of the branches, you're shakin' money outta my pockets. You're allowed to laugh while you're doin' it.'

'Shouldn't be a problem,' said The Bear. He liked Miklos. Miklos liked giving money away and he liked receiving it. In The Bear's eyes that made them a good team. 'Had a lot of trouble with the hydraulics on my blade. Get a bit rough at times.' He turned to his mates. 'What about you blokes?'

'Same here,' they said. 'Must be a fault in the design.'

'What comes after the trees?' asked The Bear.

'Victory,' said Miklos. 'So long as you keep goin'. Whatever happens you don't stop. Just go for glory, straight down the line of the road. Knock everything down. Don't stop for anyone or anything.'

'What happens to us if we accidentally squash some poor bastard?' asked one of The Bear's mates. 'I ain't goin' to gaol.'

'No one's goin' to gaol. We'll make sure you don't,' said Miklos. 'That's Arnie's job and he's not the sort to let you squash anybody he could squash himself. Arnie likes squashing people, don't ya, Arnie? But once again, I like the way you're thinkin'.'

*   *   *

Liz was exhausted by the time she pulled up outside the two-storey house that was her home and office. The clock ticked past eight and all she could think about was dinner and falling into bed. She wished she had a tenth of the energy of her passengers, who in the preceding days had done nothing more strenuous than visit the toilet.

'Look in the fridge,' she said to Summer. 'Whatever's in there is dinner.'

'I'm not hungry,' said Summer.

'I am,' said Liz. 'And you're eating whether you like it or not. And then it's bed.'

'No way!' said Summer. 'We're going out to the blockade.'

'We'll go tomorrow.'

'We mightn't be able to get through tomorrow. They might close the road.'

Liz had to concede that Summer had a point.

'There's nothing in here except the fridge light,' said Jerry. 'Hang on, there's some butter and half a packet of parmesan cheese in the door.'

'There might be some bread in the freezer,' said Liz hopefully. 'How does parmesan on toast sound to you?'

'Terrible. If you've got any Barilla I'll make a pasta.'

'In the cupboard beside the fridge. You'll find a bottle of olive oil there too.'

'Any chillies?'

'There's a small bush in a pot outside the back door. Be careful, they're hot.' Liz smiled for the first time since picking them up. 'If you make me a pasta I'll take you out to the blockade.'

'Done!' said Summer.

Liz slumped down at her desk and started listening to her phone messages. She was tempted to ring Brian on his mobile and chew his ears. He'd made everything sound so easy. Just pick up Summer and Jerry from Bairnsdale, and while you're there pick up various fan belts and radiator hoses which had suddenly become totally unavailable in Osbourne and Orbost. It seemed that every make of car and every model took a different size and the only thing they had in common was that they were usually out of stock. She'd spent the day trekking from garage to garage until she'd managed to fill most of her order, and then persuaded a sympathetic RVAC road serviceman to part with the rest. When she'd finally got to the hospital she'd copped a blast from Summer and Jerry for making them wait all day in the visitors' room in front of a television that only ran infomercials on osteoporosis and intestinal worms. By that stage Liz was tired, hungry, cold and wet through from the constant rain. She'd burst into tears.

She listened as one caller after another left a message, but there was no message from the one person she was anxious to hear from, someone she'd never met and knew only by reputation. She wanted to know exactly how imperative 'imperative' was, and why.

'Come and get it,' said Jerry. 'Pasta alla Gino and something that's trying hard to be a side salad.'

'What's wrong with it?' demanded Summer.

'What's right with it?' countered Jerry.

'Should I open a red?' asked Liz.

'I'm not allowed alcohol,' said Summer.

'And I'm off for a month on doctor's orders,' said Jerry. 'But don't let us stop you.'

'You have already,' said Liz. As bad as her day had been she wasn't going to end it drinking alone. She stuck her fork into the spaghetti and twirled. 'Hey, this is good!'

'Olive oil, garlic, chilli and black pepper. *Aglio e olio*.'

'Summer, take my advice. Marry this man.' For the first time that day Liz was beginning to feel good.

* * *

'Boom!' said Davo.

Wozza stared out through the windscreen, wishing he was back in the pub sinking beer.

'Got 'im!' said Davo.

Wozza just carried on staring through the windscreen, wishing he was anywhere else with anyone else. Anywhere but stuck in a ute with Davo.

'How about that?' said Davo.

'How about what?' said Wozza. He tried not to take any notice of Davo but every now and then he found his mouth working before his brain did.

'Boom. Right up the date.'

'What were you aiming at?'

'Its date, of course.'

'What's date?' said Wozza impatiently. Davo had pushed the passenger seat as far back as it would go and lowered the back rest so he had room to rest his semi-automatic against his shoulder and sight along the barrel. He'd been firing imaginary bullets at imaginary animals ever since Miklos got Arnie to send them down to keep an eye on the bulldozers. Wozza was not happy. He could've been drinking. Instead he was babysitting three massive hunks of metal and Arnie's younger brother. His throat was screaming out for some amber lubrication. Wouldn't be so bad if they'd given them a slab. Wozza reckoned he could sit anywhere forever so long as they kept the tinnies coming.

'Galah's date.'

'Yeah, right,' said Wozza.

'Know how many that is?' said Davo slyly.

'No.'

'Fifty-five, and I haven't missed yet.'

'Jesus ...' Wozza sighed. The kid was actually counting.

'Boom!' said Davo. 'Fifty-six.'

'Amazin'. Dunno how you do it,' said Wozza. 'I can't see a thing out there. The windows are fogged up. It's pissin' down. It's darker than the inside of a cow yet you can see well enough to shoot fifty-six galahs without missing even once.'

'I'm only pretendin' to shoot them, Wozza.' Davo grinned shyly in the dark at Wozza's stupidity. 'Boom! See?' he explained.

Wozza shook his head in exasperation. He'd never claimed to be smart but Davo made him feel like Einstein.

'That's fifty-seven, right?'

'Right,' said Wozza. 'Wake me up when you get to a million.' He leant his head against the side window and closed his eyes.

'Just keepin' me eye in, just in case, like.'

'Good on yer. Now let me get some sleep.'

'Okay.' He sighted along the barrel but didn't pretend to shoot. 'Wozza?'

'What?'

'I'm hungry.'

'So you said.'

'Know what I'd like?'

'Yeah. You've told me ten friggin' times! A sausage and egg McMuffin.'

'Yeah. Get hungry just thinkin' about it.' A fart exploded in Davo's trousers.

'Fifty-eight,' said Wozza automatically.

* * *

God knew all about wet skin, wind chill and hypothermia. He wore a heavy-duty plastic garbage bag over his upper body, with just one hole cut for his neck, and his arms folded in front of him keeping dry. He strode out like a man on a mission on tireless legs accustomed to being without transport. Despite the fact that he could barely see the road in front of him he kept up a solid pace. God hadn't intended to follow the road but skirt around through the logged forest behind the fringe of trees that lined the road. However the constant rain and darkness meant that he'd have to use his torch and that could give him away. God didn't want anybody to know he was abroad let alone where he was headed. So he stuck to the road and adhered to the caution he'd learnt tracking quolls and potoroos: every so often he stopped dead in his tracks, head up, sniffing and listening for the sound of approaching cars. He'd learnt to listen for cars up in Little Potoroo Creek, where he'd learnt everything else that now governed his life, while he sat and waited for Liz to deliver his supplies or bring the gift of Summer. Anybody watching him in action would have discarded conventional theories and come away convinced that man had descended not from apes but from kangaroos.

He walked on and on, purposefully and single-mindedly, taking to the bush once as an old VW Kombi passed by on its way out to the blockade. When at last he could hear an intermittent buzz of traffic and smell smoke from fireplaces and wood-burning stoves he left the road for good. Tracking animals had taught God how to move quickly and silently through scrub, how sometimes the quickest way was on hands and knees using the tracks and tunnels large animals used. It didn't take him long to spot his target. It was blacker even than the blackness of the night. He circled it, eyes straining, nose sniffing for telltale wafts of cigarette smoke, ears pricked for the sort of sounds humans make. He froze as a wombat began scrabbling in the dark, digging for roots. God circled it, knowing it wasn't always smart to come between a wombat and its burrow. When he was certain the only threat came from the two men in the ute parked on the opposite side of the road, he turned and crawled a hundred metres back the way he'd come, stripped off his clothes, rolled them up, wrapped them within his garbage bag to keep dry, and left them at the foot of the only decent-sized gum tree left standing. At that point all he wore was his Swiss army knife on a string around his neck.

He'd already begun to shiver as he dipped his hands into a puddle and scooped out a handful of mud from the bottom. He let the water run off through his fingers before working the mud-like dough until it reached an even sticky consistency. First he covered his body, then his arms and face. The coating of mud brought some relief from the wind but God knew how temporary the respite was. He had work to do and precious little time to do it before the cold got him. He crawled back through the scrub towards his target, pausing to pull his Swiss army knife over his head and lever open the largest blade.

He crouched, listening for any changes that might have occurred in his absence. The ute had not moved and, in the sudden flare of a match lit for a cigarette, he saw the two men and something that froze him to the spot — a rifle pointed in his direction.

* * *

'Boom!' said Davo. 'One hundred and twenty-three.'

Wozza sucked bitterly on his cigarette. He wanted a beer, needed a beer, craved a beer. They were still drinking at the pub and nobody had thought to bring him so much as a single tinnie. His throat was dry, he was irritable and it was plainly obvious that he was just wasting good drinking time, sitting there serving no purpose. He knew better but knowing better rarely proved a deterrent to Wozza. He snapped. 'That all you gunna do all night? One hundred and twenty-three, for fucksake!'

'What's your problem? May as well do something.'

'That's doing something?' Wozza knew all about Davo. His fists had taken out more teeth than all the dentists in Melbourne since Federation. With a rifle in his hands he was a total nutcase, worse than Arnie. Wozza knew he should stop right then, but he had the shits and someone had to know it. It was his bad luck that Davo was the closest. 'That's doing something, pretending to shoot birds you only pretend you can see?'

'It ain't hurtin' no one.'

'It's friggin' hurtin' me! It's driving me friggin' crazy. Boom! One hundred and twenty-four. Boom! One hundred and twenty-five.' Wozza couldn't stop himself. He started mimicking Davo and, worse, he did it in a little kid's voice.

Davo had gone to school for a while and knew what that meant. He'd had plenty of opportunity to learn. He didn't like having the piss taken out of him and his uncompromising methods of retaliation had got him expelled. He lowered the rifle and tucked the butt under his arm. He slowly turned to face Wozza and the barrel slowly turned with him. 'You wanna make somethin' of it?'

Wozza's blood froze. He could imagine the dead look coming over Davo's eyes like a third lid. Christ! He'd seen it often enough. He started to say something, to apologise while he still had time, but was too late. He felt the barrel of the rifle slam against his lips, had to open his mouth so Davo didn't ram his teeth down his throat. 'Numphhh ...' he said. He gagged as the barrel jammed against the back of his throat. He jerked back hard against the window and screwed his head sideways. With both hands he managed to push the barrel away, out of his mouth. 'Sorry!' he said earnestly. 'Sorry, sorry, sorry! Jesus, Davo, I didn't mean no harm.'

Davo stared at him, two unblinking eyes in the dark. Without warning he pulled the gun away and once more pointed it at the world outside the windscreen, as if nothing had happened. 'Thought you were havin' a go at me. Makin' out I was stupid or somethin'.'

'Nah, not me,' said Wozza. 'Not me, we're mates.' His throat hurt like hell. 'Sorry if I gave you the wrong idea. Christ, I could do with a beer.' His hands were shaking so much it was doubtful he could hold one even if he'd been given one.

'Know what I'd like?' said Davo.

'Yeah,' said Wozza. 'A sausage and egg McMuffin.'

'Nah,' said Davo cleverly. 'That's where you're wrong. Two sausage and egg McMuffins. I'm more hungry now. Boom! One hundred and twenty-four.'

'Nice shooting,' said Wozza sincerely.

* * *

God began by crawling under the last truck in the line then patiently worked his way forward. He reasoned that the risk of being caught increased the longer the job took, and he wanted to be facing his dry clothes and the blockade if he had to bolt. His hands were cut and bleeding from reaching blind up around alternators, generators, fuel and oil pumps, oil coolers, crank cases and the massive engine blocks. His entire body was painfully cramped with cold. He'd lost count of the number of times he'd bumped his head. The cold was the biggest problem. He had to lie on his back in puddles and the wind worked on his wet skin and froze him through to his bones. He lurched on to the third and last truck, his body stiff and aching, his mind beginning to numb dangerously as hypothermia set in.

* * *

'Reckon we oughta call it a day,' said Wozza.

'Arnie said we have to stay here till he comes and gets us,' said Davo. 'Always do what Arnie says or you get into trouble.'

'What good are we doin' here? My throat hurts. I need a beer. Maybe we could just go back and get some beer.'

'Arnie said ...'

'Yeah, I know what Arnie said.'

'Boom!' said Davo. 'One hundred and eighty-nine.'

* * *

God had just finished with the truck and was about to turn his attention to the last bulldozer when he realised he wasn't alone. The smell was overpowering and he wondered dully why it had taken him so long to react. 'Go away!' he hissed. But instead the wombat moved cautiously closer. The beast didn't have a very large brain or a particularly complex one, but it was interested in food and sex and it was curious to know if the muddy creature in front of it could help it with either of its desires.

'Shoo ...'

The wombat interpreted this as a come on, and came on. God had no choice but to back out from beneath the truck on his hands and knees. He was cold, his body ached mercilessly and he was feeling light-headed and dizzy. His hypothermia made him slow to pick up the sound of the four-wheel drive as it turned towards him, and he was even slower to realise the implication of the swinging beams of light. He recognised the sound of the engine and, in his cold-befuddled state of mind, even thought briefly of raising an arm in greeting.

* * *

It was just after ten and raining hard when Summer, Jerry and Liz finally hit the road for the drive out to the blockade. Liz had piled a few of Brian's old tracksuits and t-shirts and more packets of heavy-duty garbage bags on top of the pile of radiator hoses and fan belts. They drove down past the pub towards Thirsty Creek Road. As soon as she began the turn, Liz flipped her lights onto high beam. They immediately picked up the massive machinery parked by the side of the road, and something else — a pair of startled eyes.

* * *

Boom!

'Jesus Christ!' screamed Wozza.

Boom! The sound of the SKS semi-automatic in the confined space of the ute nearly blew out Wozza's eardrums.

'What the fuck are you doin'?' he screamed. Tiny pieces of glass fell like hailstones onto the bonnet and road. 'My fuckin' windscreen! You shot out my fuckin' windscreen!'

Davo wasn't listening. He was sitting forward and taking aim when the headlights went out. 'Aw shit!' he said. 'Quick, Wozza, turn your headlights on. Now!'

'Get stuffed!' said Wozza. It was one thing to pretend to shoot pretend galahs, another thing entirely to shoot out his windscreen.

'Hit the fuckin' lights!'

The rifle swung ominously. Wozza obliged.

'Not there! Over here!'

'Where?' The headlights showed nothing on the road ahead and little of Davo alongside, but Wozza could just about work out where he was pointing. He still didn't have a clue what Davo was aiming at. He hit the starter so he could turn towards the target but running the heater fan had drained the battery. His attempts at kicking over the motor just made the headlights dimmer.

'Stuff it!' said Davo. 'Bloody saw something. There were two of them.'

'Two what?'

'Dunno.'

'You shot out my friggin' windscreen and you don't even know what it was!'

'Coulda been them bloody protesters up to something.'

'Coulda been an old lady walkin' her dog! Oh shit!' Wozza heard the Suzuki drive up and pull alongside.

'What the hell do you think you're doing?'

Wozza groaned. Of all the people in Osbourne to start shooting in front of, Davo had to pick Liz.

'Thought I saw someone sneaking around the bulldozers,' said Davo. 'Arnie sent us down here to guard them.'

'You shot at somebody?' said Liz incredulously.

'Coulda just been an animal,' said Wozza.

'You don't even know if it was a person or an animal, and you still shot at it?'

'Not me,' said Wozza. 'Him.'

'You bloody idiots! You might have killed someone! Have you had a look?'

'Too bloody dark,' said Davo. 'Turn on your lights and I'll have a look.'

'No way! Not until you put down your rifle,' said Liz.

'Get stuffed,' said Davo. 'My rifle.'

'Then no lights,' said Liz.

'I don't give a shit,' said Davo. 'Anyway, here comes Arnie.'

A ute turned sharply onto Thirsty Creek Road and accelerated towards them, headlights and spotlights blazing. Liz turned and looked away down the road where Davo had been aiming. She spotted the dark spreadeagled bundle immediately, leapt out of the car and started running. Davo set off after her. The ute screeched to a halt with Arnie's head hanging out of the side window.

'Hell's going on here?'

'Davo saw something and took a coupla shots at it. Shot right through my friggin' windscreen. Right through my friggin' windscreen! Scared the livin' shit out of me.'

'So what'd he hit?' said Arnie.

'Hell do I know?' said Wozza. 'All I know is there were two of them. Liz and Davo have gone to take a look. Stupid bastard hit something.'

'What the hell's Liz doing here?'

'It was her car lights that picked up whatever it was Davo shot at.'

'Shit! Davo!' he yelled. 'You come here!' The rain was still slamming down and nobody had yet come up with a good enough reason to get him out of his ute. 'Tell me what you hit.'

'Got a wombat, Arnie. Big bastard. Right between the eyes. Look at the size of the sucker!'

'How many shots?'

'Two.'

'So what else did ya hit?'

'Whaddya mean?'

'Two shots, stupid, only one corpse.'

'Jeez, dunno, Arnie. The other one took off on me. There's only one hole in the wombat.'

'Ya stupid bastard! Here!' Arnie threw a torch at Davo. 'Go and see if there's any blood trail. If there is, follow it.' He groaned out loud when he saw Liz striding towards his ute.

'You bastards are animals!' hissed Liz. 'Congratulations on killing that wombat. He was a real threat to you.'

'Piss off, Liz. Davo didn't know it was a wombat.'

'That's right. That moronic halfwit didn't know what he was shooting at. Could have been anything. Could have been anyone!'

'Yeah well, I'll explain that to him later.'

'You do that!' She looked over towards Davo who was circling the wombat with his torch. 'What's that retard doing now?'

'Two shots, Liz. He's lookin' for a blood trail to see what else he hit. Not like him to miss, even if the target is movin'.'

'I don't believe you guys. Well, you're going to hear more about this.' Liz stormed angrily back to her Suzuki, wrenched the door open and climbed in. 'Did you follow all that?' she asked.

'Yeah,' said Summer.

'Absolute morons,' said Jerry.

Liz started up the Suzuki and turned on her headlights.

'Liz,' said Summer quietly. 'Did you get a good look at the bulldozers?'

'What?' Liz suddenly remembered what she'd forgotten in all the excitement. She leant across to the passenger side and saw the monstrous dark forms looming over them. 'My God,' she whispered. The Cats would have towered over them if their tracks had been firmly planted on the ground, but on the lowloader their sheer bulk was almost incomprehensible. She engaged gear and drove slowly past, unwilling to believe the might and power of the machines they would have to confront come morning. 'Three of them,' said Liz incredulously. 'Three! Who the hell do they think we are?'

Summer just stared out through her window, lost for words. She was a blockade veteran but she'd never seen anything like this before. All of a sudden God's precious tripods seemed puny, his network of treehouses laughable, and the pilgrimage of the fifteen hundred or so protesters a waste of effort. So much for Mourn till Dawn. She had to fight back her tears. What chance did they have? What chance did Little Potoroo Creek have? What chance did the animals and birds have? And, uppermost in her mind, what would happen to God?

They drove past Davo who was circling wider and wider in his search for a blood trail. Liz ignored him. If there ever was a blood trail the rain would have washed it away. Her mind moved on to the bigger issue of how they could possible repel an assault from those monster bulldozers. She began to feel sick to the stomach and lose concentration. The glare from Arnie's headlights and spotlights reflected painfully back into her eyes from her wing mirrors, and the little four-wheel drive plunged into potholes and bucked on corrugations she failed to spot. She rounded a bend and forced herself to concentrate as the ute's headlights were finally lost from her mirror.

'Look out!'

Liz heard Jerry's desperate cry before she realised what she was seeing. Instinctively she slammed on her brakes. The wheels locked up and the little Suzuki slewed sideways to a halt. Her heart raced and her hands shook violently.

'Christ!' said Jerry.

'God!' cried Summer.

Standing before them blocking the road, naked and muddy, arms spread like a crucifix, stood a grim-faced God. His clothes were rolled up in a bundle in one hand.

'I'll kill him,' said Liz, almost laughing with relief before it occurred to her that God was probably the other 'animal' Davo had shot at. 'Quick Jerry!' she screamed. 'Help him in. See if he's been shot!'

Jerry pushed the door open and leapt out, but God ignored him and climbed shivering and stiffly into the back next to Summer. She threw her arms around him.

'Later, Summer,' Liz snapped. 'Make sure he's okay. Make sure he hasn't been shot! Then get him dry and into one of Brian's tracksuits. You can cuddle him later.' Liz switched the heater fan onto max.

God sat passively as Summer wiped the mud and rain off him and dressed him, held his arms up for the T-shirt and for the tracksuit top. Liz began to relax. God's legs worked, his arms worked and he didn't appear to be suffering from anything worse than the cold.

'You can thank your lucky stars human eyes don't reflect light,' said Liz. 'Otherwise you'd be stretched out beside the wombat.'

Summer cut a hole in a plastic bag for God's head and began to pull it over his upper body to trap in his body heat.

'What were you doing out there?' asked Summer incredulously. 'In the rain and everything?'

God said nothing. He was totally absorbed in getting warm and his vital systems functioning again. He leant against Summer to share her warmth, snuggled in close when she put her arms around him. His shivering was relentless and violent, washing over him in waves. Summer held him tightly.

'What on earth were you doing, you silly bugger?' she asked again.

'God's business,' he said weakly.

CHAPTER TWENTY-SEVEN

Samuel Johnson parked his VW right in behind the three lowloaders and their massive cargo. He had a twenty-by-twelve-centimetre card taped to the passenger side of his windscreen with 'Press' printed on it. James Ferguson had insisted that Samuel proclaim his neutrality loud and clear in case things became overheated. The fledgling reporter also had a micro-cassette recorder, his camera, James's mobile phone and, most importantly of all, his editor's confidence. He'd reaffirmed his undying commitment to the twin journalistic pillars of impartiality and neutrality, and adopted his chief's high moral stance. He let the facts dictate the angle of his stories rather than his prejudices or the prejudices of the *Gazette's* readers.

He'd delivered a blistering broadside at the protesters over their continual shoplifting and pilfering, and was congratulated on it by shopkeepers, passers-by and letters to the editor. He thought he'd balanced the books with a damning attack on the unidentified locals responsible for shooting out Jerry's front wheel, for tipping sewage over the vegetable truck and for disabling eleven of the protesters' vehicles. To his surprise he got congratulated on that story too, and by the same people. They ignored his criticism and simply enjoyed reading about the success of their counterstrikes. They appreciated the fact that someone had bothered to keep the score and update them on the carnage. His outrage had been dismissed as token moral correctness.

'The eye of the beholder,' James had said. 'People only see what they want to see.'

The funny thing was, when Samuel went to the pub he found himself listening more sympathetically to the locals' point of view. He told himself he was only doing what James had urged him to do, and was simply rounding out his knowledge so he could mount more balanced arguments. In reality he was in danger of succumbing to a blight that affects reporters the world over: he was falling victim to his own publicity. He liked getting compliments and recognition, and wanted more.

He got out of his car to take photos of the three bulldozers. He knew they'd look brilliant in the early morning light, and they did. They looked invincible, bullet-proof, rocket-proof, bomb-proof, unstoppable. He spread a waterproof sheet on the road and lay down so that the monsters towered over him and their blades looked fifty metres wide. He brought his camera up to his eye. 'Shit!' he said. He looked down at his elbow where a pebble of glass had pressed through the oilskin, his shirt and sweater, and broken the skin. For the first time he noticed other glass pebbles scattered over the road and on the bonnet of the ute parked on the opposite side of the road. He also noticed the two empty bullet cases by the ute's passenger door. Someone had fired through the windscreen from the inside? He was pondering this revelation and the circumstances that might have caused it when he heard car wheels scrunch on the gravel behind him.

'Hell are you doin'?'

Samuel pretended to be engrossed in framing his shot and calculating exposures before calmly looking up to see who was making enquiries. He didn't recognise the young officer leaning out the passenger window of the police car.

'You got permission to take photos?'

A million smart-arse replies flooded Samuel's brain but he was wise enough to ignore them all. The last thing he needed was to be off-side with the cops. He got up and brushed himself down. 'G'day,' he said and held out his hand. 'Samuel Johnson from the *East Gippsland Gazette*.' He smiled as the young constable automatically shook his hand and introduced himself and his partner. 'Welcome to Osbourne. Come down for the blockade?'

'Nothing else would get us here,' said the constable.

'Know what you mean,' said Samuel amiably. 'I heard that your inspector wants to speak to everyone and brief them before going up to the blockade. With your permission I'd like to listen in. We did get an invite, but I like to make sure I'm welcome.'

'Should be all right, but I better check,' said the constable. 'Stay here.'

Samuel watched them drive back towards the motel and shook his head. Did he have permission to photograph public property on a public road? Did he have permission to attend a public meeting? Samuel wondered how stupid blokes had to be before they qualified to join the force. He would've laughed if he hadn't been so wrapped up in his self-importance. At least he'd learnt something from the exchange. The cops were nervous, which probably meant they'd been primed to expect trouble.

He took photos of the bulldozers and cherry pickers, and for good measure took a couple of the ute. When he walked in front of the leading lowloader to take a straight-down-the-barrel shot he noticed the dead wombat. What sort of moron would shoot out their windscreen to nail a wombat, he wondered. Then again, he wondered, what sort of moron would shoot the front wheel off a motorbike? Samuel shivered. The memory of Arnie pointing a gun at his head was still chillingly fresh. Still, all the signs were there that a good story was brewing, and the big city media had stayed away, content to let the story build some momentum before getting involved. That left James and him to tell it and sell it on. It was precisely the sort of situation upon which reputations were made. He watched the police car drive slowly back towards him and began to smile.

'You're in,' said the young constable sullenly. 'Inspector Wilson said you'd been sent a press release and you were more than welcome to attend. He said you already knew that.'

I bet he did, thought Samuel. In spades. 'Before you go,' he said, 'let me just get one or two facts right. Inspector Wilson is heading this operation?'

'That's right,' said the constable.

'Do the local police come under his command?'

'Absolutely.'

'You blokes from Melbourne?'

'That's right.'

'How many of you?'

'Twenty.'

'All from Melbourne?'

'Nah, just ten of us.'

'Any particular division?'

'The Academy.'

'Ahhhh ...' said Samuel. 'Probationers. And the rest?'

'Seconded from all over the State. Mainly country.'

'Figures,' said Samuel. 'Have you been briefed what to expect?'

'Yeah.'

'So what's your job here, as you see it?'

'To assist the contractors and loggers in the lawful execution of their duties.'

'Which are?'

'To build a road.'

'And who will you be protecting them from?'

'Them bloody ferals blocking the road. Who'd ya think?'

'Do you expect violence?'

'Yeah. We've been told to expect some violence.'

'Oh, I'm sure there'll be some,' said Samuel. 'I think you can count on that. I suppose you've noticed the dead wombat up there and the hole in the front mudguard of that lowloader. You see the real issue here is not who's going to protect the contractors, but who's going to protect the protesters.'

* * *

Police Inspector Bruce 'Wily' Wilson had one of the cherry pickers lift him up to head height so that everybody could see him, and see that he meant business. He had the build of a footballer, a face that looked armour-plated, and seemed totally nerveless. The police in his squad reckoned he could stare down a statue. Wily was well aware of the strength of his unwavering gaze and had built a blunt no-nonsense technique around it. At only thirty-six he'd come a long way for a boy from Ballarat and was determined to go further. The people who mattered had already earmarked him for Chief Inspector, and Wily had his sights set on even higher office. Right from the beginning he'd worked out that there was little future in solving crime and serving the people. Instead he'd become a dedicated servant of the people's elected representatives — the politicians who ultimately called the shots. Wily understood power and influence, respected it and openly lusted after it. He quickly established a reputation as someone who was 'reliable', which basically meant he didn't ask awkward questions, and as 'someone they could trust', which basically meant he didn't give a shit about the answers anyway. He wasn't corrupt, never copped a backhander, and never put himself in a position of owing favours. He was simply the man who could be relied upon to get unpleasant jobs done quickly and cleanly, which basically meant without attracting negative publicity. On this occasion his involvement had come at the personal request of the Minister for Conservation and Natural Resources, though Wily knew he'd really been given the job because Bernie Dwight had banged tables and insisted.

Wily Wilson looked over the motley assortment of townsfolk, timber workers, road workers and representatives from DeCaF, around three hundred in all. There was the usual bunch of thugs looking for a chance to bust heads, and he had no trouble picking them out. It worried him that Miklos hadn't bothered to attend, which was either an attempt to undermine his authority or, worse, an indication that Miklos had already drawn up a battle plan which he'd not been made privy to. Either way he realised he had to stamp his authority on proceedings and make sure everybody, including Miklos, knew he was boss. But there was nothing new about that. It was the way he worked.

'Good morning,' he began. 'For those of you who don't know me, I'm Inspector Bruce Wilson. Some people call me Wily Wilson, for reasons I hope will soon become clear to you.

'At the other end of this road there are approximately one thousand five hundred and forty highly disorganised protesters. They've dug two pathetic pits in the road which really aren't worth mentioning. Behind them they've built five tripods. Protesters will sit on top of the tripods and chain themselves to the legs. Behind them is a network of treehouses and interconnecting planks which extend a further seventy metres into the bush. Behind them there's absolutely nothing to delay the construction of the road. Let me make it clear right now that nothing up there concerns me!' Wily paused while his audience digested the information he'd just given them. He could tell he'd impressed them with the extent of his knowledge, yet all he'd done was send one of his men up to the blockade posing as a protester. He waited while a mild cheer went up, then killed it. 'Let me also make it clear that nothing up there should concern you.' He noticed the reporter clicking away below him and automatically hardened the set of his jaw and squared his shoulders. He'd seen photos of Mussolini shot from a low angle and really admired them. 'I have more than adequate resources to clear the blockade away, send the protesters packing and get on with building the road. I don't need you. I don't need any of you except those with a designated job to do. The rest of you will only get in my way!'

He glared at the sullen crowd, defying comment. Before any dissenters had a chance to start muttering he struck again. 'I want to make a few points clear. I've thrown harder bastards than anyone I see here in gaol. Make no mistake, if you interfere with what I do that's where you'll end up. In gaol and hurting! By the way, is there someone here called Davo?'

'Yeah,' said Davo through swollen and split lips. Arnie and Miklos had wasted no time explaining that shooting at unidentified targets wasn't a particularly smart thing to do.

'Good. You're under arrest. Sergeant Nugent will inform you of the charges when you get to the station, which will include maliciously causing damage to public property, namely shooting one DeCaF lowloader.'

'Fuck you,' said Davo.

'Better come with me,' said Nugget through gritted teeth.

'Anyone else who so much as picks up a rifle will join him. I don't want to see or hear any chainsaws, see anyone carrying axe-handles, or catch any of you blokes laying so much as a finger on the protesters. You bulldozer drivers will do exactly what I say, go as far as I say and not one centimetre further. And don't try to bullshit me. I'm a country boy and cut my milk teeth driving those things. You can take them boot-scooting and never miss a step. I've heard rumours and I don't want any unfortunate accidents. Okay?

'Now I'm going to drive up to the blockade so the protesters also know where they stand. And where they stand they won't be standing for long. My men have been instructed to use all reasonable means to dislodge them. However, when the protesters see who and what they're up against, I fully expect them to stand aside. Now, if any of you have any questions, save them. I'm not interested.'

'I've got a couple of questions,' Samuel called out.

'All of which I'll be happy to answer this evening. In the meantime, clean your ears out, sonny boy, and learn to listen.' Wily turned around to the operator of the cherry picker. 'Okay, bring me down and we'll get this show on the road.'

'Right away,' said the operator. He pulled levers and motors whirled. The bucket shook and trembled but nothing happened. Somebody started laughing.

'Come on!' snapped Wily. Below him, 'sonny boy' was clicking away with his camera.

'It's not engaging,' said the operator who, along with the bulldozer drivers, had also benefited from Miklos's hospitality and hoped to benefit some more. 'You'll just have to wait while I take a look at it.' He bent over and started to dismantle the casing over the motor.

More people started laughing and the laughter caught on. Wily looked around in impotent rage. The damned reporter was taking more photos and this time they weren't flattering. He cursed silently but vehemently. Somebody right up the back gave him a slow ironic wave. He squinted hard to make out his face. It was Miklos. Leaning up against the passenger door of his newly repaired Toyota with a smirk on his face.

* * *

Wily Wilson put aside his fury and indignation as he faced the protesters and tried to become the cold hard bastard he liked to portray himself as. The first meeting had ended in farce and he was grimly determined to ensure this one didn't go the same way. Experience had taught him the importance of a hard first strike. His initial reaction to the blockade was that it was quite impressive. The tripods and treehouses were well constructed and represented weeks if not months of hard work, all of which he expected the bulldozers to negate in around an hour to an hour and a half, yet he grudgingly gave the protesters an 'A' for effort. With Brian's permission he stood on the bonnet of his four-wheel drive and waited for the protesters to gather around him. He'd instructed his escort to stay in the background in their four-wheel drives and let him say his piece. He imagined the protesters would be impressed by his fearless show of strength and begin to realise the futility of their blockade.

'Good morning,' he began. 'My name's Inspector Wilson and I'm going to be honest with you to the point of bluntness. My job is to clear the way so that DeCaF can commence work on the road, and do so in safety and without harassment. That is my job and that is what's going to happen.' He paused to let the booing subside. He liked to get it out of the way at the start to give himself a clear run. He set his shoulders, stuck his chin out and leant forward intimidatingly. His body language was unmistakable.

'Piss off, pig!' one of the skinheads shouted.

'Now, before any of you start giving me more lip let me make one or two things perfectly clear. First, the law is on my side not yours, and if you obstruct me I'll throw you into gaol and I don't give a shit how hard you land.

'Second, at the other end of this road there are three of the biggest bulldozers you'll ever see, driven by three of the meanest bastards in the business. There are also about five hundred timber workers ...'

'Three hundred,' cut in Samuel.

'Five hundred!' Wily repeated, throwing a withering look at the sole representative of the press. 'Five hundred, varying from honest good-living blokes scared of losing their jobs to a bunch of brain-dead psychopathic morons wielding guns, chainsaws and axe handles. The funny thing is, when trouble starts you won't be able to tell them apart. They'll all seem like psychopaths. And you know what's even funnier? It's my job to protect them from you.

'At this precise moment the only thing standing between them and you is me. Me and my officers. Twenty-three of us. Now you don't have to be a genius to figure the odds here. I'll tell you straight out, we're not going to risk our life and limbs defending a bunch of people who shouldn't be here in the first place. We are not going to stand in the way of those bloody bulldozers when they start to rip your tripods apart. We'll do our best to see that no one gets killed or badly hurt, but you've got to understand you are not our first priority and I can't offer any guarantees as to your safety. So if you're smart, you'll make your protest then get out of the way. That clear enough for you? Make your protest then get out of the way!'

The protesters were momentarily stunned into silence. They weren't accustomed to cops being so blunt and his words had a bludgeoning effect, heightened all the more by their undeniable ring of truth. Their courage and will wavered as they were forced to come to grips with the awesome strength of the opposition. No one had expected the police to ally themselves so completely with Miklos and DeCaF. Unexpectedly someone began a slow handclap and then stopped. Everyone turned to see who it was but the perpetrator was lost in the crowd. Suddenly her voice rang out.

'Bugger me, Wily,' she said. 'You sure talk a lot of crap! Ballarat threw a party the day you left home. Why don't you tell the real truth, you pathetic self-serving hypocrite. I know and you know you're really only interested in power, promotion and banging Teddy Ayling's widow.'

Wily gasped like a beached goldfish, stunned speechless. He thought he'd been the soul of discretion where the widow was concerned. He couldn't believe his ears. He'd expected jeers, he'd expected abuse, but he hadn't expected his life story. He couldn't think of a single thing to say and it wouldn't have mattered if he could. Everyone was laughing too much for him to be heard.

'You know what else?' the voice called again, and the crowd hushed to hear the next gem. The girl pushed her way to the front. 'The widow reckons you're a dud bash.' The protesters roared. 'You know what she calls you, Wily? Little Willy, that's what!'

Wily closed his eyes and clenched his fists. He'd never felt more humiliated in his life, but at least he now knew who his tormenter was. 'Sarah Jenkins!' he shouted. 'You are under arrest!'

'Again? This time try to keep your grubby hands off my tits!' She melted back into the crowd.

As the protesters' laughter turned into jeers Summer stepped forward and climbed up alongside the inspector. A few gobs of mud splattered harmlessly against the side of the Toyota. She held her hands up for silence. 'That's enough!' she said. She didn't have a strong voice and had to shout to be heard. 'Okay. Well, we can thank the inspector for his honesty in telling us the way things are, but we knew what to expect from the fascists anyway. I would just like to point out to the inspector that at this end of the road there are over fifteen hundred dedicated people committed to saving Little Potoroo Creek. Fifteen hundred people who will do everything in their power — everything! — to ensure that no road is ever built up to Little Potoroo Creek. Fifteen hundred versus twenty-three cops and three hundred timber workers! You don't have to be a mathematical genius to figure those odds! Dorf dorf!'

The protesters cheered Summer wildly as she stepped down, only stopping when Wily raised his hands again.

'Let me tell you something and listen good. Words are a waste of breath. The Light Brigade had a better chance than you. That's what you've got to understand — you are the Light Brigade. The very, very, light brigade. Passion and bravado won't help you when the big guns open up. If you have any doubts about that, keep watching this space. Within the next couple of hours the heavy brigade will arrive and I can only repeat what I told you before: each of those bulldozers could squash a hundred of you without the driver even noticing. So make your protest and get right out of the way! You! You from the press! You hear that? Do you accept that everybody here has been fairly warned?'

Samuel acknowledged that they had, even though he couldn't see how the police could possibly justify protecting bulldozers from people and not people from bulldozers. He made a mental note to include that in his story.

'Okay, everybody. You have been warned and the warning has been witnessed. When the bulldozers start work here you are on your own! Make your protest then get out of the way as quickly as you can.' Wily glared defiantly at the protesters. 'That's all I've got to say.'

'Show us ya willy!' Ciaron shouted.

Wily jumped down to the ground and hopped, fuming, into his four-wheel drive, wondering what the hell he'd done to deserve Miklos at one end and Sarah Jenkins at the other. His driver gunned the Toyota around in a spray of gravel and set off to rejoin the rest of the police contingent two hundred metres back down the road. The driver could hardly keep the smile off his face. He couldn't wait to tell his fellow officers what the widow had called the arsehole alongside him.

'Get on the radio and get the rest up here. I want every officer here and ready for action within the hour.'

Cold fury swept Wily and he realised the only way to recover lost ground was to hit the protesters with everything he had to the limit of the law, and beyond if no one was looking. It was reckless, foolhardy and potentially career-limiting, but in his heart he knew that it was the only way to get the speedy resolution his political masters demanded. 'Tell them to bring the bus up here with all the heavy-duty bolt cutters, and as many more as they can scrounge. Miklos Bollok's bound to have some And tell them to check if there's an equipment hire place. Tell them to bring crowbars and chainsaws. Oh yeah, get everyone in overalls.'

'Sir!' said his driver, wondering why Wily hadn't just radioed his instructions through himself. He brought the Toyota to an abrupt skidding halt, as his boss had instructed him to do after watching George C. Scott play General Patton.

'Gather round!' said Wily to his escort. The waiting officers took one look at his thunderous face and leapt to obey. 'This is going to be harder than I thought, and it's going to get harder unless we put the fear of God into them. First target is the protesters sitting on the road. I want you to go in hard. New chums in first, old hands second. You two women constables, ignore the women and go for the guys. They give you any trouble, use all necessary force to make the arrest. Hit them if you have to. I want you to humiliate them. Blokes don't like being arrested by women. Call for assistance if you get into trouble, and I want immediate and uncompromising assistance from you blokes, understand? Uncompromising! You men, go for the women. Grab them by whatever humiliating part is handiest. Be as rough and as personal as you like and make no secret of your intentions. Arrest fifty, then send them back on the bus to Osbourne. Two escorts and a driver should be adequate. Then come back for more.

'Next I want the experienced officers to form a wedge and move in as a group with everyone carrying bolt cutters, crowbars or chainsaws. I want the motors running on the chainsaws. Take no notice of the protesters still sitting on the road and go straight for the tripods. Concentrate on the first one. Cut loose any protesters chained to the legs and start sawing. When you've cut halfway through, stop and give whoever is sitting on top a chance to come down. If they refuse, keep cutting. Stop and give them one more chance. If they still don't come down, quit and escort the bulldozer in. The drivers aren't to know the legs are cut. One touch from the bullie's blade should bring the whole shitfight down along with whoever's on top of it. I think, under the circumstances, that could be considered an accident. Any questions?'

'Can we take off our police numbers?'

'If they were to become displaced in the execution of your duty, Constable, I can't see that any disciplinary action would follow. Constable Maynard!'

A young probationary officer stepped forward. 'Sir!' she said.

'I think it would be advisable if you escorted that gentleman from the press and his camera to a secure position for his own protection. Somewhere safely out of focus.' He let the sniggers die down then took a long hard penetrating look at each of his officers. 'I want you all to take up position in a straight line across the road, ten metres in front of the protesters. Under no circumstances will you engage in conversation. Stand like you mean business. Take your time and pick your targets for when the bulldozers arrive. Point to them, eyeball them and let them know you've singled them out. Now get to it and don't let me down!'

'Yes sir!'

Wily waved a couple of flies away from his face and watched his officers take up position. Another idea struck him and he grabbed hold of the radio. 'Inspector Wilson here. I want every available ambulance in the district up here now! I want them here before the bulldozers arrive. Got that?' He clicked off. The trick to winning any confrontation was in seizing the psychological advantage. Despite the earlier setbacks he was convinced the protesters would get out of the way. If any lingering doubts existed in their minds the presence of the ambulances and the ruthless softening-up process would convince them otherwise. It hadn't been a good morning for him but, by the same token, it hadn't necessarily been a bad one either.

* * *

If Wily's warning hadn't worried the protesters it had scared Samuel. He was appalled at the implicit threat of violence which the line of grim-faced officers ominously maintained. Some skinheads had dropped their jeans and mooned them, but the officers had remained unmoved. Others had hurled abuse in their faces, but none of the police had reacted. Summer, Ciaron and a scruffy bearded bloke who smelt worse than a flatulent wombat had tried to reason with them, but again they were ignored. As a tactic it was very effective. They just stood there, menacing and unyielding, a physical reminder of Wily's dire warnings. Samuel put a call through to James on his mobile to apprise him of the situation.

'Don't take sides,' James warned predictably.

'You can count on that,' said Samuel.

'What are the protesters doing?'

'For the most part they're being responsible, although the atmosphere's pretty charged, as you can imagine. The organisers are walking around telling everybody to stay calm and not resist arrest. The general theme is, if anyone gets arrested they should go quietly because someone else will take their place. There's enough of them and, after all, how many people can the cops arrest? I think that's why they're being so intimidating. It's probably just a scare tactic but it's worked on me.'

'Glad to hear it,' said James. 'Just concentrate on getting good pictures. The story will pretty much write itself. Now hang up and find yourself a safe place or you're fired.'

'Again?' said Samuel. He pressed the end button, pushed the aerial into its housing and wandered over to where Wily was waiting impatiently for the bulldozers. 'Mind if I ask a few background questions?' he said.

'Be quick,' said Wily.

'Okay,' said Samuel. He took out his notepad like he'd been taught. 'Do you have much experience dealing with blockades?'

'Not much,' said Wily.

'Is that right?' said Samuel.

'Damn right,' said Wily. 'None of the blockades I've dealt with have lasted long enough.'

* * *

The convoy of trucks and lowloaders barely reached thirty kilometres an hour as it ground along Thirsty Creek Road towards the blockade. Behind it a comet tail of locals and loggers followed. Miklos drove ahead with Arnie at the wheel, listening to all the chatter on his CB radio. He couldn't understand why everyone else chose to follow the trucks and wear the mud they kicked up. Arnie kept the ute with the wide-load sign and flashing orange light one hundred metres behind him, sitting squarely in his mirror.

'Hate to think what them lowloaders are doing to the road,' said Arnie. 'With that sort of load they gotta break the surface.'

'Who gives a shit?' said Miklos. 'They break it, they fix it. That's why people pay taxes.'

'When's Cheryl getting back?' said Arnie.

'Hell's it to you?' said Miklos.

'She's me sister,' said Arnie. 'Mum's birthday's coming up and someone has to buy the old bag a present or she gets shitty.'

'Tomorrow,' said Miklos.

'Fuck,' said Arnie.

'What's the matter with you? That too soon for ya? Ya got a problem with her or something?'

'Nah, fuck Cheryl!' Arnie hit the brakes and pulled the Toyota over to the side of the road. 'Bloody convoy's stoppin'.'

'What!' said Miklos. 'Turn around.' He stared in disbelief as, one by one, the trucks pulled to a stop and the drivers jumped out, got down on their hands and knees and stared at the ground beneath their engines. By the time Arnie had turned around and pulled to the side of the road opposite them, the drivers already had their bonnets up and were staring mystified into the engine bay. Telltale coils of steam rose lazily above them. Miklos closed his eyes and slumped back in his seat. He knew what had happened without bothering to ask. What hurt most was that he knew where the perpetrators had got their inspiration.

* * *

Wily Wilson saw the flashing orange light and rubbed his hands together, if not in joy then with a certain sense of anticipation.

'Caution! Wide load,' said the sign which Wily could read clearly. He walked out into the middle of the road and put his hand up imperiously for the ute to stop.

'What kept you?' said Wily. 'I've had to shave twice just waiting.'

'Yeah?' said the ute's driver. He was having a bad day and didn't give a shit about Wily's rank. 'Well don't throw away your razor.'

Wily stiffened. He had a sickening feeling that he wouldn't like the answer no matter what question he asked.

'Someone's sabotaged the lowloaders,' said the ute driver. 'Cut the radiator hoses and taken nicks out of the fan belts so they'd snap but not immediately. Convoy's stuck halfway between here and Osbourne.'

'Any idea who did it?' cut in Samuel. He was holding his cassette recorder out for the ute driver to speak into.

Wily spun around furiously. He hadn't seen the young reporter ghost up behind him. 'You can clear off for a start! This is a private conversation which you have no right to record!'

'Fine,' said Samuel. He put away his recorder and pulled out his notebook. 'I'm going to find out what happened anyway. It's okay with me if you don't want your side of the story presented.'

Wily's face flushed, his eyes bulged and the pulse in his temple throbbed.

'No,' said the ute driver. 'In answer to your question. Dunno who, dunno when.'

'We know who,' said Wily, regaining his composure. He gestured towards the protesters. He turned back to the ute driver. 'Tell them to unload the bulldozers and bring them up here under their own power.'

'Can't do that,' said the ute driver. To his surprise he discovered he was actually beginning to enjoy the inspector's discomfort. 'Whoever done over the trucks done over the bulldozers too.'

'God help us,' moaned Wily. 'All three?'

'Two anyway.'

'Send the good one up. We can get by with one.'

'Don't think so,' said the ute driver. It was all he could do to stop smiling. 'They don't know what else the bastards did. They want to do a thorough service and check before they so much as start them up. Any idea what those things cost?'

'Dear God,' said Wily. He looked at his line of resolute officers and resigned himself to further humiliation. His mind scanned his options, fruitlessly searching for some way to withdraw with dignity.

'The pub's been told to expect a few extras for lunch. About three hundred,' said the ute driver. 'I'll tell them to save you a steak sandwich.' He backed up and flicked the ute into a J-turn which left him facing back towards Osbourne. Wily and Samuel wore the mud spray as he fire-walled the accelerator.

'I don't believe the morning I've had,' said Wily wearily. 'And I've got a feeling the day ain't going to get any better.'

'Well,' said Samuel with a finely judged edge of irony. 'Look on the good side. At last you're getting some experience.'

* * *

The protesters had stopped chanting and singing while they tried to figure out the significance of the lone utility. They sensed Wily's frustration but hadn't a clue as to the cause. The skinheads had even ceased their loud discussion in front of the police as to which of the female officers was the ugliest and whether or not they were ex-footballers in drag. Something was definitely up and they sensed that it was to their advantage. They looked on with scarcely concealed excitement as Wily executed a textbook about face and marched up to the line of officers. He took up position in front of them and ordered them to attention at the very top of his voice. In any other circumstances he would have been impressive, but the hollowness of his posturing was blatantly apparent. He puffed up his chest, squared his chin, turned his troops and marched them in immaculate line back to their vehicles. It didn't help. Nothing could have.

The protesters knew they'd won a victory and the why and the how didn't matter. They surged forwards, jeering, cheering and peppering the police cars with mud balls as they turned and drove away.

Samuel duly took photos of the retreat then stood his ground as the protesters surrounded him. The impartial observer began laughing helplessly.

'What happened?' demanded Liz.

'What's going on?' asked Brian.

Samuel forced himself to stop laughing and waited for the barrage of questions to die down. James had warned him to stay neutral and not get involved with either party. But, hell's bells, there was a limit.

CHAPTER TWENTY-EIGHT

'Maurice Connolly is scared,' said Joseph Weiss. 'He's scared that one day he's going to get in his car and his brakes or his steering are going to fail. He's scared that his wife or his kids will be in the car with him. He's scared that it'll happen right in front of a fully laden logging truck and he'll end up wearing it.' Joseph looked apologetically at the faces of the three men who sat with him, hunched around the tiny round table in the cramped office that occasionally masqueraded as the ACF's conference room.

'He's seen too many movies,' said the lawyer who headed up the Australian Conservation Foundation's legal team. 'You've done good work, Joseph. Lord knows how you tracked him down, and the tapes and transcripts are unequivocal. But it isn't evidence unless he signs a sworn statement and comes forward to testify.'

'He won't sign,' said Joseph.

'Would it help if someone else had a word with him?' The lawyer nodded towards the green party senator.

'He'd run a mile. No way he'd talk to you. I had to promise not to reveal his identity without his permission. Just getting him to talk to me was hard enough.'

'What the hell can we do?' said the senator.

'Best option,' said Joseph, 'is find him another job. He'd settle for the same deal he was on at DeCaF. Can you get him a job with a federal government department or with National Parks and Wildlife? Hell, if you could get him a job up in the Northern Territory he'd take it. Get him out of Tassie, get him a job somewhere he feels safe and he'll sign anything. He's made that perfectly clear.'

'You're talking about a man who'll have ratted on his employers, a government department and his political bosses,' said the senator. 'Somehow I can't see any other governments or their instrumentalities queueing up to hire him.'

'Can you do something overseas? New Zealand, maybe?'

'Possibly. But even if I could, it probably wouldn't happen in the time frame we're dealing with.'

'You mentioned options,' said the lawyer.

'You've seen the photos of Little Potoroo Creek?'

'Yeah, fantastic. Are you going to tell us how you got those?'

'Nope. Who took them isn't important. The fact is, I've hawked them around the media and without exception everyone I showed them to loves them.'

'So?' said the lawyer.

'They love them but they're going to leave them. Unless there's a story attached — and a bloody good one — the photos are no use to them. It's just another lost wilderness story and there've already been too many of them.'

'So make your point.'

'We go back to the media with a story, this story.' Joseph picked up the file. 'We get our guy to testify on camera with him silhouetted so you can't see his face and run his voice through some kind of modifier. We intercut with the photos to help generate suitable outrage and keep the story visually interesting, and the senator here wades in with all his evidence about colonies of spotted-tailed quolls, long-footed potoroos, leadbeater's possums and powerful owls. We create a scandal and use it to put pressure on the government to call a halt to the work while the allegations are investigated.'

'Can't win the legal battle so we win the PR battle instead. That it?' Joseph's boss finally broke his silence. 'I think you're being a bit naive. Clyde Townsend would have us for breakfast.'

'He's right,' said the lawyer. 'I don't think you'll get any channel willing to run with the story. For a start they'd check with DeCaF, who'll deny everything, and Townsend will start throwing around threats of lawsuits with telephone number damages. Before anyone will touch it they'll want to know the identity and authenticity of your man. And that brings us back to square one. You're just going to have to get him to testify.'

'You get him a job,' said Joseph. 'Then all things are possible.'

'Doesn't he realise it's only a matter of time before he gets fired anyway?' said the senator.

'Yes, but why should he quit when he can be fired and collect a sizeable termination? They'll almost certainly buy his silence to save DeCaF from future embarrassment.'

'So the bottom line is, we've got a folder full of nothing.'

'The bottom line,' said Joseph carefully, 'is that forty thousand dollars a year plus car and pension will save Little Potoroo Creek forever. Do whatever you have to do but get that man a job!'

'Steady, Joseph,' said the senator. 'You know we'll do what we can, but the odds aren't in our favour. Any chance of a court injunction to hold things up a bit?'

'I'll answer that,' said the lawyer. 'A sympathetic judge on a good day might grant an injunction, but Townsend would get it overturned. The short answer is no.'

'We've got a temporary delay anyway,' said Joseph. He allowed a rare smile to cross his face. 'Through an act of God.'

* * *

Joseph Weiss wandered lethargically back to his desk as his colleagues went their separate ways, leaving him with the problem and no better off. He hated losing and, despite all his hard work, Little Potoroo Creek was looking more and more like a lost cause. He'd been given a chance to make a difference and he'd failed. Just as he was deciding which particular red wine to assault and drown his frustrations in, his phone rang. The receptionist said a lady was on the phone who didn't want to give her name. Joseph's shoulders slumped. The receptionist couldn't have identified his caller any more clearly if she'd spelled out her name letter by letter. He picked up the phone.

'Joseph Weiss,' he said.

'We got lucky,' said Cheryl. 'The bulldozers broke down. I don't think we can count on getting lucky again.'

'Yeah, I heard.'

'So what are you doing, Mr Weiss?'

'Our man won't testify. He sang like a bird but he won't put his name to the song.'

'So what are you doing about it?'

Joseph filled her in on the meeting.

'You still haven't answered the question,' said Cheryl. 'Have you explored all avenues?'

'Yes, and I've got the photos to prove it,' Joseph said wearily. 'On their own all they do is discredit Bernie Dwight. They don't touch Little Potoroo Creek. I think Miklos would hang Bernie out to dry on this one and I reckon Bernie would cop it sweet. He'll get kicked out of office, but so what? He'll only take up a directorship with Rip, Chip and Ship. That information is only effective once we've got Miklos and DeCaF on the rack and we need something to tip the scales.'

'You disappoint me,' said Cheryl. 'I thought you were better than that.'

'I'm doing everything I can with what I've got!' said Joseph indignantly. 'Give me someone with backbone, give me hard facts, give me something I can use and I'll use it.'

'I'm going back to Osbourne tomorrow,' said Cheryl. 'I'll ring if I hear anything. Goodbye, Mr Weiss. It's a funny thing, I never picked you for a loser.' She hung up.

Joseph stared at the phone and mentally upgraded the bottle of cheap wine to two. She'd called him a disappointment and a loser. Nobody had ever called him that before. In his entire life he'd never pictured himself as a loser. He clenched his fists and ground his teeth. The trouble was he had absolutely no evidence to refute the charge.

* * *

'Come in,' said Miklos unnecessarily. Wily had stormed past Jan and was already leaning over Miklos's desk, his face purple with rage.

'You better have a damned good explanation!' Wily hadn't meant to shout quite so loudly but there was a limit to how many times he was prepared to be humiliated in one day, and the limit had long since been exceeded.

'Davo?' said Miklos calmly.

'Davo!' said Wily.

'You look like you could use a drink,' said Miklos. 'What's your poison? Scotch, vodka, cold beer?'

'You can stuff your blasted drink. I want an explanation!'

In an instant Miklos was out of his chair and around his desk. The two men were well matched in height, but Miklos's sheer bulk and obvious strength was overwhelming. He shoved his face up as close as he could to the inspector's so that their noses almost touched. 'Nobody refuses a drink with me,' he hissed. 'You drink with me or we both go outside.'

Wily held Miklos's gaze for as long as he thought was prudent. 'Scotch,' he snapped. 'Ice no water.'

'Only way,' said Miklos. 'Now sit down. You and me have got some talkin' to do.' He took a couple of tumblers out of his cabinet and was liberal with both ice and Scotch. He put one in the inspector's hand. 'Cheers,' he said.

'Up yours,' said Wily.

Miklos smiled thinly and sat down behind his desk. 'What you gotta realise is that Nugget had no grounds for detaining my brother-in-law.'

'Davo's your brother-in-law?'

'Yeah. Didn't anyone tell ya?' Miklos paused. His hard eyes observed a slight sag in Wily's shoulders and a softening of his resolve. 'Now you tell me this. How can Davo be charged with malicious damage to public property when, given the events of this morning, it's plainly obvious he was protecting it?'

'He was in possession of an illegal weapon.'

'He has a permit for a semi-automatic. He's a professional shooter.'

'Bullshit!' said Wily.

'It's a fact. Nugget has a copy of his permit. You could chuck a saddle and stirrups on some of the foxes we get down here. Semi's the only way to stop them.'

'Cut the crap,' said Wily. He had his voice back under control and his mind had kicked back into gear. 'You know damn well I was using Davo to set an example yet you deliberately set out to undermine my authority.'

'How can I undermine something you don't have?' Miklos said evenly.

Wily recoiled as if hit by an electric shock. Any pretence of control was instantly vaporised. He started to rise out of his chair, fists clenched.

‘Sit down!’ roared Miklos. ‘We’re havin’ a drink!’

Wily sat.

‘You’ve gotta nerve, Inspector, and a thicker hide than any politician I ever set eyes on. You come into my town and you think you can just take over. You make no effort to see me. You don’t even rate me worth a chat. You treat me like some country hick. Understand this, Inspector, I own this town! I am this town! Without Regional Consolidated Sawmills there is no town, there is no industry, there are no jobs. There’s hardly a prick in town who doesn’t depend on me and owe me money. All the trees you see out there are mine, no matter which way you drive. North, south, east or west. All the trucks you see out there I have a lien over. Every bulldozer and every bloody chainsaw. People get into shit in this town, they turn to me. To me! Do you get the picture?’

Wily did. To prove it he nodded.

‘Now, if you were in my position and everything you’d worked for was threatened by a bunch of drug-takin’, dole-bludgin’ layabouts, if your home and entire community was also threatened, would you sit back and let a stranger with a bunch of pimply-faced probationary constables with nothing to lose come in and take over? I don’t think so. I don’t think you would. You don’t match my idea of a wimp, Inspector, you don’t look like the type that would roll over. So why the hell do you expect me to?’

Wily stared at his glass. The Scotch had gone and he rattled the ice to draw attention to the fact. ‘Maybe we should establish some common ground.’

‘Now you’re talkin’. Bernie Dwight told me you were reliable, someone I could trust, and it’s not like him to be wrong.' Miklos noted that the mention of the local member's name didn't pass the inspector by. He slid the bottle of Scotch across the desk so Wily could help himself. Miklos waited until the pale amber had flooded the glass. The man had a heavy hand. 'Reckon your strategy's okay, Inspector, but it lacks somethin' in the execution. We have to scare those feral bastards out of the way because we don't have the time and you don't have the manpower to shift them one by one. Fact is, I have enormous manpower I can call upon. They can be pretty scary too.'

'I would have command of them?' Wily couldn't help thinking in police-force terms. He needed to know the chain of command and that he stood at the head of it.

'I don't think you want it,' said Miklos. 'You wouldn't want to be responsible for some of the things my blokes might do.'

Wily had to concede the point. 'So what do you suggest?'

'We tackle this problem together. Neither of us does anything without consulting the other. We coordinate initiatives behind closed doors. As far as everyone's concerned, you run the show, your authority is paramount, and I make sure that if any of my blokes go too far no shit sticks to you. Go by the book and do things your way, we could be here for months gettin' nowhere. Do things my way, we get a quick resolution and you go home and collect your brownie points. How many brownie points do you need to make chief inspector?'

'Makes sense,' said Wily. 'But just to make sure we understand each other, your blokes don't do anything I don't know about.'

'You have my word,' said Miklos. 'And you don't do anything I don't know about.'

'Then it's a deal,' said Wily. He rattled the ice in his glass.

'Help yourself,' said Miklos expansively. 'Stuff's not doin' anyone any good in the bottle.' He could afford to be generous. 'I'd like to make a small suggestion. The bulldozers and lowloaders won't be ready to move for three days. Whoever did the cooling system also contaminated the hydraulics. I reckon we should give the service crew four days to make sure the job is done properly. The last thing we want is a bulldozer letting us down at a critical moment.'

'Fine,' said Wily. 'Let them go in four days.'

'Good. In the meantime my boys will pay a visit in three, which you won't know about until after the event.'

'Eh?' said Wily.

'The four young constables you have posted up there to keep the peace will, of course, be caught totally by surprise. By the time reinforcements arrive I wouldn't be surprised if there wasn't a single tripod left standing.'

The blood drained from Wily's face. 'You going to lead them to make sure there are no ... ah ... accidents?'

'No, I was thinking more of a spontaneous demonstration of outrage by a population that had simply lost patience. But don't worry, my man will be leading them.'

'Not Davo, for Christ's sake.'

'Nah,' said Miklos. His face lit up in a Cheshire cat smile. 'Not Davo. Arnie. Davo's big brother.'

* * *

'Jesus, Summer, how can you live like this? No wonder you're sick.' Jerry was appalled. Nightfall had brought the rain back and effectively killed any euphoria hanging over from the morning. Dinner had been a mush of vegetables barely warmed through. Someone had tried to light a fire to sit around and keep warm by, but the sodden firewood had only produced a rank pall of smoke which had settled over the blockade site and infiltrated every tent and beneath every tarpaulin. 'The sleeping bags are wet, all our clothes are wet and the bloody groundsheet's wet. I'm bloody wet. Isn't there somewhere else we can sleep?'

'There might be some room in Matt and Georgie's tent,' said Summer.

'Let's find out,' said Jerry. They'd spent the first night together under the main tarp with a couple of hundred others, in a fug of body odour that could have stripped paint off walls. He'd put up with the snores and farts and the disconcerting sound of other people's lovemaking, thinking it was just for one night and that they'd move into permanent accommodation the following day. He hadn't expected a tent all to themselves and was reconciled to sharing with another couple. He figured he'd be able to come to some kind of arrangement whereby he and Summer could pick up where they'd left off in Melbourne. Now he was reconciled to accepting virtually anything else. Anything had to be better than spending another night under the tarpaulin.

'I know Ciaron, Sarah, Stretch and Gretta are also bedding down there, and Sky if she's had another row with Darren. Mightn't be room,' said Summer.

Jerry groaned. 'How big's their tent?'

'Four of us slept in it one night and I thought that was crowded.'

'What about the treehouses?'

'Leak like sieves.'

'I know, what about Brian's old Peugeot?'

'Where do you think Liz and Brian are sleeping?'

'The Suzuki?'

'God's got it. Maybe we can move in with him.'

'No!' said Jerry quickly. He'd seen the way God and Summer reacted with one another and realised they probably had a history. The last thing he wanted was a split in her affections. 'Let's see if we can hitch a ride back to Liz's. Have a shower and a dry bed. Brian reckons nothing will happen for a day or two.'

'You go if you want,' said Summer. 'I'm staying here. This is where I belong.'

'Arrghhh!' said Jerry.

'It's not so bad. You just put a garbage bag on over your clothes before you crawl into your sleeping bag. Keeps you dry and warm.'

'Like a big green condom,' said Jerry morosely. 'Don't suppose the two of us could fit into one bag?'

'Been done before,' said Summer. 'But only when it's really cold.'

'Let's ask around,' Jerry said unconvinced. 'Anything has got to be better than this. Someone somewhere has to have room for us.'

He looked around him at the other two hundred whiffy bodies huddled around hurricane lamps and candles, talking, singing and smoking dope, and wondered how he'd cope with another night like the last.

Even some of the diehard protesters were complaining about the Guardians.

'You get used to the smell,' said Summer. 'After a couple of days you start to stink yourself and you don't notice it.'

That was another thing Jerry couldn't get used to. Most of the protesters wore the same clothes day in and day out, living in them and sleeping in them, neither washing them nor themselves. 'What about their underwear?' Jerry had asked when Summer had explained what was normal on a blockade.

'What underwear?' Summer had replied. 'Most people don't wear any. I wouldn't bother either if I wasn't sick.'

Two hours later Summer got lucky and found some old friends from the far north coast who invited them to share their eight-man army surplus tent. Jerry checked it out and couldn't believe their luck. It was pitched on a bit of a knoll so that the rain drained away. It had a flysheet and a groundsheet that was laminated onto the tent walls and rose about ten centimetres up them. Inside the tent was probably the driest area in the entire camp, and there was absolutely no need for them to wrap up in garbage bags. Jerry accepted the invitation gratefully. Even though their inclusion meant there'd be ten in a tent for eight, there was still plenty of room for everyone to lie down.

But they'd hardly settled in and started to warm each other up with the heat of their bodies in their shared sleeping bag when the first half-drowned gatecrasher crawled into the tent.

'Our tent's collapsed,' she said. 'And it's raining harder than ever.'

Over the next few minutes five more of her friends joined her. They were so wet and miserable no one had the heart to throw them out. They brought the cold, the wet and the night in with them, and crowded into the tent so that Jerry had to battle to find space to lie down. Someone lit a meths lamp and those with spare dry clothes lent them to the newcomers who, without so much as a second thought, stripped off their wet clothes and began to dry themselves. Jerry turned away and stared at the blank wall of the tent in embarrassment, but no one else seemed to care. He screwed up his face as once again the rank dank smell of unwashed bodies assailed him. He gave up trying to sleep and sat up. Large naked breasts bobbed inches away from his face.

'This is Pauline,' said Summer.

'Hi,' said Jerry weakly. Pauline held out her hand and he shook it quickly so that she could get back to the tricky task of pulling a medium-size skivvy over her XOS body. He dropped back down on his elbow and pulled Summer down with him. 'Why do you do this?' he hissed.

'Do what?' said Summer.

'Do what!' said Jerry. 'There's a fucking sea of mud out there that would bog down a tractor. Everything's soaked, everywhere's crowded, the food's shit, and everybody here smells like cat piss on carpet. So far all anyone's done is sit around and smoke dope. This sucks, Summer, it really sucks.'

'I know,' said Summer. 'But someone's got to do it or there'll be no native bush or animals left.'

'Yeah, but it's more than that. I get the feeling you like it.'

'I do. They're all nice people, Jerry, and we all share a common cause. Everybody looks after each other. I think that's great, and right now there's nowhere else in the world I would rather be.'

'Maybe. But there's got to be a better way.'

'Let me know when you find it.' She pulled a face and ran her tongue around her mouth. 'Oh yuck! Can I borrow your toothbrush?'

* * *

When Miklos left the pub around eleven o'clock Wily was still holding court and going strong. The man could hold a drink and Miklos had to respect him for that, but that was all he respected. Miklos had the inspector pegged in the same league as a politician: self-serving, self-important and one-tenth as smart as he thought he was. As they'd walked into the pub, Wily had clearly thought he had an opportunity to re-establish his credibility and authority. He'd begun to strut and swagger as if he had Miklos in his pocket, when even dipshit Davo could see the reverse was true. Miklos had been content to let the inspector posture and had taken the chance to relax, satisfied that he had everything back under his control.

Later, as he turned into his drive, he was momentarily surprised to see the house lights on. Then he remembered that Cheryl was due home. He found her sitting up in bed, reading.

'You're back,' he said.

'That's the rumour,' she said.

'You okay?'

'So-so. You?'

'Yeah.' Miklos was uncertain what to say next. 'Can I get you anything? Coffee?'

'That would be nice.'

'How do you have it?'

Cheryl suppressed a smile. They'd been married for fifteen years and he didn't have a clue how she had her coffee. But why would he? 'Black. No milk, no sugar.'

'No worries,' he said and disappeared into the kitchen.

'Business as usual,' Cheryl said softly and felt a profound sense of relief. She hadn't expected love, warmth or affection so wasn't disappointed. All she'd hoped for was acceptance, and that had been granted. She'd been overwhelmed by the sheer familiarity of everything — her things! — the moment she'd opened the front door and walked in. Of course, her paintings were missing, but so much else wasn't, like the dishwasher and microwave, washing machine and dryer. All her married life she'd thought of the house as Miklos's and it had come as a stunning revelation to realise that it was hers as well. She was home, in her home, among her things, and all she'd needed was for Miklos not to dispute her right to be there.

'Here's your coffee. Okay?'

'Perfect,' she said.

Miklos lay down heavily on the bed beside her. He kicked off his boots. 'What are you reading?'

'The manual for my new camera.'

'Ahh ...' said Miklos. 'You got a good one?'

'Oh I did,' said Cheryl. 'A very good one with very good lenses.'

'How much?'

'A lot.'

'How much is a lot?'

'About two days in the clinic.'

'Two days in the clinic?'

'With orthodontic procedures of course, plus facials and manicures. They really are very good at charging.'

'Guess I deserve that.'

'Yes, you do, but it's done and over with. Let's forget it.'

'That's the thing about you, Cheryl. You don't hold grudges.'

'No point.'

Miklos laughed. 'You know, if I hadn't married you, Cheryl, you coulda had a great career. I would have promoted you to the board. Be great to have someone like you around the office for advice occasionally. You're smart, you're tough and people love you.'

'Do you love me, Miklos?'

'Don't spoil things, you know what I mean.'

'Yeah, I know. Thanks for the compliments anyway.'

'Meant every word.'

'How are you going with the blockade?'

'Bit of a set-back.'

'I heard. And?'

'Things have sorted themselves out. They sent us a police inspector who needed a bit of breaking in. But I've explained things and he's seen the light. We'll be ready to roll again come Friday.'

'Can't do much in the rain anyway.'

'Sunny day tomorrow and for the rest of the week. Should dry the ground out nicely.'

'Good,' said Cheryl.

'Tell you something you might not believe.'

'What's that?'

'It's good to have you back.'

Cheryl turned and looked at Miklos in surprise. 'Yeah?'

'Yeah. Man can only eat so often in the pub. Be nice to have a decent meal for a change.'

Cheryl smiled. What had she expected?

'I've been thinking about things, you and me. It ain't perfect but we seem to get along in our own way which has gotta be worth something.' Miklos lifted his hand and rested it on her leg. 'I suppose a …'

'Yes,' said Cheryl abruptly. 'It is until my ribs finish healing.'

'How long will that take?'

'What's your hurry?'

'No hurry,' said Miklos defensively. 'Could do with a good night's sleep anyway. By the way, in case you've forgotten it's your mother's birthday.'

Cheryl turned around in amazement. 'I hadn't forgotten, but thanks for the reminder. How did you know? Arnie tell you?'

Miklos shrugged his shoulders noncommittally.

'Funny you should remember Mum's birthday,' said Cheryl. 'I never forget it either. It comes exactly one week before mine.'

Miklos closed his eyes and gritted his teeth. Every time he tried to be nice it always backfired on him. 'Maybe we should celebrate. Go out to dinner,' he said.

'You serious?' said Cheryl.

'Yeah,' said Miklos. 'Why wouldn't I be?'

'Thought you were sick of eating out.'

'Once more won't kill me.'

'Okay, where?'

'There's a new Chinese restaurant in Orbost.'

'Sounds lovely. Thank you, Miklos.'

'You're welcome.'

Later Cheryl lay in bed listening to Miklos snore. Her conversation with him had restored her confidence. Miklos had used her to provide him with a family and maintain their home. Now it was payback time. She'd use him for his cheque book and for the home he provided and go her own way. It didn't really matter that her way was diametrically opposed to his as long as she was discreet. It occurred to her that she finally understood how people could become spies and double agents. It was easy. All she had to do was live two lives.

Relieved and contented she slipped dreamily into her favourite retreat, remembering every moment of her night in the cave when God had made love to her, not just to her body but to her heart and soul as well. When — however briefly — she'd been loved and wanted, and the deep well of her emotions had turned out not to be dried up after all. She hoped and prayed there was a place for God in her other life.

* * *

Summer and Jerry finally lay down to sleep from sheer exhaustion around four in the morning. Jerry had stripped down to his underpants and managed to persuade Summer to do likewise so that the dampness of their outer clothing wouldn't spread to the inside of their sleeping bag. Summer had rightly suspected an ulterior motive but complied. He'd watched in amazement as she'd removed layer upon layer of clothing, and there always seemed to be another layer underneath.

'If you leave any clothes around they'll just get trodden on or borrowed,' she said by way of explanation. 'It's easier to wear them.'

Summer lay with her back to Jerry, curled tightly in the cradle of his body, enjoying the intimacy. She giggled as Jerry struggled to contain his arousal. Memories of their night together in Melbourne, which had lured him down to East Gippsland, kept surfacing in his mind.

'Put it away,' she whispered but instead she felt him pressing harder against her. Finally she shifted position so that he could slip inside her. She felt him grow bigger and harder and pressed back against him. People were still talking quietly and others snoring. Jerry barely moved and neither made a sound but in less than a minute his body stiffened and she felt him exhale long and deeply against the back of her neck. He made no attempt to withdraw and they remained joined together as they drifted off to sleep.

The camp was late rising as a consequence of the troubled night. The sun had returned with the dawn and shone down on a world washed clean. Every leaf glistened with the brilliance of diamonds, and fragile wisps of mist spiralled upwards from the treetops as the process of drying began. Jerry woke to the sound of whip birds and magpies. He staggered through the mud to the latrines in boots and underpants and only became aware of the incongruity of his attire when he saw others dressed the same way. What struck him most was the mineral freshness in the air and the bright almost dazzling clarity. It was impossible not to greet others with the same smiling good humour they offered him. More people emerged from beneath sodden canvas as he made his way back to his tent, all minimally dressed with arms full of damp clothes and bedding. He woke Summer.

'C'mon, we've got to hang things out while there's still somewhere to hang them.'

Summer pulled on her driest clothes and gathered up the rest. In no time at all every guy rope and branch within reach was festooned and the camp looked dressed for a festival.

'Bath time,' said Jerry firmly and, ignoring Summer's protests, dragged her by the hand down to the creek. They stripped and squatted down to wash their bodies, even though the creek was swollen and running brown.

'Look around you,' said Summer. 'Look at the trees, listen to the birds, smell the air. Don't you think this is worth saving?'

Jerry had to agree. His skin tingled from the iciness of the water and the vigour of his rubbing, and his senses absorbed everything around him. Summer's innocence and vulnerability. Her girlish, bony, waif-like body. The skeletal knuckles of her spine, the ripples of her ribs and the hardness of her nipples. Whip birds sang immaculately timed duets in a world overwhelmed with mossy earthiness, with freshness and rebirth, and the filtering light lit on the goosy, blue-tinged paleness of their naked bodies. It was possible to believe they were Adam and Eve in a pristine wilderness, and that people like Miklos Bollok did not exist. That nothing beyond their immediate surrounds existed. He was overcome by strange but not unwelcome sensations, all of which were admitted in his goofy smile. 'Yeah,' he said softly. 'It's worth saving.'

'Well, Little Potoroo Creek's a hundred times better.' Summer put her arms around him and hugged him for warmth.

'You're worth saving too,' said Jerry quietly. He felt Summer stiffen in his arms.

'Not now,' she said.

'Yes now. You know I'll have to head back pretty soon and I want you to come with me. I want you to get some rest and some decent food for a change, and I want you to go back and see that doctor. I'm not saying what you're doing here isn't worth it. We both know it is. But there's more to life, Summer, other responsibilities, and your first responsibility is to yourself.'

'I belong here.'

'You belong with me. We both know it. I want you to move in with me. I'm not asking you to give up the forests or give up blockades, but there are other ways of serving the cause. It's time you got your health back and got some balance in your life. You could go to university and fight the cause with your brain. We belong together, Summer, and that has to mean something too.'

'It does, Jerry.' She hugged him as tightly as she could.

'You'll come back with me?'

'I'll think about it,' she said.

Magpies sang overhead and Summer heard distant voices and laughter. The morning sun was full on her back and she could feel its warmth seep into her body.

Across the creek a rat-like antechinus darted out of the undergrowth, sat back on its haunches and stared at her, its radar dish ears poised at the vertical. Summer relaxed and allowed Jerry's arms to support her. She didn't want anything to change. Ever.

PART FOUR

A DESPICABLE ACT OF BARBARISM

CHAPTER TWENTY-NINE

'What's goin' on?' Charlie asked Wozza. 'What are we doin' here?'

'Hell do I know?' said Wozza. 'I'm just doin' what I'm told. Like you.'

'What are all these other blokes doin' here?'

'Askin' the same stupid questions as you.' Wozza wandered off in search of Arnie and some answers. Rip, Chip and Ship's yard was crowded with men standing around in groups in the spill of floodlights, helping themselves to the meat pies and coffee topped up with Bundaberg rum which Miklos had laid on for breakfast. Some were sleepy, some hungover, but all had risen an hour before dawn as requested and arrived with an eager sense of expectation. Something was up but nobody knew what. Wozza spotted Davo sharpening the teeth on his chainsaw with a rat-tail file. 'You seen Arnie?'

'Yeah, mate,' said Davo. 'Hard to miss him.'

'Eh?'

'Behind ya.'

Wozza turned around as Miklos and Arnie climbed onto the back of a jacked-up four-runner ute. The spotlights the owner used for shooting kangaroos had been turned around to illuminate their platform. Everyone listened closely as Miklos explained what he wanted them to do. The men responded with the kind of enthusiasm normally portrayed by lynch mobs in westerns.

'Thought we wasn't supposed to do nuffin' till Friday?' someone called from the back.

'That's right,' said Miklos. 'That's what them dole bludgers up there think as well. Tough shit. You're just gunna have to go up there and spoil their day.' The men roared their approval.

'There's forty of us,' said Miklos. 'Ten vehicles ought to be enough. Use all the four-wheel drives and the utes can make up the numbers. I want ya to leave at ten-minute intervals and meet up at the seven-k mark where the logging roads cross.'

'What about the bloody road block?' asked Charlie.

'Getting to that,' said Miklos. The road block had been Miklos's idea and Wily had been quick to see its potential. Wily had set it up at the beginning of Thirsty Creek Road and kept it manned around the clock by two officers. They'd been instructed to allow the vegetable truck, water tanker and protesters' vehicles through, but no locals. The road block gave the impression that Wily was protecting the protesters from angry or drunken loggers, which was beautiful considering its real purpose was to provide him with an alibi as Miklos's stormtroopers overran the blockade. 'No one leaves here without getting a map and a designated route from

Arnie. You'll use fire trails and the old logging roads to bypass the road block.'

'What if the utes get bogged?' said Wozza. 'Some of them trails are shockin'.'

'Utes go first, four-wheel drives second. If you get bogged someone will pull you out. So get yourselves organised. If anyone's forgotten their chainsaw, see Arnie. And make sure your chainsaws have full tanks. Help yourselves from the jerry cans by the bulldozer shed. Hold it!' Miklos yelled at the men as they began to surge towards the jerry cans. 'Nobody jumps the gun, okay? You meet at the seven-k mark and go in a convoy behind Arnie. Get outta line, you answer to me! Okay?'

The men roared acknowledgement and surged towards the free petrol. Some had jerry cans of their own which Miklos knew they'd fill and use to fuel their lawnmowers or just use later in the course of their work. He shook his head at the meagreness of their aspirations. There they were, heading off to do his dirty work so that he could make millions, and all they could think of was stealing a couple of bucks worth of petrol. He spotted Arnie dragging a twelve-litre can out of his ute and called him over.

'Yeah, Miklos?'

'Arnie, what are ya doin'?'

'What?'

'What do you do whenever you need petrol?'

Arnie shuffled uncomfortably.

'Let me remind you. You fill your ute and your truck at the gas station on my account. You help yourself from the yard tanks when you need diesel or fuel for your chainsaws. Arnie, you haven't paid for petrol since Jesus Christ wore short pants. Have I ever complained?'

‘No,’ said Arnie. He was momentarily stunned that Miklos actually knew what he’d been up to.

‘So?’

Arnie looked from Miklos to the men helping themselves to free petrol and back again. Even though he got his petrol free it went against the grain to ignore the chance of getting more petrol free. ‘Thought I’d take some extra along to the blockade, just in case,’ he said.

‘Just in case what?’ said Miklos.

‘Just in case someone runs out,’ said Arnie brightly.

Miklos stared hard at Arnie. It didn’t matter that Arnie was lying, and nor did another twelve litres of fuel matter a damn. Miklos just found it hard to believe that someone could be so dumb, and the need to grab anything offered for free so ingrained. He watched Arnie steal glances towards the men around the jerry cans, as twitchy and toey as an addict needing a fix. ‘Good idea,’ he said, but his sarcasm was lost. Released and able to follow his instincts Arnie whooped like Geronimo as he charged across the yard.

* * *

Liz realised what was happening the moment she turned onto the longest straight section of Thirsty Creek Road. She hit the brakes and swung the little Suzuki in a U-turn, fishtailing almost out of control as she pointed the bonnet back towards the blockade and flattened the accelerator to the fire wall. She had a lead of about one kilometre, which translated into a one-minute warning at best. She hit the horn, hoping the sound and her urgency would carry over the three kilometres back to the blockade. If the skinheads hadn't brained and slaughtered another couple of sheep, and if the Guardians hadn't reacted and started another punch-up, if the Aboriginal activists hadn't waited to the last minute to suspend their land rights banners in front of the no woodchipping banners, and if she hadn't got sick of the lot of them, thrown a tantrum and decided to go home to check the messages on her answerphone, the surprise would have been complete. Even so she knew it was going to be touch and go.

Her hand alternated on and off the horn as she fought the steering wheel. The road was hard going for the little Suzuki at the best of times, at speed it was a nightmare threatening disaster. She took the second-last bend before the blockade, checking her mirror for a glimpse of her pursuers. Their absence meant she'd at least maintained her lead. She pounded her horn and hit her emergency button so that all her indicators flashed at once. The Suzuki lurched dangerously as she steered around the final corner and the blockade appeared in the distance. She flashed her headlights and was relieved to see figures surging forward to meet her.

'It's on!' she screamed. 'A whole bloody convoy about a minute away. Get everybody in position!' She opened the driver's door and stood on the sill. 'Move it!'

'Here they come!' someone yelled. The lead four-wheel drives swung into view.

Liz spun around to face the four young cops. 'You say you're here to keep the peace, well here's your bloody chance. Keep it!' One of them responded by hopping into their Toyota and calling for assistance.

'Liz, get the Suzuki out of here! I'll take over!' Brian had a smear of Vegemite on his top lip. 'Get someone up onto the tripods. Go!' He stood back to let the Suzuki pass. 'Okay, everybody, passive resistance. They've got to get past us and they'll get nowhere if we all stand firm. They're not going to hurt us with the cops looking on, okay? Stand firm.' His words were swallowed in a roar of revving engines and skidding tyres. The first four-wheel drives had hardly pulled to a stop before men began jumping off the back of them, their intentions clear in the grimness of their faces.

'Fuckin' bewdy,' said a voice behind Brian. He turned to find all the skinheads out of position, up in the front line instead of guarding the tripods. Worse, clubs roughly hewn from branches and the length of axe handles began to materialise in their hands.

'No!' shouted Brian. 'Passive resistance.'

'They'll be fuckin' passive by the time we're fuckin' finished,' said one of the skinheads.

'Oh fuck!' said another.

At first there was just one chainsaw spluttering into life, then a whole chorus. Brian whirled around, unable to believe his eyes. Chainsaws? The mob had formed up into two loose lines and were advancing on them with screaming chainsaws held high. The noise came at him like a solid wall, overpowering and bludgeoning. Brian couldn't help himself. He began to back up and discovered that everyone else including the skinheads was doing the same. The mob advanced, grins appearing on faces, aware of the fear sweeping the protesters. Brian didn't know what was worse, the looks of hate or the grins which suggested the mob was looking forward to inflicting serious pain and injury. He felt someone push past him. Summer! She marched out to meet the mob and stopped defiantly in front of them. She pointed her finger at Arnie as if singling him out for a thrashing.

'Stop there, you bastards!' she screamed, though there wasn't the slightest chance of anyone hearing her. She held her arms in front of her, palms flat and upright as if pushing against a wall, and that was eloquent enough for Arnie. He stopped, let his machine wind down to idle and gestured to his men to do likewise.

'You got a problem?' he yelled.

'No, you have,' Summer yelled back. 'I've got AIDS. AIDS! Know what AIDS is? Well, I've got it. It's in my blood. You guys come any closer I'll throw myself onto your bloody chainsaws and splash my blood all over you. In your eyes and in your mouths. You won't be able to avoid it. You'll all catch AIDS. One tiny speck of my blood and you're history. So come on! Who wants to be first? You!' She advanced menacingly on Arnie.

He hesitated. Davo walked up alongside him.

'What's up? What's she sayin'?'

'Fuckin' bitch says she's got AIDS!'

'So?' said Davo. He casually laid his chainsaw down on the ground, took two paces towards Summer and king hit her. Summer was unconscious before she hit the ground. The mob cheered and revved their chainsaws feverishly. Davo smiled idiotically, well pleased with himself, took two paces back and bent over to pick up his chainsaw. He noticed Arnie smiling at him in approval. That meant a lot to him.

'Arsehole!' screamed Darren, but Davo had no chance of hearing him against the rising cacophany of revving chainsaws.

'Look out!' screamed Arnie, but Davo had no chance of hearing him either. He stood and swung his revving chainsaw around just as Darren's club glanced off the side of his head, deflected onto his shoulder and crushed his collar bone. Davo dropped his chainsaw in surprise and stood wide-eyed. He was used to wearing a bit of discipline from Arnie and Miklos, but nobody in their right mind did to him what the skinhead had just done. Trouble was he failed to inform Darren of the fact. The Dick didn't hesitate. The target was just too good. His forehead collided with the bridge of Davo's nose and Arnie's little brother dropped like a culled goat.

Arnie charged at Darren but stopped short as the limitations of his chainsaw suddenly dawned on him. At idle the saw was useless as a weapon, at revs with the teeth whirling around it was too effective. One touch and great hunks of skinhead would fly off in a shower of blood, flesh and bone. What was worse, Arnie realised, with the cops looking on he could wind up on a murder charge. Just as the limitations dawned on him they also occurred to Darren, but Darren had a decided advantage. He was out of control with rage. He picked up Davo's chainsaw, revved it to the max and charged.

The effect was immediate and predictable. The mob scattered. It was one thing for them to scare people with chainsaws knowing they weren't really going to run blade through living flesh, another thing entirely to confront an out-of-control psycho skinhead with a grudge and no respect for the rules. They ran. Darren chopped and sliced but his targets were faster and better motivated. They ran for their lives and didn't look back. There was another vital piece of information they knew which The Dick didn't: when speeding chains touch together they sever instantly, and God only knew how many people they'd kill or maim before they scythed to a rest. Maybe the police knew as well, or maybe they just decided it was time they did something. They ran between Darren and the retreating mob, slowed him down enough for Brian and Ciaron to grab hold of his arms.

'Bastards! Bastards! Fuckin' bastards!' Spit flew from Darren's mouth and tears from his eyes.

'Calm down!' ordered Brian.

'Friggin' cool it!' ordered Ciaron.

'Bastards!' sobbed Darren. 'See what those fuckin' bastards did to Summer?'

'Hard to miss,' said Ciaron. 'Also saw what you did to the bastard that hit her. Now cool it!' Ciaron took the chainsaw off him and hit the kill button. 'It's all over anyway. The cops are sending the bastards home.'

'Bit early with that call,' said Brian. 'I'm not convinced they're going anywhere.'

They watched tight-lipped as the cops argued with the mob. Now that the men had had time to go over what had happened, they'd got their courage back and begun to work out tactics for a second assault. Suddenly they started flinching and ducking.

'What's going on?' said Brian.

'The artillery,' said Ciaron. 'Let's get out of here.' Rocks and mud balls flew over their heads and rained down on Miklos's little army. The men dived for cover under the trays of their utes. The cops backed away. A bottle flashed overhead and crashed into the side of a four-wheel drive. Flames erupted immediately.

'Christ!' shouted Arnie. All he could think of were the jerry cans of petrol stashed on every ute and the chainsaws with their tanks filled to the top. 'Let's get the hell out of here!'

'No!' screamed Brian as another Molotov cocktail flew overhead. 'This is a passive protest!'

The bottle fell short and exploded in flames. Miklos's mob needed no urging. Utes roared into life and men braced themselves against the deluge of missiles as they climbed back up on the trays. Every strike was met with a cheer from the protesters. Emboldened they charged, hurling everything they could get their hands on. They cheered as an axe handle smashed through a windscreen. Wheels bit gravel and the confrontation ended in an explosion of mud, scrabbling tyres and a rain of rocks and abuse.

'Unbelievable,' said Brian. 'Five minutes ago we were gone for all money.'

'Yeah, passive resistance is a wonderful thing,' said Ciaron. 'Why don't we go see how Summer is? You coming, hero?'

'Yeah,' said Darren. 'Bastards.'

'You're as white as a ghost,' said Ciaron.

'So are you,' said Darren.

'So's Brian,' said Ciaron.

'So's Liz,' said Brian. He started to giggle and the others joined him.

'So's Jerry,' said The Dick.

Liz had managed to get Summer to sit up but still couldn't get much sense out of her. A white-faced Jerry held her hand while Gretta harmonised the purpling bruise on the side of her face.

'How is she?' said Darren.

'Not good,' said Liz, and in truth Summer looked as bloodless as a corpse. 'But better than that bloke. He hasn't moved since you nutted him.'

Darren turned to examine the bloodied prone form being attended to by the Guardians. 'Oh yeah. Forgot about him,' he said.

'You forgot about him? How could you forget! You damn near killed him,' said Liz.

'Tried to,' said Darren. 'Would've if he hadn't spun around at the wrong moment.'

'You're lucky he did ... oh shit! Darren, get outta here! Go! Now!'

Darren had been in trouble often enough to know never to argue or ask questions. He caught a quick glimpse of the cops lunging for him as he bolted. The crowd defiantly closed ranks behind him.

'Come back here!' shouted one of the cops. 'You're under arrest for assault.'

'Piss off, you chicken-shit arseholes!' Ciaron thrust herself in front of the young cop, checked his progress with a shoulder into his chest and stood chin out, fists clenched, blocking his way. Skinheads and Guardians gathered around her, still spoiling for a fight.

'Out of my way or I'll arrest you for obstructing the law,' screamed the cop.

'You won't live long enough,' said Ciaron.

'You can't arrest all of us,' said Brian quietly. He pushed Ciaron away. 'If you guys had done your job none of this would have happened. Now, if you don't want to end up in serious trouble I'd advise you and your colleagues to move back to your car.' He grabbed hold of the cop's arm and gently but firmly led him away. The rest of the cops sullenly followed. 'How about sending for an ambulance?'

'We already have. That logger coulda been killed.'

'I was thinking more of the girl.'

'Oh yeah,' said the cop.

'Oh yeah,' said Brian. He let go of the cop's arm in disgust. 'The one your brave logger mate king hit. Have you thought of arresting the arsehole? He ought to be taken away in a paddy wagon not a bloody ambulance.'

'Up to the boss,' mumbled the cop. 'He was provoked. She was causing an obstruction.'

'You make me sick,' said Brian.

'Fuck you,' said the cop. 'One more thing. Get somebody to bring that chainsaw back over here or we'll do someone for theft.'

'Go ahead,' said Brian. 'Charge me. Charge anyone. I can't begin to tell you how good that'll look in the press. Now, hear me out. The girl goes in her own ambulance. The first ambulance. You want to get that arsehole to hospital you ring for another one. Otherwise he's going nowhere, and you have a fight on your hands if you think otherwise. Is that clear, officer?' Brian turned and strode away, hands shaking with rage.

* * *

'It's not too late to change your ways,' said Rainfather.

'We forgive you,' said Sister Shining Light of the Soul.

'Fuck am I?' said Davo. He stared dully at his broken shoulder which had dropped and twisted around in front of him, his left elbow supported in the palm of his right hand. His left ear, partially torn from the side of his head, hung at half-mast. Blood jellied on the side of his neck. There was pain, lots of pain, but he couldn't quite identify the source.

'You are one of the fortunate ones,' said Earthmother. 'You have had a revelation. You have been given a chance to change your life forever, to join us and become one with nature.'

'We forgive you,' said Sister Shining Light of the Soul, in case her message hadn't got through the first time. 'Come live with us. Come share our love and the love of all things living.'

Davo could hear a siren wailing, getting louder, and wondered what poor bastard had copped it this time. He forced his glazed eyes open wider and took in the Guardians for the first time. 'Fuck's that smell?' he said.

* * *

'Summer all right?' asked Brian.

Liz looked up from her desk and sighed. 'She refused to get in the ambulance and refused to go to hospital. Just about what you'd expect. The paramedic didn't think anything was broken and made her take some painkillers. Some of the skinheads have offered to do a run into Osbourne and get some Disprin. With any luck they'll come across some locals, have a fight and get some of the aggro out of their system.'

'It's a problem,' said Brian. 'You sit around waiting for weeks and then it's all over in five minutes.'

'Nothing's over yet.'

'You know what I mean. I'm grateful for what Darren did, God knows, but I can't help wishing it had gone on for a bit longer to give the troops a chance to let off a bit of steam.'

'I think we'd better have a meeting,' said Liz. 'I've been making a note of things.'

'Hope that includes posting lookouts.'

'What do you reckon? I think we should drop a couple of people way down the road with a mobile phone.'

'Do it anyway,' said Brian. 'You'll have no problem getting volunteers. This morning stirred everyone up a bit.'

'We've also got to do something about discipline.'

'Yeah, I know. The press will be here tomorrow so you can pretty well count on them playing by the book. We need to make sure we do as well. Get the veterans up front and lots of women, people who know what to do to get the sympathy vote.'

'So I take it you'll have a word with Darren and his mates?'

'Yeah, I suppose so,' said Brian. 'But we'll still need a meeting. Everyone has to know what to do and what's expected of them. We've got to get our black brothers to toe the line as well before there's a revolt. We're going to have to watch that Bobby, he's a clever fellow. He never does anything without thinking about it very carefully first.'

'Bobby?'

'The bloke that's leading the Aborigines. He's been around and I don't think there's much he hasn't learnt about politics or PR. His timing with the banners was pretty good. His crew are over there now, arguing over whose banners are entitled to fly on which trees, who got in first, etcetera, etcetera.'

'Okay,' said Liz. 'Grab some volunteers to pass the word around about the meeting. Better it's held sooner rather than later. By the way, we need more drinking water and the vegie truck's overdue.' She turned her attention back to the work on the table in front of her.

'They rang me half an hour ago. They had a puncture but they're on their way. I'll get the meeting organised, you get a tanker out here with more water.'

'Business as usual,' sighed Liz automatically.

'Yeah, business as usual.' Brian turned to go. 'Oh Jesus!' He reeled backwards, partly from fright and partly from the force of impact. He'd collided with God who'd quietly ghosted up behind him and was patiently awaiting his turn to speak. 'Stop doing that,' said Brian.

'Chain,' said God. 'We need chain. Lots of chain.'

* * *

'Five minutes,' said Miklos.

'Bit longer than that,' said Arnie defensively. He eyed the fridge in the corner of Miklos's office, longing for one of the beers it contained. There was a piece of skin missing just below his left temple where a protester's rock had found its target.

'Forty hard bastards armed with chainsaws and those dole bludgers kicked your arses outta there in just five minutes.'

'Yeah,' said Arnie uncomfortably. 'But like I explained, with all the petrol ...'

'Forty men. I give 'em breakfast. Give 'em enough fuel to run Tasmania. What do they give me? Five freakin' minutes!'

'Miklos ...'

'Shut up! Forty men with chainsaws, for Chrissakes, and the only person injured was one of ours!'

'That girl was out cold, Miklos. Davo didn't miss.'

'But Davo's the only one who came home in an ambulance. Whoever hit him didn't miss either. Shit! What is it?'

'Inspector Wilson's here to see you.' Jan was framed in the doorway. Wily pushed past her.

'I don't remember you making an appointment,' Miklos snapped.

'I'd have made one if I needed one,' countered Wily. He had a smile on his face that dynamite couldn't shift. 'Your blokes did real well,' he said. 'Nearly lasted five minutes.'

'It was a bit more than that,' said Arnie sullenly.

'Not according to my men. I've read their report. You got done like dinners, instant dinners at that.'

'So you've come here to gloat,' said Miklos. 'Okay, you've done it. Now piss off, I'm in a meeting.'

'Got to talk about my plans for tomorrow,' said Wily. 'I've got extra men and another bus ...'

'I don't give a shit what you've got,' Miklos snarled, his face distorted with rage. He rose out of his chair and gripped the edges of his desk as if to stop himself from lunging over to the other side and ripping Wily apart. 'You get out there tomorrow and do your job so I can get on and do mine. In the meantime, get your arse outta my office!'

'If that's how you feel,' said Wily. He was still grinning and enjoying himself hugely as he slowly stood and sauntered to the door. He paused in the doorway. 'Four minutes forty-five seconds, according to my men.' He giggled as if unable to contain himself. 'Let me know when you have another good idea.'

Miklos watched him go; did nothing because there was nothing he could do. He turned to Arnie. 'Piss off,' he said menacingly, waited a full second for Arnie to make his escape and slumped down in his chair. The protesters had beaten him again and he couldn't figure out where he was going wrong. He'd had trouble in the past but it had never lasted. He'd never allowed it to last. Yet he'd had disaster after disaster ever since ... ever since Clyde Townsend had come on the scene. He wondered if all the issue management stuff was making him soft. His face hardened. He had a business to run, orders to fill, and machines running below capacity. It was time to get back to basics. He decided to stay in his office and work instead of going out to the blockade the following day, certain that Wily would accomplish no more than Arnie had. For the first time he sensed the possibility of defeat, of losing to a bunch of useless layabouts, of losing Little Potoroo Creek. His anger came to the boil once more. He thumped his desk, briefly considered calling in Jan so he could work off some of his frustration, then thought better of it. It was time for tough thinking and tough actions, not for indulgence. It was time he seized back the initiative and remembered exactly what it was he needed to do. He smiled grimly. With everyone and their dog at the blockade he had the perfect opportunity to do it.

* * *

As Miklos had predicted Friday's confrontation was little more than a replay of previous protests, with Wily's troops arresting scores of passively resisting but vocal protesters in front of an audience of timber workers and their wives. It was a scenario which had been seen a hundred times before on television and the media's overwhelming lack of interest in the event seemed justified. Only two crews from competing local TV channels, a reporter-photographer team from the *Age* and a photographer from Clyde Townsend's PR company kept Samuel Johnson company.

At first Wily seemed to be making progress as his male constables mauled the tits and bums of female protesters in the process of arresting them, and his female constables did their best to humiliate the male protesters they targeted. Those arrested did not resist, while other protesters obeyed instructions and moved aside. Bit by bit the bulldozers occupied the space the protesters vacated as they were slowly drawn into God's trap. Even so, the entire confrontation would have passed without mention in the media but for the outcome of the meeting Liz and Brian had called the previous day.

Bobby, the Aboriginal activist, had embraced God's idea and also seen it as an opportunity for power sharing, a means of delaying the bulldozers with all factions receiving equal representation. Brian and Liz saw no reason to disagree. Wily simply saw seemingly endless rows of sitting chanting protesters chained together, which he instantly realised he lacked the manpower to cut loose and shift. But the media saw something that had little to do with the cause the protesters had come to champion, something much grander altogether. They saw black men and women occupying every second space in the front rows, chained together in protest with white men and women, each proudly proclaiming the other's cause. White people called for recognition of Aboriginal land rights. Black people asked for the preservation of Little Potoroo Creek for all Australians and for future generations. The media saw a spontaneous act of reconciliation and reported it that way.

Neither Brian nor Liz had any idea why the media were getting excited until Wily ordered his troops forward with bolt cutters and the photographers went wild with excitement. Bobby saw his opportunity, stood and proudly held his hands forward, inviting the police to cut through his chains. He turned to camera like a true professional and gave the video crew the sound bite they were after.

'We stand here united, black and white brothers and sisters together as one people, as fellow Australians, to make sure Little Potoroo Creek remains untouched and in the care of the original owners. Only this Victorian government and the power of the woodchip dollar can tear us apart.' Right on cue a young constable cut through his chains, an act which was immortalised on television sets and front pages right around Australia.

'You're right,' said Liz in awe. 'That Bobby is good.'

'Not quite what we wanted,' said Brian, 'but it'll do.'

'It's exactly what Bobby wanted. It was his bloody idea to chain everyone together like keys on a piano. He planned things to happen this way. For Christ's sake, Brian, get over there and start bending that *Age* reporter's ear and see if you can get your face on television. It doesn't matter who you have to stand on to do it.' Liz gave her husband a hefty shove. 'Get going! This is a protest against woodchipping not a demonstration for Aboriginal land rights. Who the hell do you want controlling the agenda — us or Bobby?'

The protesters who'd stepped aside rather than be arrested now showed their true intentions by charging forward and chaining themselves to the stalled bulldozers. Brian seized the initiative by climbing up onto the first bulldozer's tracks and leading the chant to save Little Potoroo Creek.

'Hey you!' he cried. 'Save Little Potoroo!'

'Hey you! Save Little Potoroo!' the protesters chanted back at him, right arms high, flicking their wrists back and forth in unison as if pointing at a common enemy.

The cameras turned towards Brian who held both hands up for silence and began his pitch by calling Bobby up to join him. It was a ploy which immediately gave him ascendancy over the Aboriginal leader and reinforced the impression of unity. Bobby saw what was happening and hesitated, but realised then that he had no choice but to accept and be seen to endorse everything Brian said. Everyone else who had a barrow to push crowded at their feet waving their banners. By this stage Wily had given up and was already making his plans for the following day. More than anything else he was trying to work out how he could avoid Miklos's scorn. A protester raced up and flicked his wrist in his face.

'Hey you!' screamed the protester. 'Save Little Potoroo!'

Wily was more interested in saving his flagging career prospects.

CHAPTER THIRTY

'It's not my birthday until Monday,' said Cheryl. She was wearing the camouflage make-up the clinic had given her to conceal her bruises beneath her regular make-up so no reminders of her battering would intrude on their evening out. The air in the Toyota's cabin was heavy with Chanel No 5.

'The Beijing doesn't open Mondays,' said Miklos. 'Besides I'm gunna be busy Monday.'

'Tonight's fine by me,' said Cheryl. 'I'm really looking forward to it.'

'Yeah, I can tell.'

'Yeah,' Cheryl laughed. 'It's a new perfume and I'd no idea it was so concentrated. Do you like it?'

'In moderation, maybe. Christ!' The front suspension bottomed out on a pothole. Something heavy and metallic clunked in the back. 'They're gunna have to do somethin' about this bloody road.'

'It's your trucks that broke it up.'

'Don't start.'

Cheryl decided to change the subject. 'What's tying you up on Monday?'

‘Nothing much. Just the mill. Just work. Just the need to get back and start makin’ some money for a change. Somebody has to.’

‘What about the blockade?’

‘That’ll have to take care of itself. I’ve called all the men back to work. Had them working today, as a matter of fact, to make up for the days they wasted yesterday and Thursday.’ Mikos slowed as they drove over a section of road where the hard top had broken completely away and the foundation had become rutted. ‘They don’t generally like workin’ Saturdays.’

‘What?’

‘They don’t like workin’ Saturdays!’ Miklos had to shout to be heard over the hammering of the suspension and the metallic clunks and thuds from behind the rear seat.

‘What on earth have you got in the back?’ said Cheryl.

“What’s it to you?’ They were back on a smooth section where the tar seal was unbroken and had no need to shout. His voice took on the quiet sinister tone Cheryl had come to dread. ‘What do you need to know for? I thought you would’ve learnt your lesson by now. What you don’t know can’t hurt you.’

‘I was just making conversation. That’s all.’

‘Yeah, but that’s the whole point. People can twist things, jump to conclusions, get things wrong. I don’t want to spend the rest of my life apologising to you, and I don’t think for one second you’d want me to have reason to.’

‘Just forget it,’ said Cheryl. ‘I’m sorry I asked. It’s just that …’

'Just what?'

'You don't usually have things bouncing around in the back in case you have to stop suddenly.'

'It's just some tools, Cheryl. If you're worried about a screwdriver burying itself in the back of your head I'll stop now and repack them.'

'That won't be necessary.'

'Good. Then can we talk about something else?'

Cheryl sat in silence. Miklos slowed to negotiate another section of potholes and set the tools in the back thumping again. She tried to imagine a screwdriver or set of spanners making the kind of noises she heard, but couldn't reconcile one with the other. She couldn't help wondering what it was Miklos didn't want her to see, and whether the Cheryl of her secret life had the courage to find out. In the meantime she had to remain the grateful wife of Miklos Bollok and enjoy her birthday dinner.

'How old do you think I'll be on Monday?' she asked.

'Two days older than now.'

'No, seriously.'

'Let's see. You were eleven years younger than me when we got married, right?'

'Yeah.'

'So that should make you seventeen years younger than me now.'

Cheryl laughed. 'Our two boys must think I need a bit of help. They sent me the perfume as a present. I don't know where they got the money from.'

'Can't you guess?'

'What?'

'Why do think I had to call the men back to work? Chanel No 5 doesn't come cheap, you know.'

She reached across and put her hand over his on the steering wheel. 'You can be awfully sweet when you want to be.'

Miklos just snorted.

* * *

The riot broke out moments after the skinheads roared back into camp in two old Holdens. Like everyone else, Brian knew they'd gone off on one of their hunting expeditions. Nobody liked what they did, but in Brian's eyes killing sheep and chickens served the dual purpose of giving them the meat they wanted and satisfying their blood lust. He'd expected the usual outcry from the Guardians, animal rights groups and militant vegos, but he hadn't expected a riot. The screaming and shouting convinced him people were killing each other. He leapt to his feet and raced down towards the creek, dodging guy ropes and other protesters attracted by the commotion.

'Murderers!'

'Killers!'

'Animals!'

'Bastards!'

In amongst the abuse and invective Brian could hear women crying and the solid thuds of clubs colliding with flesh and bone.

'What's going on?' he yelled. He pushed his way through the crowd, imagining broken bodies lying everywhere.

‘The poor thing’s still alive!’ cried one of the animal rights women, her eyes flooded with tears. ‘Listen to it! My God! Oh my God!’

‘Fuckin’ keep back or I’ll fuckin’ hit ya!’ One of the skinheads faked a charge at the crowd, swinging his club around and around above his head.

Brian shoved people aside as he forced his way to the front. The clearing was lit by the fire beneath the make-shift barbecue and the headlights from one of the Holdens. It took him a moment to work out what was going on. Two skinheads were standing over a bloody bundle lying on the ground. One swung his club which crunched sickeningly into a pulp of blood, flesh and bone. The sound that followed was soft but unmistakable and Brian was simultaneously sickened and enraged. ‘Let me through!’ he yelled. But the crowd was packed tight, held back by a ring of skinheads with clubs.

Another weak bleat came from the stricken sheep.

‘You bastards! Bloody bastards!’ The crowd surged forward but no one was game to try and break the skinheads’ cordon.

‘Let me through!’ shouted Brian. ‘Let me speak to them!’ As he watched a shadow pushed through the crowd and walked fearlessly towards the skinheads. To Brian’s amazement the skinheads hesitated and allowed the man through. He walked straight up to the beast, brushed its tormenters aside and cradled its head in his lap. He stroked the beast’s head once in a final gesture of comfort, then lifted its chin up to give his Swiss army knife room to do its job. Blood gushed over God’s legs and the sheep went limp. The crowd fell silent save for the occasional sob. God wiped the blade of his knife matter of factly across the sheep's back, stood and abruptly walked away.

'You bastards!' someone yelled, and almost immediately stones and mud began to shower down on the skinheads. The cordon charged and Brian was almost knocked off his feet by protesters trying to get out of the way of the flailing clubs.

'Stop it!' He yelled. 'Stop it all of you!' He pushed his way into the space between the combatants and held his arms up. A mud ball smashed into the side of his face but he ignored it. 'Somebody shine a torch on me! Who's got a torch?'

Two beams of light flickered on and held him in their beams. A trickle of mud and blood ran down his face and dripped off his chin. 'Okay, everybody, calm down! Just cool it! Okay?'

'Get out of the way, Brian,' someone shouted. 'These arseholes have got it coming to them!'

'Bloody thing came back to life as we lifted it outta the boot of the car,' said one of the skinheads. 'It's not our fault.'

'Just shut up all of you!' yelled Brian. 'I'll tell you what we're going to do. For what it's worth that poor sheep is now dead. There's absolutely nothing you can do for it. You people are going to go back to your tents, and these people ...' he glanced at the skinheads behind him, 'they're going to finish what they're doing and then they're going back to Canberra.'

'Bullshit!' someone yelled. 'They're going nowhere until we're finished with them!'

'Anyone who wants to argue can pack up as well. I don't care who you are. We're not here to fight each other and I'm not here to be your bloody referee. You're going back to your tents — now! — and these guys are packing up and leaving tonight. That's it! No arguing!'

'You kickin' us out?' said one of the skinheads belligerently.

'No, you're leaving of your own accord, but you're still leaving.'

'Says who?'

'Says me!' The Dick pushed his way forward and stood beside Brian. 'You argue with him you argue with me. Okay?'

'Place sucks anyway,' said one skinhead.

'Full of fairies,' said another.

'You keep us fairies out of it,' yelled Pete.

Somebody laughed and others joined in.

'Okay,' said Brian. 'Show's over. Back to where you came from. Dinner's about ready anyway. Now go.'

The crowd began to drift away, angry and frustrated but without option.

'Thanks,' said Brian. 'I owe you one.'

'No worries,' said The Dick.

'I guess I'll hang around here until they go.'

'No point,' said The Dick. 'I'll stay here so you may as well go and get something to eat.'

'Tell them thanks for me for the good things they did, helping erect the tripods and standing up to the timber workers.'

'No point,' said The Dick. 'They didn't do anything for you or Little Potoroo Creek. They just came here looking for some aggravation. They couldn't give a shit what side they're on. Matter of fact, I'm amazed they didn't line up against us.'

'Do you reckon they'll change sides?'

'Do you reckon those loggers would have them?'

'No, don't suppose so.'

'Christ, look at these dumb bastards would you.'

Brian looked and wished he hadn't. The skinheads had ripped the skin and wool off the sheep in strips and had begun to chop up the carcass with an axe. Blood painted the grass and bushes nearby and splatter marks covered the front of the skinheads' trousers and shirts.

'I tried a bit they cooked the other day. It was burnt black on the outside and inside it still had a pulse. They ate the lot. No salt, no tomato sauce, no nothing. Tasted like shit.' Darren spat onto the ground as if expunging the taste from his mouth.

'Reckon they'll go quietly?'

'Given a chance. Most of them want to piss off anyway. They're bored and they've got no beer. Truth is, they can start a fight anywhere so there's nothing keeping them here.'

'I'll leave them to you, Darren. Thanks again.' Brian wandered off back to the tarp which doubled as kitchen and community centre. All blockades were chaotic and riddled with competing factions, but this one seemed more chaotic than any other he'd attended. He wished there was a better way of saving the forests. He braced himself for what he hoped was the final round. Stars twinkled through the treetops in what appeared to be a cloudless sky. A sea of faces turned towards him as he pushed his way in under the tarp. Why couldn't it be raining, he wondered, why couldn't it rain the one time he needed it to? He ignored the mutterings and dark looks as he worked his way towards the centre, past rank steaming bodies, irritated by things he normally accepted. People who never washed, men who never cut their hair or trimmed their beards, women who allowed sweaty matted bushes of hair to flourish beneath their armpits. The big happy family he represented was not happy, nor was it one family, and he was heartily sick of the squabbling, pettiness and jockeying for power. Why did blockades always attract the fringe, he wondered?

'You're as bad as they are!' somebody shouted, and was backed by angry murmurs of assent.

Brian ignored them and made a small platform out of two wooden fruit boxes. They weren't very substantial and looked like they wouldn't last long. It didn't matter. He didn't have a lot to say. 'Your attention, please,' he said. 'I don't like what those morons did any more than you.'

'Funny way of showing it!' somebody yelled. Brian let it pass.

'Thing is, you'll be no use to Little Potoroo Creek, to the forest or the animals that live there if you wind up in hospital with a broken skull. If you want to push your luck with the skinheads that's where you will wind up. You may as well just walk away now. Quit. You may as well send Miklos Bollok a telegram telling him to come and help himself to whatever he wants. You lose and we all lose. Why? All because of a bunch of moronic skinheads and your own lack of self-control.' Brian paused and looked around him. People were listening resentfully, but they were listening. 'In a couple of hours from now those morons will be driving out of here and not coming back.' He paused again to let a faint cheer die down. 'They'll go quietly if we let them go quietly. So let them go quietly. They're spoiling for a fight more than you are, in fact they'd welcome the chance to bend their clubs over your heads. Let them toot their horns, do wheelies and scream abuse. Let them taunt and tease and carry on like the arseholes they are. But so what? I'm counting on you to exercise your self-control and remember what brought you down here in the first place. Little Potoroo Creek is depending on you. Now, do I have your support or shall I just pack up and leave as well?' Brian stepped down, not even waiting for an answer and not seeming to care either. He spotted Liz standing with Summer and Jerry and headed towards her.

'You got our support,' yelled Bobby.

'And ours,' said Rainfather.

Other affirmations followed but Brian ignored them all. He was too fed up to bother. He shook his head in refusal when Liz held out a bowl of pumpkin soup she'd saved for him and walked out into the night. The sweet evening air hit him like a tonic, but he needed more. He needed God to remind him why he persevered and put up with all the crap. He needed God to tell him about his cave homes in Little Potoroo Creek. He needed God to remind him that it was all worthwhile.

* * *

Over the weekend more protesters drifted away, back to jobs, university or just somewhere dry. To compensate, around half of the protesters who'd been arrested returned after having the charges against them dropped.

After all, as they pointed out, how could they be charged with obstruction when the road was already blocked by three bulldozers, three buses, two cherry pickers and half a dozen entrenched tripods. Nevertheless the resolve of the remaining protesters softened.

On Monday afternoon Jerry hitched a ride back to Melbourne on the vegie truck, having failed to persuade Summer to change her life or even accept that another life was possible for her. He knew his future lay in the city, in his parents' café and, one day, in a restaurant or café of his own. He believed hers lay in completing her education and using her brain to take the fight to the people who made the decisions. He believed she belonged by his side, though still free to fight her cause. But he failed to convince her to return with him, to take her place at university or alongside him in his bed. Summer swung first one way then the other, torn between staying and leaving, between duty and a deep affection she refused to accept was love. In the end, unable to make a decision, she made no decision and remained at the blockade by default. She made no attempt to stop him leaving because she had nothing to say that hadn't already been said, and no concession to make because she feared for her independence. She let him go because she also knew it would only get harder the longer they stayed together. She stood wrapped up in his raincoat, his farewell present to her, and watched until the vegie truck disappeared from sight around the bend. She tried hard not to be affected by his departure, tried hard to deny the emptiness she felt inside, reminding herself that she made no claims on him or anyone and nobody made claims on her. She knew it was the only way if she was to preserve her independence and remain free to campaign for her forests. But Jerry's departure only left her feeling alone, not liberated, and aching with a pain worse by far than that which Davo's fist had inflicted. She let Pete take her hand and didn't object when he dabbed at her tears with his hanky.

CHAPTER THIRTY-ONE

Tuesday morning dawned like a death in the family. The sky was filled with a high grey overcast that was going nowhere and doing nothing. It blocked the sun but brought no rain, and hovered as if waiting for the seasons to make up their minds. It was the kind of day which stupified by its ordinariness and dullness.

Cheryl rose reluctantly at six and made bacon, eggs and coffee for Miklos while he showered. She sensed something had changed in their relationship. She had no idea why. Maybe Miklos still felt guilty about the beating he'd dished out, or maybe he'd simply grown tired of Jan. Maybe the days he'd spent alone had made him appreciate what was missing. Now he came home in the evenings and seemed happy to chat about everyday things. He was even showing an interest in their two sons. Cheryl was grateful for whatever it was that had brought the change.

Yet she could not dispel a sense of unease. The blockade had not only stalled work on the road but Miklos's ambitions, and it was totally out of character for him to show so little concern. She kissed him lightly on the cheek as he left for work and he actually thanked her for making his breakfast. Cheryl neither understood the change in him nor the reason for his apparent complacency.

Once Miklos had gone she was left with another long day to fill without anything to inspire her to pick up her paintbrushes. The photos and negatives she'd salvaged paled in comparison with those she'd taken of Little Potoroo Creek and she deeply regretted the sacrifice she'd made. More than anything she wanted to drive back up to the Heights to take more beautiful photos and rediscover the feeling of exhilaration and sense of mission, to burn once again with a desperate need to paint, to restore purpose to her life. But Little Potoroo Creek was out of bounds and her mission on hold. She had a roll of film in her new camera which she was tempted to use up familiarising herself with its various functions and new lenses. But the dead sullen stillness of the day offered little by way of inspiration. She knew exactly what kind of light waited for her outside: the overcast sky sucked colour, life and contrast out of landscape and reduced everything to a flat monchrome. The idea of driving up to the blockade and photographing the protest appealed until she realised she had to be seen to align herself with Miklos and the police. What if God saw her standing among the opposing forces? What would he think of her betrayal? What would he think of her?

She stacked the breakfast dishes in her Miele and put on a load of washing, filling in time until Osbourne's only mini-market opened and she could shop for basics.

She showered and checked herself in the bathroom mirror before dressing. Credit where credit was due, the clinic really had done an excellent job.

Cheryl exchanged the usual polite nods and greetings as she worked her way around the aisles, smiling at people who no longer felt completely comfortable in her presence. People deferred to her in a thousand seemingly insignificant ways, all of which underscored her difference. She was no longer Cheryl, but the wife of Miklos Bollok. People pulled their supermarket trolleys out of her way, apologised when their children didn't automatically show the same courtesy, and never invited her to share their gossip. She lined up at the checkout behind a young woman with a baby in a pouch strapped to her front, a toddler in her trolley and two more hanging off the counter. The kids were whining for the chocolate frogs and brightly coloured sweets on pegs besides the cash register which Cheryl knew their mother had no money to buy. The situation was painfully familiar, a reminder of the years when she and her mother had been in the same position. She watched as the young mother placed generic brands of cereal, baked beans, washing powder and other basics on the counter. It appeared that even disposable nappies were a luxury beyond the woman's means and the only treat she could see for the toddlers were bottles of concentrated coloured cordial. Cheryl found herself staring into the life she'd been lucky enough to escape.

'Thirty-seven dollars thirty-five,' said the checkout girl.

The young mother hesitated, handed over two tens and two fives and rattled around in her bag for spare coins. A dollar, three fifty cent pieces, an assortment of twenties, tens and fives, but not enough.

'I'll put something back,' said the woman.

'Put the difference on my bill,' cut in Cheryl.

'Thank you, Mrs Bollok, but really it isn't necessary.'

Cheryl reddened. The young mother was clearly as embarrassed as she was, and both of them were aware that other shoppers had stopped to stare.

'Make up your mind,' said the checkout girl. 'You're holding everybody up.'

'I'll take out the cornflakes and one of the tins of beans,' said the young woman apologetically.

'No, you won't,' said Cheryl blocking the way. 'You need them, you have them and while you're at it have some of these as well.' She grabbed a handful of chocolate frogs and packs of Smarties and dropped them into the young woman's basket.

'Please Mrs Bollok ... I can't.'

'Take them,' said Cheryl. 'Please. Look at your kids' faces and tell me I'm doing wrong.'

'That's eight Freddos and five packets of Smarties,' said the checkout girl.

'That's fine,' said Cheryl. 'Put them on my bill.'

'Thank you very much,' said the young mum gratefully. 'I'll fix you up next time I see you.'

'Fine,' said Cheryl. She smiled a goodbye and turned to the checkout girl who'd begun totalling up her purchases. The mother and children paused at the doorway as an ambulance sped past with its siren screaming. Cheryl thought nothing of it. She continued on to the butcher's for some lamb cutlets. Osbourne had quite a reasonable butcher, provided you wanted what was available. While she was being served Nugget roared past in his patrol car, lights flashing and siren wailing.

'Bit of excitement,' said the butcher.

'If you find car accidents exciting,' said Cheryl. 'How's business?'

'Mincemeat, stewing steak, soup bones and sausages, the cheaper the better.' He banged her cutlets down on the scales. 'The sooner we get rid of those bloody protesters and your husband gets his papermill up and running the better.'

'I think Miklos would agree with you there.'

The butcher smiled as he dropped the cutlets into a plastic bag, turned and answered the phone. 'Hang on a sec,' he said. 'Hello? Ice? Yeah, I've got ice. Heaps. Why? What? You're kidding! Yeah, I'll shut up shop now. Be there in ten.' He slammed the phone down and turned to Cheryl, his face ashen. 'The bastards!' he said.

'What's the matter?' said Cheryl.

'Them bastards have only gone and spiked the bloody trees! Some poor bugger's had his right arm ripped clean off. They want me to bring some ice. I gotta go.' He stopped at the door of his fridge and turned back to face Cheryl. 'Look, help yourself then do me a favour. Would you close up for me? I gotta go. Fix me up next time.'

The butcher dumped ice into a plastic tub and raced out the back to his van. Cheryl leaned heavily against the door jamb as the butcher drove away, then slowly closed the door behind him. Timber work was dangerous enough without people deliberately spiking trees and she couldn't imagine how anyone could be callous enough to do it. She shook her head bitterly as if to rid her mind of the all too familar repercussions. God knows timber work didn't pay enough to justify the risks, or compensate battling families for the loss or maiming of husbands and fathers. She had to fight back revulsion as she dropped the lamb cutlets into her shopping bag, closed her eyes and made her way blindly to the door. She couldn't bear to look at the raw meat that surrounded her.

* * *

'Samuel!' yelled James Ferguson as he slammed down the phone.

'He's gone,' replied Mrs Watson.

'Gone?'

'To the blockade,' said Mrs Watson. She peered at James over the top of her butterfly-wing glasses. 'He left five minutes ago.'

'Well, get him on the mobile! This is urgent!'

'He let Glynnis take his mobile because Tim, her youngest, is sick and at home alone.'

'What's wrong with hers?'

Mrs Watson just shrugged. 'Flat battery. Maybe you should have bought two more of them mobiles,' said Mrs Watson. 'Not just one.'

'Maybe I need someone who can just do as they're told! If Samuel gets to a phone and if he phones in, tell him to get along to Diggers Hill as fast as he can. There's been an accident of some kind and people are saying that the trees have been spiked. If that's true, then God help us. I'm going there now. Just take messages.' James grabbed his hat, coat and camera and raced out.

Once he cleared town he put his foot down, confident that there'd be no speed traps or cops to book him. They'd all be headed where he was, and were probably there already. He caught a glimpse of a helicopter off to his right, flying low at full speed, and guessed its destination immediately. He drove faster. The report had been unequivocal: a tree feller's chainsaw had hit a spike; yet his reporter's instincts warned him that there was more to the incident than was immediately apparent. There'd been no evidence of extremism among the protesters, no violence or threats of violence as a precursor, and no acts of sabotage other than the mischief done to the trucks carrying the bulldozers and that was no more than retaliation. Nothing in Samuel's reports had led him to believe that the protesters were anything other than typical greenies, more obstructive than aggressive. The spiking was totally unexpected and wholly out of character. But facts were facts. Trees — at least one tree — had been spiked and the finger of suspicion was inevitably pointed towards the blockaders.

The traffic was stopped on his side of the road as he drew near Diggers Hill. He trusted that the police would accept the Press card taped inside his windscreen as entitlement to proceed on the wrong side of the road. The helicopter was in sight, its skids straddling the centre line and paramedics urgently wheeling a mobile stretcher towards it, when a local policeman motioned him to pull off onto the side of the road.

'What's happening?' asked James.

'They're just about to load the poor bugger,' said the officer. 'Apparently he's still alive and they're flying him straight to Melbourne. They're taking his arm with them in a bucket of ice so they can sew it back on.'

'I wish them luck,' said James grimly. 'You ever seen the mess a chainsaw makes?'

The cop shook his head.

'If I were you I wouldn't count on him taking up knitting. Mind if I go over and take some shots?'

'No, go for it.'

James resisted the urge to jog. Some people mightn't take too kindly to him taking pictures at all and any unseemly haste would only make matters worse. He slipped the camera off his shoulder and framed up just as the injured man was being loaded. 'Terrible business,' he said over and over, in case anybody misunderstood his motivation or wanted to challenge his presence, but the chances of being heard over the roar of the helicopter's motors and the whump-whump-whump of its rotors were remote. He clicked away as unobtrusively as possible, firing off shots as fast as he could without appearing too hasty. He stopped shooting before the helicopter lifted off and stood back respectfully as it did so. He wished Samuel had witnessed him in action so he could see how it was done. Was done, he thought bitterly. Modern sensationalist journalists showed scant respect for anyone or anything, and even less for the old skills and techniques. He spotted Nugget and walked unhurriedly towards him.

'Terrible business, Sergeant,' he said and waited for Nugget to respond.

'Those bastards are going to pay for this,' said Nugget.

'Aye,' said James. He waited a couple of beats until Nugget turned to him expecting him to say more. Experience had taught James that a well-timed pause made people listen more closely and become just that little bit more cooperative. 'Sergeant, I'd appreciate it if you would show me exactly where the accident happened and talk me through events. For the sake of accuracy, you understand. When something like this happens the community's best interests are not served by rampant speculation and wild rumour. People are going to be upset enough.'

'Sure,' said Nugget.

'Would you mind if I quoted you?' said James. 'In the interests of authenticity. I've got your photo on file though I might take another.'

'Fine with me,' said Nugget. He took James deep into the scrub where the crew had been working, pointing out the trees that had been felled earlier.

'Have you found any more spiked trees?' asked James.

'Miklos and the men working here have gone looking. Miklos has shut down the chipper and he's got people running off everywhere telling blokes to stop work. You know what they're like, independent contractors, they're a law unto themselves. Never tell anyone exactly where they're going, and there's no telling where else those green bastards might have stuck their spikes. Here we are.'

There was no mistaking the scene of the accident. Blood lay in thick clotted pools around the base of the tree. The surrounding scrub looked like it had been lightly spraypainted. Half a dozen men and a young police officer stood sullenly to one side, boots stained red.

'Oh dear God!' said James. 'It's a wonder the poor man's alive at all.'

'The paramedics gave him transfusions on the spot or he wouldn't be. See the spike?'

James suppressed his revulsion and stepped up to the trunk. The saw had barely penetrated ten centimetres. There would have been nothing to stop the blade once it had sheared, nothing but the operator's arm.

'Bastards tacked the bark back over the head of the spike,' said one of the bystanders. 'Look above the cut, you can still see the nail holes.'

'I wondered about them,' said James. As the saw had kicked back it had ripped out a piece of wood three centimetres deep and about nine centimetres long from the trunk immediately above it. He could clearly see the section of spike that the saw had struck, a silvery blaze against dark gunmetal blue. 'What do you make of the spike?' he asked his audience. 'It would have to be at least a centimetre thick. Wouldn't a six-inch nail have done just as well?'

'Yeah, maybe,' one of the timber workers volunteered. 'Depends whether you just want to bugger the saw or bugger the operator as well. Whoever did this wanted to make sure he buggered the operator.'

The rest of the onlookers murmured in angry assent.

'Maybe. But it could also be that whoever did it was really trying to wreck the chipper. I mean, imagine the damage a spike that size would do. It would reduce it to scrap metal. Break one saw, you stop one man working. Break the chipper and you stop all of them working. What do you say to that?'

'If that was what they wanted they would have set the spike higher, not at cutting height,' said Nugget. 'By the way, do you want to take a picture?'

James looked around distastefully at all the blood and gore. 'Maybe just the part of the trunk with the spike. I don't doubt that there are some journalists who'd like to see this poor man's blood splattered all over the front page but I'm not one of them. There's his family to think of.' James took his shot and stepped gingerly away from the tree, wanting to wipe the blood off his shoes against the surrounding scrub, but somehow it seemed disrespectful and the wrong thing to do. He pulled out his notepad and pen. 'Any of you know the man personally?'

'We all know him,' said Nugget. 'Colin Hayward, married, bunch of kids he's devoted to. Lives out by the yabby farm. Top bloke, real battler. Never been in trouble and he's not much of a drinker.'

'Good footballer too,' said one of the bystanders. 'Great hands. Tried out for Carlton once.' The man realised his indiscretion and stared down at his feet. He angrily kicked a stick away. 'Jesus Christ, them bastards are going to pay for this!'

'Bloody oath!' said one of his mates.

James had a sickening feeling that the story was only beginning.

* * *

James Ferguson walked back to the highway just as Miklos Bollok was leaving, but managed to persuade Wozza to show him the two other trees they'd found spikes in. They were much like the one he'd seen but without the blood. Once again the spikes had been hammered in at cutting height. He leant in closer and spotted the nailholes above their heads where the bark had been tacked back on.

'What will Miklos do now?' he asked. 'Put this whole area off limits?'

'You kiddin'?' Wozza spat into the undergrowth. 'Nah, we're just gunna have to be a bit wary from now on and check the trunks before we cut into them. If we refuse to drop them Miklos would just come out and do it himself. He'd cut us out of a job as well.'

'How hard would it be to drive a spike like that into a tree?'

'Bloody hard. They probably used a sledgehammer, something like that.'

'Yes, I agree,' said James. 'But have you noticed that whoever did it didn't miss, not even once? There's no bruising on this tree or on either of the others. Now, that is impressive. How does anyone acquire the skills to do that?'

'I dunno,' said Wozza. 'I've seen plenty of guys that accurate with an axe.'

'Aye,' said James. 'But don't you think that's an unusual skill for a conservationist?'

* * *

Wily paced in frustration as once more his men began to work their way through the ranks of protesters with heavy-duty bolt cutters. No matter how hard they worked or how much progress they made during the day, it was back to square one every morning. The protesters' supply of chain seemed inexhaustible, and Wily had no idea how to go about moving a thousand people who were not only chained together but determined to stay put. He knew they had to be replenishing their supply of chain somehow but couldn't work out how, and he was smart enough to realise he was powerless until he did. His men searched every car that passed through the road block but they still hadn't turned up a single link. He'd led a raid into the camp to find their stockpile but had come out emptyhanded. He'd asked every hardware store from Eden to Sale to withhold sales of chain to anyone who wasn't local, and to report anyone who bought up in volume. He'd even thought about starving the protesters out, but the local townspeople were adamantly against the idea.

'They'll only steal what they can't get,' the shopkeepers said, and the farmers who'd had sheep and chickens go missing added their weight to the argument.

When his walkie-talkie demanded his attention, he couldn't help snapping as he pressed the transmit button. 'What is it?'

'Sergeant Nugent is on the radio, sir. Needs to speak to you urgently.'

'Tell him to hold on.' Wily checked his watch out of habit and training. Eleven forty-three. A good police officer always knew where he was and at what time in case it was subsequently prudent to be somewhere else. He left a sergeant in charge and returned to the four-wheel drive he liked to refer to as his mobile headquarters. The officer monitoring the radio handed him the microphone. 'Inspector Wilson here. Say your piece, Nugget, and make it quick.'

Nugget did.

'Bloody hell,' said Wily.

'Yeah,' said Nugget drily. 'That about sums it up.'

* * *

Cheryl drove out towards the yabby farm wondering what on earth she was going to say. Miklos's instructions had been blunt and didn't invite refusal. No one else was available or suitable, he'd said, and beside he couldn't think of anyone better qualified to present his sympathies and offer of help. Cheryl had to concede he had a point but that didn't make her job any easier. Miklos's offer was generous and would no doubt be accepted with gratitude. Full pay and job waiting for the injured man on his recovery, either in the office or out in the yard as overseer. A hotel room near the hospital and all expenses for as long as his wife needed it. Yes, Miklos was generous, but she'd never felt less like Santa Claus, and Miklos had made no mention of what would happen if the poor man died.

She wondered who Gillian Hayward was, wondered if she knew her or would recognise her, wondered if it would make any difference if she did. She thought it would be easier dealing with somebody she didn't know, and the unfamiliarity of the woman's name brought a faint comfort. She didn't need to read the scrawl on the letterbox of the old farmhouse to know she was in the right place. Family and friends had rallied around and their cars blocked the driveway and spilled out onto the street. She sat for a moment to calm herself, took a deep breath, then got out of her car to do her duty.

A middle-aged woman answered her knock.

'Good afternoon. Mrs Hayward?' asked Cheryl. She could tell that the woman had been crying and made her assumption on that basis.

‘Yes, but not the one you want. You want Gillian. I’m her mother-in-law. Colin is my son.’ She seemed angry that Cheryl didn’t know.

‘I’m very sorry,’ said Cheryl. ‘I’m Cheryl Bollok. I’d like a few words with Gillian if possible. Only if she’s up to it, that is.’

‘I know who you are, Mrs Bollok. You’ll have to forgive me if I seem abrupt but we’re all a bit upset. Please come in.’ She led the way along a dimly lit passageway that reminded Cheryl of her childhood home. Walls lined with broad tongue and groove from a time when timber was cheap and all that was available. Cheryl heard a baby crying in a bedroom as she passed by and someone trying to soothe it. Heard a rattling sound as she passed another bedroom and caught a glimpse of tiny hands scrabbling for Smarties which had fallen out of the bottom of a treasured packet and tumbled onto the lino floor. In that instant Cheryl had a premonition that she knew who Gillian Hayward was, and was engulfed by a confusion of emotions. Sorrow and pity certainly, but behind it all horror, shame and embarrassment over her earlier unasked-for generosity. She’d meant well, but what was her gift worth now? What were eight Freddo Frogs and five packets of Smarties when the young mother’s husband lay cruelly injured, possibly even dying, his arm severed in the service of Rip, Chip and Ship, a victim of Miklos’s battles and of Miklos’s ambitions?

Gillian Hayward sat in an old armchair with a mug of tea in her hands, surrounded by concerned friends and plates of scones. She looked up and saw Cheryl and her tear-streaked face managed a weak smile of recognition.

In all her life Cheryl had never felt more ashamed.

* * *

Miklos rose from behind his desk as Jan opened his office door.

'Mr ... uh ... McPhearson to see you,' she said.

'Ferguson,' said James.

'Come in, come in,' said Miklos warmly. 'Sit down.'

'Thank you, it's good of you to see me at such short notice. It's a terrible business.'

'Yes, you could say that,' said Miklos. 'Now, what can I do for you?'

'I have a few questions.'

'And I'll be happy to answer them.'

'Thank you, Mr Bollok.'

'On one condition. I want to know who took the photographs, Mr Ferguson.'

James looked steadily at Miklos. 'I don't doubt that you do, Mr Bollok. I assume you're referring to the photos we published of you taking the hammer to your Toyota. You must realise that even if I could I would never reveal our source.'

'Even if you could? Come on!'

'A member of my staff handled the transaction. My only interest was in the veracity of the pictures, not the source. They cost me a lot of money, Mr Bollok, and under normal circumstances I would refuse to pay. That is not the way I run my newspaper. But you compromised me, Mr Bollok, and I felt the sum of five thousand dollars in cash was not too much to pay to protect my reputation.'

'Yeah, pity about mine.'

James shrugged but remained resolute.

'Ask your questions. I'm a busy man.'

'Mr Bollok, you realise no doubt that this ... ah ... accident this morning could have some unfortunate consequences if ...'

'Accident?' cut in Miklos. 'I don't know about any freakin' accident. If you're talking about what happened at Diggers Hill that was no accident. I don't want to pick up the *Gazette* and see you calling it an accident. It was sabotage and damn near murder! Call it what it is!'

'I can understand how you feel, Mr Bollok, but we have a responsibility — you and I — to make certain that tempers don't become too inflamed. There's been enough blood spilt.'

'You listen to me, Mr Ferguson, those bloody protesters out there spiked my trees! They damn near killed, maybe have killed, a man who works for me. Don't you go soft on those bastards! Don't you come in here and presume to tell me what's what!'

'There is no evidence linking anyone with the spiking, protester or otherwise, and until there is neither you nor I should go jumping to conclusions.'

'Who stands to gain, for Chrissake?!' Miklos rose out of his chair, face flushed with anger. 'We found three more trees that had been spiked!'

'Three?' said James quickly. 'Wozza only showed me two.'

'Found one in the yard,' said Miklos. He allowed his anger to subside. 'Come with me, Mr Ferguson, and I'll show you what we're up against. This was no spontaneous act. This was no act of mischief. This was deliberate, calculated, cold-blooded sabotage.'

James rose and followed Miklos out into the yard.

'There!' said Miklos. 'Write about this!' He handed a thirty-centimetre spike to James. 'Feel the weight of it. That's hardened steel. Look at the point. You could hammer it through concrete and it wouldn't lose its edge. Tell me what else you'd use something like this for.'

'Perhaps it's some kind of stake, something that has to bear a load.' James casually laid the spike on the ground, bent over and took a photo. Never ask, just do.

'Like what?' asked Miklos scathingly.

'I don't know. Perhaps a marquee.'

'Yeah, or tether an elephant. There's a big call for them around here. On the other hand, it could have been made specially to spike a tree. You think about that. Can you imagine the mess this would have made of my machinery?'

'Aye, I was wondering if that wasn't the intention in the first place. Can I see the log you took it from?'

'Sure. Right here.'

James leant over the log and examined the scar where the spike had been chiselled out. He looked for the telltale nail holes and was surprised when there were none. What surprised him even more was that the entry point of the spike was a good metre and a half above the cut. 'Whoever cut this down was a lucky man,' he said.

Miklos's eyes narrowed. 'Yeah, oughta buy a lottery ticket.'

'Something puzzles me,' said James. 'Assuming the cut was made close to a metre above ground, that puts the entry point of the spike over two metres high.'

'So?' Miklos could see where James was heading and became wary.

'And a metre and a half above the other spikes. So how did they do it? How did they get up high enough? How did they get up so high and still have solid enough footing to drive home a spike this size and do it without missing and striking the trunk?'

'How the fuck do I know!' said Miklos. He spat into the dust and glowered at James. 'Maybe the arseholes had a freakin' ladder! Have you thought of that?!'

* * *

Miklos's private line was ringing as he strode back into his office. 'Yeah?' he snarled.

'I just heard,' said Clyde Townsend. 'It's on every radio station and TV news.'

'You must be very happy,' said Miklos.

'Sure,' snapped Clyde. 'Everybody's asking questions and nobody's had time to prepare answers. You were supposed to give me some warning so we can manage this thing.'

'I've had a gutful of your managing. You managed to give me Inspector Wily. What a bonus! Face it, Clyde, all you've managed to do so far is stuff everything up.'

'And you're blameless? Tell me, Miklos, how the hell am I supposed to get my guys out of the camp before your tame copper finds their tent pegs match the spikes? How long do you think it would take for my men to get the shits with us and dob us in? If you've got any suggestions I'd love to hear them?'

Miklos hadn't given Clyde's men a lot of thought. He'd figured they'd hear about the spiking and take that as their cue to hit the road. He closed his eyes and cursed silently. He had no suggestions and his silence made the lack even more poignant.

'We got lucky, Miklos,' said Clyde softly. 'You may never really appreciate how lucky. My guys got bored last night, drove north until they found a pub where the locals wouldn't tag them as greenies, and slept in the car because they got too pissed to drive back. My secretary caught them on the mobile making their way back to the blockade. Stopped and turned them around only two ks out of Osbourne. Right now they're heading for Canberra where they're going to ditch the Kombi and split up. A few hours from now they're going to be the most wanted men in the whole of Australia.'

Miklos held his silence, unwilling to make any concession.

'Their fee just went up ten grand by the way, but I told them you'd be happy to make up the difference.'

'Guess that's fair,' said Miklos grudgingly.

'Fair? You don't understand the concept, Miklos. Fair is when partners deal openly and honestly and stick to agreements. I'll explain it to you one day. In the meantime we've got a job to do. Have you talked to anyone?'

Miklos sighed heavily. Nothing in the world irritated him more than a Clyde Townsend interrogation. 'Only one person you need worry about and I had no choice. James Ferguson, the editor of the *East Gippsland Gazette*.'

'What did you say?'

Miklos told him everything.

'Chip the log in the yard,' said Clyde. 'Make it seem like an error in communication. Get Arnie or someone to go back up to Diggers Hill tonight with a hammer and put some dings in the trunks, or at least rip the bark off so no one will ever know for certain whether the trunks got dinged or not.'

'What if a bunch of guys who are really pissed off get tanked up, drive out to Diggers Hill and rip the spikes out of the other two trees with jemmies? Sort of thing they'd do and make a bloody great mess doing it.'

'Sounds good.'

'Can't do much about the tree the one-armed man was cutting.'

'One-armed man? Jesus, Miklos, you're sick.'

'Piss off, Clyde, it was your idea to spike the trees in the first place. Nugget's posted a cop at the scene and the bloody thing's been photographed every which way.'

'We'll deal with that if it becomes a problem. Now, when is Nugget going to find the tent pegs?'

'I've got a meeting with him and Wily in five minutes.'

'Good. That means they won't get out to the blockade before three. We don't want them finding them too quickly, certainly not in time for the seven o'clock news. I want it on the mid to late evening news so the story's still fresh in the morning. That way we'll get front page. Now, are you going to release your men to the blockade?'

'What do you reckon?' Miklos said contemptuously. 'Isn't that the whole freakin' point? Get everyone pissed off. Get the whole town demanding blood. The bloody army couldn't stop them going out there now.'

'Just checking, okay? I've got the Sisters of the Forest turning up in force in mourning clothes. I've got workers bussing down overnight from every concession in the State in a show of outrage and solidarity.'

'How'd you pull that?' asked Miklos.

'We're paying them to go. Play this right, everyone benefits, that's what you've got to understand, Miklos. It's not just your show, it's the industry's. We're sending you some real hard heads.'

'Make a pleasant change.' Miklos laughed. There were moments when it seemed he and Clyde were on the same wavelength.

'Now, how's the bloke that had the accident?'

'The one-armed man? He'll live.'

'What's his background?'

Miklos told him.

'Okay,' said Clyde. 'Sounds perfect. Get Jan to fax me everything you can find out about him and his wife and kids. See if any of the kids are sick, you know, crippled or mongoloid, something that makes a tragic picture.'

'Good thinkin',' said Miklos.

'I'll get a press release down to you as soon as I've got all the facts, and another once Nugget finds the pegs. The media will be there in force to catch the action. For once, under the circumstances, a bit of over-enthusiasm on the part of your blokes will not only be acceptable but expected. Let them split a few knuckles but caution them against causing serious injury. And no more king hitting sick little girls. Public sympathy can be pretty fickle and we need to retain the high ground.'

'No problem.'

'You keep out of it. Distance yourself from the action. If the media want to interview you stick to the party line. The whole affair is regrettable. The townsfolk are rightly upset and angry, and their anger is understandable. Never justified, okay? Just understandable.'

'You know something, Clyde? Just when I think I could get to tolerate you, you have to go and piss me off again.'

'I'm just making certain we all know the rules and abide by them.'

'Don't lecture me,' said Miklos. 'I know what's required and I'll do it.'

'I'm not sure my two happy campers in the Kombi would agree with that.'

'That was then. This is now.'

'Point is,' said Clyde, doing his best to conceal his irritation, 'if we do everything right the blockade will be over in forty-eight hours. Get it wrong, we could all end up in deep shit.'

'You're pissin' me off again,' said Miklos and hung up.

CHAPTER THIRTY-TWO

The news spread from the police to the bulldozer drivers to the pro-logging groups and finally to the protesters. The reaction of the protesters was immediate and predictable. It came in three phases: revulsion, followed by indignation that anyone would think they were to blame, then dread when they realised that was precisely what everyone would think. Brian didn't have to call a meeting as everyone automatically gravitated towards the admin tarp.

'What the hell are we gunna do?' asked Rainfather.

'The first question I have to ask is, does anyone here know anything about this?' Brian looked closely at the faces around him and saw only bewilderment and concern. 'Anybody overhear anything? No? Come on, rack your brains! The cops will be here in force any minute and our best interests lie in being as helpful and cooperative as we can. I have to know if one or any of you were involved, or know of anyone who was involved. This thing is going to rebound on us in spades.'

'It wasn't us,' said the Guardians, leading all the other factions in denying involvement.

'None of us would do anything like that,' said Summer. 'You know that.'

'A lot of people have left here recently,' said Brian. 'And not everybody shared our views on passive resistance.'

For a moment the protesters stood stunned by the implications.

'Effin' skinheads!' said Ciaron. A wave of anger and helplessness swept over the gathering.

'Darren?' called Brian.

'Forget it,' said The Dick. 'If they were plannin' something like that they woulda said somethin' and they didn't or I'd know. Anyway, those dickheads didn't give a shit about woodchipping, they only came down here for a fight. The idea of spikin' trees wouldn't even occur to them, and even if it did they wouldn't have a clue how to do it.'

'Then who?' asked Rainfather.

'Nobody,' said Summer vehemently. 'We've got to believe in each other and support each other. Nobody here would ever do anything like that.'

'Summer's probably right,' said Liz. 'But we've had fifteen hundred people here and the possibility remains that someone's overstepped the mark.' She stopped as someone at the back called out, and squinted down the road past the bulldozers and pro-logging groups. A convoy of police cars snaked towards the blockade, sirens off but lights flashing.

'Take your lead from me,' said Brian. 'Cooperate and let the police do whatever they like. Don't give them any excuse to blame us. Cooperate!'

Brian moved forward to meet Wily and Nugget. He spotted Samuel Johnson standing by the bulldozers and called him over. 'Would you mind hanging around? I want it on the record that we gave full and willing cooperation.'

'Can't do that,' said Samuel. 'I'm not sure that would be very smart. I can't appear to be aligned with you. Think about it, do you want an independent observer here or not? I think the cops might prefer it if I wasn't here.'

'You're right,' said Brian. 'Can we chat later?'

'Given the chance. Good luck.' Samuel turned and photographed the police cars skidding to a halt. A small army of grim-faced officers spilled out onto the road. Brian waited until he saw Wily and stepped forward, Liz by his side.

'Inspector Wilson!' he called. Wily must have heard his shout but chose to ignore him. Two cops intercepted Brian and Liz and ushered them back to the body of the crowd. 'Inspector!' Brian called again as Wily stepped forward with a megaphone.

'Attention, please,' said Wily. 'I am Inspector Wilson and you know why we're here. In a couple of minutes my officers will move into your camp and conduct a search. No one is allowed to leave. I want everybody here to go and stand by their tent, vehicle or whatever it is you sleep in, and wait. Anyone who obstructs my men in the execution of their duty will be arrested and charged. Is that clear?'

'We have nothing to hide,' shouted Brian. 'Everyone here will cooperate fully and willingly.'

'Oh, I can guarantee that,' said Wily. 'Sergeant Nugent, get the search underway.' He turned to Brian contemptuously. 'My instructions apply to you as well. Now move it!'

'That spiking had nothing to do with us!' said Brian indignantly. One of the cops pushed him away so roughly he staggered and nearly fell. He heard someone shout 'Fascists!' and the cry was taken up. People were scared but that didn't extinguish their right to get angry. Brian cupped his hands to his mouth. 'Stay calm!' he yelled. 'Don't let them provoke you! Stay calm!' He turned angrily to the cop who'd shoved him. 'See that bloke over there with the camera? He's a reporter. Lay another finger on me or on anyone else and I can guarantee your picture in the paper.' Brian waved Samuel Johnson over. 'Can you come with us while they search under the main tarp?'

'No problem,' said Samuel. He fell into step alongside Brian.

'I know you have a job to do here, but we need to talk.'

'What do you want to know?'

'Everything you know,' said Brian.

'I'll tell you what James told me.' He made no attempt to move closer to Brian or seem to confide, but lowered his voice so that Brian could just hear him. To anyone watching it would have seemed no more than an interview on the run. Brian only heard what he had to say by concentrating on every word. 'James went out to Diggers Hill, talked to Nugget and Miklos Bollok. James has the feeling there's something fishy going on.'

'Like what?'

Samuel told him his editor's concerns.

‘Christ,’ said Brian grimly. ‘Well that rules out the skinheads. They couldn’t club a sheep to death without missing so no way they could have spiked a tree cleanly. In fact I don’t know anybody here who could have. Half the people here can’t even chop firewood. And you reckon the spikes were hardened steel?’

‘James said they could have been made for the purpose. The question we’re asking ourselves is, what do you stand to gain by doing it?’

‘Gain? Nothing! We were holding our own out here.’

‘Exactly. So who does stand to gain?’

‘They do,’ said Brian. ‘God Almighty, the cops, the whole town, everybody is going to come down on us like a tonne of bricks. The bloody Premier could send the army in to shift us and the whole State of Victoria would watch them kick our heads in on their televisions and applaud.’

‘Exactly,’ said Samuel quietly.

Brian stared incredulously at Samuel as his mind made the obvious leap. ‘Surely not ...’

‘Think it as much as you like, but don’t say it,’ warned Samuel. ‘Don’t say it to anyone. Without evidence the accusation is preposterous. You’re going to have to let us raise doubts, and James fully intends to. Whether or not anybody takes any notice is another issue. You don’t need me to tell you what will happen if you start throwing around wild accusations. In the meantime we’ll run your denial of involvement, record your horror and outrage, and extend your deepest sympathies to the victim and his family. You keep your eyes open and let me know if you find anything. I’d better go. Got to maintain my neutrality. Besides, James is putting the paper to bed and I have to ring him with an update.' He held up the old analogue mobile phone James had reclaimed from Glynnis. 'At least I don't have to walk half a kilometre up that hill to get reception.'

'See you, and thanks,' said Brian. Something about people walking up the hill to use mobile phones nagged at him briefly. His brow furrowed, then he let the thought slip away to consider the implications of Samuel's information. He shook his head. Miklos was a hard man, but was *anyone* that hard?

* * *

The police were very thorough. In the process of searching they managed to drop bedding into puddles, dry clothes into mud, and tramp wet boots over dry groundsheets. They routinely addressed the protesters as bludgers, poofters, freaks, dykes or bitches. They called the Aborigines coons, chockos and rock apes, and threatened to kick their black arses in. They kicked down humpies and collapsed tents as they checked tent pegs for a match. But the protesters took it all on the chin and kept their resentment to themselves. They didn't resist and didn't give lip.

The first significant discovery was three spools of chain beneath a pile of pumpkins. Brian turned to Liz and rolled his eyes in despair. Unwittingly they'd also given a pointer as to how they sneaked the chain into the camp and he knew Wily was smart enough to pick up on it. Wily was sure to search the vegie truck in future. They had more chain stashed away in the treehouses, but Brian had no reason to think the cops wouldn't search them as well. He cursed silently. The loss of the chain deprived them of their most effective weapon. He blamed himself for not being smart enough to hide it while he still had a chance.

'Brian.'

He turned to face Liz, alerted by the alarm in her voice. The cops had found something and he caught a glimpse of Wily and Nugget striding through the camp to investigate. Even though he only saw them briefly, the look of triumph on their faces was unmistakable.

'Oh dear God, please no...' he said and set off after them, hoping that some young cop had got excited over nothing. He had to push his way through a silent stunned ring of protesters to see what was happening. An inner cordon of police held the protesters at bay while Wily, Nugget and two young officers occupied the centre, alongside the kind of tent only a yuppy would buy. A sharp length of metal gleamed dull blue-black in Wily's hand. Nugget was on his haunches examining two more tent pegs which had neither returns nor indentations to help secure the guy ropes, and which were clearly similar to the one Wily was holding.

'Whose tent is this?' thundered Wily. 'Who sleeps here?'

Nobody moved. Nobody spoke.

'Don't waste my bloody time! Somebody must know who sleeps here!'

Brian could hear alarm bells ringing but still couldn't quite make the connection. He felt somebody suddenly pull hard on his arm and try to drag him away. He began to resist until he realised it was Ciaron and Sarah Jenkins.

'It was those two guys!' said Ciaron.

'Who?' said Brian.

'The two guys we warned you about. In the blue Kombi. The ones with the mobile phone and esky,' said Sarah. 'Nobody wants to say anything because they don't want to be the one to dob them in.'

Brian's shoulders slumped and he closed his eyes. Everything Samuel had told him began to take on substance. What horrified him most was the planning and premeditation.

'Leave it to me,' said Brian weakly. 'Inspector?'

* * *

'It belongs to two men in their late twenties, early thirties. Two outsiders.' Brian ran his hand wearily through his hair. The police had commandeered the admin area and set up teams to question the protesters one at a time. The choice of venue also meant nobody could prepare food for dinner until the police had finished. Wily thought that might add a bit of urgency to proceedings and encourage people to talk.

'Names,' said Wily.

'Like I told you, I haven't a clue. We've had more than fifteen hundred people here. All I can tell you is what I've already told you. They were misfits. Nobody had ever seen them at protests or blockades before and they kept to themselves. They had stretcher beds and a bar fridge, for Christ's sake. We've sort of had an eye on them ever since they showed up and pitched their ridiculous tent.'

'You've had your eye on them for weeks and you can't tell me who they are or where they are?' Wily looked contemptuously at Brian. 'Some poor bastard's had his arm ripped off and you're still protecting them.'

'Inspector, believe me, if I knew where they were I'd rip their balls off before you got near them. All I can tell you is they drive a blue Volkswagon Kombi and it's not here,' said Brian. 'The men on your road block would probably know it well. Even have its rego number if they've been doing their job.'

'We're going to find them if we have to fingerprint the entire camp,' said Wily. 'You could save us all a lot of trouble.'

'I can't help you,' said Brian. 'Maybe some of the others can.' He looked up as an officer approached Wily.

'Sir,' said the officer.

'What is it?' said Wily.

'Sergeant Nugent has just called from Osbourne to confirm that the tent pegs match the spikes.'

'Thank you,' said Wily. He turned back to Brian. 'Well, well. You know it's all over, don't you? You've lost. You may as well clear off now. I'd hate to be here on your side of the fence when the timber workers come calling in the morning. Bugger me, I'd rather tell my missus my girlfriend's pregnant.'

* * *

'It has to be a setup,' said Samuel. 'The tent had eight pegs supporting it. Five regular pegs and three that matched the spikes in the trees. If the cops ever find the Kombi I'll bet London to a brick that they'll find the other three regular pegs somewhere inside it. Why use the spikes when there was no need? There can only be one answer: they were meant to be found.'

'I can't disagree,' said James. 'Something similar happened in Tasmania a few years back before a Federal election. An obstruction was found on a railway line moments before it would have derailed a train. As I recall there was a protest note attached signed by a militant green group which has its base in America. As a result of the publicity the local green candidate, who had a slim lead in polls in the run-up to the election, was narrowly defeated. The letter was subsequently discredited when it was discovered that the name of the green group had actually been misspelt, and no one could produce a grain of evidence that the group even existed in Australia. Of course by then it was all too late. The green candidate had lost and that was that.'

'They're playing the same dirty tricks here!' said Samuel.

'Not quite. The big difference is, nobody was injured there. It is an enormous leap to suggest that Miklos Bollok — or anyone else for that matter — would deliberately maim one of his own. People would have a lot of difficulty buying that.'

'Which makes it all the more perfect,' cut in Samuel.

'Aye, it does.'

'We've got to do something.'

'Whatever that something is will have to wait for the next issue,' said James. 'The story at the moment is that a young man with a wife and four kids had his arm ripped off because some person or persons unknown spiked a tree he was felling. Similar spikes have been found in the camp of the protesters. That's it. Tomorrow

I want you out at the blockade to cover what happens there. That's where the story will be. God only knows how that will develop, but if there's any substance to our suspicions I'd say that the protesters are in for a very unhappy day, and that the blockade is as good as over.'

'Aren't you going to do anything?' asked Samuel bitterly. 'Are you just going to let them get away with it?'

'Ah … the impetuousness of youth. I didn't say that,' said James. 'I have an editorial to write and I might give it just a little more prominence than usual. If I like it I might even be tempted to send it to a few of my fellow editors in Melbourne, Sydney and Canberra. Will that help you sleep better tonight?'

'Another Scotch will help more.'

'Help yourself,' said James. 'And pour one for me. You know there's only one thing I value more than a Scotch at the end of the day.'

'I know,' said Samuel wearily. 'Your objectivity.'

'My neutrality,' corrected James. 'That is my greatest asset. You ought to try it sometime.'

* * *

Joseph Weiss slumped despondently on his sofa watching the late news, his only company a steadily emptying bottle of red wine. He'd caught the early news and current affairs programs, switching from one to the other like a three year old who's just discovered the joys of the remote control, his despair growing by the minute. The TV channels had used Cheryl's beautiful photos of Little Potoroo Creek, but their glory and majesty had been overwhelmed by the horror. Joseph knew ancient trees and endangered wildlife didn't matter a damn compared to the tears of a lovely young mum with four little kids and a husband whose arm had just been ripped off in an act of inexcusable brutality. He searched for some glimmer of hope, some good news, but instead bad piled on bad through a release of information carefully orchestrated to dominate the evening's viewing and generate a groundswell of outrage. Colin Hayward had survived, but he'd been resuscitated twice on the way to hospital. His arm had been carefully packed in ice in the hope of reconnection by micro-surgery, and the viewing public crossed their fingers and held their breath, praying for the miracle to happen, only to have their hopes dashed by the horrific nature of the injuries. Doctors muttered about missing tissue and the public anger grew. The *pièce de résistance* came with a late newsflash that identical spikes had been found at the blockade. When Bernie Dwight's face appeared on the screen for the sixth time, mouthing sympathies he didn't feel for the victim and his family and damning the protesters for their 'despicable, unconscionable and cowardly act of barbarism', Joseph switched off his TV.

He rang Liz to demand an explanation or perhaps pick up a piece of information that might put a new spin on events and help him try to salvage the situation, but only succeeded in reaching her answerphone. He rang on her mobile only to be informed that her phone was out of range or not switched on. His bottle of Jacobs Creek made another much-needed contribution to his glass. It was time to accept the unacceptable, that the battle was lost, that another precious and irreplaceable wilderness had fallen to the bulldozers, and that he had failed.

He sipped his wine but all he could taste was the bitterness of defeat. He tried to excuse his failure. Perhaps Little Potoroo Creek had always been destined to be destroyed, perhaps that's why he was given it, a project to cut his teeth upon and learn. Perhaps it had always been a lost cause and he was too inexperienced to realise it. But he knew, in his heart, that none of that was true. Cheryl had brought a scent of victory, a promise of a victory he no longer dared hope for, and he had let her and everyone else down. There had once been a chance, Cheryl had offered him a chance, and he hadn't the wit to exploit it. He stared at the blank screen and memories of Bernie Dwight's smug face reared up in front of him. Could he really have lost to men like that? Could he be beaten so easily and comprehensively by the likes of Miklos Bollok, Clyde Townsend and a man who couldn't utter a word without someone else's hand up his bum moving his lips?

He grabbed his phone and dialled a number in Tasmania, letting the phone ring until a sleepy voice answered. He stated his case with firmness and passion and implored the man to change his mind and testify before it was too late. Maurice Connolly told him to go to hell. Joseph hung up feeling he was already halfway there. He stared bitterly at the phone, wondering what he could do to force the man to testify. Desperate times demand desperate measures, Cheryl had said. He wrote a note on the pad by the phone to ring his private detective once more and snapped his pencil with the weight of his disgust.

CHAPTER THIRTY-THREE

The cold reached into Summer's bones and, for a moment, she dreamt she was back in the squat in Melbourne with the wind howling in from the Southern Ocean. She shivered and reached for God, to snuggle against him and cuddle him as she'd done throughout the night, to draw both warmth and comfort. But there was no comfort to be had and God's place on the mattress had grown cold. Summer forced her eyes open and looked around the treehouse. A cold sullen greyness seeped through the cracks like ground mist, heralding a new day which held little promise. There was no sign of God. Summer burrowed deeper beneath her blankets, wishing she had thought to bring her sleeping bag up to God's abode, or had more clothes to put on. Where was God?

She tried to ignore the cold and find refuge in sleep, but it had touched her bladder and she couldn't ignore her need. At one stage during the night she'd considered pulling on her boots because her feet were so cold, and had reached out and pulled them over to the side of her bed. Their dampness had discouraged her then, but now she pulled them beneath the blankets and jammed them onto her feet, reluctant to surrender any warmth until she no longer had a choice.

Summer looked at the rope which was the usual means of descent and wondered if her numbed hands were up to it. The alternative was to climb down from branch to branch until she reached the primitive ladder which extended from the lowest branch to the ground. Neither method appealed, but the rope was quickest and she thought it might chafe some warmth and feeling into her hands. But would her hands have enough feeling to support her? She was about to take the plunge when she spotted God beneath her, dragging something through the undergrowth. He was naked and soaking wet.

'What are you doing?' yelled Summer. God paused and looked up at her.

'Come and help,' he said.

Summer forgot her reservations, grabbed hold of the rope and slithered to the ground. 'You're crazy!' she said, and started to laugh. 'It's freezing! What are you doing?'

'Getting my chain,' said God. 'I hid it in the creek.'

'You're a genius,' said Summer.

'I'm cold,' said God. 'Help me get the rest.'

'I'll be down after I've had a pee.' By the time Summer made it to the creek God had fished out the last lengths of chain and was feeling around with his toes in the murky brown water to make sure there was no more. Summer ordered him out, peeled off a sweater and gave it to him to use as a towel.

'Somehow we'll have to figure out a way of joining the short pieces up with the long pieces,' said God. 'That's the only way it'll work.'

'Just get dressed,' said Summer. 'Brian can send somebody to pick up all this stuff. There's a fire going over in the kitchens and our first job is to get you warmed up.' She shivered as a light breeze licked around her. 'And me, for that matter.' She waited until he'd finished dressing and took his hand to lead him away, but God resisted.

'Summer,' he said quietly. 'Will you stay with me?'

'What do you mean?'

'Will you stay with me today, on the tripod?'

'Of course, if that's what you want. Why?'

'It's important, Summer. It may be our last hope.'

* * *

'He did what?' said Brian, not even trying to hide his delight. 'He's a bloody genius!'

'I've told him that,' said Summer. 'But right now he's just cold.'

'He'll be right, look at him.'

God crowded the fire that Brian had lit, with a mug of hot tea clasped tightly in his hands.

'What are your plans?' asked Summer.

'We're in for a testing day and our only hope is for us all to stick together, every one of us chained together, a thousand people who can't be moved.'

'What about their bolt cutters?'

'Take forever to separate a thousand people,' said Brian optimistically. 'And there's another plus. I can't see timber workers, no matter how pissed off they are, taking swipes at blokes whose arms are chained to their sides. They'll come here looking for a fight, looking for any excuse to kick our heads in, so we've got to be absolutely sure we don't give them the opportunity.'

'Fair enough,' said Summer. She sipped her tea, glad that it wasn't the herbal stuff she had to drink when Gretta, Ciaron or the Guardians were around.

'What are your plans?' asked Brian.

'God wants me to stay with him on his tripod.'

'You've done enough. I was going to suggest you stayed in the background. I'm a bit surprised that God wants to stay back there as well.'

'He says it's our last hope.'

'Our last hope? What's he on about?' Brian turned to look at God and wondered what the hell he was up to.

* * *

At seven-thirty Nugget arrived in his patrol car, bringing with him a bus filled with police officers and equipment. Protesters immediately raced into position so that they didn't surrender any territory before the confrontation even began. Nugget ignored them. Instead he had his men unload the chainsaws and bolt cutters from the bus, while others armed with axes and mattocks headed off through the curtain of trees by the side of the road into the logged area behind. This was something new and the protesters looked on with growing apprehension. They couldn't help noticing that the cops, who'd been growing increasingly bored as the days passed by, now moved with a sense of urgency and purpose.

But if the cops' attitude had changed so had the protesters'. Gone was the confidence and resolve that came with the deep-seated belief in their rightness and the justness of their cause. In its place was nervousness, and apprehension bordering on fear. Somebody started singing 'We shall not be moved' and others joined in. Their dirge wafted across the camp.

'Stuff me!' said Stretch. He was sitting on the trunk of a fallen tree, picking at his guitar while trying to explain the inspiration behind the first hit song he ever wrote, oblivious to the fact that the girl who constituted his entire audience didn't give a stuff and was simply bathing in the afterglow of having spent the night with someone who bordered on fame. 'Brian!' he yelled.

'What's up?' said Ciaron, crawling out of a tent with Sarah Jenkins close behind.

'Listen to that shit,' said Stretch. 'This ain't a protest, this is a wake!'

'Then do something,' said Ciaron. 'Brian's off doing something else.'

Stretch stood and handed his guitar to his starry-eyed friend. 'Hell no! We won't go!' he yelled.

'Fuck's that got to do with anything?' said Ciaron. 'The Vietnam War's over. We lost, remember?'

'Just do it,' said Stretch.

'Hell no! We won't go!' they yelled, and yanked people out of tents and away from whatever they were doing to join them. Together they marched on the protesters who'd taken up position blocking the road. 'Hell no! We won't go!' they chanted. More people joined in and they soon drowned out the battle hymn of the born loser. The chant seemed to energise the protesters, and attracted the attention of the cops who had no trouble recognising the challenge in the voices.

Stretch raised his hands for silence and everyone looked at him expectantly. He turned to face the cops who were now watching them cautiously. He singled one out, a big humourless bastard who was just spoiling for a fight, and pointed his finger at him. 'Hey you!' he shouted. 'Fuck you, pigs in blue!' His followers cheered and picked up on his chant.

'Fuck you! Pigs in blue!'

Some of the arrogance and cockiness went out of the cops. Nugget decided that Stretch would be the first bloke arrested, and that he'd have a little chat with him later back at the police station.

* * *

The Channel Nine chopper landed behind the screen of trees just on eight-thirty, which explained what the cops had been doing there. Channel Seven's chopper landed five minutes later. Brian began to wonder exactly to what degree events were being orchestrated when a Channel Nine outside broadcast van rolled up with a police patrol car as an escort. His wondering was cut short when almost immediately a police helicopter arrived and passed low overhead. It was clear that its role had also been predetermined when it returned to hover right above the protesters' heads. It only stayed in position for a minute but it seemed an eternity to the protesters being battered by the whump-whump-whump of the blades and the rotor wash. It moved slowly away and began hovering around the edges of the blockade, down as low as fifty feet, intimidating everyone beneath and drowning out the chants.

The protesters could have accustomed themselves to the police helicopter if that was all they had to deal with, but Wily denied them the chance. With impeccable timing he led a cavalcade of police cars and buses, their lights flashing and sirens wailing, into view of the blockade. Behind the police cars trailed the busloads of timber workers from Osbourne and all over the State, all of whom were armed with placards drawn up and supplied by Clyde Townsend's company. Weitzler and Hand had also supplied sticks to mount the placards on, but most of them had been discarded for more substantial pieces of wood, the sort that wouldn't break or bend if they came into contact with someone's head. When Wily reached the blockade, vehicles were still streaming around the bend almost a kilometre behind him.

As soon as his car slid to a halt Wily was out and ordering his troops into lines three deep, facing not the protesters but the new arrivals. This unexpected turnaround, more than anything else, scared the protesters who suddenly felt gratitude towards the men they'd spent most of the morning abusing. Overhead the police helicopter whipped dust up into their faces and hammered away at their resolve.

'Move back! Move back!' The loudspeaker on the helicopter burst into life and the protesters were stunned to realise that, for once, it was the pro-woodchippers who were being addressed, not them. Even more alarming was the forest of placards appearing behind the police lines and the angry roar that reached them over the sound of the helicopter. The roar swelled to the kind of volume associated with football grand finals as the helicopter drifted and wheeled away to the landing area. Its departure was barely noticed.

Brian and his helpers moved among the protesters, preaching passive resistance and providing reassurance. They had to shout to be heard by people squatting right at their feet. Brian had helped chain people together but his dream of a thousand people made inseparable had vanished with the last of the chain before the job was even half completed. He'd set aside the smaller lengths of chain, the trimmings left behind from previous days as the police with bolt cutters had moved among them, so that the volunteers on the tripods could chain themselves into position and make it hard for the police in the cherry pickers to dislodge them. Other protesters bound themselves to the main body with rope and tape, but Brian knew their efforts would be more symbolic than useful and cursed himself repeatedly for not having had the forethought to also hide the new chain in the creek. There again he wasn't entirely to blame: he had a lot to think about, and the least God could have done was share his idea.

He turned at the sound of another loudspeaker and heard Wily ordering the timber workers back. But the only people taking a backward step were the police, and Wily's voice had a kind of insincerity that seemed to invite the timber workers to disregard his instructions. Brian was certain his performance was entirely for the benefit of the TV cameras. He saw rather than heard the bulldozers start up, saw the black smoke explode from their exhausts, and saw the police lines buckle as if the timber workers had been given a signal to push forward. He could see the faces of the men opposing him and realised he was staring at a lynch mob. The timber workers were screaming, swearing, hurling abuse and demanding vengeance for their fallen comrade. They wanted blood, and if they'd taken any of Brian's at that moment they would have been stunned by its iciness. How could he offer reassurance when he had none to give?

'Hey you!' he yelled. 'Save Little Potoroo!' No one responded. He reached down and grabbed people by their jackets and screamed into their faces. 'Hey you! Save Little Potoroo!' A few joined him, but in a desultory fashion, and the chant died as quickly as it began. All eyes were on the line of police and the tidal wave of violence behind them. The police line wavered and Brian groaned aloud as Arnie broke through. He couldn't hear what Arnie was screaming, but he was close enough to see his face clearly and realise that Arnie had every intention of making the day the highlight of his life. But before Arnie reached the front line of terrified protesters one of them rose to meet him. Brian recognised the shaven head immediately and felt a flicker of hope. Darren had deliberately placed himself among the protesters chained together at the front so that once again he could single-handedly repel the enemy, and this time under the watchful eye of the TV cameras. The Dick was bad, but was he as bad as Arnie?

A hush descended over the blockade as the two men shaped up to each other.

'I know you,' said Arnie. 'You were that mad bastard with the chainsaw.'

'I know you too,' said The Dick. 'You were that chicken-shit arsehole that ran away.'

Arnie lunged at Darren with both arms. The Dick slipped in close as he'd done a hundred times before, weight moving forward onto his toes, shoulders giving impetus and face averted. He slammed his forehead in the direction of Arnie's nose. His execution was perfect in every respect bar one — he took his eyes off Arnie. Arnie's counter was immediate and immaculately timed. Later many of the onlookers would claim that they head-butted each other simultaneously, but that wasn't the case. Arnie hit Darren the instant before Darren expected to hit Arnie, and that decided the outcome. The Dick hit the ground unconscious, his entire forehead split open as cleanly as if Arnie had struck him with an axe.

That was all the mob needed. Their roar of triumph drowned out the protesters' cry of despair. The police line crumbled and the loggers surged forward. Their method was uncomplicated. They simply grabbed protesters by whichever part was handiest and dragged them out of the path of the bulldozers. Men and women alike screamed in pain as the chains crushed against ribs or threatened to rip off limbs. People were dragged to both sides and the protesters in the middle begged to be cut free before they were torn in half. The police did their best to oblige.

* * *

'Oh Christ!' Samuel screamed into his mobile. 'They're going to kill someone. It's like a battlefield.' Samuel had taken up position on a small rise to the side of the blockade. It seemed the ideal place, and the rest of the media had also headed instinctively towards it and set up. The slight elevation suited the cameras and was close to the thick of the action. It never dawned on anyone that they might be too close.

'Just tell me what's happening and keep out of it!' said James.

'Bloody hell! They've started throwing things!' Samuel raised his arms to protect his head against wayward missiles. 'I'm going to have to go somewhere safer. One of the protesters just sent an axe handle cartwheeling into the loggers. A couple of guys copped it full in the face. Christ! Now I'm copping it! I'm going to have to call you later!' He switched off and was about to retreat from the firing line when a rock smacked into the face of the Channel Nine reporter alongside him. The reporter clutched his face and dropped to his knees. It was only when Samuel saw his hand-held microphone spill onto the ground that he realised the man had been going out live on air. He picked up the mike instinctively and turned to face the camera. It turned towards him, held on him, and the blinking red light drove any thought of self-preservation out of his head. He stared straight down the lens and started talking.

'This is the scene at Thirsty Creek Road, at the battle of Little Potoroo Creek.' With his first words Samuel wrote the front-page headline for every newspaper in the country. His next words set the tone for every electronic news broadcast and current affairs program. 'It is a scene of bloody carnage and a scene that shames Australia. It is a day when the mob came to rule.' The red light kept flashing and words issued from his mouth and Samuel knew only that destiny had finally found him. The producer gestured to him to keep talking and he did.

He kept talking when the camera left him and panned slowly over the battlefield. Kept talking when it zoomed in on close-ups of the injured. But it would come back, Samuel knew. Oh yes, it would come back!

* * *

'We've got to do something!' screamed Summer. 'We've got to help!'

'My job is to stay here,' said God. 'Your job is to stay with me.'

Summer wiped the tears from her eyes with her sleeve. She was beginning to understand why God had chosen to occupy the last of the tripods. He'd known. From her elevated position she could see everything that was happening, and see the course of their defeat. The thousand protesters that Wily had failed to shift in a week of trying were beaten, broken and scattered. Bulldozers and cherry pickers occupied the space they vacated, and ambulances followed close behind. The police were gradually restoring order, but at the front line they still seemed content to let the loggers do their dirty work for them.

'Summer, come in behind me.' God spoke softly but the edge in his voice warned Summer against argument. She did as she was told. God perched where the three legs of the tripod intersected, then reached his hands up as high as he could, wrapped them around the two leading poles and took hold. He kicked both his legs off the tripod and hung down, each leg parallel with one of the poles. 'Bind each of my ankles to the poles. Quick as you can.'

Summer had no idea what God was up to but did as he asked.

'Tighter,' he ordered. Summer was already worried about cutting off his circulation. By the time she'd finished the strain was clearly showing on God's face.

'Good,' said God. 'Thank you.'

'What about me?' asked Summer.

'I have one more job for you, Summer, and you're the only person in the world I can trust to do it.'

'What?' said Summer.

'One last job,' said God. 'Then I want you to get down. I'll tell you when I'm ready.'

Summer turned back to check the progress of the bulldozers, certain now that God was up to something she wouldn't like, but she hadn't a clue what. The protesters had gathered protectively around the legs of the first tripod, but to no avail. The timber workers simply sliced through the ropes that bound them to the poles and dragged them away screaming. The lead bulldozer surged forward and struck the tripod with its blade. Whether the knock was deliberate or accidental made no difference. Summer screamed when she saw the tripod begin to topple, but nowhere near as loudly as the two women who'd tied themselves to the top of it. When the police in the cherry picker came to remove them, the two women couldn't get aboard fast enough. Barely a breath later, the bulldozer flattened the tripod as if it had been made of matchsticks. The sitters on the second tripod watched terrified as the first tripod disintegrated, and abandoned ship. The second tripod fell. The protesters on the third tripod were more resolute and defiantly held the line. The bulldozer paused to let the cherry picker past. Resolute or not, they were easy pickings for the police.

* * *

'Not since Tiananmen Square have we witnessed scenes anything like these,' said Samuel. 'The blockade to save Little Potoroo Creek from woodchipping is almost over, crushed not by tanks but just as mercilessly by bulldozers.' The producer gave him the wind-up signal. 'On this saddest of days, this is Samuel Johnson, *East Gippsland Gazette*, for Channel Nine News.'

'Fan-bloody-tastic!' said the producer. 'I don't know where you sprang from, mate, but you're doing great. Don't move. The director's on line. He's got a queue of people waiting to interview you.'

'No worries,' said Samuel.

* * *

'What're we going to do?' screamed Summer.

'Do exactly what I tell you. Look at me, Summer.' God cupped Summer's jaw in his hand as if he was holding something indescribably precious. 'I asked you to stay with me because you're the only one I can trust to do what needs doing.' He smiled at her sadly.

The police had begun to remove the first of two protesters clinging to the top of the fourth tripod. God reached into his shoulder bag and took out a ten-centimetre nail. 'Do this for me, Summer, and for everything Little Potoroo Creek means to us. Do this for the animals. Do this for the trees. Promise me.'

'What?' said Summer, her mind whirling, fearing the worst but not believing God would go through with it.

'Hold the nail over my left foot.'

'No!' said Summer. 'No way!'

'Please,' said God gently. 'Do it for me.'

Summer reached down, her hand trembling, and held the nail point first against God's foot. The suddenness and force with which he struck it took her totally by surprise. She screamed. She hadn't even seen him reach into his shoulder bag for his hammer, hadn't even been aware that he had one with him. God groaned and sucked air in through his teeth. He hit the nail again, and again, driving it into the pole. Someone was screaming and it took Summer some moments to realise it was her. It didn't sound like her, but then she'd never really heard herself scream before. She turned to look up at God but her eyes were blinded by tears. She felt him pressing another nail into her hand.

'Now the other foot, Summer. Now!'

Summer screamed again as the hammer fell. Twice, three times. God pressed two more nails into her hand. She had to strain to hear his voice. Holding the nails was the most horrific thing she'd ever done in her life, but God was about to ask her to do more.

'Left hand,' he said weakly, and offered her his hammer. 'Now, Summer! Now!'

'No! No!' Summer reeled back, unable to even touch it. She wept without restraint. 'I can't! I can't!'

'Do it!' he begged. 'It's the only way.' God could not conceal the agony he was in.

'I can't! Don't make me!'

'Don't put me through this for nothing.' A spasm racked his body and a tortured moan escaped his lips. 'Please, Summer, please!'

Summer grabbed the hammer from his hand, unable to deny him any longer. Her justification and only hope for salvation lay in the belief that the sooner she did what she had to do, the sooner his ordeal would be over. She swung the hammer for God and drove the nail clean through his hand. The second swing missed and smashed into his wrist. They both cried out. The third and fourth struck home.

'The other hand,' said God. 'Now, now! Oh dear God ...'

Summer clenched her teeth once more and, sobbing uncontrollably, completed the job.

'Go now!' said God. 'Leave me!'

* * *

'Oh no!' said Samuel. 'Oh my God, no! Look what he's done! Get the camera around! Get the camera around!'

The clouds parted for the first time in days and the sun lit on God's face. The cameraman had no difficulty zooming in on his target.

'Bloody perfect,' he said. 'Bloody fantastic!'

* * *

Summer fell down as much as climbed, tumbled helplessly into the arms of stunned fellow protesters. She was aware of sobbing and crying and people shouting. Ciaron's strong arms were around her, hugging her to her breast. The bulldozers had ceased their roaring and the engines ticked over in idle as if put on hold. It seemed to Summer that the whole world had stopped and was holding its breath. She wiped her eyes with her sleeve and dared to turn and look up at God. In that instant she understood exactly why he'd done what he had. The cross was the wrong shape, an X rather than a T. But God was crucified all the same.

The police and loggers stood by, stunned and uncertain how to proceed. In those precious moments God hung on his cross for all the world to see, a solitary, tragic, heroic figure, his blood seeping down his arms and feet in little crimson rivers, his eyes screwed closed, the veins and muscles in his neck knotted in torment, his mouth frozen open in a silent scream.

The media devoured the image.

CHAPTER THIRTY-FOUR

'Why do ya reckon a bloke would go and do somethin' like that?' said Miklos.

'Buggered if I know,' said Arnie. 'Hell, if I'd known that was what he wanted I'd have done it for him.'

'I'd have held the nails for ya,' said Miklos.

They both laughed. Miklos's Toyota was stalled in Thirsty Creek Road's very first traffic jam. The road was blocked with cars, utes, vans and buses carrying timber workers who'd come to do a job, done it and now wanted to find a pub where they could have a decent drink and boast about it. The blockade was over. God's tripod had fallen, along with his treehouses and the trees that had harboured them. Nothing stood between the bulldozers and Tathra Heights above Little Potoroo Creek except four to six weeks of clearing and road building. There was little the protesters could do except drift away home or stand by and watch. They talked about regrouping and chaining themselves to the bulldozers at night, or lying down in their path, but the will to fight on had gone, been bashed out of them, and even the most optimistic had to accept that nothing they did from then on would delay the bulldozers by more than a day at the most.

'That bulldozer driver did all right by ya,' said Arnie.

'Yeah,' said Miklos. 'Wondered when he was going to give me a return on my investment. Hate to have to keep him and his mates in food and beer for the rest of my life.'

Arnie laughed. 'You see that bloke I nutted?'

'Saw the meat wagon that took him away. Bloke told me his brain was oozing out.'

'Yeah?' said Arnie. He thought that was a good thing. The car in front moved off and they followed. 'Gunna take all day to get to Orbost if it stays like this.'

'What's ya hurry?' said Miklos. 'We won. Even uphill's downhill from here.'

It was mid-afternoon before Miklos dropped Arnie at the pub and drove to his office. Jan was waiting for him, eyes full of reproach and bottom lip pouting. Miklos groaned silently.

'Everybody's been trying to ring you,' she said.

'Don't sulk,' said Miklos. 'You know that gives me the shits.'

'All the TV and radio stations, all the newspapers. I haven't had a minute to myself.'

'Yeah?' said Miklos. Her immaculate make-up and nails showed the benefit of hours of dedication. He pushed open the door to his office and walked straight to the fridge for a beer. 'Well just keep telling them I'm out. I don't want any calls.'

'Clyde Townsend wants to talk to you urgently. Shall I get him on the line for you?'

'No, I'll use my direct line.' He twisted the top off his beer and took a long pull.

'Sometimes I think you don't need an assistant!' said Jan.

'Know something?' said Miklos. 'Sometimes so do I. Now get the hell out and shut the bloody door behind you.'

Jan stuck her chin up imperiously and strode out of his office, down the hallway and out of the building. Miklos smiled, ambled across his office and slammed his door shut. He wasn't sorry to see Jan go. If she'd stayed she'd have done all she could to make his life miserable, and he didn't want anything to spoil his day. He figured he'd take her a bottle of Bailey's later and reacquaint himself with her magnificent tits. For the first time in ages he believed things were back under control and felt good about it. He finished his beer and opened another. Outside his office Jan's phone was ringing virtually non-stop. It reminded him of the call he had to make.

'Miklos?' said Clyde Townsend. 'Where the hell have you been? The shit's hitting the fan down here!'

'What do you mean?' said Miklos coldly.

'What do you mean what do I mean?' said Clyde. 'You ought to know. You were there!'

'Okay, some of the blokes you sent down got a bit carried away. Arnie split some dumb prick's head open. Big deal. Don't tell me you didn't expect something like that.'

'What I didn't expect,' said Clyde, 'was some crazy to nail himself to a cross! I don't know who's advising that guy but he's a bloody genius! Public sympathy's turned, Miklos, and that's a dangerous thing. All the media's talking about is that guy hanging there crucified, and it doesn't help to see bulldozers working around the tripod flattening trees while the doctor and medics are trying to get the bastard down. Every green group in Christendom is on air and on the bandwagon.'

'Slow down,' said Miklos. 'What are you sayin'?'

'What I'm saying is that the public and the media are changing sides. They're changing their minds about who is right and who is wrong. And when they get serious about changing their minds, politicians usually follow.'

'So what are you gunna do about it?'

'Everything is what I'm doing about it, but it's all uphill. Today nothing's working but I'm hoping for better press tomorrow, provided we don't make any mistakes. Everyone's forgotten about the poor bloke who's just had his arm ripped off. That's yesterday's news. Nobody cares about his family. I've sent out bulletins from the hospital. I've had a crew film the family moving into the hotel next to the hospital. I even sent out an unattributed story saying the youngest girl had fallen and broken her arm and that the hospital was going to put her in the same room as daddy. Nobody's used any of it. I've even thought of sending someone down to run over the family dog!'

'Stop whining and do the fuckin' job you're paid to do,' said Miklos. 'Things are fuckin' up your end, not down here. Down here's sweet. We're shiftin' dirt. Issue management is supposed to be your department. You're supposed to be the expert, so fix it.'

'Sometimes, Miklos, you amaze me with your stupidity. You've left me a lot to fix.'

'Bullshit.'

‘Listen, and listen good. Stuff up now and we’re all in big trouble.’

‘Go on,’ said Miklos.

‘I’ve got a guy in the Channel Nine newsroom. He rang to warn me about a tape going to air this evening. Know a guy called Samuel Johnson? A reporter from the *Gazette*?’

‘I know him,’ said Miklos. ‘Pimply-faced kid. Wet behind the ears.’

‘That was yesterday. Today he’s a star. Somehow he got himself in front of the camera and he hasn’t stopped talking since. He may be a twerp but the camera loves him. He’s confident and he oozes credibility. All of the big guns in news and current affairs have interviewed him and he’s hurting us with every word. According to my man, who’s seen the tape, he’s blabbing on about all the dirty tricks that have been played on the protesters since the blockade began. You remodelling your Toyota, people cutting their radiator hoses, dumping sewage on their vegetable truck, shooting front wheels off motorbikes, every bloody chapter and verse. Now he’s putting two and two together and asking whether the whole business with the spikes isn’t just another dirty trick. Why would anybody in a brand new tent be using hardened spikes, which aren’t suitable to hold guy ropes, instead of the tent pegs which were supplied and are purposely made for the job? Why would anybody spike trees and then leave such an obvious clue behind? Where were the occupants when the police came looking? Who tipped them off? Why were they driving a stolen Kombi? Do you want me to go on?’

‘I get the picture.’

'So far it's only questions. He's said nothing we can litigate against to shut him up. Whatever happens we all have to stick to the party line.'

'Thanks for the scoop.'

Clyde ignored him. 'Who knows, Miklos, besides you, me and Bernie?'

'Only the two clowns you sent camping.'

'You sure about that?'

'Yeah, unless you've told somebody.'

'Like I would.'

'So you've got nothing to worry about. Anything else?'

'Some good news. Inspector Wilson has come under the hammer for the way he handled things. The TV's making it look like the police gave the loggers an open go at the protesters. There are shots of women being punched and dragged screaming over rocks. They're comparing it with Tiananmen Square. The government will make him the scapegoat and take the spotlight off us.'

'So where's the problem?'

'There are plenty of problems,' said Clyde.

'For you, not me. The spiking's a dead issue. People can think what they like but nobody can prove a thing. Besides, nobody's seriously gunna believe that we go around spiking our own trees and maiming our own people.'

'True, but things are changing. When that crazy crucified himself he also hammered nails into us. The road's not built yet and I'm worried that, unless we strike quickly and take the initiative, our gutless politicians will have a change of heart.'

'Yeah? Well, you and Bernie just get in there and remind them that I've got a contract — a signed contract — and I'll sue the shit out of them if they renege. Remind them also that there are a lot of unemployed voters down here depending on me for jobs and a whole lot of local businesses counting on me buildin' my papermill. Just ask them which one wants to go on television and tell them it ain't gunna happen. Bugger me, Clyde, do I have to do your bloody job as well?'

'No, I'll do my job. I'm going to need you to talk to the media soon but not yet. Silence can be interpreted as guilt. As soon as we work out the angles I want you talking till your tongue turns black.'

'As if I haven't got enough to do.' Miklos slammed the phone down. He no longer felt he had everything under control. He no longer felt he was having a good day. Outside his office Jan's phone rang incessantly, reminding him that Australia wanted to have a word with him, but the time for talk had gone. It was time to keep his head down and dig like crazy. It didn't occur to Miklos that this was also the strategy employed at Gallipoli.

* * *

Cheryl sat in the gloom in front of her TV, oblivious to everything except the image on her screen. Her eyes were red-rimmed and exhausted of tears. She made no effort to turn on the lights, make coffee or make dinner, but sat paralysed by the horror and the weight of her shame. God gave everything he had to give for Little Potoroo Creek, but all she gave were her precious photos and her pathetic ambitions to paint them. God risked his life, but she was not prepared to risk the comfort and security of her home. God had touched her with his love and now he broke her heart with his pain.

The six o'clock news began with God alone on the cross and cut to a clearly distraught Samuel Johnson, delivering his commentary for the fifth time that day. Cheryl knew every frame and every word yet could not drag her eyes away. She watched the doctor administer anaesthetics and painkillers, knew his every move before he made it. Watched as police, paramedics and protesters lowered God gently from his cross, glimpsed his beautiful face as he was loaded unconscious into the ambulance, saw Summer helped in alongside him, and suffered her shame all over again. She should have been there, should have helped, should have done more so that one man would not have had to do so much.

It was the phones that had alerted Cheryl as she returned from a futile morning in Orbost spent buying toys and sweets for Gillian Hayward's kids, only to discover when she went to her house that they'd all gone to Melbourne. Unable to find Miklos at work the media were trying his home. She'd no sooner got rid of one caller than another rang. She'd disconnected the phones and turned on her television to see if she could find out what all the fuss was about. And then she'd seen God.

When the news finished and led into the current affairs program Cheryl genuinely believed that nothing else that day could possibly shock her. But it did. She sat up and began to take notice when Samuel Johnson started raising questions about the spiking and the identity of the alleged culprits. It took her a moment to grasp where the questions were headed, but once she did the implications sickened her. She stared at the screen in horror, terrified that the reporter was touching on a truth too awful for her to bear. When the TV cut to a close-up of the spikes she screamed as if a giant hand had reached inside her and wrenched her soul from her body. She knew exactly where she'd seen them before.

* * *

Joseph Weiss worked tirelessly, collating and dispatching reports and studies he'd prepared but never thought he'd have the chance to use. His advocates and the media devoured everything he sent them and demanded more. Against all odds a miracle had occurred, and they had their opponents on the run. He had no time to stop and contemplate the nature of a man who could so literally nail himself to his cause. He simply accepted that God had single-handedly turned the tide of public opinion, and that the best way he could honour him was to do his best to make sure his suffering was not in vain.

However Joseph held no illusions regarding what God had accomplished. Public sympathy had turned purely on emotion not on fact, and emotion rarely endured. They had two days, maybe three at most, to force the government to order a halt to further road building. In the meantime he knew Miklos would have the bulldozers working non-stop through every daylight hour while Clyde Townsend bent, distorted and created facts to suit the woodchippers' cause. Yet, provided there were no mass shootings, earthquakes, fires or any other cataclysmic event in the coming days to divert attention away from Little Potoroo Creek, Joseph believed they were in with a chance, slim though it might be.

God had given them an opportunity to resurrect the issue of the impact study prepared by DeCaF. All around him staff and volunteers worked the copiers and fax machines to exhaustion. Dinnertime had come and gone but nobody had time to either notice or care. The coffee had run out but nobody had done the dash to the corner deli. It didn't matter. Nobody had time to make it or drink it. Outside Joseph's window cars backed up in glowing red queues while their drivers did battle with the rain and each other. It was a good night for not going anywhere, which was just as well.

When his phone rang it was a green senator in Canberra, ringing for new material to introduce into the Senate. He'd only just hung up when it rang again, this time with a news producer asking if he'd kept a copy of God's letters to the *Age*. Joseph had and promised to fax them over immediately. He opened his press cuttings file, found the two articles and glanced quickly over them to ensure they'd work for the cause and not against it. His lawyer's eye flicked quickly through the first letter, then pulled up, stunned by the prophetic first line of God's second letter. Joseph's mouth fell open. How far ahead had God planned? How had he known?

'Dear Editor,' it said. 'Any day now I will face my Calvary.'

Joseph instantly grasped the news value and shouted the first thing that came into his mind that would guarantee him immediate attention. 'Rape!' he yelled.

Faces appeared in his doorway, some anxious, others grinning idiotically.

'You and you,' he said pointing at random, 'drop what you're doing. I want quality photocopies of this cutting sent to every TV channel in the country and a copy faxed to every newspaper and radio station.'

'Wow!' said the volunteer who took the cutting. 'Wow!'

Joseph smiled. 'What you see here is living proof of the wow factor. If it impresses you it will impress Australia. Now get on with it!' He was about to ring the news producer back when his phone rang again. He snatched it off the cradle. 'Joseph Weiss.'

'Know any good lawyers?' said a voice softly, but all Joseph could hear was a cry for help.

'Where are you?' he asked.

'A service station outside Bairnsdale.'

'Are you okay?'

'Yes.' A pause. 'No. I'm not.'

Joseph heard a sob of anguish that chilled him to the bone.

'Joseph, there's no one else I can turn to, nowhere else I can go.'

'That's okay,' said Joseph hastily. 'If you didn't turn to me I'd accuse you of being anti-semitic. Now, listen to me. You've got a bed for as long as you need it, a hot dinner waiting, a lawyer who listens and someone who thinks you're absolutely wonderful.'

'Who?' said Cheryl hesitantly.

'Me. Now move it!' Joseph rang off. He slumped back in his chair, eyes closed and head in his hands. The strongest woman he'd ever met was on the verge of losing it. The wife of the man who was his most implacable enemy wanted refuge in his apartment. The question was, why? Were there more revelations or had Miklos simply used her as a punching bag once too often? He shook his head to clear it. There were too many questions and the answers were still two hours away. In the meantime he had producers and editors to call, lobbyists to arm and a wave of sentiment to ride.

He asked the receptionist to call him at ten even if it meant dragging him out of a meeting. With the mountain of work to do he knew his departure would hardly be greeted with joy. His phone rang at nine-fifty but it was his private detective not his receptionist. Joseph listened, not knowing whether to feel relief or disappointment as the detective described Maurice Connolly as a quiet family man who kept to himself, didn't drink or smoke, and appeared to have no other vices or skeletons in the closet. Only when the detective told him he was wasting his time and money because Maurice Connolly was a devout Catholic and regular church-goer did Joseph realise he'd been given precisely the information he needed. He whooped with joy. The detective hung up mystified.

Joseph stopped off at a gourmet take-away for dinner, opened one of his few good bottles of red and settled down to wait for his visitor. When Cheryl finally rang the buzzer and he opened his door to her he was relieved to find her in one piece and unharmed, but relief turned to concern the moment he looked into her eyes. His smile froze. She was clearly on the verge of exhaustion, not just physically but emotionally, as if the drive to Melbourne had drained the last of her reserves. He barely had time to open his arms to catch her as her carryall slipped from her hand and she slumped forward. Joseph held her tightly, supporting her, and waited unmoving and unspeaking until the silent sobs building in her body ran their course and finally eased. He waited until she lifted her head from his shoulder before guiding her to his sofa.

'I'm sorry,' she whispered.

'Don't be,' he said. 'Being a friend means never having to say sorry. It says so on my secretary's calendar. I've made up your bed in my wine cellar, which the real estate agents insist on calling the second bedroom. I've also left a towel on top. Why don't you have a shower and freshen up while I make coffee and get dinner. I'm a lousy cook but a sensational re-heater.'

Cheryl managed a weak smile. 'That guy who you said thinks I'm wonderful — he's not too bad himself.' She let Joseph help her to her feet. 'Give me ten minutes.'

Joseph expected Cheryl to pick at her dinner but instead she ate everything on her plate and didn't object when Joseph refilled her glass. He wasn't to know she hadn't eaten since breakfast. He waited until he'd served coffee before beginning to question her.

'What happened?' he asked tentatively.

Cheryl looked down at her coffee as once more she felt the weight of her burden. 'Don't make me tell you tonight. Please, Joseph, I couldn't face it. I have a plan which I think might work, but I'll need all your help, and the best lawyer you can find.'

'Aren't I good enough?'

'Plenty good enough.' Cheryl smiled. 'But I have another role for you to play. I want the best lawyer money can buy. I want a hard-nosed in-your-face smartarse, someone you respect and whose discretion we can trust completely.'

For a brief instant Joseph caught a glimpse of the Cheryl of old. 'Someone who could front Miklos. Yeah?' Cheryl nodded. 'Have you met my father? He's very charming until he doesn't have to be.'

'Is he involved with the Foundation or actively interested in conservation?'

'My father? No way. Just the usual lawyer things. Power, money and position.'

'The trouble is, he's involved with you.'

'So that rules him out. I'll find you someone else. Mort Feldman. My father can't stand him, which is the highest recommendation he can give. Are you sure you don't want to tell me what this is all about?'

'Not tonight.'

Joseph's eyes narrowed. 'What are you up to?'

'Please don't ask. Just get me the best lawyer there is.'

'I have. Mort Feldman. Can't you even give me a hint?'

'No. I'm sorry.' The cloud of despair that had enveloped Cheryl when she'd arrived settled over her once more. Her shoulders slumped and she buried her head in her hands. Joseph rose immediately, went to her side and crouched down with his arm around her shoulders.

'What's the matter?' he said. 'Why won't you tell me?' She refused to look at him or take her hands away from her face and he had to strain to hear her.

'I'm too ashamed,' she whispered.

* * *

James Ferguson's light was the only one still burning as Samuel parked his car. He opened his door wearily and prepared himself for the bollocking he had coming. He had no idea how to apologise, where to begin, or what to say. James had given him a chance and he'd dumped him the instant a better offer had come along. He found his boss at his desk, feet up and a tumbler of Scotch in his hand. A chair and another tumbler sat on the opposite side of the desk. Samuel slumped down into the chair and let James pour him a double. He sipped long and deep, closed his eyes and let the golden fluid find its own way down. It stung the back of his throat but not unpleasantly, reached his empty stomach and spread its glow through his body. The way it soothed him, whisky could have been invented with tired reporters in mind. He braced himself for James's onslaught.

'You know,' said James, 'when I was about your age I met a young lady who swept me off my feet the instant I saw her. She was gorgeous. Hair like strands of gold, eyes like saucers and bluer than a summer sky. All the boys fancied her. There used to be a dance in the church hall every Saturday night and one day I plucked up the courage to ask her to go with me. I was the happiest man alive when she accepted. She told me she'd meet me there and we agreed a time and place. I told everyone I knew about my good fortune and all my friends and their girlfriends came along to witness my finest hour. Of course she failed to turn up. I found out later she'd jilted me because she'd had a better offer from someone older and richer who'd taken her out to dinner.'

'Ouch,' said Samuel.

'We took down your copy off the television.'

'I'm really sorry, James.'

'And of course you did phone in between interviews.'

'What can I say?' Samuel hung his head.

'Did they offer you a job?'

'Yes.'

'And what did you tell them?'

'I said I'd speak to you first.'

'Did you now?'

'Yes,' said Samuel.

'Then you're a bigger fool than I thought.'

'What?'

'Seize the opportunity, lad, like you seized upon that microphone! I can't tell you how proud you made us all feel. Samuel Johnson, *East Gippsland Gazette*, for Channel Nine. Samuel Johnson, *East Gippsland Gazette*! Ha! Lad, you should have been here to hear the cheers! Now finish your glass and we'll drink to your new career.'

Samuel drained his glass and held it out for a refill. 'You're a giant among men, James. I'm going to miss you. It'll be like losing a father, best friend and mentor all at once.'

'So long as you don't forget what I've tried to teach you. Put your heart away, Samuel. Put it in a box and hide the key. Use your brain and maintain your impartiality. That's the only path to the truth, and no matter what anybody else tries to tell you, finding the truth is what makes great reporters. Nothing else. Never sacrifice content for style. By the way, I think you did an excellent job of raising doubts about the spiking. Obviously something of me has rubbed off on you.'

Samuel averted his eyes and stared down at his Scotch. 'Don't tease me, James. I had no idea I was going to end up on television.'

James's eyes narrowed. 'It was you, was it? I thought I must have left my computer on.'

'I called in on the way to the blockade and ran off a copy of your editorial. I thought if I knew where you were heading I could maybe dig out more information for you. Maybe even use it as a starting point for the stories I phoned in. They were your words I said to camera, James, your ideas. They were all there in my mind and just came spilling out.'

'My words, eh?' James leant back, a smile edging across his face. 'My ideas, my editorial. Now why do I feel so pleased about that? Maybe I should have gone on television myself.'

'You're not angry?'

'I'm flattered. You've done well, lad, very well indeed. It isn't every day television runs with my editorial.'

'Do you think it will do any good?'

'For a while, maybe. Long term, who knows?'

'We've got them on the run,' said Samuel indignantly.

'We? Who is "we"? Not me, and if you've been listening to a single word I've been saying, not you either. If you mean the protesters have the woodchippers on the run, that's true for tonight but it could all change tomorrow.'

'What do you mean?'

'Come on now, don't be naive! For every person who uncovers a truth there are ten or a hundred and ten spin doctors hell bent on corrupting it, distorting it for the benefit of vested interests. I read in the *Age* the other morning that there are one hundred and twenty thousand reporters in America charged with the job of reporting the news, and one hundred and fifty thousand people engaged in issue management, bending and corrupting the news the reporters report. And don't think for one second it's any different here. You've seen first-hand how Miklos used us to try and influence the media against God. Tonight the protesters have the upper hand, but who knows what will happen tomorrow. The only certainty is that truth, as always, will be the first casualty.'

'So it's all been for nothing?' Samuel stared glumly at the ice melting into the dregs in his tumbler.

'I didn't say that. This has just been another phase in a battle that's far from won. Get out there and keep telling the truth, not how you want it to be but how it is. That is the only way you'll be of value to yourself, to Channel Nine, and to their long-suffering viewers.' James reached for the bottle of Scotch. 'One more for the road?'

* * *

Miklos snatched up the phone and jammed it to his ear. 'Where the fuck are ya?' he snarled.

'Miklos? It's Clyde.'

'Shit!' said Miklos. 'Thought it was Cheryl.'

'What's up?' said Clyde warily. 'Cheryl's not missing, is she?'

'Not if you know where she is, because I fuckin' don't.'

'Miklos, this could be important.' Clyde twisted his hand to look at his wristwatch. The hour hand had almost climbed to midnight. 'When did she go missing?'

'Hell do I know? I got home half an hour ago. No lights on, doors unlocked, no dinner and no Cheryl. Now you know all I know.'

‘Could she have gone to visit friends?’

‘She doesn’t have any friends.’

‘A movie maybe?’

‘She rents a video.’

‘Is anything missing? Her clothes, a suitcase?’

‘How the hell would I know?’

‘Jesus, Miklos, you’re not being very helpful.’

‘And you are?’

‘Think for a minute, Miklos. Could she know about the spikes?’

‘No way.’

‘You sure?’

‘Yeah, I’m sure.’

‘Did you ever take them home? Miklos?’

‘No. Wait a sec, not in the house. Wrapped up in the back of the Toyota.’

‘So she could have seen them?’

‘Why would she look in the back of the Toyota? Besides, they were wrapped up.’

‘She ever use your car?’

‘No way.’

‘Ride with you?’

‘Only once. To dinner in Orbost. She slept all the way home.’

‘Then we’re probably okay. There’s probably a simple explanation for her absence. But if she’s not back by morning, I think it’s time to start worrying.’

‘Fuck off.’

‘What if it was her that took the photos of you smashing your car?’

‘We’ve been through that. It wasn’t.’

‘What if she’s secretly on the protesters’ side?’

'She isn't.'

'What if she's been eavesdropping on your conversations and searching your car?'

'You're askin' me if I trust her. No, I don't. I tell her nothin' except to keep her nose out of my business. I don't discuss business or do business at home when she's around. She has nothin' to eavesdrop on and doesn't search my car. I'm not paranoid like you, but I am careful. Okay? Now was there some other reason you rang me or did you just want to piss me off again?'

'Yeah, I rang you for a reason. We want you to make yourself available to the media tomorrow morning from six in your office. This is what I want you to say.'

Miklos listened and took down notes. He liked what Clyde wanted him to say and it was pretty much what he would've said anyway.

'Okay?' said Clyde.

'Yeah. Anything else?'

'We've got a few surprises in store. We've generated enough stuff to muddy the water so people won't know what to believe. By the day after they'll lose interest. I've also got the government to commission an enquiry into an environmental impact study done for the Bellbird concession in the Central Highlands.'

'So what? How does that help me?' asked Miklos.

'Can you see this government holding two enquiries simultaneously?' said Clyde patiently. 'Besides, the fix is in. We know we can win Bellbird. Overall things haven't turned out to be as bad as they seemed at first.'

'Glad to hear it.'

'Keep me informed about Cheryl.'

'You got the hots for her or somethin'?'

'I hate loose ends.'

'I'll tell her what you called her.' Miklos hung up. He looked balefully at the microwave and wondered if that was what Cheryl used to make cheese on toast.

CHAPTER THIRTY-FIVE

Summer awoke to a house on tiptoes. Her head felt heavy and fogged by the sedatives the hospital had given her, but that didn't entirely explain the overwhelming lethargy that had invaded her body. A powerful owl stared at her from a long out-of-date calendar, letting her know she was back in Liz and Brian's spare room. She had no idea what the time was, other than that it still wasn't time for her to get up. A folded towel sat on the foot of her bed as a gentle reminder that Liz required her to shower. She closed her eyes. Showering required more energy than she could even begin to imagine. Sleep beckoned, but then so too did an image of God in pain and sudden memories of a hammer in her hand driving nails through his bleeding palms. She cried out.

'Sum, you awake?'

She opened her eyes and found an anxious Pete hovering over her.

'I didn't wake you, did I?'

Summer closed her eyes and shook her head so slightly that Pete wasn't certain she had.

'Liz and Brian are working in the office downstairs and I'm under strict instructions to make you two boiled eggs and toast, and to stay with you until you've eaten every bit. I'll make you a nice cup of tea as well. Stay there and don't move.'

Summer wished she had a choice. More awake now she remembered being taken in to see God, his face grey against the whiteness of his pillow, his lips moving leadenly. She remembered leaning over him, straining to hear his words, and the egg-shape of his clumsy bandaged hand reaching for hers. In the end he'd only said two words and that seemed to satisfy him for he slipped easily into sleep.

'Thank you,' he'd said.

The two words had fortified her as she'd fought off the sedatives and insisted on sitting up to watch the late night news and witness the swing in public sentiment. At some stage she'd succumbed and someone had carried her up the stairs and put her to bed. God had been right in one respect in that he'd captured the cameras and focussed sympathetic attention upon their cause. But had he stopped the bulldozers? In the blur of the aftermath of God's crucifixion she recalled the bulldozers working around the tripod, ripping out the trees with their treehouses. How far had they gone? Were they still working?

'Time to sit up,' said Pete. He carried a tray with two already decapitated eggs, a little straw basket which he'd lined with a paper serviette and filled with buttered toast cut into soldiers, a pot of tea with two cups, sugar bowl and tiny jug of milk, and two pink roses with the tips of their stems wrapped in silver foil.

He placed the tray on a chair while he helped Summer sit up. 'I've got the hens on standby in case you need more.'

'What's happening?' said Summer.

'I'll tell you,' said Pete. 'Between eggs. Now, do you want me to feed you? Eggs are very good for breast development, you know.'

Summer smiled.

'It's true. It's all the hormones they feed the chickens to make them grow quickly. If I hadn't stopped eating eggs I'd have been wearing a bra by now.'

The eggs were perfect and the toast still crisp. Summer didn't think she was hungry but each mouthful made her anxious for another. The first egg disappeared and the second followed, taking all the soldiers with them. Pete poured the tea and it tasted fantastic, and all the better for not being herbal.

'Jerry rang,' said Pete. 'He saw you on television being loaded into the ambulance. He wanted to know how you were.'

'Did he say anything else?'

'He's found a new bike he wants to buy when the insurance comes through. Apparently the insurance company is chasing up the police in Orbost. But, no, he didn't mention that he'd found another girl, fallen in love or got her pregnant.'

'Did you give him my love?'

'I gave him our love.'

Summer laughed.

'I told him he has a very cute butt and we miss him terribly.' Pete gently took Summer's hand. 'And you do, don't you?'

Summer's smile faded. Thinking of Jerry and the reason she'd had to let him go reminded her of all her unasked questions. 'He has a job in Melbourne. I have a job here.'

'You won't always be here,' said Pete. 'And he won't always hold the door open for you.'

'I'll be here until we win! And when we win I'll be somewhere else, fighting for another forest until there's no more woodchipping.' Her eyes had started to water again but both of them knew it wasn't for the forests.

'The forests don't ask for this much sacrifice, Summer. You've done your bit and no one can ask you to do more. You belong with Jerry, Sum, and it's time you grew up and finished your education.'

'No. I'm needed here. Until logging's stopped I'll always be needed.'

'All blockades do is draw attention to areas of land under threat. No blockade has ever stopped a logging company or saved a forest. Those decisions are made elsewhere by bringing pressure to bear on governments.'

'That's not true!'

'Yes it is, and you know it is.'

'That's not true,' said Summer once more, but the vehemence had gone from her voice.

'You've got the brain and the charm, now go get the education. Go back to Melbourne. Go back to Jerry. Go back and see your doctor in the hospital and get your health back. Then you can use all your resources for the cause and use them more effectively.'

'Maybe,' said Summer. Pete wasn't sure whether she'd given in or was just too worn out to argue. 'How're we doing?'

'The ACF is pushing for a moratorium on Little Potoroo Creek. It said so on the morning news. They're mounting a new challenge based on the environmental impact study.'

'Are the bulldozers still working?'

'There's nothing to stop them. Not yet, anyway. Ciaron and Sarah Jenkins have gone back out there to join what protesters are still left, but they'll only be nuisance value and they'll probably get arrested. The *Gazette* devoted the front cover and first four pages to God and the spiking. It's incredible. Whoever wrote the stories stopped short of pointing the finger at Miklos Bollok and his thugs, but not by much. There are pictures of spiked trees without a mark on them and a picture of a spiked tree trunk in Rip, Chip and Ship's yard with the spike more than two metres off the ground. They're suggesting that only somebody who works in the industry would have the skills to knock the spikes in so cleanly.'

'I knew it wasn't us,' said Summer.

'Liz and Brian have been ringing the *Gazette* trying to get copies of the photos to send up to Melbourne. All they've done since six this morning is talk on the phone.'

'Good on them,' said Summer.

'Do you want to know about Darren?'

'Darren!' said Summer. 'I'd forgotten all about him.'

'His head was split clean through to the skull and he has a hairline fracture. In fact he has a number of hairline fractures. They had to sew him up inside and out so he's had around forty stitches. All up, fifty-three people ended up getting treated at hospital. Some with broken bones, but mostly for cuts. But for what you and

God did it would all be over. You were incredibly brave, Summer. I couldn't have done it.'

'God was brave.'

'So were you. Now, everything's under control so all you have to do is go back to sleep for a while. I'll wake you up if anything exciting happens. Want me to ring Jerry?'

'Yeah.'

'What will I tell him? Summer?'

But Summer had closed her eyes and a heaviness had descended with her lids. She began to frame an answer but in the process lost the thread and lacked the will to go looking for it. She slept through to mid-afternoon when the sun broke free of the cloud cover and shone through her window onto her bed. Whether it was the warmth of the sun or the extra sleep, Summer awoke feeling refreshed and strong enough to brave a shower. For no reason that she could think of she felt optimistic. Maybe it was an accumulation of things: the stories in the *Gazette*, the fact that Liz and Brian were downstairs beavering away for the cause, or simply the fact that she felt better. But she had the sense of having made a decision and she always felt better after that. Positive vibes began to course through her body.

After she'd showered she made her way downstairs, expecting to find smiles and a charge of positive energy radiating from smiling faces. Instead she found Liz and Brian in defence mode, gathered around their radio. Pete was channel-chopping the TV looking for news bulletins.

'Hi, Summer,' said Liz. 'How're you feeling?'

'I'm fine. What's going on?'

'The counter attack,' said Brian. 'Every crank in a dog collar has been on air accusing God of blasphemy and sacrilege. We've even had a representative from the southern Baptists call from America to condemn God for what he did.'

'Claimed to represent the Baptists,' said Liz. 'Could've been anyone.'

'Doesn't matter,' said Brian. 'They've even dug up some Catholic and Anglican church leaders to put in their two cents' worth. Meanwhile Miklos Bollok is on air telling everybody it wasn't a cross but a tripod and only sensation-seeking media could make it anything but a tripod. He's saying there's nothing holy about God, nor good about him. Once again God has become the crazy man who escaped from an institution, lives in a cave and who poisons anyone who comes near him. Give them another couple of hours and they'll have him molesting little boys and dishing out drugs again. It's an organised campaign to discredit him.'

'He's accused God of starting the dirty tricks by sabotaging the bulldozers and lowloaders,' said Liz.

'That's ridiculous,' said Summer. 'They're lying.'

'Of course they're lying,' said Brian patiently. 'But by the time we prove they are, it'll all be over. Liz and I have spoken on damn near every radio station in Victoria and dozens more interstate. So has James Ferguson at the *Gazette* and that reporter friend of yours. But every time we try to correct a lie, Miklos and his mates come out with another. They've even organised phone-ins to jam the radio stations' switchboards so ordinary listeners can't ring in and give their opinions. Just listen to this.' He turned to the radio. 'Recognise the voice? She claims to be just a housewife and have no involvement whatsoever with woodchipping, but she's one of the Sisters of the Forest, and we know damn well who's pulling her strings. It'll be the same all over the State.'

'We've got to do something,' said Summer. 'We can't let God down.'

'We're doing everything we can,' said Liz. 'Apparently James Ferguson is going on TV at six-thirty to talk about the spiked trees. Maybe that'll help.'

'News headlines!' shouted Pete. They all turned to the TV as the familiar face of the news presenter filled the screen.

'Tonight angry church leaders speak out against the crucifixion at Little Potoroo Creek,' said the announcer. 'Doubts cast on the character of the man who calls himself God. And woodchippers dismiss photos of spiked trees as deliberate fraud. More at six.' The announcer's face disappeared and was replaced with another selling washing machines at ridiculously low prices, which were exactly the same as they had been the previous week.

'Christ, they're good,' said Brian. 'They're covering all their bases one by one. Liz, see if you can get James on the phone.'

'Phone's ringing now. Hello? James? Did you see the news in brief? What's going on?' As Liz listened her shoulders sagged and she slumped down in her chair. 'Thanks,' she said and hung up.

'What did he say?' said Brian.

'They're going to say that James, unwittingly or otherwise, took photos of the wrong trees. Apparently

Weitzler and Hand, the PR company that acts for the woodchippers, have been distributing pictures of trees that have had the daylights bashed out of them with little arrows showing where the indentations are and where the spikes were.'

'Were?' said Brian quickly.

'Removed for evidence according to the blurb, but they didn't say by whom. The tree trunk in the yard was mistakenly fed into the chipper and is out of the debate. The only tree that appears unscarred is the one that injured poor Colin Hayward. "Appears" being the operative word. According to the police sergeant who investigated the accident, one Sergeant Nugent, the side of the tree out of sight of camera was as badly knocked about as the others. So they're claiming that, rather than being the work of experts, the spiking is clearly the work of amateurs. But nobody has yet explained why Colin Hayward, who's been cutting down trees since he left school, didn't notice anything suspicious.'

'Surely nobody's going to buy that?' said Summer.

'Sooner or later the truth will come out,' said Brian. 'It usually does. Unfortunately it's more likely to be later, and too late for Little Potoroo Creek. Our only hope is that the government will stop work on the road until an enquiry is held. That's if they're forced into holding an enquiry.'

'They'll have to hold an enquiry,' said Summer desperately.

'The problem is,' said Brian, 'they've just announced they're going to hold an enquiry into the Bellbird environmental impact study. Nobody can reasonably ask them to hold two.'

'What are we going to do?' said Summer. Her positive vibes were as exhausted as she was. She slid down the wall and sat cross-legged on the floor. 'Please don't tell me what God did was for nothing.'

* * *

Cheryl switched off the television and stared into the remains of her coffee, too angry to even contemplate bed. Any lingering doubts she'd had about going through with her plan had vanished over the course of the evening. She'd watched with disgust as Clyde Townsend's tactics had unfolded. James Ferguson and Samuel Johnson had performed valiantly and credibly on current affairs programs, but their every argument had been countered. James's dispassionate objectivity had been matched by the woodchippers' outrage. On the late news a succession of churchmen blustered to camera, accusing God of blasphemy, a psychiatrist described God as 'seriously disturbed', and her husband calmly heaped the blame for every misfortune that had ever befallen Osbourne onto the protesters, dismissing them all as 'a lazy misinformed ratbag rabble'. Her disgust turned to bitterness when she realised the extent of the manipulation she and the rest of Australia had to contend with; just days earlier, like everyone else, she would have accepted the news at face value. Her anger flared with the last news item when she saw the Hayward children once more crying in grief. Their pet kelpie had been run over and killed. The driver had not stopped.

She'd just decided to make fresh coffee when a tired, weary, but nevertheless excited Joseph Weiss finally arrived home. He saw Cheryl was still up, dropped his bag and his armful of files onto the table, and threw his arms around her. In his enthusiasm it seemed right and proper to kiss her so he did.

'Well?' she said.

'We're in with a chance!' said Joseph. 'We've spoken to all the interested green groups, spent the whole bloody day in conference and on conference phone, and they've all finally agreed to our compromise position and agreed to let the ACF negotiate on their behalf.'

'I never had the slightest doubt.'

'Let me tell you, getting everyone to agree to anything is a first and nothing short of a bloody miracle, particularly as I couldn't tell them what was going on.'

'You've done your part.' Cheryl stared at him with an amused smile. 'Are you going to ask if I've done mine?'

'Sorry!' Joseph returned her smile with a rueful one of his own. 'When you didn't call I just assumed everything was on track. So, how did it go?'

'I guess you'll find out tomorrow. Mort Feldman is a very clever man. He said he'd been waiting all his career for a moment like this.'

CHAPTER THIRTY-SIX

Miklos Bollok stood at his office window watching timber trucks delivering the logs felled by the bulldozers and crew who were clearing the path for the road. One part of his life, at least, was under control, but it was the other parts which preoccupied him. Cheryl could have vanished into thin air for all he knew. Nugget had run a check on road accidents and hospital admissions and drawn a blank. Jan had compounded matters by resigning, saying she was leaving Osbourne and going somewhere where her talents would be better appreciated. It hadn't taken Miklos long to put two and two together and come up with Wily. He couldn't even begin to see what Jan saw in the inspector, or imagine what sweet-talking bullshit he'd fed her. His first instinct had been to clip her across her petulant face and give Wily something to remember him by, but in the end he couldn't be bothered. He didn't mind that Jan was boring and stupid, but lately she'd become possessive and demanding and that was something he couldn't abide. Her use-by date had come and, more than anything, he felt relief. He paid her out and told her to beat it. Nevertheless, Jan's departure was another change in his life, another uncertainty when he already had more than enough to deal with. As hard as he tried, he couldn't figure out where Cheryl might be, and tried to remember if she'd said something about going bush with her camera. The trouble was, she could have. He didn't keep her around for conversation and didn't bother to listen half the time she spoke to him. But it was nice knowing she was there. He noticed Arnie down in the yard, looking across at him and waving, indicating that he was heading to the pub for lunch. That, Miklos figured, was the best offer he'd had all day. He turned immediately and closed his office door behind him.

Arnie brought him up to date with the bulldozers' progress as they wandered up the street and through the car park. 'We're going to do all right outta this road buildin',' he said. 'Taken some great logs to the sawmills and got heaps for the mill. No levies on any of 'em.'

'Yeah, I heard,' said Miklos. 'Your sister say anything to you or your mum about going out into the bush to take photos?'

'Mum's said nothin', and I don't even remember when I last spoke to Cheryl. Hey, look who's here!'

Nugget didn't even look up from his beer as they joined him at the bar.

'Had a thought,' said Miklos. 'Cheryl might've gone bush to take some pictures. If that police chopper's still around, do you reckon you could get them to take a bit of a look around?'

'Mate, I couldn't get them to do anything even if I wanted to.' Nugget stared morosely into his half-empty glass, picked it up and downed his beer in a gulp.

'Fuck's the matter with you?' said Arnie. 'Miklos is askin' for a favour. You got a problem?'

'Yeah,' said Nugget. 'You could say that.'

'Wily giving you a hard time?'

'That idiot.'

'Then what, for Chrissakes!' said Miklos.

'I've been fuckin' suspended!' said Nugget. 'That's what! Remember that bludger who had his front wheel blasted off by them two dickheads in Orbost? They've just been arrested and now my bosses want to know why I didn't investigate or submit a report since I was first on the scene.'

'So why didn't ya?' asked Miklos.

'What do you reckon? Anyway, it gets worse. Wily's dobbed me in over the tree spiking for failing to secure and protect evidence.'

'You just can't trust some people. Here, let me get ya a drink.' Miklos waved Macka over. 'Three beers and a jug.'

'Reckon I might be knockin' on your door for a job.'

'Can't see you fellin' trees,' said Miklos. 'Don't waste your time.'

'I was thinkin' more of security, you know, looking after the mill and stuff.'

'Who the fuck's gunna steal logs?'

'Someone might want to break into your office.'

'And steal what? The kettle? There's nothing there anyone would want to nick.'

'C'mon, Miklos, you're loaded. What's one more name on the payroll?'

'What do you think I am? The bloody SPCA? A retirement home for failed coppers?'

Nugget put down the beer Miklos had bought him and slowly got up off his stool. 'Ya just gunna hang me out to dry, is that it?'

'Ain't my problem,' said Miklos. 'You got yourself in the shit, you get yourself out of it. I don't want you hangin' around the yard like a stray dog turd.'

'Well fuck you!' said Nugget.

'Watch it!' said Arnie. He grabbed Nugget by his shirtfront.

'Let him go,' said Miklos. 'The man doesn't want to drink with me. He won't get the chance to walk out on me twice.'

Nugget looked close to tears as he headed out the door, shoulders drooping and head bowed.

'Bastard hasn't paid for his beers,' said Macka.

'Always was useless,' said Miklos. 'Useless as a spare prick at a wedding.'

The office receptionist caught Miklos's attention as he returned from the pub. 'I've got some messages for you,' she said. 'One of them's urgent. From a Mr Feldman in Melbourne. He said something about a moratorium.'

* * *

Clyde Townsend had the nation's papers spread out on a table in front of him checking for stories about the spiking and Little Potoroo Creek. Editorials were demanding an enquiry, but apart from that the story appeared to be losing steam. He felt he deserved full credit for his efforts in muddying the water. He was feeling quietly satisfied with himself when the phone on his private line began to buzz. He picked it up.

'Who the hell's Mort Feldman when he's at home?'

'Afternoon, Miklos.'

'Don't piss me about, Clyde.'

'Miklos, everyone knows Mort Feldman. He's the principal of Feldman, Harden and Eldridge. He's a legal top gun. No social graces but a brain the size of Ayers Rock. He could get an acquittal for Attila the Hun if the money was right. Why do you want to know?'

'He wants to see me, you and Bernie in his office tomorrow at eleven.'

'What! Why?'

'Something about mediating a solution to Little Potoroo Creek to avoid the necessity of an enquiry.'

Clyde Townsend felt a cold shudder go through his body. 'What did he say? What were his exact words?'

'Jesus, Clyde, what do you think I am? A freakin' tape recorder? He said he wanted to see us in his office at eleven tomorrow. He said the minister and his principal adviser will also be there and two greenies from the ACF. He said we could kiss goodbye to ever logging any of our concession if we didn't show. You got any problem with that, you ring him. And when you find out what the fuck is going on, you ring me!'

'Okay!' Clyde snapped back. 'One other thing. Any word from Cheryl?'

'No. Not a peep.'

'Christ Almighty, Miklos, I hope she's got nothing to do with this.'

'Cheryl? Why the fuck would she?' Miklos slammed the phone down.

Clyde hung up slowly and looked around the room at the piles of newspapers and clippings. Suddenly none of it mattered a damn. Filled with foreboding he picked up his phone and dialled Feldman, Harden and Eldridge. Mort Feldman was not available.

CHAPTER THIRTY-SEVEN

Mort Feldman struggled to stand one hundred and sixty centimetres. In compensation nature had given him in girth what he lacked in height. He stood waiting in the anteroom of his firm's main conference room as his secretary ushered in Miklos Bollok. He saw a king-sized edition of himself. They eyed each other off, instantly recognising in the other the qualities they prided in themselves.

'Mort Feldman,' said Mort Feldman. He held out his hand to Miklos. 'Just shake it don't break it.' Miklos took his hand and couldn't suppress an ironic smile.

'This is Clyde Townsend,' said Miklos.

'We've met. Such a promising career wasted,' said Feldman.

'You had your chance,' said Clyde defensively.

'And this is Bernie Dwight,' said Miklos.

'Another great performer,' said Feldman generously. 'Tell me, do you make Townsend wear a glove when he sticks his hand up your arse?'

'What?' said Bernie.

'Skip it,' said Clyde.

'Come on through,' said Feldman. 'Everyone else is here already. Everyone has a nameplate on the table in front of them. Find your seat and do your own introductions.' In the last sentence all semblance of joviality drained from Feldman's voice. The effect was chilling. The three newcomers skipped introductions and sat. Feldman sat at the head of the table and slowly scanned the faces before him before speaking.

'I know the minister's busy, as in fact are the rest of us, so I don't suppose anyone will mind if I skip the usual formalities. Let me state my interest right from the start. I'm here today and I've invited you here today because I'm being paid to.'

'By whom?' snapped Clyde.

'None of your business. You'll get your chance to talk; right now I hold the floor.

'You've all read the editorials and the minister has confirmed that he is under immense pressure to declare a moratorium on logging not just Little Potoroo Creek but the entire concession granted to Regional Consolidated Sawmillers, or Rip, Chip and Ship as it's better known. The moratorium would stay in place pending an enquiry into the granting of the concession in the first place, and subsequent events which you're all well aware of.

'Naturally the government is resisting and resisting for two principal reasons. One, holding an enquiry can't help but give credence to the allegations that Rip, Chip and Ship — and indirectly Townsend's firm, Weitzler and Hand — were involved in the tree spiking, and just about everybody in Australia wants that not to be the case. It is hard to imagine anything more callous or heinous.'

'Get on with it,' said Miklos.

'Two, all sides in this dispute, including the government, though perhaps I should say especially the government, are well aware that the environmental impact report prepared by DeCaF is a fabrication, a farce, a farrago of half-truths and outright lies.'

'I reject that assertion!' said the minister.

'Really?' said Feldman disinterestedly. 'We all know that it would take very little to tip the balance and place the government in a situation whereby it has no choice but to declare a moratorium and hold an enquiry. The trouble with an enquiry is that nobody can know for sure where it will lead or where it will end.' He picked up a document from the table in front of him and held it up. 'Gentlemen, this will tip the balance. It is a subpoena. It subpoenas a certain Maurice Connolly who co-authored DeCaF's report.' Feldman looked up to gauge reaction to the subpoena.

The minister's mouth worked but no sound came out.

'You can't do that,' said his adviser. 'We have to commission an enquiry before you can subpoena him.'

'Quite right,' said Feldman, 'and you've just commissioned one. Maurice Connolly also worked on the Bellbird report. I think you'll find our interrogation quite wide ranging. Shall I continue?' Mort Feldman allowed himself a slight smile. 'Maurice Connolly will be obliged to testify as to the integrity of the study done for Tathra Heights and Little Potoroo Creek. He will be obliged to testify under oath. Under oath, gentlemen. Oh yes, we all know Mr Connolly has expressed his unwillingness to testify on many occasions, but now he has been deprived of choice. He will testify. In light of this fact, it may be a matter of some interest to you to learn that this same man is a devout and practising Catholic. That will be uppermost in his mind as he gives his testimony, under oath and before God. Is anyone here prepared to bet on him telling porky pies, because if anyone is I'll gladly take your money.'

Feldman looked slowly around the assembly as if looking for takers but, in reality, allowing the effect of his revelation to sink in. The minister had turned white and his adviser matched his colouring. Bernie Dwight twitched, Clyde Townsend looked dumbstruck and Miklos just appeared bored.

'So what's the deal, Feldman?' said Miklos. 'You got a point to make or do you just like hearing your own freakin' voice?'

'A compromise, gentlemen. I am offering you a compromise which, in the true nature of such agreements, satisfies nobody entirely. You will all have to give a bit, but in my opinion, given the circumstances, I believe the ACF is being overly generous.

'This is the deal. The ACF withdraws the subpoena and you reach an agreement which allows Miklos to log around sixty-six per cent of his concession and preserves the upper reaches of Tathra Heights and Little Potoroo Creek for all time. Rip, Chip and Ship can log up to the three-fifty metre mark but nothing beyond. The government declares all land beyond that mark a national park.'

'Sounds reasonable,' said the minister.

'Eminently,' said his adviser.

'No deal,' said Miklos. The minister looked as if he was about to burst into tears.

'Jesus,' said Clyde Townsend grimly.

'I haven't finished,' said Feldman. He gave Miklos a look of undisguised loathing and disgust. It bounced off Miklos but its possible significance wasn't lost on Clyde Townsend.

'Oh Christ!' he murmured.

'Before anyone else responds,' continued Feldman evenly, 'I have some photographs I'd like you all to look at.' He picked up a bundle of brown envelopes and began handing them out, first to Joseph and his boss, then to the minister and his adviser, then to Miklos, Clyde Townsend and Bernie. Each person's name was typed on a label stuck to the front of the envelope.

'You dumb shit!' whispered Clyde Townsend to Miklos.

'Fuckin' shut it!' said Miklos.

'Little Potoroo Creek,' said Feldman. 'Now, someone tell me that it's not worth saving.'

Joseph opened his envelope and, once again, could only admire Cheryl's photographic skills, even though he'd seen her photographs many times before. The minister and his adviser didn't have to look at the photos. The last thing they needed was Maurice Connolly to testify; they knew they'd need more than luck to survive an enquiry. Nevertheless they pretended to study the photos intently.

'Beautiful,' said the minister. 'We had no idea Little Potoroo Creek was so ... so ... worthy of preservation. It does rather tend to put a new complexion on things.'

'Absolutely,' said his adviser.

Miklos opened his envelope and stared in disbelief at the photo it contained. Clyde opened his and saw the same as Miklos — not a picture of Little Potoroo Creek but a photo of four hardened steel spikes resting in the rear of Miklos's Toyota.

'Oh shit!' said Clyde quietly though he desperately wanted to scream.

'Oh shit!' said Bernie almost simultaneously as he looked at the photo which showed him blowing kisses to two girls whose combined ages would have struggled to reach thirty.

'Beautiful, aren't they?' said the minister, eager to find agreement. Bernie nodded, too stunned to speak. 'They remind me of the work of those two Tasmanian fellows, Olegas Truchanas and Peter Dombrovskis.'

Miklos looked up and smiled wryly. They were two names he'd heard bandied around before.

'May I draw your attention to the photos beneath,' said Feldman smoothly.

Joseph, his boss, the minister and his adviser found more of the same, more shots of Little Potoroo Creek. Bernie found more of the private detective's photos, including one which had been shot through his bedroom window and showed a naked girl sitting on his crotch. Miklos found a summary of Cheryl's petition for divorce demanding custody of their two boys, the family home and contents, her Landcruiser and a settlement of two million dollars to be paid over ten yearly instalments. His eyes narrowed as he took in the details. He allowed a grim smile as he realised what the motive was behind the ACF's apparent generosity in leaving him more than sixty per cent of his concession to log. They hadn't set the figure, Cheryl had. His ex-bookkeeper was just making sure he had the income to meet her divorce settlement.

‘Do we have a deal, Mr Bollok?’ Mort Feldman flung the question like a shot from a gun. He made no attempt to hide his contempt.

Miklos scowled and tore the incriminating photo and summary in half and stuffed the bits back into the envelope they’d come in. He looked around contemptuously at the men who claimed to be his friends and allies, and at the fear and desperation in their faces. He turned to Mort Feldman and tossed his envelope along the table with enough force to knock a water glass crashing to the floor.

‘Yeah,’ he said. ‘You’ve got your freakin’ deal.’

CHAPTER THIRTY-EIGHT

The hospital entrance was hung with streamers and the floor was littered with corks from the cheap champagne Pete had organised. Ciaron and Sarah Jenkins were holding hands and didn't give a damn what the locals thought. A young nurse was all over Darren on the pretext of examining his scar. Gretta had given up trying to harmonise God's injuries and had found patients elsewhere to attend to. Earthmother and a couple of her acolytes had gone with her. Rainfather and the remaining Guardians clustered around the doorway where the breeze picked up their distinctive odour and carried it to every nook and cranny, sparing no one. Matt, Georgie and Sky were practising techno under Stretch's direction. Summer, Lyndal and Austrian Anke fussed around God's wheelchair talking non-stop. Lyndal held God's bottle of sherry, Summer his glass. Jerry had ridden down from Melbourne on his new Ducati and had his arm around Summer, making firm his intention to never let go again. Beaming protesters milled everywhere. The noise level was loud enough to be a threat to the health of the other patients. The hospital was tolerant but also practical. They gave the gathering an hour to say their piece and go.

The party was on the point of breaking up when Cheryl quietly edged into the hallway holding a bunch of native wildflowers. Summer was first to spot her. 'Cheryl!' she screamed. 'We did it! We did it!'

'Yes, I heard,' said Cheryl. She looked through a gap in the gathering towards God who was tucked up in his chair, surrounded by adoring women, his bandaged arms folded across his chest. A slow smile of recognition spread across his face and Cheryl felt herself go weak at the knees.

'You should've been there!' said Summer breathlessly. 'We gave it one last shot. Two hundred of us chained to the bulldozers. It was fantastic! They thought they'd beaten us but we came back. You could see them give up. The cops just stood by and did nothing. We stayed there all morning, singing and chanting, and they didn't even try to start the bulldozers or unchain us or anything. Around lunchtime one of the cops came up to us and told us we'd won. Said Little Potoroo Creek was going to become a national park. He brought his radio over so we could hear it for ourselves. We did it! Dorf dorf!' She threw her arms around Cheryl and hugged her.

'It really is great news,' said Cheryl, extracting herself from Summer's embrace. 'Would you mind if I had a word with God?'

'Okay, everybody, time's up.' Brian started pushing people towards the door. 'Say your goodbyes and get out of here.'

'Not you, Cheryl,' Liz added hastily.

Cheryl stood by while everybody farewelled God. His eyes left her as each of his visitors said goodbye, but they always came back. And his smile got bigger every time. When Summer's turn came to kiss him Cheryl could clearly see the closeness that existed between them, and recognised it for what it was — the fondness of good friends, nothing more.

'He's all yours,' said Liz meaningfully.

'Thanks,' said Cheryl. She could have sworn Liz had winked.

'No,' said Liz. 'Thank you.' She reached across, kissed Cheryl on the cheek and spoke softly into her ear. 'We'll never be able to thank you enough. Nobody else knows about your involvement except God. I thought he was entitled to know.' She squeezed Cheryl's hand, turned away abruptly and left.

Cheryl stood silently looking at God until the echo from Liz's footsteps were long gone, then walked across the hall towards him. She felt naked and exposed, as if her hopes were emblazoned across her forehead in neon. Her footsteps bounced off the bare hard walls and ceiling so loudly that she could have been wearing clogs. She leant over God and kissed him gently on his lips. Her tears splashed silently onto his forehead.

'Hello,' she whispered.

'A divorce settlement?' said God. He gazed up at her in wonder, his whole attention focussed on her. His smile broadened as he cupped her face gently in his bandaged hands. 'Where are we going to live, Cheryl?'

'Wherever we like,' she said. 'Wherever we bloody well like.'

Also by Derek Hansen

SOLE SURVIVOR

When Rosie Trethewey – disillusioned doctor turned market researcher – unexpectedly inherits a shack on the remote northern tip of Great Barrier Island, she decides it's time to begin a new life.

Arriving at her new home, Rosie finds she has two neighbours sharing the wilderness.

One is Red O'Hara, a refugee from horrific wartime experiences on the Burma Railway. The other is Angus McLeod, a retired policeman who's abandoned a society he sees as soft and contemptible.

Rosie's sudden appearance panics Red and Angus. They both fear she'll disrupt their ordered lives.

And they're right.

In this inspiring novel of survival, love and conflict, three loners are forced to come to terms with themselves, each other and the encroaching world.

ISBN: 0 7322 5747 6